PRAISE FOR ASHERWICK

You'll be on the edge of your seat as fear and desire partner in a dangerous dance. With ever-increasing suspense and an abundance of scorching hot interludes, this book proves to be even more exciting and tantalizing than its predecessors.

- *Indies Today*

I adored this story. Ms. Westill has created the most fantastic world with these amazing characters... I love the complex mystery, the romance, the world itself, and all the fabulous characters.

- *Baroness Book Trove*

Westill's books never disappoint. They're suspenseful, romantic, sexy, and mysterious, and the writing pulls you into this unique and captivating world from the first pages.

- *One Book More*

... much better than the box that genre put it in. I thoroughly enjoyed the intrigue of the mystery interspersed with the sexual tension between the characters.

- *BookSirens Reader Review*

Absolutely loved it! What another great read. Everything you need in a book and the spice is amazing!

- *Booksprout Reader Review*

ASHERWICK

GEN-HEIRS: THE GUARDIANS OF SZIVERIA

SARAH WESTILL

To the extent that the image or images on the cover of this book depict a person or persons, such person or persons are merely models, and are not intended to portray any character or characters featured in the book.

All rights reserved. No part of this publication may be reproduced, distributed, or transmitted in any form or by any means, including photocopying, recording, or other electronic or mechanical methods, without the prior written permission of the author, except in the case of brief quotations embodied in critical reviews and certain other noncommercial uses permitted by copyright law.

This is a work of fiction. Names, characters, places, and incidents either are the products of the author's imagination or are used fictitiously. Any resemblance to actual persons, living or dead, businesses, companies, events, or locales is entirely coincidental.

ASHERWICK

Gen-Heirs: The Guardians of Sziveria – Book 4

Copyright 2022 by Sarah Westill

ISBN 978-1-955293-08-2

Cover Design by For the Muse Designs

❀ Created with Vellum

OTHER TITLES BY SARAH WESTILL

GEN-HEIRS: The Guardians of Sziveria

(in reading order)

Levkaseon – A Prequel

Wintersfall

Raiventon

Kynhaven

Asherwick

Ericksen - A Wintervail Special (Nov. 2022)

Survaine (April 2023)

Bella and the Beast Master

(A Gen-Heirs World Novella Series)

Frozen Flowers Fallen

For world maps be sure to visit www.sarahwestill.com

To get the latest updates, follow Sarah on Instagram

@authorsarahwestill

DEDICATION

For my husband, who has always seen beyond my insecurities and encouraged me to be me.

Welcome to the Gen-Heirs World

In the distant future, a major cataclysmic event not only reshaped the world as humanity knew it but left entire lands uninhabitable. As generations of survivors struggled to endure a fight for territory and resources, humanity regressed into what became known as The Primal Years. A dark and dangerous time that lasted for centuries.

Slowly, civilizations formed into the new nations. Limited means of transportation and communication began to develop in a resource-poor world. Powerful countries arose known as Sziveria, Ruthenia, Italyssa, Westica, and Cairo. New cultures, with their own standards of honor, became global powerhouses.

By 830 PCE, strong talents are now inherited traits, passed down through genetics. The recipients of an unavoidable hereditary legacy are known as Gen-Heirs. Trains, ships, carriages, and if one can afford them, small magnetically powered vehicles move people. Radios are the only means of quick communication besides handwritten messages. Heated water is a luxury. Extreme drops in temperature and harsh arctic winds have forced most food growth indoors, in greenhouses. A dangerously lethal virus known as Human Rabies Syndrome (HRS) plagues the globe. The inhabited world is growing at a slow rate, each unique country striving to exist in harsher, cold climates, and those who survive have become ruthless in their quest to thrive in this new, forsaken world...

THE RANKING SYSTEM:

Guardians of Sziveria

Queen / King Elect
    Prince / Princess Elect
    Arch Guardian
    Prince / Princess
    Shield Guardian
    Master Guardian
    Primary Guardian
    Key Guardian
    Guardian (anyone who serves the realm)

Other Key Terms –

First Intelligence Office (FIO)
    Sziverian National Investigative Division (SNID)
    Haven City Enforcement Services (HCES)
    Medical Science Officer (MSO)
    Medical Science Investigator (MSI)
    Uninhabited Zones (UZ)
    Human Rabies Syndrome (HRS)

PROLOGUE

Sunrise Cliffs, Italyssa
October 7ᵗʰ, 834 P.C.E.

NATHALIA SEARTAVOS ASKED THE IMPOSSIBLE OF HER DAUGHTER. Sylphine stared at her mother and tried to form a coherent thought, or intelligible words. Both failed her. Warm ocean air fluttered past vivid blue curtains the same color as the sparkling water beyond. The entire floor was open to the outside. Yellow sandstone tile reflected the mid-afternoon sun, drenching the entire space in an ivory glow. Paradise on most days. Today, the Land of Sun and Wind had become a nightmare in the making.

"I'm sorry, you wish for me to do what?" Sylphine asked slowly. Perhaps she'd misunderstood.

Nathalia licked her lips and reached for her daughter's hands. "Listen carefully, my dove, either you go and convince your promised to go through with the marriage, or you *will* be forced into a union with Leone Cyrano."

"*Mitaika*, none of this is making any sense. *You* aren't making any sense. Why would I be forced into anything?"

Serene patience settled over Nathalia's beautiful face. The breeze circling the room teased the long, still-blonde length of her hair. "When our country was planned, the founders needed a way to ensure every man and woman would do their duty to our infant country and create families. They passed a law decreeing that if anyone was not married by their twenty-first year, a petition could be placed for a union. You're twenty-four and unwed. The Cyrano family placed such a petition before the House. They granted the request." Her mother's gem-green eyes shone with fear and desperation. "Please Sylphine, return to Sziveria. Persuade your Key Guardian to finally marry you."

Somehow Sylphine managed not to reach for her left arm, which held not one but two promise bands. Seven months ago, Jonathon Hunter had literally tossed his band away in anger and disgust, dissolving what had been a perfect arrangement for them both. Or so she had thought. Life was much more complicated than the make-believe she'd tried to force their relationship into. They'd both paid a high price. Sylphine swallowed. She couldn't go back to Jonathon.

"I'm afraid that isn't an option. I will just tell Mr. Cyrano I don't wish to marry him," Sylphine stated.

Nathalia's hold tightened to discomfort. "The law doesn't work that way. Once granted, he has the right to marry you, regardless of our refusal."

Disbelief choked Sylphine. "What? How can that be? They'd allow me to be raped. Because that's what would happen if I marry a man I do not wish!"

Her mother blew out a heavy breath. "When the law was made, they didn't care about that. They only cared about the population growing. The law hasn't been used for over a hundred years now. But we both know the Cyrano's have been desperately trying to get into this family for a very long time."

When a merger failed between the Cyrano's and Seartavos's, the Cyrano family decided the next best way to get their hands on the shipping empire was through marriage. To date, none of the Seartavos line had taken to what the Cyrano's had to offer, including Sylphine. Ten years older than her, Leone had been after Sylphine since she grew breasts at fourteen.

When she'd become legally old enough to wed at seventeen and had her celebration of life party, he'd immediately tried to convince her marriage was essential. He'd make her happy, and she needed him to ensure the future of Sun Wind Trade and Commerce thrived. Sylphine had answered by quickly becoming engaged to the first of many mistakes. When possible, she'd managed to remain in an engaged relationship to keep the Cyrano's at bay. At least until she realized her unique genetically inherited ability of being able to experience another's emotions at a touch, had been being taken advantage of by the men who'd promised to love and honor her.

What would happen if she were to marry a man who didn't even claim that much? Sylphine shivered. At least Jonathon, who'd agreed to a completely false engagement, had never touched her. Not even to hold her hand. Sylphine never knew how he felt about her, and until the moment he'd bitterly dissolved their relationship, she hadn't wanted to know.

Breathing away regret and heartache, she knew she had to be honest with her mother. "I'm afraid Jonathon wants nothing to do with me."

Nathalia stilled. Her beautiful eyes searched Sylphine's face. On a tug, she forced Sylphine onto the nearest chaise lounge, positioned to take in the most of the breathtaking cliffside view. "I thought this one was for real. You said he would last."

Sylphine worked her bottom lip between her teeth. A seagull let loose a cry and swooped low on a steady breeze. "He… lost someone he loved. I couldn't help him. Everything fell apart."

"You are a Sympath," her mother said in disbelief. "How could you fail him?"

Shame burned her cheeks red. "I never let him touch me. I couldn't help him process, or even understand what he was feeling. He didn't speak of his loss. He was so angry."

"His anger should have been no surprise. Death is a void; you know this. But we can celebrate life if we know how to see past the loss and embrace the love." Nathalia shook her head. "He will be better now. You can still go to him. Don't you care for him?"

Caring, Sylphine had learned the hard way, wasn't enough. "*Mita*… I can't marry," Sylphine whispered. Hating the tears that burned her eyes. "Please, help me find a way out of this law."

Tears shone in Nathalia's gaze. "There is no way out other than marriage to another before he can serve the petition. My dove, if you don't want him, you *must* choose another."

A heavy knock sounded on the tall, thick wooden door to Sylphine's bedroom suite. Nathalia leapt off the lounge and rushed across the room. The long, sheer layers of her lavender to dark purple gown floated behind her. The bells around her ankles joined the tranquil flutter of the curtains. Sylphine closed her eyes and tried to focus on the familiar sounds, and the salty, fresh air.

"Erico, what is it?" her mother asked, her voice laced with anxiety.

"There is an envoy here from the Cyrano's demanding to see Young Mistress Seartavos."

"Where is Acrisius?"

Sylphine rubbed her damp palms on her thighs. If her father could have fixed this, he would have already. Since her mother was the calmer of the two parents, apparently, she'd been sent to try to talk reason into her daughter. The situation appeared to be as bleak as Nathalia painted.

"Master Seartavos is speaking with the envoy, Mistress. He told me to tell you if Young Mistress Seartavos doesn't wish to leave with the men, she must depart via the tunnels. There is no other way."

Nathalia's shocked gasp preceded the slamming of the door. "They are coming! Sylphine, my dove, hurry!"

Shoes came flying at her from the right. She squeaked and grabbed for them, hugging the buttery-soft leather to her chest. Her mother's bare feet slapped across the stone floor to the other side of the room, where a door connected to the next room. They rushed through the second floor, and took stairs down to the basement level, which were cut into the stone face of the cliff. Like the house above, the lowest level opened out to the ocean, drenching the dark space in glowing light.

"*Mita*, what am I supposed to do?" Sylphine asked breathlessly, chasing after her mother's fleeing form down a long tunnel.

"Get to a ship bound for Sziveria, doesn't matter what kind, you can't be in a passenger manifold or any manifest."

Shocked, Sylphine stopped. "What? You want me to... stowaway?"

Her mother turned and reached for her. In the dimly lit space, her eyes were colorless, but desperation was no less evident in them. "You must. If the Cyrano's know where you've gone, they will intercept you. Please, tell me, do you want to escape him or see what your fate will be in their hands? I must know. You either have to go through with getting to Sziveria, and to your promised, by any means you can. Or you need to stay here and face the petition."

The enormity of her situation crashed around her like the tunnel caving in. Either she left her home, the safety and love of her parents, or she found herself forced into a marriage to a vengeful, greedy family. "Oh, summer sun, this is really happening to me."

Her mother squeezed her arms. "Yes. And either you get to Jonathon, who can keep you safe, or another. We can't protect you here. Is there anyone else if not him?"

Sylphine realized even if there was, which there wasn't, she wouldn't want anyone else. She shook her head. "No, there is no one else. But Sziveria is a three-day ocean journey. How am I supposed to sneak on and survive that without food or water?"

Nathalia licked her lips and hastily began removing her jewelry. Her earrings, bracelets, and three rings fell into Sylphine hands. "Use these to purchase passage from a crew member. Try not to use them all, but if necessary, do it. And when you're on board, hide. Do not let anyone know where you've gone to sleep your nights. Sneak into the galley the first night and take only what you need to live, nothing extra. One meal a day, my dove, do you understand?"

Fear coiled in her chest. Sylphine nodded when her mother pressed again. "Okay, yes."

"When you reach Sziverian shores, do what you must, but get to Jonathon. Radio us when you arrive so we know you're safe."

When her mother pulled her, Sylphine dug her feet into the stone. "*Mitaika*, I don't have my papers; they won't let me in."

The heavy pound of booted feet echoed near the bright entrance to the tunnel. Nathalia hissed and yanked Sylphine's arm hard enough to cause her to stumble.

"There is no time," her mother urged. "You will have to seek asylum when you get there. Your Guardian is an enforcer, he can help, I'm sure. All that matters now is your safety."

"They wouldn't hurt me, would they?" Surely, if Leone wanted her as his bride, she'd arrive to him healthy.

"It's not you that I worry about after the contract ceremony, my dove." Her mother's voice was grave, her fingertips digging into the flesh of Sylphine's arm to the point of pain.

Sylphine ran to keep pace. Her mother's words echoed in her mind. "You think he'd hurt you after he had me as his wife?"

"I know he would. How else would the Cyrano's gain control of Sun Wind?"

"Come with me, *Mita*!"

They stopped at the opening. Cracks of light broke through the rickety door concealed behind a wall of ivy. Her mother caressed her cheek to her jaw. "I can't leave your father, you know this. We will be fine, as long as you're safe. Your father is very powerful here. Once you're away, we can begin to try to battle the petition, but not before. If they are able to serve it to you, all will be lost." She pressed a kiss to Sylphine's forehead and then pushed the door open. Brilliant light flooded around them, making Sylphine's already tear-filled eyes burn. "Go."

1

A FINE MIST BLANKETED HAVEN CITY, COVERING THE GROUND IN a haze and swirling in the air. Not for the first time, Sylphine wrapped her arms around herself, longing for sunlight since leaving the warmth of Italyssa. She tried to focus on the angry driver screaming profanities and demands for raimarks she didn't have to pay for the journey she'd needed from the MagnaRail station to the Enforcement Services East Street Division. Jonathon Hunter, also known as Key Guardian Asherwick in Sziveria, worked in the building as an investigator.

Sylphine had been foolish enough to think the driver would be charitable since she'd asked to be brought to an Enforcement precinct. The livid red of his jiggling cheeks, and the spittle coating the lower half of his dark beard, revealed exactly how *benevolent* he was inclined to be with her. Hunger gnawed at her stomach, and she knew if she itched anymore at the seams of the course gown she wore, she'd bleed.

"Mister, I am very sorry. Just let me go inside to my promised, and he will gladly pay you."

The man pointed at the tall, bleak building. "He's in there?"

"Yes, he is a Master Tribunii with Enforcement Services, and a Key Guardian."

He looked her over, narrowing his dark eyes to slits. Sylphine pulled her shoulders back and raised a brow. Despite her poor attire and filthy state, she was an heiress, and she knew how to look like one.

Shaking his head, he sighed. "I go in with you."

Knowing she had no other choice, Sylphine agreed. At least she was in Haven City, safe, despite the sketchy travel means she'd endured, very near to the man who would help her out of a deep hole she'd found herself stuck in. Again.

The usual bustle of the division precinct was subdued in the later evening hours. Sylphine strode with purpose to the front desk, all the while aware of the suspicious glare of the driver at her back.

Under normal circumstances, she would have gone straight to the Hunter residence. But her situation was anything except ordinary, and she refused to put Jonathon's sister, Ramsey, in danger. While the chances of the Cyrano's knowing she was in Sziveria at this moment were minuscule, the risk remained. Hopefully, since Jonathon seemed to live at the East Street Division, her waking nightmare would soon be over.

Taking a deep breath, Sylphine approached the front desk. She pasted on a smile and rested her arms on the tall reception counter. A woman looked up from a word puzzle spread out before her in the newspaper. Annoyance made the creases on her face more prominent. Her grayish-blue eyes took in Sylphine, and with a sniff, she returned her attention to the puzzle.

"This isn't the overnight shelter. It's two blocks," she lifted her pen and pointed to the left, "that way."

Sylphine kept her shock internal and shook her head. She figured she looked terrible, but not *that* terrible. "No, I am not...."

The woman glanced up again. A sagging, gray-streaked bun shifted on the crown of her head. "Clothing distribution is on the first Friday of every month, during business hours."

Sylphine opened her hands and shook her head again. "No, I do not need..."

"Look lady," the receptionist snapped, "unless you have a crime to report, we don't have anything for charity. I'm sorry. Go to the shelter, they have everything you need."

The driver coughed. Sylphine resisted the urge to shoot him a glare. Smoothing her fingers along the polished surface of the counter, she tried again. "I need to speak with MT Hunter. Please."

"Is this concerning a case?" she asked, leaning forward, her gaze filled with suspicion.

"I'm his promised, and I need to speak with him. Now, please. You can tell me where his office is, I will get there myself."

"MT Hunter left about an hour ago." The woman returned to her puzzle. "If you're his promised, you can get to his house, can't you?"

Sylphine sensed more than saw the driver close in behind her. The frustration rebounded off her in waves. "You said you'd get my money for your fare."

"Yes, and I will," Sylphine assured. She looked back at the receptionist. "Please call MT Hunter. Please. I have no way to get to his house. I took a hired carriage here. I swear he knows me. I have had a terrible journey. I was robbed, and I fell off the pier in Port Anchor. East Street Division is closer from the rail station than Jonathon's house."

The woman stared for quiet seconds, flipping the pen idly between her fingers. She pointed it at Sylphine with a glare.

"If I radio him and you're lying, I will be the witness this man needs against you to put you behind bars for theft."

Anxiety curled in her chest. *Please, please don't hate me so much, Jonathon.* "Very well."

On a long-suffering sigh, the woman twisted in her seat towards the long row of radios. During normal business hours, there would be an operator for each station. She retrieved a huge binder from underneath the counter and flipped through its pages. Moments later, the static of an undesignated outbound signal flared. With quick skill, she designated the call. The signal chirped.

"MT Hunter, Key Guardian Asherwick," Jonathon's voice said over the line.

Sylphine almost slumped in relief.

The receptionist shot her a sideways glower. "Hello, MT, this is Gweneth at East Street Division. I have a woman here claiming to be your promised. She insisted I call."

Tense silence crackled on the line. Gweneth's stare scathed. Sylphine held her breath.

"Who?"

Jonathon gaped at the radio in his hand. Surely, he'd misunderstood the East Street Division's evening receptionist. "Can you please repeat?"

"Yes. She says her name is Sylfa Seartava."

Tilting his head back, Jonathon chuckled deep in his throat at the awful butchering of a name that still managed to make his pulse race more than he cared to admit. "Sylphine Seartavos?"

"Yes."

Jonathon held the receiver against his chest in thought. Why was Sylphine in Haven City, and why did she go to the precinct and not to the house like she used to? She also still claimed to be promised to him, when over six months ago he'd called off their engagement. He hadn't seen her since that dark night. Alarm snaked along his spine. Something bad must have happened. "I'll be there in a few moments."

"Copy."

The faint click of the transmission ending echoed in the dim office. Jonathon sighed and reached for his jacket. His luck would have something happening the moment he walked into the precinct, and him not in uniform to handle the situation. The golden yellow threads of the Enforcement Services crest, his name, and dual rankings over the left breast glimmered faintly as he shrugged into the black coat. HCES in large block letters screened onto the back in the same golden shade made clear what the front didn't. Haven City Enforcement Services: Investigative Division was printed in smaller letters underneath.

He clipped his badge and gun onto his belt. Despite the effort being futile, too many hours had passed since he took a shower this morning, he tried to tame the thick mess of hair on his head. Silence greeted him in the foyer. He glanced up the stairs, where his sister remained in her room, as usual. Shaking his head at her extreme antisocial behavior, he left the house.

Brisk night air swirled heavy with moisture. Jonathon strode with purpose to his Ariot parked beside the house. The sleek silver lines of the two-seater vehicle glistened in the gaslights lining the street. Jonathon's income bracket made the magnetically powered vehicle well outside his means. He was fortunate that as the Master Tribunii for his team, and overall lead investigator for the East Street Division violent crimes unit, he needed a mode of transportation not reliant on beast or man.

With the flip of a small switch next to the steering column, Jonathon started the process to power his ride. The soft hum of motion reverberated through the Ariot. Carefully, Jonathon eased onto the road. It would take a few more minutes of generated power to light the filaments of his front lights. Until then, the glow of the street lamps would do. The streets were mostly deserted this time of night. Soon, the cold arctic air from the north would make traveling this time of day impossible for anyone but those who had an Icekutian breed of horse and lots of layers. Early autumn brought frosty nights, but not enough to hamper travel.

At East Street Division, he pulled into a front parking space. During the day, hired rides lined the curb. Only one carriage waited outside, and as Jonathon bounded up the steps, he noted it was empty. An angry female shriek followed by a male roar loud enough to be heard outside had Jonathon rushing the remaining distance to the doors. He yanked on the handle and a whoosh of air rushed past him.

A tall, heavy, bearded man had his hands wrapped around the upper arms of a smaller, disheveled woman. Tangled, matted hair of an indeterminate color hung in thick cords down her back. A faded burlap dress drooped off her frame, at least a size too big. The man gave the woman a harsh shake.

"Where is my money?" he barked, glaring at Gweneth. "Get an enforceman here now, I want her detained for theft."

Crossing his arms, Jonathon settled his weight onto his heels. "I'm an enforceman. What has she stolen?"

Wide eyes, the shade of a summer ocean snapped in his direction. Jonathon's breath caught in his chest. He stared at the raggedy woman in disbelief. "*Sylphine?*"

She nodded but made no effort to pretend she didn't look like a vagrant. "Hello, Jonathon. Thank you for coming."

The musical lilt of her voice never failed to send a delicious shiver down his spine. Jonathon shot the man holding her a dark glower. Fisting his hands, he stepped forward. The man peeled his fingers from her arms and took a slow step back. "She owes me raimarks. Said you'd pay them."

Jonathon looked Sylphine over again. Every piece of jewelry that normally adorned her was missing. Her rings, earrings, the enticing beads, feathers and ribbons in her hair, necklaces, and bracelets, except… He narrowed his gaze on her left wrist, where two silver bands enclosed her wrist. Interesting. Everything else was gone.

"How much?"

The man grumbled an amount. When Jonathon arched a brow at the cost, the man sputtered, "I've been waiting here almost an hour. That's at least two additional fares she cost me by not being able to pay."

Jonathon sighed, but didn't argue. He had questions he couldn't ask until he had the lovely Miss Seartavos to himself. The driver accepted the raimarks without another word and fled the building.

"Is there anything else?" Jonathon asked Gweneth.

She shook her head, her limp bun flopped around. "No, MT, nothing."

Giving a nod of thanks, he grasped Sylphine's fabric-covered elbow before she could protest and hauled her towards the doors. On a quick glance, he noted the angry red skin on her chest, wrists, and he imagined anywhere else the course material touched.

Outside, he released her. She put several feet between them, ensuring he wouldn't be able to grab her again. Old anger flared through him. Why had he expected anything would have changed? He motioned towards his Ariot.

"Explain to me how you'll allow that terrible dress to touch you, but I can't," he asked, opening the door for her.

Startled, she froze mid step on the sidewalk. "The dress can't take over my senses."

"Only rub them raw."

Picking up the faded brown length of skirt, she stepped onto the street. Without another word, she slipped into the

Ariot. Jonathon sighed and closed the door with more force than necessary. Once inside, he reached for the switch and then stopped. Twisting in his seat, he faced her.

The faint light from a nearby lamp washed her in subtle shadows, bringing attention to the tangle of her hair and the smudges of dirt coating all her visible skin. Still, even beneath the filth, Sylphine's beauty outshone any other woman he'd met. The gentle angles of her jaw, cheeks, nose, and chin were made for staring. Her sensual, full, naturally pink mouth was made for kissing. Something even now he had to practice real restraint to keep from attempting. And the tragedy of a dress she wore hid a body made for a man's hands. Jonathon flexed his fingers over the wheel. But the hands touching her would not be his.

"All right, what's going on? No lies, and don't evade my questions," he ordered. "I don't see or hear from you for almost seven months, and then you show up at my work looking like," he waved his hand around, "this. Start talking."

2

———————

IN THE DARKNESS OF THE ARIOT, SYLPHINE HAD HOPED TO FIND A sense of security. But with every breath she took, Jonathon's very masculine scent of cedar, warm musk, and *him* scattered her thoughts. The sheer presence of him invaded her space. And his voice... She squeezed her eyes shut. His rich, deep timbre caused her heart to clench.

How she'd missed him.

Tears of relief burned her eyes. She breathed through the annoying flash of emotion. Breaking down in front of her former promised, fake as the arrangement may have been, wasn't something she could personally afford. Jonathon Hunter wasn't the kind of man to ignore a woman's distress, no matter how much distance he wanted between them. He'd be compelled to somehow soothe her.

EXHAUSTED AND RIDING THE EDGE OF HYSTERIA, SHE DIDN'T think she'd be able to deny the potential comfort his touch could provide. The rush of emotions that would accompany the attempt would be her undoing. Her own emotional state teetered on the brink of a meltdown. She didn't need to deal with his too.

Already concern, annoyance, and something she couldn't identify shifted in the air around her, brushing her skin with tiny flutters. If she were to touch him, those same feelings would arc straight into her. Taking a deep breath, she focused on the haze swirling outside and not on the tense vibrations within the small vehicle.

"A dangerous rival of my father made threats against us. My parents were concerned about my safety, so they sent me here." *To you.* Sylphine wasn't ready to divulge everything. Not yet. She flexed her fingers into the coarse weave covering her thighs.

"What happened on the way that you've lost everything? Where you robbed?"

"Not exactly." A heavy sigh rushed from her. "There was not any time for me to pack or even get enough money to purchase passage. I bartered to make my way here."

The faint drum of his fingers on the narrow dash drew her attention to him. In the low light, his features were muted. Most would consider Jonathon to be average in looks. His hair was short and dark brown, but not so short her fingers wouldn't disappear into the depths, and his eyes dark blue. Not overly tall at six-feet, he had a solid, lean frame that served him well chasing criminals. A strong jaw, defined cheeks, and a nose a little too big for his face kept him from crossing into overly handsome. His lips... Sylphine shifted her focus back outside. They were perfect. Nothing average about the curves of his mouth.

If she stared too long, all the fantasies she'd conjured over the years she'd known him would surface. One thing she knew very well about MT Hunter, he was wickedly good at what he did for a living. He'd see the desire written on her face and the language of her body. Then he'd ask again why only a dress could touch her skin. And she'd have to shamefully confess because she'd be a disappointment to him. Best to not even broach the topic again.

"You don't have any bags."

The statement made her peek at him. She shook her head. "No, I have nothing, except what is at your house."

His fingers stopped drumming. "How did you get into Sziveria?"

Normally all the baubles, bracelets, rings, necklaces, and anklets Sylphine wore provided a sense of security. She felt beautiful, sensual, and desirable, adorned in things that flashed and chimed with each move she made. All the things she wasn't in reality. They also gave her something to fidget with, in nervous circumstances. Like this one. She cleared her throat.

"Well, I may have jumped into the Sovereign Channel at Port Anchor."

Silence blanketed the interior. When Jonathon remained motionless, Sylphine chanced a glance at him. He stared at her, eyes wide, jaw relaxed in clear disbelief.

"You..." Words failed. He tried again. "You entered the country *illegally*?"

"Is that a problem?"

He twisted to face the steering wheel. His hands wrapped around the wooden frame until his knuckles stretched white over bone. With an aggressive swipe, he flipped the switch to power the Ariot. "No problem at all," he muttered between clenched teeth.

She couldn't stop from rubbing her thumb along the promise bands around her left wrist as he pulled onto the road. One hers, one used to be his. When he'd tossed the band away in a fit of justified anger, Sylphine hadn't been prepared for the hurt his action caused her heart. Nor had she been willing to say goodbye to their relationship.

The thick silver bracelets were the only things she hadn't been able to part with, no matter how desperate she became for food or shelter over the two-day journey from Port Anchor to Haven City. The safety of the MagnaRail allowed her to rest, at least. The bands had become her only link to Jonathon over the months, a source of comfort. Now, he sat beside her, close enough to touch if she dared. She pressed her hands together between her knees.

"I have documentation with the Immigration and Import Regulation Agency since Sun Wind has government contracts. I am sure there will be no issue obtaining copies, if you feel I need them."

His hands flexed over the wheel. "I do, very much, feel you need them."

"All right, I will get them."

A heavy breath rushed from him. "You know I'm an enforceman, right?"

"Yes."

He pointed at his chest. "I'm a Master Tribunii."

"I know."

"And a Key Guardian."

"Yes."

"I am going to be harboring an undocumented traveler. At. My. House." Each word was emphasized by the pounding of his palm against the steering wheel. "What am I supposed to say?"

Sylphine looked at him. "Who will ask?"

He shot her a glance and snapped his teeth together. She arched a brow in challenge. "How do you normally come into my country?"

An uncomfortable slither raced along her spine. "I arrive at Port Scarbrough."

When she didn't continue, he urged, "And?"

She pushed her toes into the hard floor of the Ariot. "And an Emissary greets me. Welcomes me to the country."

He waved his hand.

Sylphine shifted in discomfort. "I'm given a dossier if I'm here on business, and social invitations and event tickets if I'm here just to visit."

"Someone always, *always*, personally greets you. The heiress and liaison for one of the most powerful trade companies in the inhabited world. You do not just *show up* in Sziveria."

Astonished, Sylphine stared at him. She had no idea he knew so much about her process of entering his country. "Yes, you're right, they all know me. Arch Guardian Immetana is a friend. She will help if I need her to. I will tell them I was robbed, my papers stolen. I am in distress, so it's close enough. Immigration and Import will help."

He slid her a sideways glance again. "You say that as if you're convincing yourself."

Sylphine watched the dark houses slide by. Maybe she was convincing herself. Without the papers, Leone Cyrano would have no trouble taking her out of the country. Even with them, if he had the right documentation, and she was still unmarried, he'd be within his rights to haul her back to Italyssa. A knot twisted in her stomach.

Why couldn't she be one of those courageous women? The ones who spoke their every thought, and put a voice to their every fear, taking away their power? If she were, she'd have spilled the truth to Jonathon the moment he'd asked. Even now, she tried to think of a way out of her situation without dragging him down with her. Biting her lip, she struggled to keep tears away. She'd figured out what to do. She had to.

* * *

Jonathon hung his jacket on a peg behind the door and slipped out of his boots. Sylphine stood in the dark foyer, arms wrapped around her waist. She looked lost. Alone. Focusing his attention on lighting a lamp, he pushed down the urge to gather her into his body. The offer for comfort would be rejected, and in his frustrated state, he'd likely lash out. He knew better than to even try.

"Go upstairs and get out of that excuse for a dress you're wearing before your skin chafes anymore. I'll make you something to eat," he said, motioning towards the stairs with the smoking match between his fingers.

She remained motionless, her gaze fixed on a point only she knew. Jonathon tossed the used matchstick into a small metal box beside the lamp and considered his options. Walk past and let her decompress in her own time, or risk getting closer and having her panic on him. Slowly, Jonathon approached her from behind and to the side, beyond her peripheral vision. Once she was within reach, he brushed his fingers across her shoulder. A startled jump twitched her frame. On a gasp, she glanced over her shoulder.

Jonathon took a safe step back. "I know you're exhausted, hungry, and filthy. Let's handle one issue at a time. Go change and come back down. I'm going to make you some food."

When she stared at him and made no effort to move, Jonathon grasped her shoulders and urged her closer to the stairs. The warmth of her body seeped through the rough material under his fingers. He wanted to flex, to know if she felt as supple under his hand as she looked to his eyes. Instead, he let her go. Finally, she shuffled forward with a nod.

Jonathon waited until she disappeared upstairs before rolling his sleeves up and heading to the spacious kitchen. After lighting enough lamps to work by, he set out everything he'd need to make scrambled eggs, fried bread, and chopped fruit. He lit the stove and set the necessary pans on the warming cast-iron top. While he waited for the pans to heat, he chopped fruit for a bowl. The faint shuffle of slippers sounded behind him.

Slyphine ambled in and sat at the circular, wooden table in a nook overlooking a small greenhouse at the back of the house. Only darkness and a faint reflection from the kitchen offered a view this late at night. She gathered the edges of her pink cashmere robe over her lap but didn't bother adjusting the gap at the top, revealing a dark blue silk underdress. The bust pulled tight over her generous breasts and did nothing to conceal the angry expanse of exposed skin on her chest.

Sighing, Jonathon set his knife down and reached into a cupboard to his left. He pulled out a small glass jar of amber-colored salve. He crossed the short distance to the table and held the medicine out to her. Sylphine gave him a wary stare, but plucked the jar from his palm.

"What is this?" She inspected the container as Jonathon returned to the food preparations.

"Something to soothe your skin." He sliced the knife blade cleanly through apples. "I could help you apply it, if you want."

A choked gasp joined the pounding of the blade, and he glanced in her direction. Her fingers curled around the jar pressed between her breasts. The shockingly vibrant shade of her teal eyes stared at him. He managed not to smile.

"I-I will be fine, thank you."

Jonathon shrugged. His gaze flickered to the matted length of hair, normally light brown streaked with shades of gold. "What about your hair?"

Her fingers brushed the back of her head, where it looked as though a family of rats had made a home at some point in her journey. "Ramsey has said she will help."

"Help with what?" Ramsey asked. She sniffled and then

yawned. Her thick, cotton robe hung open over a long, light blue nightgown.

"Brush my hair," Sylphine answered.

His sister snorted. "The whole street is going to have to come help with your hair." She sat heavily in a chair. The legs screeched across the tile. "How are *you* handling this disruption to your chaos?"

Jonathon glanced at her when the room remained silent. "Is that question for me?"

Ramsey stared at him with her brows lifted. "Who else lives in a state of constant motion? I certainly don't. So?"

He returned to his task, adding more ingredients since Ramsey joined them. "Fine."

Ramsey made an *I-don't-believe-you* noise. Since Jonathon didn't quite believe himself, he didn't defend his reply. For now, he'd focus on something other than the beautiful woman he couldn't touch sitting illegally in his house.

The two women chatted about nothing important while he finished. When he was almost done, Ramsey placed the settings, fussing every time Sylphine attempted to help. He placed a bowl of heaping scrambled eggs, a plate of fried bread, and a bowl of fruit in the center of the table.

The comfortable silence while they ate was a familiar one. Jonathon never figured out why the Italyssian heiress preferred their company, and their average home, to the luxuries of the embassy or even the suites at one of the top hotels Haven City had to offer. She never complained about the food he or Ramsey cooked. Right now, Jonathon would have believed himself a gourmet chef the way she attacked the meal.

Ramsey paused with a forkful of eggs halfway to her mouth. "When was the last time you ate, Fi?"

Sylphine waved her fork around, shoving a piece of bread into her mouth. She took a long gulp of water before answering. "I had some soup two nights ago, when I landed ashore."

"Soup?" Ramsey asked.

Sylphine nodded. "Yes. Well, what passed for soup to the *alkaligo* family. I did not take much."

Ramsey scrunched her face in contemplation. "*Alkaligo*?"

"Small, or little, I think is your word," Sylphine supplied and then took another large bite of eggs.

"How did you lose your clothes?" Jonathon asked between bites.

"I told you, there was no time to pack. What I had was ruined by the time I reached Port Anchor. My swim in the Sovereign Channel destroyed it." With her fingers, she picked up a piece of apple.

Jonathon tried to remain neutral as her tongue wrapped around the fruit and her fingers disappeared into her mouth. Everything in him tightened. He averted his attention back to his plate. "And the dress you had on?"

"The mother supplied for me. A generous gift. She only had one other piece of clothing. I gave her both my earrings for the meal, the gown, and enough raimarks for the MagnaRail."

He chanced a glance back up at her. "I think you were the generous one," he said gently. "Those earrings will feed that family for a month if she's smart."

Sylphine set her fork down with a heavy breath. "I have a box full of them, both here and in Italyssa. At the time, the value of what she offered was greater than the value of two pieces of silver."

Ramsey yawned. "Well, Fi my dear, if you want those knots out, we best get to it. I'm ready to go back to bed."

Jonathon rose and gathered up the dishes. Nothing remained except a piece of bread. Sylphine watched, her expression torn.

"It's okay," Jonathon said, motioning with his head to the door. "Go on, I'm used to cleaning up."

Hot water poured over Sylphine. She groaned and let the spray cleanse away the wretched experience of her travels. No one would think less of her if she cried. Safe, warm, fed, Sylphine wanted to give into the desire. However, she knew once she started, stopping would be near impossible. She'd blubber like a baby until she passed out from exhaustion.

With her hair saturated in conditioner, Sylphine cut the water and wrapped in a plush cotton robe. Ramsey waited in the bedroom, behind a screen Sylphine used to partition off a dressing area. She waited behind a chair, a thick comb in her hand. A yawn stretched her pretty face, and she waved for Sylphine to sit.

The Hunters lived in a modest, two-story house. Four bedrooms upstairs, and a library, study, sitting room, dining room, and kitchen downstairs. While Sylphine knew she could stay in more luxurious rooms larger than their entire house, something about their private residence comforted her. She wanted to attribute it to Ramsey being the sister she never had, but she feared if she examined the reason too closely, she'd have to admit to something else entirely.

Yes, she mused as she took her seat and let Ramsey begin tackling the chaos that was her hair, the small home held the promise of family. A concept her parents had lived out so well together, showing her what true love looked like on a daily basis.

Over the years, Sylphine had been forced to acknowledge the rare gift of passion her parents shared for each other. In the early days of her youthful, adult years, she had figured the first man to arouse desire was *the one*. Frowning at her reflection in the mirror, she tried to push away the unwanted memories of dissatisfied lovers. Of men who, after sating their lust a time or two with her body, walked away from the love she'd believed they'd held for her. Desire, it turned out, was a sorry substitute for passion, a lacking factor in every relationship she'd attempted.

In disappointment with herself as a woman, and in every man who'd revealed her frigid nature, Sylphine had latched onto the Hunters and the safety they offered. Jonathon had never tried to be anything more than a friend, and Ramsey's reclusive nature made her a quiet oasis in an otherwise loud world.

"So," Ramsey began, picking the comb through a tangle. "Why are you here looking like this, really?"

Sylphine smoothed her hands along the barren top of the vanity. How much did she dare reveal? "An old family rivalry discovered an ancient Italyssian law it seems and they are trying to enact it against my family."

The brush paused for a moment. "Are you in danger?"

"Sort of. My parents are mostly the ones in jeopardy."

"Oh, Fi, I'm so sorry. I know how close you are to them. Leaving them behind must have been terrible."

Sylphine patted Ramsey's forearm. "Yes. I have to try to reach them first thing in the morning. Is the radio still in Jonathon's study?"

Ramsey returned to brushing. "Yes. And one in his bedroom."

A faint blush crept onto Ramsey's cheeks. Sylphine met the woman's lavender gaze in the mirror. "His bedroom."

Shrugging nonchalantly, Ramsey separated a section free of knots over Sylphine's shoulder. Water dripped down the edge of the robe in cold rivulets. "I was simply telling you where else he has one. Of course, he'd need one in his room if HCES needs to reach him while he's sleeping."

"And you think I'd go into his room?"

"It's just a room."

Tension stiffened Sylphine's spine. *Just a room.* Sure... right.

A room Jonathon slept in, dressed in. A space that would smell of him, warm and masculine, inviting her to imagine things she had no business imagining.

Not once had she dared to even stop in the doorway and look at the chamber so personal to him. His study was enough. Chaotic files, papers, and books, along with the things important enough to surround himself with. Pictures of his parents, he and his sister as children. His certifications and awards that wouldn't fit in his small office at work. Knowing more of him on the surface would make her want to explore more of him all together. A danger she couldn't afford.

"I will use the one in his office, as usual."

Ramsey shrugged. "Whatever you want. I figured since you still wore his promise band, both of them, his bedroom wouldn't be off limits."

The bracelets chimed as Sylphine lowered her hands to her lap. Her gaze met Ramsey's in the mirror again.

"Did he ask you why?" Ramsey's warm, sympathetic eyes remained fixed on Sylphine in the mirror.

Sylphine shook her head. "No, I didn't expect him to, though. After all, he is the one who ended our falsehood of a relationship." She brushed her fingers along the cool, metal bands. "I seem to be the one having trouble letting go."

Ramsey set another chunk of combed hair over Sylphine's shoulder. "Are you sure it was so fake?"

Sylphine scoffed and resisted rolling her eyes. "Of course. I never even allowed your brother to hold my hand. Everything we presented outside this house, and even within, was for show, to keep suitors away. Something I thought we both wished enough to continue until questions were asked about why we hadn't contracted in marriage yet."

A long rush of air escaped Ramsey's mouth. "When Cora Dandridge died… something changed for Jonathon."

Even in death, the woman's name managed to make Sylphine frown. Until Cora, she hadn't thought herself a jealous person. Then she'd observed Jonathon's easy, flirtatious nature around the beautiful journalist, and Sylphine had wanted what she couldn't have. The traded mischievous touches, hidden smiles, and relaxed laughter she'd seen him share with Cora. When the woman had been murdered, something had fractured in Jonathon. Sylphine had been unwilling to help him pick up his broken pieces. A mistake she regretted to this second.

"Do you think he loved her?" Sylphine whispered.

Another heavy sigh left Ramsey. "I don't know. They'd bantered and argued for so long, I think he missed a close friend. Perhaps he loved her, but not the way I know she wanted. Which I'm glad for. She would have torn his heart out."

"Why do you believe that?"

"Miss Dandridge went through men like I go through books. Somehow, she was careful enough not to contract HRS. How I haven't figured out, but she did. Jonathon doesn't play those games. He never has. But I think if she'd managed to convince him, he would have fallen hard for her. She was a force of nature I often envied."

Sylphine considered the words. "Perhaps he could have helped her settle down."

"We'll never know. Would you have wanted to see them together?"

Horror made Sylphine recoil in the seat. "No! I would have sm—" Sylphine snapped her mouth closed.

A glimmer of triumph shimmered in Ramsey's eyes.

"Smacked her? Smashed her face in? Smote her where she stood with an evil glare?"

Sylphine couldn't help laughing. "Stars no, what would Haven City think of me if were to behave so..." She searched for the word she needed in her mind in Sziverian. "Tactless?"

"Oh, it would have been glorious. I can see the headlines in the gossip section of *The Chronicle* now. Italyssian Heiress Unleashes Island Passions."

Laughing harder, Sylphine shook her head. "You are impossible. Island passions?"

Ramsey waved the comb like a knife. "The poor woman wouldn't have known what hit her. Too bad."

"No, thank goodness. What would your brother think?"

"That he was worth fighting for?" Ramsey asked softly, tugging at a new knot.

Sylphine's smile faded. "He *is* worth fighting for."

"Just not for you?"

"I don't deserve, nor have the right, to fight for your brother."

Ramsey reached around and grasped Sylphine's arm. Under the calm, still waters of Ramsey's personality, tendrils of determination and a hint of anger filtered into Sylphine. She wanted to snatch her arm away before the emotions became stronger and un-ignorable. The two promise bands shone in the dim light of her room. One simple, the other etched with beautiful vines and inlaid with aquamarine stones.

"You are the only one who ever did have the right to fight for him. As for deserving?" Ramsey released her. "I don't know. I used to think you did. But you're so scared of yourself, perhaps you need to figure out who *you* are first."

3

The faint crackle and hiss of radio static competed with the rapid pounding of Sylphine's heart. She pressed the transmit button and tried again. *"Pata, Mita, akse tva piakestei risanstor."*

Like the other three attempts, radio silence greeted her request to please answer. Sylphine sniffled back the threat of tears and pressed the microphone to her forehead. The options available to reach them beyond a transmission were limited. By letter or by a communications center, either could easily be intercepted, and she'd lose the one edge she currently had. Sooner or later, someone would recall her promissory engagement to Jonathon, and they'd come for her. Sylphine needed all the time she could get before that happened.

Faint currents of concern, fatigue, wariness, and a strength of authority shifted in the air around Sylphine. A floorboard hadn't creaked, nor had she heard the study door open, but the intensity of Jonathon's emotional presence swirled like an eddy around her. Bracing herself for the gale force of the eldest Hunter, Sylphine carefully set the microphone back into its holder.

No one *felt* like Jonathon Hunter to Sylphine.

No one.

The first time Ramsey had introduced her to the Key Guardian Asherwick, the dominance of his emotions had almost knocked her over. She'd politely refused a physical connection. She still lacked the courage to reach out and simply touch him, in any capacity. Surviving such an onslaught would surely be the equivalent of withstanding a hurricane near the eyewall.

And yet… as she swept her gaze over his pristine attire, she couldn't help but wonder how swift his passions would turn. From the worry that seemed to be a constant companion to something else, something brighter, hotter. Joy, hope, desire, and dare she dream he'd ever feel it for her, even love.

At times such as now, when her world crumbled into terrifying dust around her, she considered forgetting how frightening being swept away by someone else's state of mind could be. The helplessness of losing herself as another's passions coursed through her body. For a single, crazy moment, she wondered what being swept into Jonathon's full range of emotions would be like. To experience the world through him completely. Sylphine fisted her hands and held them tight in her lap. No. She couldn't afford the distraction or the toll such an event would take on her.

Jonathon stopped at the corner of the desk, crossing his arms over his broad chest. The sleeves of the white dress shirt he wore pulled tight across his biceps, showing off defined muscles. He was clean shaven. Every strand of his dark brown hair was combed neatly in place. In a few hours, after the stress of his job weighed him down, his hair would be the first thing to become disheveled.

He braced a hip along the edge and looked her over.

Sylphine resisted the urge to fidget under his appraisal. "Did you reach your parents?"

"No," she sighed. "Nothing but static."

"Are you dressed to be seen?"

The change in topic took her off guard. He lifted his brows in question and straightened, adjusting his cuffs. Sylphine took a deep breath and glanced down at herself. Despite the overlapping layers of lace, silk, and cotton in various shades of rose pink, she still had the sensation of being exposed. She touched the naked strands of hair, normally layered with feathers, ribbons, and beads. A few bracelets dangled from her wrists, but she had nothing on her ankles or around her neck.

"I suppose," she said. "Why?"

"We need to go make sure you're legal."

"Ah." Of course, they did. "Did you sleep last night, harboring me?"

His velvet blue eyes warmed. A tinge of his amusement brushed past her. "I slept very well knowing you were under my roof, though I won't say it was uneventful."

Heat burned across Sylphine's cheeks. Somehow, she managed to keep her attention above his waist. "I see your humor has returned."

A smile transformed his face from good-looking to dangerously handsome. Jonathon had a dimple on his right side and perfect, straight white teeth. Sylphine swallowed. She'd forgotten the power of that smile. His mirth, now laced with happiness, heated her inside. A welcome break to the cold fear previously clinging to her.

"Slowly, yes, appears to be." And then he winked. And she forgot to take a breath.

When she remembered she needed oxygen to survive, she gulped in air too fast and choked. Sputtering and coughing, she turned away, mortification burning her cheeks. Jonathon reached close enough for his arm to brush hers. Sylphine froze, expecting a stronger wave of emotion from him. Only a sense of awareness and the heat of his body settled over her.

"What's wrong?" he asked, opening a small, top drawer.

Sylphine considered lying and saying nothing, but as she glanced up at met his curious, yet concerned gaze, she couldn't. "I… I expected to feel your emotions, more than I already do."

His focus shifted to where his arm almost rested against hers. "Because our arms touched?"

Sylphine frowned and moved closer to him, until she brushed along his forearm again. "Yes."

"Why?"

"I'm a Sympath," she said, moving away from him.

He rolled his eyes, and removed two objects from the drawer. "I'm very aware of your Gen-Heir talent. Somehow, I have a feeling *you* aren't aware of *how* it works." He shook his head and sighed, clipping a badge, and then a gun to his belt.

"I don't know how that's possible, but damn, it makes a lot of sense," he muttered with another head shake.

Confused, Sylphine tilted her head and looked up at him. "What do you mean?"

He shifted the waist of his pants to accompany the added weight. Sylphine realized she was watching a routine he did almost daily. He hadn't donned his tie yet or a jacket. The private nature of his actions had her cheeks flaming again. Though he didn't seem the least bit bothered, as though it were the most natural thing in the world for him to get ready for work in her presence.

"Do you trust me?" he asked, breaking her musing.

"Yes," she said without hesitation and realized she meant the word.

His jaw flexed in thought. "Why have you always been so leery of me then?"

"I'm overwhelmed when anyone touches me," she admitted.

He lifted his hand, palm facing towards her. "Do this."

Taking a deep breath, she obeyed.

"Now, you remember, you trust me."

He leaned over her. Both his hands braced on the arms of the chair, locking her in place. Alarmed, she pressed into the seat. They'd never been this close before. She'd never allowed it. He inhaled deeply. The first shift in his mood feathered across her skin, a faint sense of desire. The all too familiar sensation around men made panic threaten. Sylphine swallowed against the lead fist in her chest. Jonathon was different. He wouldn't be like *them*.

"You smell good, like sunshine, flowers, and I don't know what," he whispered.

"Salt, my ocean," she supplied.

"I always wondered how you'd smell." Another one of his devastating smiles crossed his face. "You never let me get near enough until now."

Up close, the rich blue depths of his eyes reminded her of the purest cuts of sapphire. His warm, woodsy masculine scent invaded her senses, adding an intriguing mixture of her own desire to the traces from him. "I thought I wouldn't be able to handle... you."

"Dangerous words to say to a man." His gaze flickered to her mouth.

The anticipation his fleeting glance to her lips caused shocked her. Sylphine had never invited a kiss before, yet they'd always happened anyway, with her powerless to stop them once the rush of lust invaded her senses. And she, a frigid lump of disappointment for a man's needs. The reminder served like a cold splash across her heated skin.

"Only to one who can't control himself."

The corners of his lips twitched again. "Good thing I have that in abundance."

"Do you have a point to all of this?"

"Ah, yes, my experiment for you."

Before she could realize his intent, he kissed her cheek. The brush of his lips to her skin sparked a tingle that rushed straight to her belly. When he straightened, he looked at her curiously.

"Well? Did that overwhelm you?"

Sylphine blinked. The touch of his mouth hadn't sent a current of feelings through her at all. No, what he *had* done had been all within her, a response she felt all on her own. "No."

"Touch my hand, or my neck, or my face. Anywhere you like."

The strong cords of his neck beckoned her touch. The steady beat of his pulse thrummed near the folded collar of his shirt. A sudden dryness coated Sylphine's throat. Her hand trembled as she gathered the courage to do what he asked. Unable to bring herself to touch him fully, she skimmed her fingertips along the warmth of his neck. Immediately, his myriad of emotions sizzled across her nerves. Sylphine gasped and dropped her hand before she could fully process even one of them.

"See the difference?" he asked. A wicked gleam lit his eyes. "Now kiss me. Same thing. Choose a spot."

"I don't…" She shook her head and let out a harsh breath. "I don't think that is a good idea, Jonathon."

Annoyance bracketed his mouth. "I promise I won't attack you."

"I know, but," she took another deep breath, "it is not very proper for me to do… that."

His touch swept along the two bracelets on her left wrist without touching her. "And yet you still wear my promise.

You're under my roof again. Why the concern about propriety now?"

Indeed. In fact, she'd done far more with other men. She wasn't a white-laced virgin. Embarrassment for all she *had* done made her flush. Compared to that, what he asked was downright chaste. But this was Jonathon Hunter. Safe Jonathon. Allowed only in her dreams to be everything she wanted and everything *he* would want from her. Broken illusions were treacherous things.

He didn't move. Patiently he waited for her to make her decision. Licking her lips, Sylphine lifted in the seat, drawing nearer to him. The cedar notes of his cologne grew stronger closer to his skin, blending in an enticing way with his natural male scent. Sylphine closed her eyes. Kiss him? She wanted to *taste* him. Surprised by the strength of the impulse, she clenched her teeth together to keep her tongue firmly in her mouth.

She couldn't resist taking another deep inhale as the edges of his collar teased her chin. Her lips pressed to the pulse now pounding in his throat. A male groan of longing vibrated under her kiss. The noise sent a thrill straight to her toes. No man had ever made that sound with her before.

Fascinated, Sylphine sat back and stared at him. His eyes were closed, every muscle in him tense. Then he touched her. A simple sliding of his fingers down her cheek and the rush of emotions she'd been expecting when she kissed him flooded into her. Sylphine froze, a cry lodged in her throat. His hand fell away.

"It's touch alone," he said, his voice strained. "Your hand or mine, has to be skin-to-skin contact. Clothes act as a barrier. I'm not sure how it works, but I know that much. Now, you know too."

Jonathon took a shuddering breath. He straightened, spinning away from her. Sylphine watched his retreat, but made no effort to call him back. She glanced down at her hands. Memories of all the times she'd been overcome by a flood of male emotions danced through her mind. In the haze of being overtaken, she could barely recall fingers wrapping around her wrist, her forearm. The first man to claim he loved her had once wrapped his hand around her neck right before he kissed her. She frowned. Had they known what they were doing to her?

In Italyssa, her genetically inherited gift was rare. In fact, she didn't know one other person who possessed it. Her mother believed the ability came from her mother's side. Family history documented her great-grandfather had been a Sympath. He'd used his *gift* to swindle people.

Nathalia Seartavos had different plans for her child. The street-raised daughter of a con man saw a talent in her daughter not to take advantage of others but to help. She'd tried her hardest to impart pride and honor in Sylphine. A lack of knowledge had made learning her talent difficult. Sziveria appeared to have more Sympaths. Knowing she wasn't alone, a freak among a population of dancers, artists, winemakers, and musicians seemed almost freeing.

"We need to be going," he said over his shoulder as he strode from the study.

Sylphine bit her lip. Being closed up inside Jonathon's small Ariot would be twice as difficult now. His scent still lingered in the air around her or perhaps refused to leave her mind, like the man himself.

WHAT IN THE *ARCTIC* HAD HE BEEN THINKING? JONATHON stared out the windshield while he waited for Sylphine at the curb in his Ariot. The hesitant flutter of her lips across his neck continued to burn a path straight to his groin. He shifted in the seat, adjusting his pants, again, before she climbed in. He didn't think she'd appreciate the all too masculine act.

Polite custom dictated he open the door for her, but he wasn't in the mood, or condition, to stand waiting. He'd struggle to keep his hands to himself, with her sitting only inches from him as it was.

Brisk morning air swept into the small cab when she opened the door, sending her unique, exotic scent ahead of her. Jonathon filled his lungs with ocean, flowers, and a brightness exclusive to her. Now clean, her bronze skin, two shades darker than his, glowed in the blooming light of day. The bohemian style of her gown accented every full curve of her figure. She slipped her fingers down a thick lock of hair, drawing attention to the missing ornaments normally mixed in with the rich blonde. Large silver hoops dangled from her ears, flashing as she slid inside. Her hand fell to her chest, where necklaces of various lengths made of silver, gold, and glass beads usually graced her neck. She sighed. Jonathon kept from grabbing her hand for comfort.

"It'll help sell you being robbed," he said quietly. When her eyes widened in question, he motioned up and down. "You missing so many parts of your wardrobe."

"Ah, yes." Her fingers curled into her chest. The sad frown filled her eyes as she focused out the window. "I lost four of my *Naenzi's* when I jumped in the water at Port Anchor."

The memory of her showing the importance of all the ornaments in her hair by dancing for him flashed through his mind. Even though the event occurred over a year ago, the vision of her twirling, hips swaying, feet moving to a rhythm set in her mind, the ribbons, beads, and feathers creating a rainbow of color around her, seemed real enough to touch. The provocative show had been to teach him how the Blessings of Beauty, or *Naenzi te Kordelka* in her language, worked to make her beautiful to suitors in her native land. Jonathon didn't think Sylphine needed any help being *more* attractive.

Greater, however, were their personal significance. They were gifted on her birthday every year of her life until she married, by a female family member. Each one was a memory, an offering of love. And she'd lost four. Jonathon's chest tightened. He shifted the Ariot into gear.

"I'm sorry." He gripped the steering wheel to keep from reaching for her.

"I should have given them to my *Mita* before I left her."

"I'm sure you weren't thinking you'd somehow lose them."

He waited at an intersection for the traffic patrol to guide the next crossing. Beside the Ariot, a horse pawed impatiently at worn brick, leading a cart full of produce. The driver expertly handled the beast, keeping him in line, and in his lane. Their turn arrived, and Jonathon pulled ahead of the horse.

The headquarters for the Immigration and Import Regulation Agency were on the outskirts of town, near the main MagnaRail station. Most imports not checked at Port Scarbrough were inspected once they reached the rail station. Several nations had embassies near the Agency as well.

Jonathon tapped the wheel. "Would your embassy have your documentation, since you do business here so often?"

A guarded expression crossed her face. "I would rather avoid my embassy, if possible."

Unease grew in the pit of his stomach. What wasn't she telling him? "Why?"

Her attention remained out the window. An almost indiscernible shift moved her closer to the door, further from him. She must have sensed his displeasure and suspicion. Something she didn't like. Too bad.

"I do not know who the Cyrano's own. I cannot risk them

finding me." Her gaze flitted briefly to him before returning to the view outside. "My parents' lives depend on my remaining unfound."

Jonathon glanced her way again. She hadn't mentioned the name before. "These Cyrano's are threatening your parents?"

"Yes."

"Very well, they will be a last resort."

"Thank you."

They made the rest of the journey in silence. Jonathon found a parking space behind the monolithic granite building. A perfect square, with a glass domed courtyard in the center, the structure was a throwback to early Sziverian architecture, when civilization still learned the power of creating something impressive with labor.

The midmorning sun had worn away most of the frost in the grass and along the window panes, but a few shadows created a haven for stubborn glittery remnants of ice. Jonathon surveyed the bustle of Guardians, most working for the IIRA, and a few civilian support staff hurry up the sidewalks and stairs into the building or to their vehicles to take them to an assignment.

Jonathon's great-grandfather had worked as an agent in this building. Had earned the ranked position of Key Guardian Asherwick for his service. In doing so, he'd secured a future with a choice for the generations that followed. To continue in civil service or serve in a seat in the Hall of Laws. To date, the Hunters had chosen service over a seat.

The morning's rays still hadn't warmed the air enough to send away the chill of night. Jonathon shrugged deeper into his jacket and shoved his hands in his pockets, using his hip to close the door. Sylphine unwrapped a shawl she'd had tied around her waist and swept the long, thick layer of fabric across her shoulders. Birds chirped a melodious song, flitting between parked Ariot's and tree branches, looking for a morsel of anything worth eating.

On the other side of the building, carriages for hire lined the sidewalk waiting for fairs. Groups ambled down the steps, taking the first ones they came to, loading up, and being carted off. Horns *meeped*, and men yelled in protest as slower horses pulled into traffic crawling by. Sylphine shaded her eyes and watched as an Ariot whipped around before a driver could cut him off, causing the horse to rear up in protest.

Shaking her head, she fell in step beside him. "I always wonder how an Ariot would stand up to being trampled by an angered horse."

"Hurts the horse," Jonathon offered. "The metal and glass tend to tear them up."

A visible shudder ran through her. "How awful."

"There aren't any Ariot's in Italyssa?"

"No, we have horse-drawn carts, bicycles, or our feet. Our streets aren't big enough to share much more."

"Outside of Haven City, bicycling is more common. Those who can't afford anything more still travel that way in the city, but it can be dangerous."

Her attention shifted to the crowded street. "I can see."

Inside, the chaos wasn't much better. Though the rush of people and loud shouts to be heard above the noise was less than what Jonathon dealt with on a daily basis at his HCES office. Sylphine approached the reception area, where five workers dealt with official visitors, and the uninvited. A young man handed a temporary visitors' badge to a stern older woman, who snatched the thick printed card on a lanyard from his hand. Nose in the air, she picked up a suitcase resting at her feet and stalked off.

The young man heaved out a sigh. When his dark eyes

noticed Sylphine, they grew bright, as did his smile. "Miss Seartavos! We weren't told to expect you."

"Not to worry, Harris. Key Guardian Asherwick and myself were not expected this morning." She stepped up to the counter, smoothing her hands along the surface until her forearms took her weight.

Harris's attention briefly flickered to Jonathon before returning to the beauty displayed before him. Jonathon understood and managed to keep a smile in check. Hands still in his pockets, he waited behind Sylphine. He didn't figure she'd need his help obtaining her documents.

Something close to relief relaxed the receptionists face. "Oh good, I didn't think I could handle two upset women in a row."

Frowning, Sylphine seemed to watch after the retreating form of the woman who'd walked off. "You know I do not cause trouble."

"Who was she?" Jonathon asked out of curiosity.

A flush darkened Harris's cheeks. He set about searching through a collection of files. "Shield Guardian Northclyffe."

Jonathon immediately sought out the now barely visible form of the woman, walking with stiff purpose towards the wide granite stairs leading to the floors above. "The First Prefect for Riaville Enforcement Services?"

"Yes, apparently, *she* was expected this morning."

Sziveria had four major cities, though Haven City was the most populated, three others were large enough to have Shield Guardians who served as First Prefect for Enforcement Services. Riaville was the last bastion of civilization before the Tabrias Mountains split the country. Most of the residents made the long train ride to one of the three prisons for employment in the Northern Boundary or worked the massive shipping yards and docks of Port Tabria.

Jonathon had a thick folder on his desk with pages of

supposed prisoner transfers. Only, the transfers never actually happened. The inmates were shipped off to work as slave labor, in several nations where resources were likely being stolen from what were believed to be Uninhabited Zones.

The point of transit out of the country was believed to be Port Tabria, where Shield Guardian Northclyffe had dominion. Jonathon hadn't found the time yet to review the documents, but perhaps someone else held suspicions at the Agency. Or, worse yet, perhaps someone was as corrupt as the previous Shield Guardian for the Haven City Enforcement Services had been. Either Northclyffe herself or someone within the IIRA.

Jonathon didn't care for either prospect.

While he'd been musing and plotting conspiracy theories, Sylphine had finished explaining her dire situation. Harris seemed sympathetic and handed her a visitor's badge and instructions on where to go to hopefully procure her legal documentation. He'd told Sylphine he'd wait for her in the lobby. Once she disappeared into the crowd, Jonathon faced the desk again.

"Is there a radio I can use?"

"You want me to say what again?"

Sylphine stared at Jonathon over the top of the massive radio capable of achieving overseas communications. Even though he'd explained what she needed to do twice now, she was so nervous about messing up, she couldn't think straight. If she somehow botched this, her parents, and her hiding location, would be in jeopardy.

While she'd been obtaining her documents, thankfully a simple endeavor, Jonathan had attempted to send a message from the Agency to her parents. Sylphine had been shocked and grateful for his concern and efforts. If the message didn't come from his home, but rather from a known business venture, he'd explained, it'd probably be delivered without much question. When the connection had gone through, however, the person on the other end couldn't understand any words he spoke. Since Jonathon didn't know but two or three words in Italyssian, he'd had to wait until she finished.

Patient as ever, he folded his forearms on the radio and looked over the top at her. "Something your parents would know is you. Maybe something they call you, or a favorite food you enjoy as a family. Say the shipment of whatever *that* is has arrived. The missive will be coming from Sziverian Import and Immigration Agency, so they'll know you made it here."

The operator connected the call and gave a thumbs up when the line picked up. Sylphine held the microphone to her lips and spoke her message. The shipment of doves had arrived safely. Because the message came from the Agency, Sylphine added all documentation was in order.

When she finished with a nod to the operator, she glanced up to see Jonathon giving her a peculiar look. She flushed and tucked a lock of hair behind her ear. "What?"

He shook his head as if waking from a daze. "Nothing. I just forget how…." His attention shifted to the operator, and sighed. "Never mind."

Sylphine stood as he straightened. She thanked the operator again, keeping her hands clasped behind her back to discourage any offerings of contact. Jonathon motioned for her to precede him from the room. Outside, the sun made a valiant attempt to warm the air, but the chill on the breeze reminded Sylphine she was a long way from home. At the Ariot, Jonathon held the door for her. She slid into the interior, gathering the long length of her skirt between her legs as she settled.

The door didn't close after her. Confused, she glanced

up and found Jonathon lounging against the open frame, his arms braced over the edge of the door. He watched her, his dark gaze looking over every inch of her. Sylphine clasped her hands between her knees and took a long breath.

"What?" she asked when he failed to move.

"What was the message you sent?"

Sylphine looked at the windshield, the awareness of him made her heart kick. She'd seen a similar look in others. Similar, but not the same, and she wasn't sure what the difference was in him. "I said the doves had arrived."

"Doves?"

"Yes." She fidgeted. "Can't you get inside?"

"I'm not quite ready to be so close to you yet."

The admission made her focus snap back to him. Their eyes locked for several intense seconds. A sudden, strong urge to *touch* him had her pressing her knees together, holding her hands hostage. Coward that she was, Sylphine closed her eyes on a shuddering breath and turned her head away. The Ariot bounced with the force of the door closing.

"Why doves?" he asked as he entered the vehicle.

Sylphine propped her arm on the door and rested her chin in her palm, thankful for the return to civility. "My mother calls me her dove."

He grunted and powered the Ariot. "Bird of peace."

Sylphine couldn't help the little sarcastic snort that escaped. "Bird of elegance, not peace."

"Are you not a negotiator?" He turned the wheel with stealthy precision, arcing them backward out of the parking spot so fast she squeaked in alarm.

Unused to the speed in which he maneuvered, Sylphine grabbed the first thing she could reach, which happened to be his arm. "I am in favor of my father's company, yes."

A humorous glint sparkled in his eyes. His fingers tapped

on the steering wheel. "I guess *my hawk* doesn't have the same ring to it."

The heat of his skin through the jacket tingled along her palm. The sensation of his firm muscles flexing as he wove through traffic made her breath catch. Sylphine snatched her hand away. "No, I suppose not."

He weaved and darted between horses and other Ariot's too slow to make the same bold moves. Sylphine sucked in her breath, her heart in her throat.

"Why the rush?" she asked.

"I'm late. I have to get you back, and get to the precinct before my MP reams me a new one."

Sylphine tried to process his words. She remained confused. "*What* will he do?"

Jonathon glanced at her. She squealed and waved at the road. He laughed and turned his attention back to driving. "He'll yell at me until I'm properly subdued."

Her eyes widened in disbelief. "Subdued? Would he believe that about you?"

He shrugged and pulled into the driveway. "Wouldn't matter. I can play the part if I need to. If he's mad and I'm at fault, I will 'Yes, Master Prefect' with the worst of them."

Sylphine shook her head on a chuckle, reaching for the door handle. "I cannot see you saying 'yes master' to anyone."

"Prefect," he corrected with a wink. "Master *Prefect*."

She dropped her gaze to his jacket, where his dual ranks, *Master Tribunii Hunter* and *Key Guardian Asherwick*, were embroidered in deep, golden letters. "Does anyone call you master?"

The moment the question escaped her mouth, she regretted the words. All traces of humor fled from his face. His mouth set into a grim line. He sat very still.

"I control no one, Sylphine," he said softly.

Even though he had no way of knowing her dark past, she couldn't help the hitch in her throat or how the words resonated within her. All she could do was nod and escape the Ariot before he noticed how deeply his admission had affected her and asked questions she couldn't answer.

Outside, the brisk air welcomed her. She sucked in a lungful and closed the door with her back, leaning against it for a moment before venturing to the house. The two-story residence blocked the sun making its slow journey across the sky, casting a hard, cold shadow. Her shoes crunched on the loose pebbled path. The *whoosh* of the magnetically powered car accelerating sent a tight discomfort through her chest.

Jonathon was gone.

FEET POUNDING ON THE PAVEMENT, JONATHON IGNORED THE shouts of protest and screams of distress as he flew by other pedestrians. He pressed a finger to his ear, trying to make out the crackled words coming into his coms unit.

"Left, Hunter, left!" a woman shouted through the earpiece. *"Rainier, he's coming towards you, down Old Beekman Row."*

Jonathon turned left, barely avoiding a trash can toppled over in front of a gate. He glanced at the street sign as he ran past and did a quick search of where Old Beekman was in relation to him. At the next alley, he cut across, upsetting a horse pulling a small cart. He waved in apology before he disappeared down the dank, narrow lane. A cat hissed and scurried from his path, while a dog barked in frustrated anger through a window.

"Is he still on Old Beekman, Ericksen?" Jonathon asked, releasing the transmit button.

"Yes," she replied. *"We can't get a vehicle down it. Too narrow. FG Wackerly is understandably upset. We must rescue his hat."*

Jonathon shook his head and couldn't hold back a grin at

the Tribunii's dry tone. He pressed the transmit button. "Tell the FG not to worry, he has two MT's on the task."

"Don't worry, MT. I've told him the hat is as good as his again."

His team normally worked navigable streets and avenues. The restricted rows of tightly packed dwellings that barely passed for houses weren't something they were used to. Jonathon had enforced these areas as a First Guardsman; however, he knew all the little cut-overs and side paths.

Sweat dripped down his cheeks and coated his back. They'd been chasing the would-be burglar for eight rows now. Aside from whatever he'd snatched from the crime scene he'd stumbled into, he'd taken off with First Guardsman Tray Wackerly's hat.

Since guarding the house against looky-loos was the FG's first street assignment, and not only did a burglar get in but managed to pilfer a part of his uniform, Wackerly was having a bad day. Jonathon and his team weren't helping by teasing the kid. Even though he deserved every bit of their good-natured torment.

The thief's bright blue shirt caught Jonathon's attention the second he emerged from the alley. Jonathon put on a burst of speed. Cries of alarm and annoyance tipped the man off to Jonathon's presence. The thief pushed and shoved people to try to slow Jonathon down. Used to the tactic, Jonathon quickly maneuvered around the human obstacles. Before the man could down another narrow side street, Jonathon launched himself forward. He crashed into the robber, sending them toppling into a rotting fence.

Wood splintered underneath him and fragmented in the air. Jonathon landed hard on something that refused to give under his weight and forced air from his lungs in a painful rush. The thief cursed, tumbling into the dirt-filled yard. Before the man could fully rise, Jonathon grabbed his leg and yanked, sending him sprawling face first into a bucket filled with something thick and dark. The thief reared up, gasping and sputtering, clawing at his face in panic.

Laughing between catching his breath, Master Tribunii Marck Rainier stopped at the broken fence, bracing his hands on his thighs. "Well, that's one way to catch a crook, Hunter."

Jonathon gave the burglar another yank, removing cuffs from his hip with his other hand. "I'm glad I have your approval."

Marck motioned with his fingers at himself. "Here, I'll handle that."

Jonathon didn't argue, grimacing as a sharp pain radiated from his side when he handed over the cuffs. Marck tossed the dust-covered First Guardsman cap onto Jonathon's lap, along with a small aluminum cooking pot. Melted down, the pot had some value. To Jonathon, it wasn't enough to warrant the prison time. The situation was clearly different to the thief.

"Hey!" the crook shouted as Marck yanked his arms back. "Why you taking me in?"

"You stole something," Marck answered, the cuffs clicking into place. "Therefore, you go in."

"I didn't steal nothing she'd be needing. She's dead," he argued, his feet scrambling for purchase when Marck hauled him up.

"You'll get the chance to make your statement at the Accusation Hearing. Until then, you'll have plenty of time to perfect your account in a holding cell at South Row Division."

The crook sputtered in protest, his words lost in the cacophony of neighborhood noise as they disappeared into the crowded thoroughfare. Sighing, Jonathon forced himself to stand. He slapped the patrol cap against his thigh to remove some of the dust. Holding the pot handle in his other hand, he ambled down the street barely big enough for the parade of delivery carts inching their way through.

People wove between the horses and carts, some patient, some not.

At the end of the street, Tribunii Melody Ericksen leaned against a dark silver Ariot, arms crossed. Chestnut curls framed her round face, amusement danced in her spring-green eyes. Beside her, First Guardsman Wackerly rolled a pebble with the toe of his boot, his visible skin three different shades of red. Jonathon plopped the hat on the young man's tawny head. He reached up with both hands and held the cap down.

"Don't lose it again," Jonathon said, chuckling. He held out the pot. "Evidence will need this when you go to the Accusation Hearing."

FG Wackerly took the handle, his pale blue eyes wide. "You won't do the process?"

Jonathon shook his head. "Wasn't on my watch he stole."

The reminder brought a new level of flush to the kid's cheeks, still full of youthful pudge. He pulled his hat off, further mussing his hair. "Yeah, okay."

Jonathon shifted his attention to Melody. She nudged the young First Guardsman in the ribs. Wackerly grimaced and stared at her in confusion. Wanting to avoid the forced gratitude he knew she was about to make the FG attempt, Jonathon eased back away from them.

"Did MT Rainier say if he needed me anymore to process the scene at the house?"

Melody straightened from the Ariot and looked around. When she didn't seem to see who she was looking for, she shrugged. "I think so, weren't we finished when the FG here lost his hat?"

Wackerly sighed in dejection. Shaking his head, he climbed into the Ariot. Jonathon chuckled. "This will follow him his entire career."

Melody grinned. "Yeah it will, and I for one, can't wait.

We need something fun at South Row. We aren't like you East Streeters, all easy ranked guardian crimes and complaints."

Jonathon managed a smile. "Is that what you think?"

She waved an arm around the chaotic street. Vendors shouted. A woman tossed a slop bucket from a second-story window. Skinny dogs slunk between slow roving carriage wheels, searching out any morsel of food. Someone stepped in an unidentifiable pile and cursed. A baby cried on a stoop while a woman beat a rug over a sagging porch rail. No, his Division didn't work in one of the poorest areas of Haven City. He worked among the deceit and treachery of a class meant to protect the nation who only seemed to want to protect themselves. Somehow, that seemed worse.

Sprinkled in between the wealthy homes and businesses of successful merchants and Guardians, were a few middle-class rows. Among the carefully maintained houses and manicured side yards, a sinister threat spread like an invisible shadow.

"It's what I want to think." Her gaze lingered over the lives unfolding around them in their daily tasks. "This place is bleak enough. They don't need none of the magic lily dust mess, too. I'd prefer to remain ignorant of the stuff, and the secondary crimes it seems to be responsible for."

Jonathon understood. He didn't want to know about the pink powder that had destroyed so many lives either. "I'm surprised it didn't hit here first, actually."

She bristled, swiping a curl out of her face with an angry sweep of her hand. "Why? Because poor must mean they need a way to escape their miserable reality?"

Jonathon settled his weight onto his back leg, glancing over the top of the Ariot to a man smoking a cigarette, waving a tan glass bottle in the face of anyone who came near. "Because the population is denser here. The row known for sex-hustlers is two down, and we both know they prefer their clientele as sedated as possible. How many times have you conducted a search in this area and came away with illegal substances?" He nodded with his chin towards the man across the way. "I bet if I walked across the street, that man would finally notice my jacket and take off."

Her jaw worked, and she shot a defiant glance over her shoulder. "Maybe, maybe not. Could be a jar of water he claims cures everything."

"Might be, sure. My point is whoever started circulating magic lily dust did it for profit to start with." Jonathon opened his arms, ignoring the sharp pain in his side. "They won't find much profit here. Not when, as far as we can tell, it's all being imported."

Uneasiness scrunched up her face. "They'll start cutting it with something."

"Yes," Jonathon agreed. "And I think they did. I think that's what killed the woman in your case I was sent here to help with."

"And someone didn't want us to know, so they made it look like murder."

Jonathon inclined in his head. "Very good. I can see why MT Rainier is looking for a Master Tribunii position for you."

She flushed at his praise. "Maybe yours will open up since you're due to make First Tribunii."

A swift breeze blew down the street, ruffling Jonathon's hair, carrying the stench of greasy food and waste. Good thing he needed a shower when he went home. "I have no desire to be FT. I like solving cases, not sitting in an office all day."

"Maybe someone else, then." Her green eyes gleamed. "Isn't the MT for forgery, embezzlement, and robbery at East Street being promoted? Solving bank and merchant offenses would be a nice break from violent crimes."

"Let me know if you apply. I'll talk to the MP over the unit."

Her back straightened. "You'd do that?"

"Of course." Jonathon smiled and winked. "We MT's have to have each other backs."

Casting a coy smile, she tucked a curl behind her ear. "I'm not MT yet."

"You will be."

"We usually go eat after a team case, you should join us," she said, her gaze flickering from his eyes to his mouth and beyond.

Jonathon studied her for a moment, from the enticing blush of her cheeks to her small, lithe frame, and knew, given nurturing and time, they could see if something would bloom between them. Melody Ericksen was driven to climb the Enforcement ladder, and within a few years, she'd succeed and outrank him. Not necessarily an issue.

No, the bigger issue Jonathon grudgingly had to admit: she wasn't Sylphine. Perhaps that was a good thing. Though, when his mind conjured his perfect woman, all he could see was lush curves and, when unguarded, a teasing promise in ocean-green eyes. Jonathon wanted what he couldn't have. And sadly, he wasn't willing to settle for less either.

With a declining smile, he took a step farther from her. "I appreciate the offer, but I need to get back home."

Disappointment shifted across her face, replaced quickly with an upturn of her mouth and a stiffening in her shoulders. "Cases to review?"

Jonathon nodded. "Always."

She looked at him for a long moment and then nodded. "I don't give up easily, you know."

A crooked smile twitched across his lips. "You wouldn't be a good investigator if you did."

5

———

THE ECHO OF A DOOR CLOSING JOSTLED SYLPHINE FROM SLEEP. Alarmed, she bolted upright. A paper fluttered in her vision, and she gasped.

Where was she?

She tried to glance around, but the paper flapped in her field of view again. Reaching up in exasperation, she touched the sheet and realized it was stuck to her face. Booted footfalls sounded outside the door, and she squeaked in distress. That's right, she'd come to Jonathon's study to use his radio in another attempt to reach her parents. In aggravation when she'd failed, again, she laid her head on the desk and must have fallen asleep. And apparently drooled, because now one of his papers was glued to her cheek.

No, no, no! He could *not* find her like this!

Sylphine snatched the paper off her face and slapped it to the desk. Using her thumb and middle finger, she attempted to remove any remaining evidence she'd fallen asleep with her mouth hanging open. Jonathon paused when he walked into the study, his hand in the process of removing the objects from his belt. An odd look crossed his face before he continued. He looked— Sylphine allowed her gaze to wander the length of him, from his messy hair to the sweat-streaked dirt coating his face and clothing— drained.

"What happened?" she asked, rising.

At the desk, he dropped the items into a drawer with a shrug. "Nothing."

Sylphine took a deep breath, allowing his mood to fully surround her. Frustration, annoyance, a hint of anger, and fatigue. "Not nothing," she whispered, meeting his stare with a defiant tilt of her chin.

He slowly reached for her. Inhaling in alarm, she shied back. Shaking his head, his disappointment reached her before the expression crossed his face. "I was just going to smudge some of the ink off your face. What happened to you?"

Gasping, Sylphine rubbed her fingers on her cheek. The tips came away black. She tried not to be irritated with herself over her reaction towards Jonathon, but years of being over-whelmed by the touch of another had ingrained a fear in her she couldn't seem to overcome. Not even for him, no matter how much she was beginning to want to.

"Is it away?" she asked, rubbing again and seeing nothing.

A half-smile tilted Jonathon's lips. "Gone. Is it gone," he corrected. "And no, it's not."

His brows lifted in a questioning manner as he leaned closer. Sylphine breathed deep to gather courage. Bracing a hand on the desk, she nodded. Without a mirror, she wouldn't be able to clear what she assumed was smudged ink from her face.

Jonathon reached into an inner jacket pocket and pulled out a dark blue handkerchief. After covering his fingers in the fabric, he swept the cloth down her cheek, rubbing at persis-tent areas. Deep concentration pinched his forehead and bracketed his mouth. The expression was a common one for him. Time and again, she'd observed him pouring over files with the same intense look on his face. With his focus directed at her, an odd flip trembled in her stomach.

Sylphine's eyes wandered his face, down his neck to his chest and beyond. The sensation deepened in her stomach. Would he look the same, overcome with passion? Or different? Again the desire to touch him, to run her fingers down his cheek, to his strong jaw, took her by surprise. Not for the first time in her life, Sylphine's so-called *gift* brought forth bitter regret. If she were normal, she'd be experiencing how the shadow growing along his jaw felt under her fingers, how his pulse beat at his neck, or even in his chest.

Instead, she tried not to be swept away by the emotions radiating from him seeping into her without a single brush of her hand to his flesh. He straightened, inspected his work, and then nodded.

"All gone." He tossed the cloth onto his desk and picked up a sheet of paper. He flipped it back and forth with a frown. "Hope this wasn't important."

Heat rushed into her cheeks. "I am so sorry. I tried to call my parents, and I fell asleep when I laid my head down."

"Still no answer?"

She shook her head. "Nothing."

Concern shone in his dark eyes. "I'm sorry. Perhaps I can try from my office?"

"If they took their radio, it will not matter. I am beginning to believe that's what happened."

A grimace scrunched his face as he slipped out of his jacket. The annoyance she'd sensed earlier returned in force, followed by a sliver of anger. He turned away from her. Dirt and something darker streaked his white shirt. Twisting, he inspected his side, not visible to her. His softly uttered curse made her brows raise. She blinked in thought, processing quickly why he'd be irritated and angry. The reason dawned like light spilling through a window.

An injury.

Sylphine grabbed his arm and pushed, forcing him to face her once again. A small red bloom stood out against the dingy white cotton. Gasping, she grabbed the shirt and yanked. The smooth skin of his abs tensed, outlining the defined muscles just beneath the surface. Above his hip, a ragged cut marred his side, but the injury wasn't the only issue. Something dark and jagged protruded from his skin.

Before she could stop herself, she touched him. "Wha—" She didn't get the chance to finish her thought as the irritation from his wound and anxiety, likely from her touch, held her captive.

He stepped out of her reach. His shirt fluttered back over his stomach. "You really do get lost, don't you?"

The contact severed, Sylphine took a deep breath and met his worried gaze. "I... I do not know how to stop it from happening."

"And how do you feel, when it happens?"

She tilted her head, not understanding. "What do you mean?"

"Your personal feelings. You still have them, yes?"

Waving her hand, she dismissed his question and pointed at him. "I am not the one with something sticking out of my body. You need a medical scientist."

Jonathon shook his head, hanging his jacket over the back of his chair. "I'm fine. I have tweezers upstairs. I'll get it out. Probably a piece of the fence I went through."

"You said nothing happened!"

He shrugged, untucking his shirt the rest of the way. "I wasn't lying, nothing unusual happened."

"Having a chunk of wood in your body is normal?"

Sighing, he headed from the room. "Wood, a knife, a fork.

What else." He looked contemplative for a moment. "Broken glass, a nail, a letter opener, a garden trowel, one of those li—"

Sylphine stared at him in horror. She held up her hand to stop him from continuing. "No, no more. People did all that to you?"

Another shrug. "Sure. When people are desperate, they'll do anything."

He disappeared into the dark foyer. Seconds later, the creak of a stair filtered into the space. Sylphine stared at the darkened doorway in disbelief. Of course, she knew his job wasn't exactly safe. He was an Investigator for Enforcement Services. He went after violent criminals on a near daily basis. However, she'd always figured he handed someone orders to apprehend said offenders, not go after them himself.

Gathering her courage, Sylphine chased after him. The thought of him yanking the chunk of wood from his side alone caused pain to blossom in her chest. How was she supposed to help, though, when she couldn't even touch him? Deciding she'd address that issue when faced with it again, she slipped into the open door of his room. Light split the darkness from a doorway to the right.

He stood with one foot braced on the edge of a tub, shirt unbuttoned, torso turned to examine the injury. Sylphine flexed her hands, looking him over. His earlier question came to mind. *How did she feel when she touched someone?*

Underneath the surface of the emotional vortex she'd been sucked into, the heat of his skin under hers flickered in her mind. The play of his muscles tensing when she'd been so close to his wound. There had been no time to consider how *she* was affected by the physical contact.

"Let me help," she said.

He glanced over his shoulder in surprise. Slowly, he

lowered his foot to the floor. "How can you when you won't touch me?"

She regarded him for a moment as he voiced her concern. "You think I can, though. You believe I can touch you and not be stunned."

"I know another Sympath. He has excellent control over his talent, so yes, I know it's possible." He crossed the short distance to a row of cupboards across from a small pedestal sink. "But I don't know how he was taught or how to help you learn."

Leaning a shoulder on the jamb, she crossed her arms. "I want to help you."

Silver glinted in his hand. Tweezers. He held them out to her. "I admit, it's in a tough spot. If you think you can help, go ahead. Otherwise, I'll get Ramsey. Won't be the first time she's had to fix me."

Sylphine straightened and accepted the tweezers. He turned, pushing the shirt out of the way and bearing his side to her. In the brighter light of the bathroom, the angry wound made her gasp. Dried blood mixed with dirt streaked down to the waist of his pants. The large splinter protruded grotesquely from his skin. She stared at it, working her bottom lip between her teeth.

"I think it will bleed when I pull it out," she said with worry.

He went back to the cupboard and pulled out a handful of cotton bandages. "Okay, ready for the inevitable."

Sylphine perched on the edge of the tub and took a deep breath. She poised the sharp points over the splinter and frowned. How was she supposed to maneuver without bracing herself on him? Flexing her jaw in thought, she steadied herself on his hip, covered by his pants. A stillness surrounded him. Concerned, Sylphine glanced up.

His eyes were closed, shoulders pressed back. Nervous

anticipation and the faintest hint of desire he couldn't hide tingled along her skin. The bright lamps over the sink washed his bared torso in stark relief, outlining the subtle plains of muscle he earned in the situations that resulted in his current injury.

Faint white scars broke up the expanse of his abdomen, adding a curious, rugged appeal. Sylphine wanted to trace them, kiss them. Learn more completely how the man displaying them earned the badges of courage. Once again, the strength of her interest in Jonathon as a *man* stunned her.

The men previous to him, with whom she'd made the mistake – or rather allowed them to overwhelm her into acceptance – of taking them as lovers, had never fascinated her the way Jonathon did. Perhaps because they'd moved everything too fast for her to see them as anything more than a disappointment in the end. Jonathon gave her an opportunity. Distance to study. A chance to wonder.

All dangerous things.

Shaking her head at her fanciful thoughts, Sylphine focused on her task. "Are you ready?"

His gaze shifted to her. If his emotional state weren't an open book, his shadowed eyes would leave her wondering what he was feeling. "With you down there like that, I'm ready for anything."

Sylphine let his words sift around in her mind until their meaning dawned. If he were to turn and face her, the seam of his pants would be level with her mouth. The idea sent a wicked flash of hunger across her nerves. Both that he considered it and that she imagined it. A hot flush crept up her neck, setting her cheeks aflame. "Jonathon Hunter!"

He brushed the tail of his shirt behind his back, exposing the wound more clearly for her. "Yes?"

Words failed. Shaking her head, she sighed. "You will make me have to get Ramsey."

His attention slid away from her. "I'd rather not think of my sister right now, thank you very much."

Laughter bubbled up in Sylphine, and she smacked his thigh. "You are terrible."

He glanced down at her again and winked. "Only with you."

The banter was indeed common. Jonathon had never shied from teasing her in the most tempting of ways. "How did I get so lucky?"

He shifted his weight on his feet, angling his body to see his injury better. "I don't know. I guess because I know you don't take me seriously, so I can."

A trace of disappointment accompanied his words. Sylphine wanted to tell him that's all he'd ever feel when it came to her if she did take him seriously. A dissatisfying memory. The depressing thought forced her back to the task, which had slipped from her mind, again. Jonathon was remarkably gifted at distraction.

"How did you function with this in your side?" she asked, her fingers curling into his pants while she carefully nudged the tweezer tips around the sliver. The solid muscle of his thigh tightened under the fabric.

"I hurt, but I didn't know anything was wrong until I took my jacket off and saw the blood. I didn't have time to check it before I was home." He hissed, his body jerking when she made an attempt to dislodge the wood.

She mirrored his reaction and cringed. "I am sorry."

He let out a long breath. "No, it's okay. Quick pull, all right?"

Nodding, she braced herself and the tweezers again. This time, once they were in position and she felt the solid mass between the pincers, she gave a hard tug. The thick splinter slid free. Fresh, bright blood welled from the small puncture wound left behind. She inspected the jagged chunk of wood.

"Tell me you saved a small fortune in diamonds or maybe rescued a child when this happened?"

Hoarse laughter rumbled from his throat. "Afraid not. A Guardsman's hat and an aluminum pot are quite safe."

"What?" she asked in disbelief.

"Yep." He blotted at the seeping wound. "Was sort of nostalgic, actually. I hadn't chased a petty criminal through the South Rows in years."

Sylphine searched his face. "You had fun."

A smile tugged at his lips. "Arctic, yeah, I had fun."

"If you like chasing thieves through the streets, why don't you go back to being a street enforcer?"

He held up a bloody cotton square. "Bad for my health."

"I still have the salve you gave me in my room. I will be right back."

Sylphine found the ointment on her dressing table. She returned to Jonathon's bathroom to find him pulling a gauze roll from the cupboard. He held it out to her.

"Trade you," he said, motioning with the roll to the little jar in her hand.

She held the roll while he applied the medicine to his side. He shrugged the shirt completely off when he was finished. Sylphine resisted the temptation to lick her lips and swallow against the sudden dryness in her throat. Her heart kicked as she took in his strong shoulders and the flex of his biceps.

"Help me wrap this around my waist, please."

Sylphine blinked away her stupor and stepped the rest of the way into the bathroom. He held a square to his side and waited for her to unroll the gauze. She went around to his back. Using his free hand, he helped wrap it around his waist. Sylphine tried not to breathe him in, the smooth expanse of his back close enough for her taste if she wanted. Deep inside, she knew he'd let her. Knew he'd let her do a lot more if she wished.

Somehow, she managed to behave herself. At each pass of the gauze, while she waited, she took in his bathroom. Clean. Organized. So different from the chaos of his desk and the bookshelves in his office. His bedroom was thankfully dark, so she had no idea, aside from the hint of light that outlined what appeared to be a huge bed, what his space looked like.

"All finished," he said, tying off the excess. "Thank you."

Before she could walk around him, he was looming over her. The rich depths of his blue eyes filled her vision. The flash of exhilaration was the only warning she had when his mouth descended. A firm, lingering press of his lips on hers left her shocked. She stared at him as he straightened, a wicked grin twinkling in his eyes and playing on his mouth.

"You didn't drown, did you?" he asked.

Her hand shaking, she pressed it to her mouth and shook her head.

When he leaned close again, she dropped her hand and closed her eyes. His lips brushed hers in a tender, whispering kiss. Pulling, teasing, but demanding nothing. She returned the gentle exploration. Her hands clenched into her dress to keep from gliding along his warm skin to his shoulders. An exciting little quiver danced in her stomach, a new sensation all her own, not created from someone else's emotions. She focused on it while his lips moved over hers.

Cool air swept across her face and mouth. Surprised, her eyes fluttered open to find him staring at her with an odd expression. She swallowed. Heavy dread settled in her stomach. Had she been cold for him, too? "What?"

"How did that feel?"

"Different… strange," she admitted, a little breathless.

"Good different?"

Flushed, she nodded. He didn't appear to be disappointed. "Yes."

Seemingly satisfied with her answer, he stepped aside.

Sylphine hesitated. She met his searching stare. "How did it feel for you?"

He arched a dark brow. "You couldn't tell?"

"I can tell your emotions, yes." Frowning, she realized in that moment, she hadn't noticed him, only herself. "But I... I did not sense yours."

Leaning forward until his breath brushed across her mouth, he whispered, "I can't wait to kiss you again, that's how I feel."

6

MUTED MORNING LIGHT FILTERED IN THROUGH THE KITCHEN windows overlooking the small greenhouse the Hunters kept cultivated. Sylphine stared out over the rows, kept in order by narrow brick paths, her elbow propped on the small kitchen table, chin on her palm. Ramsey grew all the household's herbs and what produce she could manage. Simple things, like peppers and squashes. The *thump-thunk* of Ramsey's knife on a cutting board filled the room as she diced her peppers to mix into a batch of fritters she planned to fry with bacon. The wonderful smells wafting from the stove weren't what held Sylphine's attention, though. No, that distinction was left to the man of the house.

The one who's kisses Sylphine couldn't stop thinking about.

Previous to Jonathon, every kiss she'd received had been accompanied by a hand wrapped around her wrist, or her neck, or even braced on her bare thigh. She'd been a recipient, not a participant. Until last night, she didn't know there was a difference. Now she did, and she wondered what else she'd been denied because the men who'd claimed to love her had stolen her responses with their own.

Sylphine shoved the unpleasant memories from her mind and focused on Ramsey's kitchen ministrations. Still clothed in her nightgown and robe, wild black curls tied behind her neck, the youngest Hunter worked a knife like she'd been doing the task all her life. Sylphine knew how to cook a few basic Italyssian dishes, her mother had insisted, but otherwise, cooking wasn't her strength or passion.

"Why don't you have a cook?" Sylphine asked.

Ramsey glanced over at Sylphine. The knife stopped thumping against the board. "A couple years ago, Jonathon almost died. Since then, he's been worried if something happens to him, I won't have enough to live on and care for the house. So, he invests his Key Guardian income, and we live off his Enforcement pay. What's left goes into a savings account for emergencies. Having more than a housekeeper here a couple days a week isn't in his budget planning."

Sylphine's arm collapsed to the table. Her heart roared in her ears. "What do you mean Jonathon almost died? When was this? How?"

Shoulders tense, Ramsey returned to her chopping. "About six years ago. Some scab shoved him out a third-story doorway. The balcony was rotted away. He fell, smashed through a second-story balcony, which slowed his descent enough to keep him from dying when he hit the brick. He spent three weeks in the hospital recovering. If they hadn't had a genuine Medical Scientist on staff, he probably wouldn't have made it."

"A genuine Medical Scientist? What is that?"

"People can be trained in medicine sciences, like in anything, but a genuine Gen-Heir medical talent is rare. They can touch a person and *know* what is wrong with them internally. Jonathon had a collapsed lung, four fractured ribs, a dislocated hip, a broken arm, and a severe concussion. He needed stitches in five places and remained unconscious for three days." Ramsey's voice shook as she recounted the memory. Even across the kitchen, her distress seeped past Sylphine.

Sylphine's throat went dry. His words from the night before echoed in her mind. *Bad for my health.* "Is that why he stopped being a street enforcer?"

Ramsey nodded, a little sniffle sounding from her. "Yes. When he finally woke up, I begged him to change jobs. I wanted him to go occupy his Guardian seat. No one would think less of him, and he'd still be doing an important service to our country."

A heavy knot formed in Sylphine's stomach. At the horror of knowing Jonathon had come so close to being nothing more than a memory to introduce to Sylphine, not a man. She slid her hands across the table, leaning forward. "Oh Ramsey, I am so sorry. It must have been awful for you."

"I tried to explain I couldn't lose him too, you know?" Her lavender eyes settled on Sylphine, shining with tears. "Do you think he'd ever listen to you?"

Sylphine pulled in a lungful of air. Slowly, she shook her head. "I'd never ask it of him. He loves his job too much, and he's too good for the people of your city to lose. Besides, that was years ago. Surely, he has been safer now?"

Ramsey dragged in a shuddering breath. "I suppose. Remembering makes me fearful. I'm sorry, I didn't mean to put that on you."

Straightening in the seat, Sylphine pulled her hands back. "I understand."

"Have you reached your parents?" Oil sizzled as Ramsey dropped fritters onto the pan.

"No, nothing."

"Maybe there's a neighbor you can reach who can go check on them?"

Sylphine considered her suggestion. The Seartavos property was flanked mostly by vast vineyards that spread away from the cliff's edge, with a sprinkling of small houses between them. None of the smaller residents could afford a radio. Perhaps one of the vineyard owners, but she didn't know their transmission numbers. However, she knew two of the family names enough to perhaps write to them.

"Maybe. That is an excellent idea, thank you," Sylphine acknowledged. Ramsey beamed her a smile.

Jonathon's presence swept into the room ahead of him, a torrent of positive, bright happiness. "Good morning, lovelies."

The uncharacteristic vibes radiating from him had Sylphine's spine straightening. "You are in a good mood."

He cast a grin her direction but stopped behind Ramsey. The young woman tilted her head, exposing her cheek for a quick peck from her brother in an obvious family ritual. Jonathon tugged her messy ponytail, earning him a growl and snap. Ramsey pointed an oil covered slotted spoon at him.

"Keep messing with me and no fritters for you," Ramsey warned.

"We both know you won't let me starve, so don't make idle threats." He tugged her ponytail again.

How would being included in such teasing feel? A yearning spread through Sylphine. She'd been a guest in this house for years, but always on the outside, the way she preferred herself to be. Witnessing their love, their bond, Sylphine began to regret her decision to keep this family outside her self-appointed bubble.

Jonathon snatched a slice of crispy bacon before Ramsey could pop his hand with the spoon. He laughed, spinning away from her and towards the table. His jacket fluttered away from his body, revealing he was ready for the day ahead. When he finished his turn, worthy of the most graceful dancers of her country, who knew Jonathon had *that* in him, a small box had appeared in his hand. Still grinning like a young boy, the delight stronger with him closer, he set the box on the table in front of her.

"What is this?" she asked, drawing the container closer.

"Something from Ramsey and me," he said, sitting across from her. Ramsey slid a plate in front of him with a fried egg, fritters, and bacon. He smiled up at her in gratitude.

Sylphine eyed the box and then him with a small amount of suspicion. "And this is why you are so happy this morning?"

A flare of heat and teasing light simmered in his gaze. "Other reasons, too."

Shifting her focus back to the box, she tried to stop the flush of answering heat in her cheeks and through her body. The all-to-wonderful memory of his lips whispering across hers made the warmth deepen.

"Are you all right?" Ramsey asked.

Sylphine looked up and met Ramsey's concerned stare. A plate was poised in her hand, ready to be set down. Sylphine started, and quickly moved the box out of the way. "Yes, I am sorry."

"Sorry for what?" Ramsey lifted her brows in questioning. "You haven't even opened the box yet and you're already red in the face. Don't you get gifts at home?"

Sylphine chanced a glance at Jonathon. He gave her a look that said *well?* Punctuating the playful gaze with a wave of his fork. Would serve him right if she came right out and said her blushing was thanks to the kiss he'd given her last night. Ramsey would probably drop the plate right there onto the floor. Since Sylphine didn't want to see food wasted, she simply pasted on a shallow smile.

"I have never received a gift from *you*," she specified.

Ramsey cast a suspicious stare as she set the plate in front of Sylphine. "You are a terrible liar."

Jonathon coughed. Ramsey pounded on his back. He waved her away, reaching for something that wasn't there. "Coffee," he managed to get out between fits. "Please."

The swish of her robes and nightgown accompanied her progress across the kitchen to the stove, where a fresh pot of coffee brewed. She returned with two steaming mugs, setting one down where she'd take her breakfast. Moments later, Sylphine had a small glass of fresh juice in front of her.

Ramsey took her seat with her plate, motioning with her fork to the box. "Open it."

Nervousness fluttered in her stomach. What were the Hunter siblings up to? The urge to shake the box pulled at her, somehow, she resisted. Tucking a stray lock of hair behind her ear, Sylphine stared at the simple brown box.

"It won't bite," Jonathon said, using his fork to squish his fried egg into a puddle of yellow and white.

Carefully, Sylphine popped the top off the gift. A colorful array of textures lodged her breath in her throat. With reverence, she gently pulled a long, orange ribbon laden with shimmery blue beads free. A little clip at the top allowed the ribbon to secure anywhere in her hair she wanted. Tears stung her eyes. She hugged the hair decoration to her chest. Inside the box brimmed with more feathers, beads, and ribbons.

"Where did you find these?" she asked in shock, looking between Jonathon and Ramsey.

"Italyssa Town," Ramsey answered. "Have you ever been?"

"I have heard of it," she admitted. "But most of my visits are so full, I have never had time to go."

Ramsey smiled, scooping smooshed egg onto a fritter. An action mirrored by her brother. "I will have to take you, if you start to miss home."

Start? Sylphine hadn't stopped missing home since the moment her foot stepped out of the tunnels leading away from her family house. "I would like that very much, thank you." Her fingers brushed along the supple edges of several vivid blue and deep red feathers. "What is the occasion, for my *Naenzis*? It is not my birthday."

Jonathon set his fork down, his plate cleared. "One for each year Ramsey and I have known you. I know they won't replace the ones you lost or the value of the memory, but I... we... wanted you to have them."

Sylphine pulled the rest of her beautiful treasure out of the box. She sniffled back the tears that wouldn't go away. "They are amazing, perfect, thank you both, so much. This means... everything to me."

Ramsey propped her chin on her head and regarded Sylphine. "Maybe I should start wearing them."

Unable to wait, Sylphine clipped the first ribbon adornment into her hair. "Then people would notice you."

Ramsey's mouth twisted into a sideways grimace. An unladylike grunt sounded in her throat.

Jonathon pushed his chair back with an eye roll, sighing. "Oh no, what would you do, Ramsey?"

Ramsey glared at her brother. "Maybe I'd just find me a husband to spite you."

"Spite me? Dear sister, I'd rejoice if you left this house long enough for a man to notice you."

Spine straight, Ramsey's glare intensified. "Maybe I already have."

Jonathon leveled a stare at his sister. "Oh, really? Do I know him? What's his name?"

A deep flush crept up her pale cheeks. "You don't know him."

"Do I?" Sylphine asked, curious.

Ramsey huffed and slammed her chair back hard enough to send the legs screeching across the hardwood. "Fine! I was lying, happy? There is no man. No one knows him."

Her angry footfalls from the kitchen echoed around the now silent space. Sylphine let loose a long breath.

"She is very difficult about leaving this house," Sylphine remarked, her attention on the empty entryway and foot stomps up the stairs.

Jonathon ran his hand down his face. "Yes. And the sad part is only a small handful of people ever caused her trouble. But the ones who did were harsh in how far they took things."

Sylphine had never known the full reason for Ramsey's shunning of society. And unless she found a husband within the next ten years, she'd live forever with her brother, alone and without a family to call her own. The thought was a sad one. Of course, Ramsey may not even want those things, like Sylphine did.

Giving in to the pull of her curiosity, Sylphine asked, "What happened to Ramsey?"

"She never told you?" Jonathon asked in surprise.

A distant look clouded her ocean green eyes. "I do not think so."

Jonathon considered that. Like him, Ramsey had inherited the strong protect and defend Hunter gene. The instinct had cost her. "She probably worried you'd turn out to be like the elite here if you knew."

Her head tilted. "Elite? If she felt that way about me, why did she invite me here so many years ago?"

"Well, you are," Jonathon couldn't help but point out. "As for why, I have no idea. When she invited you into our home three years ago, I was simply notified. Honestly, I was thrilled anyone had managed to get past the barrier she'd erected. It wasn't until, I don't know, almost a year later I learned exactly *who* you were. By then, the arrangement the two of you had was already routine."

She fiddled with a ribbon. Crystal beads glittered in the delicate light, filtering in through layers of glass. "And you did not research me yourself, Mr. Lead Investigator?"

"No, Ramsey is an adult. I trust her judgment, and I didn't feel you'd pose any sort of threat to us." When her beautiful gaze landed on him, the faint glow of morning illuminated the delicate planes of her face, and made her bronze skin far too tempting, Jonathon amended, "Not a physical threat, at least."

Her cheeks warmed, her attention returning to the small collection arranged before her. "What happened? Can you tell me?"

Needing something to do other than imagine his hands on her skin, Jonathon snatched the coffee cup off the table. He crossed the kitchen and distracted himself with the promise of another caffeine infusion. Pouring rich, black liquid into the mug, he attempted to ground his thoughts.

Sylphine Seartavos was so far out of his league, he knew better than to be contemplating *anything* concerning her. Especially the kiss he'd dared last night. The temptation of her full, sensuous mouth finally within reach proved more than he could resist. And like the idiot he'd shown himself to be, he'd allowed himself a taste. Now, he craved more. He wanted to know how her tongue would feel sliding along his. The texture of her skin beneath his touch as he skimmed his hands over all the smooth contours of her body. How she'd respond.

A fire burned beneath her surface. Contained. Held in check. Why he didn't know. But her unspent passion wasn't for him to ignite or even experience. At least not now, and never if she wouldn't trust him. Trust what they could have. Could be. Jonathon inhaled the fragrant steam coming from his cup and curbed his wayward thoughts before his body visually betrayed his thinking.

"If it's some family secret or too personal, I understand," she said softly, breaking his concentration.

Jonathon glanced at her, then returned his attention to the coffee. He spooned sugar into the inky liquid and carefully stirred. "No secret. Anyone in Haven City's social scene would love to tell you their version. As for personal," he shrugged, "can't really claim that either, since the incident was reported in the *Haven City Chronicle*. Extensively."

She sat back in the chair and regarded him. "A scandal?"

"On multiple levels," Jonathon admitted, returning to his seat.

Her tongue slid across her lips, leaving a tantalizing sheen behind. Those lips under his, supple and accepting, flashed through his mind, as did the very shocked reaction she'd given after. As though she'd never been kissed before. Which, of course, was ridiculous. No way in the artic had Jonathon been her first kiss.

He sipped his coffee in a slow pull, cautiously to keep from burning his tongue. "Have you been kissed before?"

Surprise widened her eyes. She blinked multiple times. "I... We are talking about Ramsey."

"Have you?"

A deep, crimson stain blossomed across her cheeks and down her neck. To her credit, she didn't look away from him. "Of course I have. What a silly question. Now, what about your sister?"

"Before last night?" he pressed.

She fidgeted in her seat. "Yes, before last night. Many times. I do not wish to talk about kissing."

Jonathon couldn't help but grin. "Why not? It's a fun thing to talk about. It's a fun thing to do."

"Key Guardian Asherwick," she snapped with a heated stare. "I will not be discussing this with you. Now, are you going to answer my question about your sister or not?"

"Uh oh... Asherwick, huh?" He tsked and shook his head, taking another drink. Whatever she was hiding would remain concealed. For now. "Very well, I seemed to have crossed some imaginary line with you." Before she could get defensive— and by the sudden straightening of her spine, he knew she was— he said, "Ramsey helped convict a Primary Guardian of multiple counts of rape."

Horror darkened her face. Tears welled in her eyes. "Oh... Ramsey."

Jonathon held up his hand. "No, you misunderstand. She *helped*, not because anything happened to her. Had it, there would have been nothing left for them to ship off to prison."

Sylphine pressed her face into her hands. A deep, shuddering breath shook her shoulders. She peeked from between her fingers. "You would have broken the law to revenge her?"

The mix-up of her words took him a moment to comprehend. Despite the gravity of the conversation, a smile tugged at him. "*Avenge*, not revenge. Yes, I would have broken the law to avenge her, and that's because no one would have found out. Blackbain would have simply disappeared."

She watched him closely. "You are not lying."

"Nope." He ran his index finger along the rim of the mug. "Does that bother you?"

Her focus shifted to his caress along the edge of porcelain. Jonathon stopped, and she breathed slowly as if waking from a daze. Her gaze lifted to him. "No, it does not bother me. So, helping convict a man of rape cast her from your society? Why?"

"Joel Blackbain was very prominent in the top financial circles. He made a lot of powerful people a lot of money. And I do mean *a lot* of money. Not only did Ramsey have to deal with the fallout of turning on *one of her own*, but the resentment of costing some a small fortune in loss." Jonathon sighed and shook his head. "I figure most of it has died down, but Joel's brother, Sean Blackbain, who was named Primary Guardian Wintersfall in the absence of his brother, returned home over a year ago. The family name may have brought back some old feelings in some of the more elite households. Ramsey chooses to not worry about any of it by simply staying home."

"How upsetting." Her cheeks puffed before she blew out a loud breath. "Now I understand why she only went to foreign dinner events with me. There was a limited chance of her encountering anyone who may hold a grudge."

"Yes, and I appreciate it more than you know that you managed to get her to do that much."

"I will try harder now." Her attention shifted to the colorful array on the table. "Thank you, again, for these."

"You're welcome. I'm glad they made you happy," Jonathon said in all honesty. "Is there anything else you need? Ramsey can take you to Italyssa Town today if you'd like."

She shook her head, the light playing off the sun-kissed strands of her hair. "No. I *need* to know my parents are safe, but I have no way of doing so."

Jonathon could relate to that driving anxiety. He hoped Sylphine's situation would play out completely different than the way he and Ramsey's lack of communication from their parents had so many years ago. "I will think of a way."

"I may write to one of our neighbors. Perhaps they could get a letter from my parents to return to me."

"That's not a bad idea. But, when you do so, if anyone is watching, they'll know the letter came from Sziveria."

A frown pinched her pretty face. "Yes, but I am starting to not care."

"You are safe here. I promise."

Something shadowy passed across her eyes before she turned her attention to the windows. Once again, he had to wonder what she wasn't telling him.

7

SYLPHINE WATCHED IN A SORT OF MORBID CURIOSITY AS RAMSEY attacked dirt in the greenhouse as though it were some vicious foe needing to be annihilated. Dark flecks of damp earth flew from the ground in clumps. Silver tines flashed in the bright sun streaming through the open top windows.

"What are you doing?" Sylphine finally asked, dodging a large clod sailing her direction.

"I'm tilling," Ramsey answered with a grunt.

Sylphine leaned forward, bracing her elbows on her thighs. "Is that what it's called?"

Confusion twisted Ramsey's face when she glanced up, still hacking away at the ground. "What is what called?"

"Assaulting the poor dirt. Tilling?"

Ramsey paused, blinking down at the crater she'd made.

Sylphine sighed. "What is really going on? What's wrong?"

Collapsing back onto her rear, Ramsey draped her arms over her knees and regarded Sylphine for a quiet moment. She pointed the tines Sylphine's direction, her gaze narrow. "I will tell you if you're honest with me as well. I know you're keeping some dark little secret in that head of yours."

Anxiety rolled through Sylphine. "How do you know?" She titled her head and studied Ramsey. "Are you *sure* you are not a Sympath as well?"

Ramsey snickered and dropped the trowel. She clapped her hands together, dislodging dirt. "You aren't denying it. And no, not a Sympath, or anything close. I just know you, and you're stressed out."

"My parents are essentially missing."

"Yes, but why did you have to leave at all? You could have faced the challenge as a family." Ramsey shook her head. "No, something else is going on. What is it?"

A sense of vulnerability made Sylphine lift her legs onto the bench and wrap her arms around them. Resting her chin on her knees, she met Ramsey's concerned stare. "There is a primal law, from the earliest days of my country, that mandates if a man or woman is not married by their twenty-first year, someone could petition and be granted permission to marry that person, against their choice."

Ramsey's mouth dropped open. "What? How? Why would they do that?"

"Our country was tiny when we started. Forging families, keeping close ancestral records was vital. No one could afford to go unmarried and hope our nation would survive. The law rarely had to be used and fell out of practice at least a hundred and fifty years ago. A family rival learned of the law. I am twenty-four years of age. Because they had grounds for the petition, it was granted to them."

The same horror Sylphine had felt reflected in Ramsey's lavender eyes. "Does Jonathon know?" When Sylphine remained silent, Ramsey pressed, "Have you told my brother?"

"The problem is not his, Ramsey," Sylphine whispered, hugging her legs tighter.

"Are you just going to hide here forever then? Is that your big plan, Fi?"

Sylphine frowned and looked away from the livid heat in Ramsey's gaze. She hadn't put a lot of thought into what she'd do or how to handle the mess. What were her options, short of hiding out and disappearing to another country? She had the means. She could make a withdrawal in Sziveria and disappear anywhere. Eventually, the family would give up. Their heir needed to marry and couldn't wait forever. Perhaps she'd even meet someone who could love her. Until then, however, what?

"I hadn't thought about it," Sylphine answered honestly.

Ramsey stood, brushing dirt from her clothing. "Maybe you should. This is your future, no one else has any say in it."

Sylphine mulled those words over in her mind. "What is the largest book distributor in Haven City? Would they carry books from my country?"

"Mr. Harold's. He owns Harold's Book Emporium in Extilis Square. We just call it Mr. Harold's, everyone knows what we're talking about." She smiled. "Books, lots and lots. If you can't find it there, it's not in Sziveria."

"Perfect. Then that is where we need to go."

Ramsey's face slid into an emotionless mask. "I can tell you how to get there."

"Anyone can tell me how to get to Extilis Square. Even I know if I want to buy something and be seen doing so, I go to Extilis. What is wrong?"

Ramsey shrugged. "I prefer to do my shopping expeditions elsewhere, is all."

"And you say *I am* the one hiding?" Sylphine snorted and shook her head, standing. "How long have *you* been hiding,

Ramsey? You will not even shop where someone may see you."

Red suffused Ramsey's cheeks. Her hands balled at her sides. "You don't know what they say to me."

Sylphine lifted her chin. "Let them say it. Words are only weapons if you allow them to be."

Ramsey's jaw flexed. "Fine. I will go with you." She glared and pointed a stiff finger at Sylphine. "But if someone is mean to me, I'm blaming you."

Sylphine laughed and grasped Ramsey, pulling her forward. She looped their arms together. "Yes, my dear sister, I will be responsible for your hurt feelings, should they happen."

A pitiful sniffle came from Ramsey. "Good. I'll remind you when it happens."

Sylphine tsked. "It is not so bad as that, is it?"

"Worse," Ramsey said without emotion.

At the foyer, they separated. Ramsey went upstairs to change from her dirt-covered dress, and Sylphine went into the library, which was her designated space when in the Hunter home. Pulling a small mirror from the desk, she checked to make sure all the *Naenzi's* she'd clipped into her hair were still secured. Losing the four from her family had been crushing. She didn't know how well she'd handle losing the special gift from Jonathon and Ramsey.

As she slipped her fingers over the delicate decorations, she wondered which ones were from Jonathon. If he had any say, or if he cared, or if Ramsey had chosen each one. Taking a deep breath, she frowned at her reflection. She shouldn't care. Yet as her finger caught on a crystal bead, she did.

Shaking away her fancy, she dropped the mirror back into the drawer. No good would come of wondering which adornments Jonathon may or may not have given.

The swish of fabric preceded Ramsey into the room. A dark, drab gray gown covered her neck to ankle. A simple gray hat sat atop her head. Her glossy black curls were tamed into a braid. No necklaces, bracelets, or even a pattern to break up the boring shade of her dress.

"What is this?" Sylphine asked, waving her hand up and down.

"My clothing. Are you ready?"

Glancing down at the bright array of blues fading into vivid greens of her own dress, Sylphine scoffed. "Everyone will notice you if you stand next to me. We could not be more opposite."

"That's the point. They'll think me a companion and pay me no attention." Ramsey lifted her slightly pointed chin. "Are you ready?"

Sylphine wanted to argue again. Ramsey wasn't her companion, not in the sense she wanted people to believe. The woman was no one's servant. Sighing and shaking her head, Sylphine grabbed her bag. "Yes, fine. But you will tell me why you want to be viewed as beneath me. I do not like you wishing to be seen that way."

"I did say I would."

Ramsey radioed a carriage service and the ladies opted to wait outside at the curb for it to arrive. The late afternoon sun dipped below the roofs of the houses lining the street. Cool air toyed with the edges of Sylphine's dress and the ends of her hair. Birds fluttered about, oblivious to their chilly environment. Sylphine wrapped her shawl tighter around her body, an involuntary shiver trembling along her limbs.

"How do you tolerate such cold all the time?" she asked, searching the shadowed road for their ride.

Ramsey glanced at her. A frigid burst of air pulled a curl free from her braid. She dashed it away with an annoyed flick of her wrist. "I don't know any different. This is actually rather nice out. No frost on the bricks or the leaves."

The seasons in Italyssa rarely varied. They may get a month, maybe two, of nights as cold as the days in Sziveria. A few nights of hard freezes necessary for their vines and fruit trees to flourish. Sylphine had always tolerated her days, weeks, or sometimes months away by knowing soon she'd returned to the sunshine drenched beaches and vineyards of her homeland. Now, she had no idea when she'd be able to go home or what situation she'd be returning to. If she focused too hard on both, panic would suck her under.

A nice hired coach stopped before them. A man jumped down and opened the door. They were helped inside a clean, plush interior, complete with a burgundy carpeted floor and curtained windows. Lap blankets were folded neatly in the center of each seat. Ramsey settled across from Sylphine, arranging the blanket over her legs. The rich red stood out against the dreary gray of her gown.

Once the carriage rocked into motion, the muted clop of hooves and rumble of wooden wheels over brick filling the cab, Sylphine cast a pointed look at her dearest friend. "All right, begin talking. I am waiting."

Ramsey took a long, slow breath and turned her attention to the passing houses rolling by the window. "I sent a bad man to prison. Helped at least a dozen women find justice. No one but them cared, however, because the scab I helped convict made a lot of people wealthy. Once he was gone, they lost their thread to the markets and industries he knew how to manipulate and play for the greatest gain. Along with that, some of them couldn't understand how I could turn on one of my *own*." She sneered the word on a growl. "Like we're some different species from the rest of the country."

Exactly as Jonathon had told her. "And you let them control you? To take away your freedom because of that?"

A warm flush crept along Ramsey's cheeks. "No. For a year I kept on, ignoring the spiteful words and the way I'd be invited, but ignored or ostracized when I arrived at a luncheon or tea invitation."

"And you grew tired of it all," Sylphine guessed.

"Well, yes of course I did." The frown deepened on Ramsey's face. She shook her head. "That wasn't why, though."

Sylphine waited quietly. Across from her, Ramsey's stiff frame radiated anxiety and dejection. The tendrils of negative emotion stirred a desire to calm and comfort within Sylphine. She reached across the distance and laid an encouraging hand on her friend's knee. Months ago, a similar, turbulent storm had churned around Jonathon. Perhaps if Sylphine had been brave enough to reach out to him then, as she was now for Ramsey, things would have ended differently between them. The reminder made her ease her hand back, a knot tight in her chest. Sylphine couldn't go back and fix her mistake. She could only learn and grow from the moment forward.

"I was promised to be married," Ramsey whispered. "He *promised* he'd protect and love me, look after me and keep me safe. I was the only woman for him, blah, blah, blah." She snickered a disgusted sound and shook her head. "Such a liar he turned out to be."

Familiar pain stretched through Sylphine's chest. Men had made those same promises to her and taken from her body with their words of love, their emotions leeching into her until she couldn't tell who truly felt what. Then, when they'd grown bored, they'd left. Sylphine figured she should be thankful they walked away instead of subjecting her to the dangers of a roving lover. Breathing out a long sigh, she focused outside.

"I am sorry. I know how it feels. The sense of betrayal."

Ramsey's face scrunched. She shook her head. "My

brother didn't betray you. I know he could have handled his outburst better, but he was hurting."

"Jonathon could not betray me, Ramsey. He made no promises. If you remember, I was the one who begged him to pretend. I…" Sylphine took a moment to gather her thoughts, fiddling with the velvety edges of her shawl. "I was unaware he wanted or expected more until it was too late, and I was too much of a coward to allow it."

"You've been promised, for real?" Ramsey asked, eyes wide. "How do I not know about these men?"

Heat suffused Sylphine's cheeks. "There is nothing to know. They are *izrasmet*, scum."

"*Izrasmet*," Ramsey repeated with perfect pronunciation. "Scum. I like that, it's perfect, isn't it? They *are* scum. Anyway, after he did that, I was too ashamed to be seen out in public again. The ridicule would have been twice as bad. Now, I'm just used to minding my own. I prefer my simple, solitary existence."

Sylphine frowned. "It is depressing and no way to live your gift that is life."

Ramsey squared her shoulders. "I happen to like my pitiful little life, thank you very much."

"It is yours to live," she conceded. "But there is more to each day than the walls of your house. If nothing else, begin going to parks, enjoy the outside."

"Jonathon helps at a children's home for the kids who are orphaned or need to be placed after a crime he investigates. I've been thinking about helping there, too."

"You should! What a wonderful thing, Ramsey."

A small smile graced Ramsey's lips. "I know some children can be cruel too. The world Jonathon pulls them from isn't kind, but he's said more than once a gentle word and heart can be the change they need to live a different life than one they came from."

"He is correct," Sylphine said. "Cruelty breeds more cruelty, especially in the next age. I have seen what generations of brutality can do. I do not wish that for anyone."

"Why did your man leave you? I can't see anyone walking away from you."

Your brother did. Sylphine bit the words back and shoved the pain of dejection deep down. She forced a nonchalant shrug. "I was not what they wanted in the end."

"They?" Ramsey's brows rose in question. "As in more than one?"

Sylphine held up her fingers. "Three. Not counting Jonathon."

A choking cough escaped from Ramsey. She pressed a hand to her chest. "What?"

Mortification made Sylphine look back out the window. Crowds were beginning to appear on the sidewalks, and the carriage, and slowed to a crawl. They were nearing their destination. "I found out the difficult way I have terrible flavor in men."

Despite the seriousness of the conversation, Ramsey giggled. Sylphine glanced at her in disbelief. "It's *taste*, Fi, you have terrible taste in men."

Sylphine snapped her fingers and pointed. "Yes, that. Exactly. I am no good at knowing the bad ones."

"My brother is not a bad one."

Sylphine's heart lurched. "Maybe I am the one who is no good for him."

Ramsey scoffed. "You don't think that, do you?"

The carriage rocked to a stop. Sylphine ignored Ramsey's question, waiting on the door to open so she could make her escape. She had no desire to explain to Jonathon's sister how disappointing the man would find her *if* they did happen to marry. The embarrassment she'd suffered at the hands of other men whose love had shown her once unfulfilled lust was discovered, the rest faded away.

One man she could discount. But three? No. Clearly, she was lacking. She couldn't go through another humiliating relationship ending due to the frigid nature they'd all accused her of having.

The door opened on a rush of chilled air. A white gloved hand appeared, and Sylphine accepted the help from the carriage. Ramsey followed, paying the driver and the carriageman who'd attended them.

Thick groupings of shoppers and business people meandered down the sidewalks, disappearing into shops and eateries. Pastries in the window of one shop caught Sylphine's attention. She pointed them out to Ramsey, who promised they'd stop by before they headed home.

Mr. Harold's Book Emporium took up nearly an entire block. Three stories of brick, filled with floor-to-ceiling wooden bookshelves. A little bell rang as the door closed behind them. Dust motes danced in the air. The windows barely cast in enough light to penetrate the depths. Lamps hung from the ceiling, shedding weak yellow-tinted light in the center of each aisle. No one looked up from behind the desk. The musty scent of paper and ink, leather and wood, filled the space.

"Welcome to Mr. Harry's," a bored voice intoned. "The directory is to your left at each staircase. Our complete inventory is listed alphabetically by subject and author."

"Thank you, Toby," Ramsey said with a smile.

The man looked up. Not much older than Ramsey, he smiled a crooked smile and pushed his glasses up his nose. Pretty golden eyes mixed with shades of green peered beyond the lenses. A thick mop of red curls fell across his forehead and over his ears. "Miss Hunter! Been awhile since we've seen you around."

"Yes, I know." She grasped Slyphine's arm and tugged her closer. "My friend is looking for Italyssian law books. Do you carry any?"

He scratched at the peach scruff along his jaw. "Well, if we do, and I'm not promising anything, they'd be on the third floor with all the other foreign works that grand-daddy likes to collect."

"Thank you, I appreciate it."

He leaned over the counter stacked high with tombs and watched them head towards the stairs. "Anytime, Miss Hunter."

Sylphine grinned at Ramsey on their way up the dark stairs. Ramsey squinted at her. "What?"

"He likes you."

Ramsey snorted. "Sure."

"Well, he does."

"You could feel it, could you?"

Sylphine shook her head. "No, I did not need to. Do you think he answers anyone else's questions?"

"My parents brought me to this shop from the moment I could read. Toby was running around with toy cars then. We've known each other almost all our lives." She leaned close and whispered, "He once showed me where his grand-daddy keeps the lusty books."

"What are those?"

Ramsey's cheeks turned an outrageous shade of red. She shook her head until curls bounced free. "Let's just say I couldn't look my parents in the eye for almost two weeks. I've never ventured to that part of the store again. If he liked me in that way, he would have tried something then."

Curious about these books that were apparently for a specific audience, Sylphine made Ramsey stop at the top of the stairs. "What are they? Crude words?"

Red still scored Ramsey's full cheeks. "Crude words," she leaned close and whispered, "even cruder pictures."

Sylphine tried to imagine a crude picture. She'd heard of them but had never seen one before. One of her former lovers had once spat in her face she should look at them some time to learn something. The barb had stung, but now Sylphine couldn't help but wonder if he was right. "And you looked at them?"

"I was fifteen. I couldn't help myself."

"Do you think," she swallowed to gain some courage, "Jonathon likes them?"

Ramsey recoiled and rushed up the next set of stairs. The heavy pounding of her feet echoed in the narrow passage. "If he does, I don't want to know. At all. Ever." A visible shudder raced down her body.

Sylphine chased her up the stairs. "Do you think men like them, though?"

"I have no idea who likes them, Fi. Not me. If you want to know Jonathon's opinion, you'll have to ask him. Leave me out of the conversation."

Sylphine froze midway to the next step. The thought of asking Jonathon anything concerning sex left Sylphine's heart pounding way too fast. Especially because she knew he'd answer, with limited hesitation, if any. At the third-story landing, Ramsey stared down.

"Well?" she asked, hands on her hips. "Are you coming?"

Sylphine shook away her thoughts and rushed up the remaining steps. The final floor of the book emporium was even darker than the ground floor. Only a handful of lamps chased away the heavy shadows cast by rows upon rows of overflowing bookshelves. A fine layer of dust coated the floor, showing recent traffic. Tiny particles floated in the air, shimmering and dancing on an invisible breeze. One of the windows must be open. They looked over the domain, and Sylphine frowned.

"Where do we begin?"

Ramsey glanced around. "I'm not sure. Maybe look for Italyssian words?"

Unsure, Sylphine rubbed her hands on her dress and searched the chaos spread out before them again. Searching every row seemed a daunting task. "Is there a directory up here?"

"I don't think so."

Sylphine took a bracing breath. She needed to find a law book. She'd search every title if that's what it took. "Very well."

"Tell me what I'm looking for and I'll search one side of a row, while you search the other."

Sylphine spoke the words for law, legal, contracts, mandates, decrees and regulations, wanting to make sure everything was covered since she didn't know under which title the old primal law may be found. Ramsey watched her lips intently, nodding to each word and then repeated them back in perfect recollection. Sylphine pushed aside the niggling sensation of Ramsey's ability to repeat without error. She'd analyze the strange phenomenon later.

They started at the right side of the room, quickly eliminating rows upon rows of languages Sylphine recognized, and some she'd never seen before. They all fascinated Ramsey to the point of Sylphine having to pull her to the next aisle. Finally, almost at the end of the room, they found the three shelving units dedicated to Italyssian literature. Pulling out all the possible options, they stacked them in the center of the walkway between shelves.

Hours later, the sun so low on the horizon, Sylphine could barely make out the words on the pages anymore, surrounded by books, she sagged against the shelves behind her in defeat. She let the book she'd been researching from tumble to the floor in a flutter of pages and a solid *thunk* on the hardwood.

"The same," she told Ramsey when the woman's curious lavender eyes glanced up from her open book. "I am in so much trouble."

Sighing, Ramsey carefully closed her book. "Okay, so what does this mean, exactly?"

"Either I run for my entire life, or I marry him. I have no other options." Sylphine tried to keep her voice even, but the tears stinging her eyes made the attempt difficult.

"Or you marry someone else." Ramsey set the book to the side, fixing Sylphine with a serious stare. "You can do that too, right?"

Despondent, Sylphine held her hands out. The two silver bracelets on her left wrist jingled together. "Who would I marry, Ramsey? Who?"

"You know who," Ramsey answered gently.

Sylphine sniffled and shook her head. "This is not your brother's problem. I already told you that. I will not ask him to fix it for me."

"What if he wants to," she argued, her chin lifted in defiance. "You won't even give him the option. You're making the choice for him. Will it hurt to at least tell him what's going on?"

Unable to stop from touching the promise band Jonathon had once worn, Sylphine looked away, not wanting to focus on the man who'd always been a safe haven, even if he was a powerful storm of emotion. She couldn't begin to hope anything could be salvaged from what she'd broken so many months ago. Sure, he seemed to be back to his teasing self, but Sylphine knew better. He'd want promises she couldn't keep. Worse, he'd want more than she could offer.

Shaking her head, Sylphine pulled her knees into her

body, wrapping her arms around them. "He shouldn't even be faced with the choice. I cannot do that to him."

The creak of a floorboard sounded somewhere in the room. Sylphine looked at Ramsey, who'd twisted to try to see beyond the shelves giving them a sense of seclusion. The shop had to be close to closing soon, with the light dying and the bitterly cold Sziverian night's looming in the near future.

"Sylphine Seartavos, this is Vayden Dossett. I have been hired by the house of Cyrano to bring you home," a deep male voice called out. "Please do not resist."

Ramsey turned around, her eyes wide, skin pale. She made urgent motions with her hands. Sylphine shook her head, not understanding what any of this meant, other than the Cyrano's were involved, which wasn't good. Ramsey carefully crawled the space between them.

On a hushed whispered, Ramsey said, "He's a reward seeker. He's stated his intent and can legally remove you from Sziveria. We have to leave. Now."

Prickles danced along Sylphine's skin. *Oh no.* They'd found her.

Sylphine crept behind Ramsey, who knew the overall layout of Mr. Harold's far better than she did. Every now and again they'd freeze, listen, and then begin moving again. They were on the second floor, weaving through book cases, trying to avoid the reward seeker who continued to state his purpose with each creak he made chasing after them.

No one, not even Enforcement Services, could stop him from boarding a ship with her bound for Italyssa. Knowing she could be legally kidnapped terrified Sylphine. She'd never considered the situation in all the dreadful scenario's she'd played through in her mind.

Ramsey peeked out from around the corner of a bookcase

and then motioned. They darted across the distance to the stairs. Their feet sounded far too loud clomping down. Sylphine's heavy breaths rushed in her ears, joined by the rapid pound of her heart. Toby's eyes grew wide at their hasty appearance.

"Is everythin—"

"Fine!" Ramsey rushed out, dashing for the door. "Mouse… it was a mouse."

A tall, dark-haired man, with intense eyes materialized in front of the exit. Sylphine knew he didn't simply appear, but the effect was all the same. He blocked their escape. A slow predatory smile spread across his face. A long, black coat draped from his broad shoulders. Black pants and shirt insured he could hide in any shadow.

Ramsey skidded to a stop, her arms held wide. Sylphine bumped into her. The man waved a folded paper in the air. Ramsey took a slow step back, forcing Sylphine to do the same.

"Sylphine Seartavos, I am Vayden Dossett. I have been hired by the house of Cyrano to return you to Italyssa. Please do not resist," he stated for what felt like the hundredth time to Sylphine's stressed nerves. He took a cautious step closer to them, his fingerless gloved hands held up in a non-threatening manner.

Sylphine looked around for another entrance. Surely a store filled with flammable material had more than one method to depart. "Is there another way out?" she whispered.

Ramsey continued to walk backward, urging Sylphine to do the same. "Through the lusty book section. So people can make their purchases and leave without being noticed."

A black curtained off portion of the store came into view. Ramsey sped towards it and snatched the partition aside. Sylphine didn't have the luxury of allowing herself to be shocked at the number of patrons in this section of the emporium. At least ten people milled about between the shelves upon shelves of depraved titles. Aside from the occasional turn of a page, everyone remained silent, as if in their own bubble. And why wouldn't they? What would they talk about? Sylphine had an insane urge to giggle at the ridiculousness of her situation.

Ramsey dashed between empty rows, and Sylphine followed, ignoring the odd looks they received scurrying past customers. The exit came into view. Relief almost made Sylphine cry out. They were going to make it. Someone grabbed her wrist. The tips of their fingers pressed between the bones in her forearm, sending a shaft of pain up her arm, mingling with an influx of frustration and determination that didn't belong to her. Sylphine twisted her arm on a cry and tried to break free. Her feet slid along the polished hardwood floor.

"Oh no you don't!" Ramsey bellowed, sliding by, a heavy book in her hand.

"What th—" Vayden's words died as Ramsey bashed a book against his shoulder. He released Sylphine. She scrambled away, searching for someone, or even something, to help.

A young man three aisles over glanced up. The bold, golden print on his black jacket gleamed like a beacon in the light he stood under. First Guardsman Tray Wackerly. An enforcer. Sylphine ran to him and grabbed his jacketed arm. "My friend needs help, please!"

The book he'd been holding fell from his hands when she yanked him to the row Ramsey was in. Grunts of disbelief and pain sounded from the shadowed aisle. The enforcer skidded to a halt. Cheeks mottled red from excursion and anger, Ramsey continued to pound the heavy book against the reward seekers hunched shoulders.

Tray held his hand out, his pale blue eyes wide. "Miss! Miss, please stop hitting that man."

Ramsey glanced up, glared at the enforcer, and hit the seeker harder. Sylphine squeaked and covered her mouth. What had happened to her sweet-natured friend?

"Miss, please! If you don't stop I'm going to have to take you in!"

When Vayden attempted to escape Ramsey's onslaught, she kicked her foot out, catching him in the shin. He howled and picked up his foot, hopping and grasping his injured leg. Ramsey took the opportunity to smack him in the center of his back.

"Is hitting him with a book illegal?" Sylphine asked, her heart pounding harder.

"Well yeah, it's illegal," he said, holding out his hand to the chaos being rendered by her friend. "She's assaulting him. If she doesn't stop, I will have to take her to the nearest division."

Sylphine raised a brow. "Which one would that be?"

"East Street." The enforcer slid his hand through his tawny hair, distress emanating off him in waves. "Miss! Please stop hitting him!" He ran to break them up, shouting, "No, don't kick him again!"

Sylphine bit her lip and pulled a book off the shelf behind the enforcer. Jonathon was at East Street Division. If this enforcer could bring them there safely, Sylphine would get more precious time to figure out how to escape from the Cyrano's and the reward seeker they now had after her. "I am so sorry," she said a second before slapping the title across the unsuspecting man's back.

"What in the arctic!" Tray spun around, eyes blazing. "What are you doing?"

Sylphine smacked his arm. "I am assaulting you, yes?"

"What?" He snatched the book out of her hand. "Stop it!"

Sylphine grabbed another one. Tray's gaze narrowed on her.

"Don't do it," he warned.

Tray took a step back. Sylphine followed, raising the book. He shook his head. Not wanting to truly hurt him, she brought the book down in a controlled arc, smacking his forearm. He yelped and pulled his arm back, glaring. For good measure, Sylphine thumped the book against his bicep.

"That's it!" he snapped, snatching the book from her hand. When Sylphine went to grab a new one, he grasped her upper arm and pulled her to the center of the aisle, away from the books. "Stand right here! Do *not* move!"

Tray pivoted on his heel and did the same to Ramsey, forcing her to stand beside Sylphine. The two ladies clasped their hands in front of themselves as if they'd rehearsed the move, staring at young FG Wackerly with big eyes.

"What is wrong with you two?" he asked on a growl, holding up a book. "You do not just beat random people in a book store."

"We're ready to go now," Ramsey stated calmly.

"Go?" Tray asked, helping Vayden straighten.

"To East Street Division," Sylphine prompted.

"Leave this man alone. I am returning to my shopping," Tray stated, fixing his jacket.

Ramsey sighed, looked at Sylphine, who frowned, but gave a slight nod. Sylphine reached right, while Ramsey reached left. They each pulled out a book and held it up. Tray's eyes widened, he held up his hands.

"Now wait, wait! I said—" They didn't give him the chance to finish. Sylphine smacked his right exposed hip while Ramsey struck his left thigh. FG Wackerly growled, dropping the book he'd taken from Sylphine and snatched the new titles from their hands. "Outside, now! Both of you! You want to be taken to East Street, fine by me, that's where we're going."

Sylphine heaved out a sigh and turned. She could feel the

sharp, angry gaze of Vayden on her back. "Jonathon is going to be so upset with us."

Ramsey shrugged. "I don't care. You aren't being carted off with Mr. Kidnaps for Money there. That's all that matters. Let my brother be angry, at least you're safe."

8

—

A QUICK KNOCK SOUNDED ON JONATHON'S OPEN OFFICE DOOR. He glanced up from the assortment of open files on his desk. Someone bumped into the young woman waiting for entry, knocking her beyond the threshold. Jonathon sighed and motioned for her to enter the rest of the way.

"I am so sorry to bother you, MT Hunter, but there's a situation down in holding they need you for," she said in a near shout to be heard over the chaos filling the corridor beyond.

Frowning, Jonathon braced his forearms on the desk. "In holding?"

The young woman nodded, the light blonde curls around her face bobbing. "Yes, I was told to come collect you immediately by an FG Wackerly? He said you'd know him."

"Do you work down in holding?" he asked. Women weren't usually assigned to handle the rougher side of enforcement work down in the basement.

"I handle in-processing." She swept an errant curl from her golden-brown eyes.

"Ah. Very well." Jonathon stood, gathering his jacket. He

slipped the coat on while following behind her through the crush of people filling the hall.

They fought through the heavy traffic of the stairs until it thinned nearing the basement, where only a trickle of people floated up or down the stairway. The wide steps ended on a long stretch of bleak, gray hall. Narrow windows along the top of thick cement walls, covered in bars, mirrored the reflection inside from the darkness beyond. During the day, they'd spill weak light into the entrance for the division's prisoner hold.

The young blonde pushed through a set of double doors and then slid behind a tall counter. She motioned with her head. "He's waiting just around the corner there."

"Thank you, Miss…"

She cast him a dazzling smile. "Emily Grant."

Jonathon inclined his head in gratitude. "Miss Grant."

Around the corner, a familiar, young tawny-haired enforcer paced in front of another set of double doors, thicker with a heavy bolted lock. Jonathon couldn't help but grin. "First Guardsman Wackerly, did you lose your cap again?"

The young man stopped and stared like a trapped mouse in a corner. His gaze darted first to the closed doors for the holding cell, the corner Jonathon had emerged from, back to Jonathon's curious stare. The FG licked his lips, his hand lifting to his hatless head. "Um, no MT Hunter, I didn't lose it again."

Jonathon crossed his arms over his chest. "What's going on?"

The young First Guardsman glanced at the doors again. A bead of sweat slid down his temple. "I didn't know who they were when… when I processed them or I never would have done so."

"Who?"

"They were hitting me with books MT, and this other guy,

I have no idea who he was, but they were slapping, and thumping. I told them to stop, but they wouldn't. They just kept at it. Hitting, hitting, hitting, over and over again. I didn't know what else to do. I detained them and brought them here for processing," Tray said in a tumble of words almost too fast to understand.

During the tirade, the young man's face turned an alarming shade of red. Jonathon held his hands out in a reassuring manner. "Whoa, slow down. It's all right. Who did you have to bring in?"

Tray pressed a shaking hand to his chest. "Oh, I can't breathe," he wheezed out.

Concerned, Jonathon stepped closer and patted the panicking young enforcer on the back. "Hey, it's okay."

Shaking his head, Tray sniffled and tried to take another deep breath. He rubbed his chest harder. "I'm so sorry, MT."

"Tray, come on, relax, what's going on?" Jonathon said, trying to diffuse the tension vibrating off of the rookie enforcer.

"I detained your sister and a woman, who said she is your promised," he said in a tiny voice and winced.

Somehow Jonathon managed to remain neutral. He huffed out a lungful of air and took a step back. "I see." He recalled back to Tray's rapidly executed confession. "They were hitting you with *books*? Where at?"

"Mr. Harry's, in the lusty book section," Tray said and then clamped his hand over his mouth. "I mean, at Mr. Harold's, MT."

"I'm sorry they did that," Jonathon stated in a calm tone, one he wasn't feeling. *What in the arctic?* "Do you wish to accuse?"

Tray blinked quickly. "Accuse?"

"The women for assaulting you."

"No!" Horror widened Tray's eyes. "Absolutely not. I

don't know why they did it. They calmed down the moment they knew I was bringing them here. I will not accuse your sister or your promised, Master Tribunii. I would never do that."

Jonathon sighed. "FG Wackerly, they assaulted an enforcer for Haven City Enforcement Services. I'm sure there are other witnesses. I won't hold it against you, but they knowingly broke the law."

"They are accused of nothing," the young enforcer stated, chin lifted.

"Very well. Please go inform Miss Grant the women may be processed out, no accusation is being leveled against them."

"Of course, MT. Thank you." Tray bowed, and Jonathon bit back another sigh.

"No, thank you, FG. I don't know what would have happened if they'd pulled this stunt with another enforcer. They're lucky."

Tray nodded before disappearing around the corner. Jonathon flexed his jaw, removing a set of keys from his pocket. He unlocked the huge bolt holding the door secured and slid it free. Five faces turned at the sound of the heavy door swinging open. Two of them were huddled on opposite ends of a long bench, together in their own unit. Misery darkened their faces, though Ramsey looked more annoyed than concerned. Sylphine's brightly colored, layered blue dress stood out in stark contrast to the drab surroundings. Ramsey all but blended into the wall behind her. If not for her dark hair, he may not have even noticed her.

The woman looked up at his entrance. Three men in a unit at the end of the room watched, but remained silent. Sylphine curled into herself while Ramsey jumped up, coming to the bars. Her fingers wrapped around the metal. "We didn't have a choice, Jonathon."

Fisting his hands on his hips, Jonathon surveyed his contained sister. "Beating an enforcer with a book. Really, Ramsey?" He shifted his attention to Sylphine, who'd turned a pretty shade of pink. "Really?"

"I'm sorry," Ramsey stated.

Jonathon shook his head and unlocked the gate to their cell. "Let's go. You can explain everything once we get to the house." He leveled them both with a hard stare. "*Everything.*"

Ramsey shoved Sylphine through the opening first. She stumbled and crashed into Jonathon. On instinct, Jonathon reached out and steadied her. The warm, generous curves of her body pressed into his. Her hands fisted in his jacket to find purchase.

"She has to stay with you or this was all for nothing," Ramsey said, flicking a curl from her eyes. "I'll ride back in a hired carriage."

"Was that necessary?" Sylphine asked, straightening away from Jonathon.

"Yes," Ramsey chirped, her teeth flashing on a smile that didn't reach her eyes.

Sylphine uncurled her hands from his jacket and stepped away, glaring at his sister. Cold air filled the space her body had occupied against his. Jonathon ground his teeth together. He didn't want to care about how good she'd felt. How much he'd imagine such a moment, only for it to be frustratingly brief. Their surroundings snapped back into focus. Now was not the time to be pondering missed opportunities.

The two women stared each other down. On a heavy sigh of annoyance, Ramsey turned on her heels and strode from holding. Jonathon frowned.

"What's going on?" he asked, the unusual tension radiating between them alarming him.

"Nothing," Sylphine answered much too quick.

Jingling the keys in his palm, he swept his hand towards the door. "Then, let's go."

THEY MADE THE RIDE TO THE HOUSE IN UNEASY SILENCE. Jonathon had a list of questions he wanted to ask, but Sylphine made no effort to engage in conversation. Since Jonathon wanted his sister's input as well, he waited out his curiosity. Stopping short of the driveway, he waited until Sylphine turned his way, her beautiful face scrunched in confusion.

"Are you okay?" he asked gently before she could ask her own question. "Before we go in and hash out why exactly the two of you decided to gang up on a poor First Guardsman with books, I just want to know if you're okay."

She visibly swallowed and took a deep breath. "I am okay now."

"But you weren't before?" he asked cautiously.

She shook her head, the little feathers, and beads in her hair twinkling in the streetlight.

"Okay," he whispered, not pressing for more. He guided the Ariot into the small space next to the house and killed the power with a switch.

Sylphine leapt from the vehicle and rushed to the house before her door had a chance to finish swinging shut. Jonathon used his foot to prop his door open and watched her hasty departure. The light from the front windows spilled across the glittery frost saturated bricks of the front steps. How she managed to make it up so quickly without slipping, he'd never know.

Icy night air wrapped around him, heavy and bone aching in its intensity. Still, he sat, lost in thought, wondering what could have prompted two rational women to go ballistic on an enforcer. Unsure if he even wanted to know because once he did, he'd have to do something about the situation, he was certain. Breathing in another lungful of cold air, he released it in a huff of swirling vapor. He couldn't put off the inevitable forever.

Keys in hand, he used his hip to close the vehicle door. Once inside, he secured the front door and slipped off his jacket and shoes. Hushed, urgent conversation filtered out from the library. Jonathon paused in the foyer, catching bits of their discussion.

"...be foolish... tell him," Ramsey bit out.

"No... not being foolish... responsible," Sylphine countered with equal frustration.

"... responsible... your life at... coward."

Jonathon slipped closer, hoping to catch more coherent segments.

"... not a coward, stop... such!"

"...weren't... admit you need my brother."

"I never said I did not *need* your brother. He does *not* need me," Sylphine ground out loud enough for him to hear every word, her voice shaky.

Jonathon raised his brows. He stepped into the room. Both the women looked his way. Sylphine gasped. Jonathon kept his focus on her. "Since when?" he asked.

Sylphine shook her head, confused. "Since when what?"

"Since when haven't I needed you?"

Ramsey's eyes widened, and she cast Sylphine a triumphant I-told-you-so look. Without another word, his trouble-making sister slipped from the room. The door closed with a faint snick behind her. Sylphine's chest rose and fell with stressed breaths. Her wary gaze followed his progress deeper into the room. To her credit, she didn't shrink away as he closed the distance between them. He'd expected her to.

"I have this thing about people making choices for me," Jonathon admitted in a low voice. "I don't like it."

She swallowed, her hand reaching for the back of the chair nearest to her. "I will remember that."

Jonathon moved around the chair opposite her, across from her desk, allowing her the opportunity to take a position where she could feel more in control. Maintaining eye contact, he slowly sank into the seat. "Tell me what happened today. The truth."

On a bracing breath, she moved around the desk, taking her seat. She spread her hands over the empty surface, as if visually collecting thoughts before her. "A reward seeker by the name of Vayden Dossett is after me."

Jonathon crossed his ankle over his thigh and rested his elbow on the arm of the chair. He had a lot of practice keeping an impassive expression regardless of how shocking someone sitting across from him said. "Go on."

A flicker of surprise crossed her face. She composed herself quickly. "Very well. The family Cyrano has been after the Seartavos business for... forever, it seems. Generations. They've offered partnerships, investments, property around the inhabited world, even marriage."

"And your family has always refused?"

Her face settled into a stern sigh. "My family has worked hard to get where they are. They built an empire by being smart. The Cyrano's are greedy, they always have been. They want easy money and the recognition our name would bring. Their company is..." she waved her hand and made a sour face, "weak. In six generations, they have managed to maintain only three ships, while our fleet has grown to over fifty. They are jealous and desperate. If they don't do something soon, the competition will eventually force them out. They cannot survive on three ships and have competitive rates unless they ship contraband."

"How is this relevant to the reward seeker?" Jonathon asked, tapping his fingers on his ankle.

She rubbed her hands on the desk again. "There is an old primal law in my country that allows a family to petition another family for marriage through our government. The petition is non-negotiable if it is granted."

"And the Cyrano family did this to you?"

She nodded grimly.

"Won't they be overtaken if they marry into your family and merge the companies?"

Sylphine shook her head. Sadness darkened her eyes. "I am the last of my family. The last Seartavos that can inherit."

Jonathon considered her words carefully. "And if they force you to take their name with the marriage, they can force a company takeover."

"Yes."

"And the book emporium?" he asked, still tapping his ankle.

A faint flush crept into her cheeks. "Ah, yes, Mr. Harry's. I was hoping to find a law book that would have a way out of the petition."

"No luck?"

"No."

"So essentially, you're a runaway bride, and the Cyrano's hired a reward seeker to bring you home."

Annoyance flickered across her features. Her jaw tightened. "I am a petitioned, involuntary bride."

Jonathon wrapped his fingers around his ankle and relaxed in the seat. "True as that may be, legally, the Cyrano's have the upper hand. If you leave this house and Dossett states his intent and gets you, there's nothing I or anyone else can do."

She braided her fingers together. "Ramsey told me."

"There is absolutely no way out of the petition?"

A little noncommittal shrug jerked her shoulders. She didn't meet his stare.

Jonathon narrowed his gaze on her averted face. "Or is there?"

When her eyes finally lifted, wariness shone bright within the ocean-tinted depths. Silence stretched between them. The muted light from the two lit wall lamps deepened the bronze hue of her skin. Even lost in worry, Sylphine Seartavos's beauty didn't diminish. Jonathon wanted to climb across the desk to her. He wanted to gather her in his arms and fix everything broken. But he couldn't. The first move had to be hers. Jonathon wasn't in control of her destiny or her life. She was.

So, he waited.

He had an inkling about what would cut the ties of the marriage petition she'd been forced into, and he hadn't quite decided how he felt about it. Or how he'd respond if his suspicion turned out to be correct. Deciding to try a different tactic, Jonathon shifted in his seat, bringing his other arm to rest on his bent knee.

"All along, this has been the situation, hasn't it? Do you think this family has hurt your parents because they can't find you?" he asked.

"If they do anything illegal, like here in Sziveria, I can nullify the petition. But I'd have to return to Italyssa to find out," she said, her attention shifting to her hands.

"And if you return, and nothing happened…"

"I will have to marry Leone Cyrano."

Hearing the man's name spoken on her lips made a knotted fist in the center of Jonathon's chest. He didn't want her to be anyone else's wife. At some point in their fake engagement, Sylphine had become *his*. He'd had the ridiculous notion of saying to her *hey, let's make this thing between us official*. Stupidly, he'd harbored the fantasy she'd welcome more from him, that she'd be as excited at the prospect of a real, actual relationship together.

All of his hopes shattered the night he realized she couldn't even stand the thought of him *touching* her, let alone sharing a life together. Now, the choice had been taken from her. Either she married this Leone, or she ran for the rest of her life.

Or...

Jonathon took a deep breath. He allowed the thought he'd been tamping down to materialize. Or she could marry him. "Were they able to present you with the petition?"

She shook her head. "No. My *mita* sent me from the house before they could."

"And the reward seeker handed you nothing?"

"He held up a folded paper."

"But never handed it to you?"

"No."

"The paper could have been his authority for the summons to return you to Italyssa," Jonathon mused.

"Or it could have been the petition, which would also have given him authority, yes?" She caught her index finger in one of her ribbons, wrapping around the delicate turquoise length.

"Sure," Jonathon said, shrugging. "Thankfully, that didn't happen. But now you're stuck in this house until you have a new plan."

The ribbon fluttered back among the golden threads of her hair. "A plan. I have not had much luck with those so far."

Jonathon shifted his foot to the floor and leaned forward, elbows on his knees. He leveled his gaze on hers across the length of the barren desk. "Aside from committing a criminal act, is there no other way out of the petition?"

The tip of her tongue darted across her lips. Jonathon's gut clenched, his focus shifting to the glossy fullness of her mouth. The tease of a kiss he'd stolen in his bathroom last night hadn't been near enough. The memory of the shy brush of her lips across his throat when he'd tested her ability to sense emotion had him shifting back in his seat to alleviate the sudden tightening of his pants.

She swallowed, moving his attention to the delicate lines of her throat, which inevitably led to him looking lower, to the full mounds of her breasts. Allure, all wrapped in a stunning package he couldn't touch. Whatever had happened to Sylphine in the past had left her fearful. While Jonathon wanted to be the man who'd show her how wonderful, how different, *they* could be, he wasn't sure if she would ever welcome what he could offer.

"There is one other way," she admitted, her words slow and careful.

Jonathon held his hands open. Somehow, he managed to remain outwardly calm, while inside, his nerves bunched and teemed. He wondered if he were far enough away or if she could sense the tension coiled in him.

When he didn't speak, waiting for her to put a voice to the words neither seemed willing to speak, she cleared her throat. "If I were already married, the petition could not be met."

"Italyssa would recognize the marriage?"

"Of course, providing the union was indeed legal."

Jonathon sat up. "Is there someone else you wish to marry?"

Red swept across her cheeks. She pressed her lips together. A visible tremor jittered across her arms. "I..." She blew out a heavy breath.

"If I offered, how would you reply?" he asked.

Tears welled in her eyes. "Jonathon, you do not want to be married to me."

Jonathon's heart clenched. "What did I tell you moments ago about someone else deciding what I want or what I need?"

Her jaw tightened. "You do not know me well enough to make a rational decision."

"Do you know me well enough to?" he countered.

"It is different for me," she said, her chin lifting in defiance.

"Why?" He stood and pressed his palms on the desk. "Because I can't lie to you? Because you've let yourself get just close enough to decide whether I'm good or bad?"

"Because you are Jonathon," she said as if he should know exactly what that meant.

He stared at her and quirked his brow. "I'm me? That's your big argument for why you know me well enough to marry me? I could say the same. You're *Sylphine*."

She recoiled and stared at him as if a second head had popped from his shoulders.

"You are sexy," he began before she could speak another word. "You are smart. You are beautiful. When you want to be, you are funny."

Slowly, he rounded the desk, inching closer to her. "You think you can't tolerate my moods, but you have for years. Only last year did you build a circle around yourself no one was allowed to enter. I respected that."

Jonathon forced the chair to turn until she faced him, and he hunched before her. He slid his hands up her clothed thighs. Despite the layers of fabric, the heat of her skin seared his palms. Her muscles under his fingers tensed. A subtle gasp escaped her lips. Alarm and something else, something she buried too deep before he could grasp it, flickered in her eyes.

He rose until his mouth hovered over hers, his hands slipping to her hips. "However, you should know, I won't be in an unconsummated marriage. If you want to marry me, if you agree, we *will* be together."

• • •

Panic gripped Sylphine. Here the man of her literal dreams stood, offering her *everything*.

I cannot do this to him.

She wanted to rail against the unfairness of her situation.

How did she tell him she wouldn't come to their marriage bed an eager, innocent woman? She'd squandered that already. Someone else had taught her lessons in intimacy. While she knew deep in her heart, whatever Jonathon had to give her would be different, she didn't figure what she had would. The shame of her past hurt like a knife to her heart.

His mouth was still so close to hers, the heat of his breath fanned across her lips. In a longing she had never experienced before, she wanted to lean forward and taste his kiss again. Deeper. Longer. More. She pressed herself back in the seat.

"And if I cannot?" she whispered, refusing to meet the intensity of his stare.

He brushed a lock of hair behind her ear. A simple, yet intimate action that left Sylphine's breath lodged in her throat. "Then we will try to find another way out of your situation."

A knot of anxiety formed in her chest. She breathed through it. "How?"

Jonathon straightened and shifted away from her. He perched on the edge of the desk, near enough to touch if she were brave enough to reach for the impossible. Yet he sat far enough that the withdrawal of his presence, his warmth, and tantalizing masculine scent went with him.

The void was enough to make her grasp for what he had left behind – the eddy of his emotional currents. Frustration. A hint of desire. Confusion. And the one she didn't want to feel or recognize hurt. Proof he was still reachable to her on some level.

Only Jonathon emitted a variety of emotions at once. Everyone else focused or dealt with them, in the singular. Not this man. Sylphine desperately wanted to get into his mind. To know how he managed to remain so stoic while a veritable storm churned inside him at any given moment. He had been correct when he'd called her on her ability to deal with him. For over a year, she had. The complexity of him called to her. Though, she had no business wishing for anything concerning him. Had she not turned down his very real, very tempting offer? And here she sat, grasping for any slip she could take. The level of her pathetic nature had reached critical heights.

Jonathon crossed his arms over his chest. The sleeves of his shirt tightened along his biceps, defining the solid muscle beneath. All Sylphine's concentration went into not staring. Thanks to his physically demanding job, Jonathon Hunter was a premium male specimen. All the other men in her life had been soft, living privileged lives and doing the bare minimum to keep from looking weak. There was nothing *weak* about the man outwardly relaxed before her.

"I'll start with criminal activity. If I find anything, you can present it before your governing body. You did say they won't force you to marry a criminal, correct?" he asked.

Sylphine nodded, unsure how to feel about his help or why he'd offer. "Yes. But Leone isn't his father or his uncle. The crime would need to be his."

Jonathon shrugged. "Let me see what there is. There may be nothing, or there might be more than you ever wish to know. I'll have to do some research."

"I understand. Do you need anything from me to help?"

"A list of known business associates. Investors, clients, the person who handles their logistics, even their accountant. Anyone you can think of."

She blew out a heavy breath and rubbed her damp palms on her skirt. "What if I do not know all that?"

"Remember what you can." He gave a small, encouraging

smile. "Though as a competitor and family enemy, I can't imagine you don't know everything there is to know about their business and those they align with."

Yes, she did. The Cyrano's entire industry was wrapped up neatly in a folder within her home office. Likely discovered and disposed of by now if the worst she feared had happened. Shoving aside the dark thoughts, Sylphine nodded again. She'd do whatever was required of her, no matter how minuscule the chance, if it kept Jonathon from being wrapped up in her drama. "Okay, I will write down everything I can remember about them."

He unfolded from the table. The light caught on the black matte finish of the gun at his hip. Another reminder he wasn't some rich boy playing at being a man. "Don't open the front door or be visible if either Ramsey or I have to answer. You can go into the conservatory, there is a brick wall between it and the street. If Dossett climbs over or breaks inside, he's trespassing, and I can detain him."

Wouldn't that be too easy? Sylphine picked at a layer of lace on her thigh. "I will be careful."

He tapped his knuckles on the desk. "Good."

"Why did you offer me a second chance?" she asked when he went to round the desk as if to leave, the words tumbling from her with a rush of emotion. "Why are you willing to be tied to me?"

"Why are you wearing my promise band?" he deflected with a wave his hand her direction.

Sylphine slid her hand over the two silver bracelets. "I could not stand to remove mine," she answered quietly.

His sapphire eyes darkened. "Why?"

Because you are the only man who allowed me to be myself around you. The words formed on her tongue and died in a flash of fear. "I just... could not."

For long seconds, he remained silent, his gaze sweeping

over her face in a quiet thoughtfulness. Sylphine resisted the urge to squirm under the weight of his focus.

"I am not him, you know," he said so quietly she almost missed the words.

Sylphine blinked. "Who?"

"Whoever hurt you enough to fear men. I'm not him. I've told you that before, yet I feel like I need to remind you."

The dark night so many months ago loomed in her memory. Jonathon stating with conviction *I need you.* Sylphine too panicked at the waves of torment flowing from him to allow even the simplest touch of comfort. Her own emotions had disabled her instead of someone else's. In that moment, her past had controlled her, had forced the potential of something special out of her reach.

She swallowed, her fingers still brushing the sleek metal of his band. "I am sorry."

His head tilted, and his brows drew together in confusion. "What for?" Sylphine lifted her eyes, meeting his. He blew out a long breath. Understanding crossed his features. "Ah. That. You have nothing to apologize for. I was in a bad place. I'm the one who should have apologized a long time ago."

Sylphine shook her head. "No. You had every right to be upset with me. I was your promised." When he opened his mouth, she held up her hand. "Fake as we may have been, I was still your friend, too. I *knew* you were suffering. We both know I cannot claim ignorance on that, and I left you to suffer alone."

"My pain was not your burden to bear," he said softly.

"Whose burden was it then?" she asked, rising. "If not mine, then Ramsey? Did you talk to her?"

He shook his head, his mouth a tight, grim line.

"Another friend then?"

Still, he remained silent. Sylphine's heart clenched.

"No one, Jonathon?" She took the few steps between them tentatively. "Did she mean so much to you?"

OLD WOUNDS THREATENED TO BURST AT SYLPHINE'S INQUIRY. He didn't pretend not to know who the *she* in question was. Cora Dandridge. Jonathon had to look away before he said something foolish enough to undo everything he'd worked towards in the short time he'd been in the library. Finally, *finally,* she was really talking to him.

Cora would have listened. She would have taken my hand and held me through my tears if you'd *been the one to die.*

But he couldn't say that. Not now, maybe not ever. The words weren't fair to either of them. However, he couldn't lie to her either. Not because she'd sense it, but because if they were to build a foundation, he wouldn't start the cornerstone on a falsehood.

"She meant a lot to me, yes," he said.

Troubled shadows flickered in her gaze. "Did you love her?"

Jonathon raked his fingers through his hair. Tricky question. He glanced at her before sighing. "Do you really want to talk about this?"

"I do." She held her hands open. "If you will. I want to understand."

Right. She wanted to understand why he'd lost his damn mind so many months ago. Why his normally shatterproof façade fractured in an uncharacteristic outburst of anger and bitterness. He collapsed in the seat nearest to him.

"Did I love her," he repeated with a long exhale. "I think I could have if she'd have let me."

Sylphine put the desk to her back. Her fingers wrapped around the thick edge. "Why would she not let you?"

A question he had no answer to. One he'd been asking

himself since Cora's death. He shrugged. "I don't know. Cora liked the high of pursuing. The back and forth. The maybe or maybe not. She enjoyed teasing."

"You enjoy teasing," Sylphine said with a small smile.

He returned the gesture. "I do, yes. So we had fun. We teased, and she tempted, and I asked for more than she was willing to give. In the end, it didn't matter. She wouldn't listen, and I felt stronger for someone else."

Indecision flickered in her eyes. She chewed on her lip. Jonathon had to tamp down a smile threatening to break free. He knew she wrested with what question to ask first. What didn't Cora listen to, or who did he care more about than her?

"Was her death horrible?" Sylphine asked quietly, leaving him shocked and frozen. She flushed and tucked a strand of hair behind her ear. "I am sorry, you do not have to answer."

"No, it's okay." Jonathon shook his head to clear his thoughts and ground his emotions. "Just give me a minute."

He clasped his hands together and pressed his index fingers to his mouth. Closing his eyes, he tried to forget the mutilated body of the copycat murder to Cora's death. A still-open case that haunted and angered him whenever he allowed his memory to drift to the event. The real life visual to a report he'd requested from Westica had been his undoing the night he'd literally thrown his engagement to Sylphine away. Not that they'd been heading anywhere except to an uncomfortable end to their fictional relationship anyway. He'd simply sped the process up by unleashing a torrent of frustration, rage, hurt, and grief all at once.

"Yes, her death was extremely horrible. I've been an investigator for almost six years, and I had never witnessed the violence that was inflicted on her. I threw up after reading the report. That a person could be so cruel...." He sighed and dropped his forehead to his clasped hands. "The horror is without equal. I knew her, knew her twin brother, knew their bond and what had been torn away from him. Then it hit me that *I'd* never see her again. Never hear her laugh, never tell her to behave herself, never tell her no, ever again."

"I am sorry you lost her," Sylphine said in a mere whisper.

Jonathon sank his head further along his hands. "Yeah, me too. Though, I'm sorrier Mason lost her. I would lose my mind if something happened to Ramsey, and she's not my twin."

Scrubbing his hands down his face, he breathed out the guilt and grief of losing Cora Dandridge to an unknown enemy. He flopped back in the seat, relaxing his legs and resting his arms on the chair. "You know, she was jealous of you."

Sylphine stared in wide-eyed disbelief and pointed at her chest. "Of me?"

Jonathon nodded.

She scoffed and rolled her eyes. "That is just silly. Whatever for?"

Jonathon lifted his hand enough to point at her wrist. "For that."

Blinking, Sylphine twisted the bands and glanced down at them. "Because I was your promised?"

He nodded again.

"Did she know we were not really going to marry?" She continued to twist and slide her fingers along the bands in an almost sensuous caress that left Jonathon mesmerized.

"No one knew, Sylphine, except you and I." *And even I had my moments where I chose to forget.*

Slim as the chance may be, Jonathon was being offered the impossible again where she was concerned. Even though he had nothing to give her but a small house and a low-ranking Guardian position in society, a far cry below the shipping empire she grew up in. No, the daughter of Italyssa, raised in sunshine and ocean waves, would be giving up a lot to choose him. And he was selfish enough to accept any length of time he could get with her. Another opportunity to call her *his* wasn't something he wanted to allow to pass by. But in the end, the choice wasn't his to make.

He drummed his fingers on the arm of the chair in an attempt to distract himself. "Wasn't that the point?"

She pulled in a deep, shuddering breath. "I suppose, yes. I just thought… if you cared about her…."

"I didn't want her in my bed," he stated, meeting her stunned gaze. "So there was no need to correct her assumption."

Sylphine's breath lodged in her throat. Her heart pounded a heavy thump in her ears. The intensity of Jonathon's focus made tingles dance along her skin. She swore he touched her, yet he hadn't moved from the seat, and she still leaned against the desk. Awareness crackled between them like a living thing. The whisper of desire and longing slid across her skin, leaving no mistake as to *who* Jonathon wanted in his bed.

"You know why I'd want to be tied to you. I know you can feel me," he whispered, his gaze heated. "The bigger question is, would you want to be married to me?"

Jonathon wasn't the first man to look at her with lust blazing in his eyes. He was, however, the first man to look at her with *desire*. As if he wanted more from her than what could be sated after a few moments. And oh summer sun, the temptation of the man sitting before her was almost more than she could tolerate. An intriguing pulse beat at her center, making her conscious of her own blossoming hunger. A sensation she'd briefly experienced before, but had been overcome when another touched her.

The answer of *yes* was on the tip of her tongue. But nerves kept her from voicing the truth. She wanted everything Jonathon offered with frightening desperation. And if she agreed, she'd have to lay out a few personal facts of her own, and she wasn't ready for the rejection he may give if he knew.

She took a deep, grounding breath and met his fierce stare. "Will you give me time?"

"I will give you some time," he answered, slowly rising from his chair. "Under one condition."

Sylphine's already racing heart pounded harder. She tilted her head back to meet his gaze. "What?"

He leaned close enough for her to see the tiny sparks of lighter blue in the depths of his stare. "You let me kiss you."

"How long will you give me?"

"You and I both know you don't have much time. If my search comes up empty, you're in the same situation you've been in since your arrival in Sziveria. Aside from that, I won't wait long. You know what I'm asking." He settled his palms on the desk beside her, caging her against the long, solid length of his body. "Are you considering saying yes?"

A tremor of anticipation raced through Sylphine's body. Instead of answering, she met his gaze with a lifted chin and somehow dug some courage from unknown depths. "Why do you wish to kiss me?"

He arched a brow. "You have to ask that?"

Irritation flared inside her, and she glared. "You are not a man who follows base needs. You have reasons for everything you do, Jonathon Hunter. I will ask again, why do you wish to kiss me?" Because she knew with every fiber of her being, the kiss he'd bestow on her wouldn't be the same as what he'd already given her. No, mixed in with the flickering wisps of his desire were undercurrents of determination and curiosity.

"Is this the heiress I'm seeing?" he asked playfully, straightening but not putting any distance between them. His fingers toyed with a *Naenzi* near her ear, the tiny shells and beads chiming together. "The Sylphine Seartavos presented to the world of merchants and governments?"

The reminder of her position within her industry, and within nations, had her shoulders squaring. "Would you prefer I be her?"

He leaned close until his breath feathered along her ear and ruffled her hair. "I would prefer *you*. Just you. Only you."

Despite the fluttering of her stomach urging her to turn her head enough to meet his mouth so close, she kept her focus on his shoulder. On the faint ripples in the white fabric. On the way the seam stretched over the muscled breadth. Her fingers flexed along the edge of the desk. She wanted to touch him. To know how all that coiled strength would feel under her fingertips. Even more, she wanted to slip her hands through his hair, discover how the softness would shift along her palms, hold him close and experience if he'd be different. If she'd feel more than his unsated lust compelling him to take what he wanted from her.

Her breathing grew heavy, adding to the anxious pound of her heart. "Why are you not answering me?"

"I believe it was you who shirked my question first." He shifted his head lower, until his breath whispered along the sensitive skin at her neck. Still, he didn't touch her.

Sylphine swallowed to keep from whimpering at the torment of his being so near and yet restrained. "*Saie*, I am considering."

"Does that mean yes?" He'd moved a little lower. His lips brushed the edge of her collar bone. Sylphine jerked in surprise as a stirring awareness traveled along her nerves, coiling deep in her belly.

"Y-yes."

"I want to kiss you," he began, his lips trailing up her

throat to her jaw, leaving a cooling yet fiery trail, "because I want to know if you'll let me."

"A test."

He straightened enough to peer down at her mouth. Sylphine licked her lips. His fingers tangled in her hair but never touched her skin.

"An experiment in trust," he corrected. "I can't be married to you if you don't trust me." His fingers slid from her hair to her shoulder and lower to her arm. His dark gaze lifted, and he made no effort to hide the intensity of his longing.

"I trust you," she whispered, knowing in her heart she meant every word. She *did* trust him. Should have always known she could.

He lifted his hands, palms out, showing them to her, and then he set them back on the desk, leaning into her as he did. Expectation shivered along her spine. Instinct had her wanting to close her eyes, but curiosity kept them open. He moved in, his gaze dropping to her mouth a second before his lips brushed to hers. The tip of his tongue traced along her bottom lip. A quiver danced low in her abdomen. Of their own accord, Sylphine's eyes drifted shut, and she opened herself, craving the emotional connection to him with a strength that shocked her.

Desire, satisfaction, and most surprising of all, admiration shifted around her. The knowledge of his unspoken praise encouraged and before she could second guess the decision, she parted her lips. His tongue swept into her mouth, and his emotions drifted away like dust in a breeze. Sylphine lost herself in the tangle of their mouths. In an unhurried, undemanding exploration. Pulses of yearning flared to life at her center. She wanted, needed, more.

A whimper escaped her. She pressed her body to his. His mouth slanted over hers as he took her queue and shifted closer, forcing her further back onto the desk. The firm heat of his torso crushed against her, making her aware of the annoying layers of clothing she'd never cared about separating her from a lover before.

But Jonathon wasn't her lover.

The admission caused a fist to squeeze around her heart. Oh, she needed so much *more*. Fire burst through her veins, sending a shaft of warmth straight through her. Somehow her feet left the floor. Somehow her hands were on Jonathon's hips as she dragged him closer.

More.

Her knees parted, settling him between her thighs. Closer still, until the proof she wasn't alone in the torturous passion raging between them pressed against her core. Once, twice, he ground his hips to hers, and the pleasure at the action caused Sylphine to gasp and tighten her hold on him. The sensation was addictive. She deepened the kiss, drawing them further into the haze of hunger swirling like a vortex around them.

Then he was gone. Cold air filled the space where he'd once stood. Confused, she opened her eyes. Her fingers still gripped his waist in a tight hold. She blinked, meeting his shocked stare, and then glanced down. She sat on the desk with her legs open. He stood between her parted knees, where her skirt had gathered, riding high on her thighs in her obvious excitement.

His chest rose and fell in heavy breaths. The intensity of his unspent desire still darkened his eyes, focused so completely on her, she shivered. "You will say yes and be my wife," he growled out and then turned and left.

9

"Well?" Ramsey asked, glancing over her shoulder as she chopped whatever was on the cutting board in front of her. The scent of sweet baking dough, cinnamon, and citrus filled the room. "Are we going to be sisters or not? I was good and didn't bother you last night, but now I'm dying to know this morning, and you have to tell me."

Sylphine dropped into a chair and buried her head in the crook of her arm on the table. Sleep had been elusive as fevered dreams of Jonathon kept waking her, leaving her aching in a part of her body she'd never ached at before. She'd almost woken him in her annoyance and demanded to know what he'd done to her, because there was no mistaking her situation was entirely his fault.

"Hmm, that's not promising," Ramsey stated. Sylphine peered over the top of her arm. Ramsey frowned fist on her hip. She waved a spatula. "What is wrong with you? Did it go that badly with him?" Her frown deepened. "Was he mad? He was mad, wasn't he?" She tsked and stomped her foot. "I *knew* I should have stayed and told my version of the story."

"No, he was not upset."

"Then what is all this pouting about?"

"Not pouting, I am tired."

"Oh." Ramsey turned, setting the spatula down. She opened a cupboard and removed a cup. "I'll get you some coffee."

Ramsey set the steaming cup of midnight liquid on the table in front of Sylphine. "I know yesterday was a difficult day. We'll get it all worked out."

"I'm not sure how much you can work out," Jonathon stated, making them both straighten as he strode into the room, a newspaper in hand.

Every nerve in Sylphine's body went on high alert. The real memory of his mouth on hers mixed with the tantalizing images of that same mouth moving over her naked skin from her dreams. She forced her attention to the coffee, pulling the hot cup closer in an effort to focus on anything except him.

The paper slapped to the table. Sylphine jumped, her gaze lifting to meet his unhappy stare. "You have a problem," he stated.

"What?" Ramsey asked, reaching for the newspaper. She unfolded the daily. A frown to match her brothers darkened her face. "Oh, no."

Sylphine straightened, grasping the cup between both her hands. "What is it?"

Ramsey's face twisted in clear disgust. She held the paper out for Sylphine. Curious and a little worried, she accepted the paper. The bold title at the bottom of the society gossip pages caught her attention. *What is an Heiress to do?* After the title was a scintillating tale of a certain Italyssian shipping Heiress and her quest to find something steamy to read while on the shores of Sziveria. Mortified, Sylphine's cheeks flamed, and she glanced up to look between the Hunters. She held up the paper, speechless.

"It's okay," Ramsey said with a cringe.

Sylphine shook the paper, her eyes wide, her breathing growing shallow.

"I know it looks bad," Ramsey admitted holding up her hands. "But really, it's a tiny article in the societal pages."

"Everyone reads this," Sylphine argued, panic building. "Oh no, no, no! Everyone, Ramsey!"

"Some people prefer *The Havener*," Ramsey said in a placating tone. "And not everyone reads, or even believes the gossip section."

Groaning, Sylphine dropped her head onto the table. "I am never going to be able to do business in this country again."

The trickle of coffee pouring into a cup made Sylphine lift her head. Jonathon glanced in her direction and gave a weak smile.

"It'll be all right." He set the pot back on the stove. Crossing to the table, he sat in the chair next to her, blowing into his cup. "If it makes you feel any better, I still want to marry you."

"Ah, I knew it!" Ramsey squealed, clapping her hands together in delight.

Sylphine ignored Ramsey's happy outburst, her attention still on Jonathon, who stared at her with amused curiosity. "I bet you do. Everyone will think you have found the perfect wife."

Jonathon's eyes glittered with mirth. "Yep, I won't have to slink around the lusty book section by myself anymore. We can go together."

Sylphine sat up and slapped him with the paper. He laughed, shielding himself with his shoulder. "You want those books, you do not need me then, do you?"

He laughed harder. For the first time in a long time, he looked his age of twenty-eight. Handsome, young, vibrant, and full of life. Sylphine's heart clenched. How would he look on her ocean's shore, with the wind toying in his dark hair and the sun at his back? He leaned close, breaking her fantasy, and whispered so only she could hear, "Actually, I'll need you all the more. They call them *lusty* for a reason, my heiress."

If whimpering wouldn't have betrayed her, she would have given in to the need. But then Jonathon would know he'd gotten to her, and Ramsey would know they were sharing some secret lovers' language. Neither needed to know how warm his words made her. Focusing on her cup, Sylphine took a slow inhale. "I suppose it is a good thing I am stuck in this house for a while. This ridiculous article can go away."

"Coward," he said with a snicker.

Sylphine lifted her chin and met his smiling gaze. "You do not play fair."

"Nope." He took a sip of his drink and winked. "Never have, never will."

"Who wrote the article?" Ramsey asked, meat sizzling in a pan on the stove in front of her.

Sylphine cast a quick glance at Jonathon. A flicker of sadness crossed over his face before he seemed to focus on something across the room. Over a year ago, the name under the title would have been Cora Dandridge. Swallowing her discomfort, she checked the writer's information underneath the title. "Delanee Ralston?"

Ramsey turned, her mouth open in shock. Grease dripped from the spoon she held. "Ralston? Delanee Ralston?" Sylphine nodded, and Ramsey looked at her brother. "The Arch Guardian's Delanee?"

Jonathon took a sip of his coffee before answering. "Yes. She took over Cora's position about seven months ago."

"Brilliant," Ramsey muttered in disbelief. "First, *The Chronicle* had an untouchable with Cora since she was

Kynhaven's sister, now they have another one in Delanee since she's the Wolvenguard's sister. Incredible."

Looking at the journalist's name in neat, tiny print, Sylphine frowned. "What do you mean, an untouchable?"

On a sigh, Ramsey returned her attention to the pan. "No one can say anything negative or even really complain. The Ralston family is pretty much unrestricted in what they can do, short of killing someone, and then," she glanced at Jonathon, who frowned, "they may still get away with it."

"They wouldn't get away with it," Jonathon stated.

Ramsey shrugged. "Anyway, Delanee can write whatever she can dig up, and us underlings are powerless against her mighty pen. At least she seems to write the truth, regardless of how unsavory the content seems to be concerning her subjects."

"I do not want to be her subject," Sylphine countered with a groan. "This is a *dezastrafi*."

"*Curi seruanta*," Ramsey agreed. Both Sylphine and Jonathon gaped at her. Ramsey lifted her brows. "What?"

"When did you learn Italyssian?" Jonathon asked.

"I didn't." Ramsey began arranging plates for food. She seemed completely oblivious to the fact she'd spoken another language.

"What did you say?" He looked at Sylphine. "What did she say?"

"For certain," Sylphine answered. She exchanged a look of apprehension with him. Ramsey had been exposed to Italyssian in mass at the book emporium the day before. Sylphine knew of one specific genetic inherited talent that allowed such easy absorption of a previously unknown language. One Jonathon likely wouldn't be thrilled over.

He leaned close, concern in his dark blue gaze. "Did you teach that to her?"

"No, but she helped me look through texts yesterday, at Mr. Harold's."

"Just searching through words?"

Sylphine nodded. Nope, Jonathon wasn't pleased at all.

He flexed his jaw, his stare intent. "Please don't tell anyone."

"I won't," she whispered.

Ramsey clicked her tongue as she set their plates on the table. "Already sharing secrets. How sweet."

Sylphine straightened, accepting her plate of fried ham and sweet glazed rolls with a gracious smile. "No secrets."

"Mhmm," Ramsey said, a doubting crook lifting her brow. She went to the counter to retrieve a bowl of fresh fruit, and returned with her plate and the bowl. Attention on her brother, she jabbed her fork into the meat. "If you're contracting, why is she still wearing your promise band, and hers."

Sylphine placed both her hands under the table, her fingers wrapping around the touching bracelets. Jonathon cleared his throat and relaxed back in his chair.

"We aren't contracting," he said. His words were executed without emotion, but the flare of annoyance from them wasn't lost on Sylphine.

"Oh." Ramsey looked at Sylphine, distress pinching her face. "But I thought..."

"Talk only," Sylphine stated. "I am sorry if you were confused."

Fork poised elegantly in her hand, Ramsey glanced between Sylphine and her brother, a deep frown furrowing her forehead. "Talk? What is there to talk about? Did you think of someone better who could get you out of your situation?"

Sylphine flushed and pushed her food around on her plate. "No one better, no. But Jonathon has an idea."

Ramsey lifted her fork and snapped it back and forth. "I

have an idea, too!" she proclaimed. "Marry! All problems are solved. The end."

"Ramsey," Jonathon stated in warning. "Enough."

"A contract is a big deal, Ramsey," Sylphine said to her plate, not wanting to see the expression on either sibling's face.

A rapid knock echoed from the front of the house. Sylphine jumped, her fork clattered to her plate. Jonathon glanced over his shoulder and then pushed his chair back. He gave Sylphine a stern stare when she met his gaze. "Don't move."

"You wouldn't have to worry about who's at the door if you were already married to him," Ramsey argued as Jonathon left the kitchen. "You are being silly, Fi. He offered, didn't he?"

"I told you, he is going to do some research for me." Sylphine tried to hear what was happening out in the foyer, but only Jonathon's muffled greeting of surprise could be caught. Since he didn't seem upset, the person must not be the reward seeker.

"And you're going to hide away in this house, is that it?"

Sylphine regarded the empty doorway before leaning forward to keep her words quiet. "I will not put your brother in a relationship that may be a mistake. How many times must I say so?"

A woman's voice filtered into the room ahead of the front door closing. Jonathon's warm laughter followed the unknown woman's words. Sylphine snapped to attention in her seat.

Ramsey frowned, looking over her shoulder. "Yeah, well, he won't wait forever. Maybe you should consider that, too."

. . .

JONATHON ACCEPTED THE FOLDER FROM MELODY ERICKSEN WITH a grin. "Must have riled MT Rainier to ask for my help. Again."

She shoved her hands into the back pockets of her black uniform pants. The action forced her small breasts to strain across the fabric of her dark shirt. A huge smile graced her pretty face. "He did tell me to remind you it's not *help*, it's *assistance*."

"Of course, he did." Jonathon tapped the folder against his thigh. "Are you on your way to the division or on your way home?"

The enforcer rocked back on her heels. "Home. I thought I'd drop that off and then see if you wanted to go for some coffee or maybe a walk? I could tell you more about the case."

The calculating side of Jonathon made him want to answer in the affirmative. He glanced at the doorway leading to the kitchen, wondering if Sylphine lurked out of sight, listening. If he agreed, and the Italyssian heiress cared for him even a little, her jealousy may prompt action towards their relationship. However, as he turned his attention back to Melody, he didn't want to use the woman that way. She had the youthful hope he'd once held about love. The bright thought of a future with someone she could find herself caring for.

Jonathon motioned to his office. "Maybe another time for the walk. I'd accept knowing more about the case, if you're willing?"

She flashed a coy smile as she passed by him, twisting on the balls of her feet for a moment to face him. Her shiny, brown curls twirled around her face. "I'm always willing." Then she spun back around and continued in front of him.

Heaving a long sigh, Jonathon followed behind her, wondering at his luck concerning forward women. Or perhaps it was his plague, he mused. The one woman he *wanted* to be bold, was the one cowering in his kitchen. He clicked his tongue at the pitiful dilemma. He knew a passionate, strong-willed, confident woman lurked inside Sylphine. Plenty of times in the past, when she'd leave for a function or a job for her company, the heiress would come forth. Jonathon had to figure out why she was hiding now and how to bring her back. Or, more importantly, how to reveal her when they were alone.

Melody peeked out from the doorway to his study, reminding him of other current tasks that needed to be addressed. Opening the folder, Jonathon joined her. She'd found a seat in front of his desk, and he edged around the work cluttered surface. Taking a seat, he set the information down and began carefully reading the reports.

"Is the body still at the morgue?"

"Bodies," she corrected grimly.

Frowning, Jonathon flipped through more pages until he found the information for the multiple homicides. "A mother and young son."

"Yes." Melody shifted, crossing one leg over the other. "MT Rainier is used to dealing with punches and knife wounds, not calculated, obvious premeditated murder."

Sadly, Jonathon dealt with intentional crimes almost daily. How the wealthier side could be more animalistic than the city's poor and often downtrodden population, he hadn't figured out yet. Bracing his forearms on the desk, Jonathon immersed himself in the case, reading quickly over the facts.

The family had been in a public park on the outskirts of Haven City, barely inside the city authority, near Old Caris Road, which put it in the jurisdiction of the South Row Division. Caris was a small town where those who worked but didn't wish to live in Haven City resided. The suburban population swell had led to a rail line being run about twenty years ago and a new road. The residents still enjoyed the perks of a large city without the population issues. However, it seemed a big city problem followed this family on their afternoon excursion.

As he read the report, a niggling unease grew in his stomach. The family of four had been relaxing in a small clearing at the edge of the park, away from the walking trail enough to be secluded. The mother and teenage daughter had been reading, the younger son playing with a set of wooden cars in the dirt not far away. The father had been doing work in a set of ledger books.

In the report, the father said he heard three shots. He'd been carrying a firearm, but the gunfire had come from the park, and he didn't want to return fire into a civilian occupied area. His wife had taken a hit to her chest, his young son one to the stomach. The third round appeared to have gone wide. In the chaos, his teen daughter went missing.

"A double homicide and a missing person? I can see why Rainier would want help. Why not reach out to the Sziverian National Investigative Division?"

"The SNID has been requested, but you know those take time. The father is understandably upset. Neither the wife nor the son, died immediately," Melody answered with a heavy sigh. "It's heartbreaking."

"A loss of this magnitude always is," Jonathon agreed, returning to the report. "I don't see his interview."

Melody frowned and blinked. "I filed it myself at the precinct. It's missing?"

Jonathon flipped through all the pages. "Yes. Along with… damn… all the witness testimony is missing."

"That can't be right."

Melody jumped up and rounded the desk. The sugary scent of strawberries and jasmine floated ahead of her. Youthful and sweet. Jonathon wondered at the sudden sense of something *missing*, like the clean breeze of an ocean.

Shaking away the odd musings, he focused on the concerned gaze she shot his direction when she stopped beside him.

"Why would he ask me to give you a case file with half the case missing?" she asked.

A dark, alarming suspicion formed in Jonathon's gut. Calmly, he closed the file. "I need you to return to South Row and check the original file. Don't mention anything to anyone. Write or radio me with what you find."

Worry shone in her bright green eyes. "What's going on?"

"Maybe nothing. Will you do it?"

She nodded. "Yes, of course, I will."

Jonathon stood, and she took a quick step back. She tucked a curl behind her ear and gestured to the folder. "Seems useless now. Do you want me to take it with me?"

Shaking his head, he slid the folder out of her reach. "No. I can still review the information I do have."

With another nod, Melody made her way from the office. Jonathon followed to see her out. At the front door, she paused, her hand on the knob. "If you change your mind about the coffee or the walk…."

Jonathon braced his arm up. "I'll tell you first."

Melody smiled. "I hope so."

"Isn't this sweet?" a deep, male voice said from behind Melody.

Gasping, Melody twirled around fast enough to send her dark curls fanning out in a halo around her head. Her hand went to her empty hip, where, when on patrol, her weapon would rest. "What do you want, *reward seeker*?" she snarled in contempt.

Vayden Dossett's unusual colored golden-blue eyes glared at the young enforcer. "Nice to see you too, *Guardian Ericksen*," he said with equal disdain.

Her spine went straight, her hands fisted at her sides. "I prefer Tribunii Ericksen."

A cynical smile twisted on Vayden's lips. "I'm sure you do."

Jonathon quirked a brow, wondering at the hostility between the two. "What can I do for you, Dossett?"

Vayden's gaze slid from Melody to Jonathon. "I heard a rumor you might know where Sylphine Seartavos is hiding."

His left arm still braced on the door, Jonathon shifted his weight to his right foot and regarded the reward seeker. "And you think I'd betray her trust?"

Vayden shrugged. "You know I'm within legal rights to send her back to Italyssa. I'd prefer to do so with minimal attention, and therefore embarrassment, to her. The woman's promised is understandably worried about her well-being."

"Yes, I am," the words left his mouth before he could censor them. "And she won't be going anywhere."

Melody glanced over her shoulder with a gasp, her eyes wide in disbelief. Her gaze moved to his empty wrist and then back to his face. Understanding, along with a darker, unrecognizable emotion, flashed across her face before she shuttered her expression. "You heard the MT, you won't be getting anything from here." She flicked her fingers in a dismissive motion. "Go on."

Vayden chuckled a dark, sardonic sound. "Looks like you won't either." He winked and clicked his tongue to his teeth. "How disappointing for you, *Guardian*."

A deep, shuddering breath trembled through Melody's torso. Vayden turned after casting another mirthless smile in her direction. Jonathon rested his hip against the jamb and crossed his arms.

"Why doesn't he like you?" he asked.

Melody looked down at her feet. She swept the toe of her shoe along the front step. "I made the mistake of going to see Madelaine Fenwick."

"The matchmaker?"

Dark pink flared across her cheeks. "Yes. I didn't want my parents in charge of finding my mate. But, I didn't realize Ms. Fenwick doesn't look at genetics to decide who she recommends."

"What do you mean?" Jonathon asked, confused.

Melody still stared at her shoes. "Whether someone is a Gen-Heir, or gen-common." She looked up, her cheeks still flaming. "Vayden Dossett was her recommendation, but he's gen-common. I'm a Gen-Heir."

Jonathon frowned, trying to remember what he knew about the reward seeker. "But his mother is Amari Dossett, Shield Guardian Terravine."

Melody sniffed. "Yes. His father, Grayson, is gen-common. My parents said their marriage was quite a scandal when it happened. Their youngest daughter is their only Gen-Heir progeny, and will likely fill Amari's role in two or three years."

"And I'm assuming the recommendation from Ms. Fenwick didn't go well?"

Melody lifted her chin, her jaw clenched. "No. I refused the meeting."

Jonathon glanced at the now vacant walk where Vayden Dossett had strolled away from the house. "Ah. I see. He wasn't good enough for you." Jonathon looked back at her. "And I am?"

Turning her face into the faint breeze, her curls blocked her from view. "My parents only had me to see our name honored. I have an obligation to my family."

Jonathon couldn't help but quirk a corner of his mouth in a smile, not unlike the ones Vayden had cast her way. "Perhaps it's a good thing I couldn't go on that walk with you. I won't be anyone's fulfilled obligation."

"Not all of us have the luxury of marrying over emotions," she stated in defiance.

Brilliant sun saturated the quiet street. Birds bounced from naked tree limbs, singing to each other in twittering melodies. Jonathon looked over the tranquil scene and took a deep breath, letting the frigid, late autumn air fill his lungs. "I'm sorry you feel that way."

She pushed hair from her face and took a step down. "I-I'll radio if I find anything about the case."

"I appreciate it."

Jonathon waited until her Ariot disappeared before returning inside. Sylphine stood alone in the foyer, her arms wrapped around her waist. In the darkened space, she looked small. Lost. He eased the door closed. The muffled click of the latch catching broke the silence. Sylphine looked up, her sorrowful stare meeting his.

"Would I not be an obligation?"

"No. You're a choice. *My* choice," Jonathon stated. He took a cautious step closer, pleased when she didn't shift away. "I want you. I want us."

Fatigue tore through Sylphine. She was so tired of fighting. Weary of denying her attraction to this man and to the future he offered. Why bother anymore? The reward seeker would keep coming around. The Cyrano's would never give up on owning her or the company her father's family had worked hard to build. If she could shoulder her pride and her fears, Jonathon offered a way out of her dilemma.

Sylphine glanced at the empty stairs. While she knew Ramsey would never judge, the personal heartache she had to disclose wasn't something she wanted the young woman to know. "Do you mind if we go to the library or your office?"

"How about the greenhouse?" he asked, pointing to the narrow corridor that led outside.

"Yes, okay."

They walked into the warm, humid outbuilding. Golden, morning light filtered through glass panels. Somewhere a pane was open, letting in birds, who searched the grounds and trees for morsels to eat, calling in musical chirps to each other. Sylphine took a deep inhale of the moist, earthen air. A wave of homesickness brought her to the nearest bench, where she collapsed, sighing. She scooted enough to allow Jonathon to sit beside her. He didn't. Instead, he found a single wicker seat and plopped it down in front of her.

"All right, what's going on?" he asked, sitting, his elbows braced on his knees.

Sylphine brushed her fingers along a feather, whispering against her cheek. She looked over the neat, tended rows of Ramsey's garden, unable to meet Jonathon's stare. "I... there is something I need to tell you."

He shifted, settling his weight back in the seat. "Okay, but why?"

"Because you may change your mind about," she took a deep, bracing breath, "wanting to be married to me."

"Doubtful."

Sylphine risked a glance his direction. The annoyed expression on his face matched the frustration emanating from him. However, an underlying current of curiosity said he wanted to know despite his claim. "Perhaps."

He stretched a long leg out in front of him and braced his arm on the chair. "Very well, say whatever you think will change my mind for me."

Dryness suddenly coated her throat. She swallowed to try to ease the sensation and licked her equally dry lips. Her heart threatened to pound from her chest. What would he think of her? Would he look at her with contempt? Disgust? Or maybe even pity? Rubbing her tingling hands on her thighs, she focused on the sun glinting from a still damp leaf near her.

"As my husband, you will not be my first lover," she said quickly while she had the nerve.

When silence followed her declaration, she chanced to look at him. He stared at her with an expression of expectation and waved his hand. "And?"

Sylphine blinked. "And…"

Did she dare tell him the rest? Gnawing on her bottom lip, Sylphine focused past him to the exterior brick wall of the house. Yes. She had to. Starting their marriage on a lie could, no *would*, ruin everything.

"And they did not want me anymore after having me. I am not, that is, I have never been…." Red flared across her cheeks. Acid churned in her stomach. "I was not… pleasing to them."

"Were they pleasing to you?" Jonathon asked.

Startled, Sylphine stared at him. "What?"

He tilted his head and regarded her. "Did *they* please *you*?"

"I—" Words stuck in her throat. After all, she'd confessed, he asked if her former lovers were any good to *her*? "Do you not care about the rest?"

"The rest?"

She nodded. "Yes! My having been with others? My being a terrible lover? Those things."

"First of all," he began, leaning forward and clasping his hands between his knees, "you won't be my first either, so why would I be upset? Secondly, I'm not convinced about the other concern you seem to have."

An unexpected bloom of jealousy burned in her chest at the thought of Jonathon in the arms of another woman. Shaking off the unwarranted emotion, she met the warmth of his stare. "You should be concerned. We cannot undo a contract."

"No, we can't, you're correct. However, unless we choose, contracts aren't forever. There's a reason couples are encouraged to start small and increase their years with each renewal."

Sylphine brushed her fingertips along the promise bands on her left wrist. "I know, it is the same in Italyssa, though we do not recognize anything less than five years."

Jonathon raised a brow. "Five-year increments?"

"No, just anything five years or over." She couldn't help but grin. "Some couples are truly adventurous and start with six years."

He returned her smile. "What did your parents start with?"

"My father says forever, my mother says five years." She shrugged. "Neither will change their story, so I have no idea."

"I bet it was forever."

Sylphine chuckled. "Yes, probably so, knowing my father."

"Have you said all you need to say?"

Her smile faded. Once again, she met his gaze, concern gnawing in her belly. "You really do not care I have known… others?"

"Do you?"

Confused, Sylphine tilted her head and touched her chest. "Do I care about my having previous lovers?"

Jonathon looked down at his clasped hands. "And me."

"Why would I?"

A small smile curved the corner of his mouth. "Because it seems to matter to you."

"Well yes, I am a woman, and we do not—"

"Take lovers?" he chimed in when her voice faded. "Of

course, women do. I'm assuming these men meant something to you at one point?"

Sylphine nodded, her voice lost.

He sighed in a sad, long exhale. "That's more than I can say about the women I've been with, who were simply used and used in turn. No emotional attachment or promises made."

"Always?" Sylphine asked, wondering how in his entire life, Jonathon had never cared enough about a woman to want her in his life long term. At least, not until her. A little flutter trembled in her stomach at the realization.

"You already have the answer to that," he said softly, giving confirmation to her inner musings. "Now, why have you believed a lie about yourself?"

Unable to stand being still, Sylphine leapt up and paced to the narrow path. "It is not a lie. If only one said as much, perhaps, but…" She shook her head, wrapping her arms around her waist. "Three?"

Jonathon didn't rise. Instead, he stretched out again, lazy, relaxed. He folded his hands over his stomach and regarded her with a calm gaze. "And how were they to you?"

The quiet expression on his face eased some of her high-strung nerves. "I do not understand the question. You asked me earlier."

"Yes, and you didn't answer then, either."

"I am not sure what you are asking," she admitted.

"They seemed to have plenty to say about you, but how did *they* fair as lovers?"

Sylphine's cheeks burned. She presented her back to him while she composed herself. "I cannot believe we are having this conversation."

"I'm thankful we are. I appreciate you being honest, I know this can't be easy. Please, answer me."

She twisted a scrap of lace from her skirt between her

fingers. Carefully, she considered her past experiences, short as they were, of the men in her life. Quick bouts of stolen moments at events, in library's, offices, and even the dark recesses in greenhouses. Once, her first promised had managed to convince her of a quick go in a carriage. Then again, had she been convinced? All she could recall from all the hurried couplings she'd experienced, were being held tight by her wrist, her arm, once even by her throat, with his thumb pressing uncomfortably into her jaw as emotions of lust and unsatisfied sexual hunger flowed into her.

An ache pulsed between her eyes at the flow of unpleasant memories. She touched her forehead. "I do not know how they were. I cannot seem to remember much."

Jonathon's gaze narrowed. "What do you mean?"

Rubbing her temples, Sylphine tried to organize her thoughts. "I mean, it is all of them. How they felt. What they wanted, and thought they needed."

"Is that why you put so much distance between us? Were you afraid I'd do the same?"

Shame made her look away. "I was afraid any man would do the same. I realized my Sympath ability was being used against me when my last promised tried to force himself on me and almost succeeded, when I fell under the influence of his emotions. Had his sister not accidentally walked in, I would not have been able to stop him."

"And now you're scared."

She heaved out a long breath, staring down at her hands. "And now I am terrified."

He stood and held his hand out. "Come on."

Sylphine stared at his open palm.

"If you want to marry me, you're going to have to start trusting me at some point. I told you I won't be in an uncon-summated marriage."

Nervous dryness made swallowing difficult as Sylphine regarded him. "Now?" she squeaked out.

Jonathon laughed. "No, not now. We aren't even married yet."

Still staring at his hand, she asked, "Then what?"

He shrugged, his hand continuing to wait for hers. "You'll have to trust me."

On a long inhale, Sylphine slipped her hand into his much larger one. The heat of his palm seared hers, and the flood of his satisfaction and happiness flowed into her, making her smile. Cooler air from inside the house rushed past as Jonathon opened the door. He led her into his office. Releasing her, he waved to one of the many seats in the messy space and then disappeared.

Sylphine glanced around, unsure how Jonathon managed to find anything when papers, files, books, and journals were stacked haphazardly on every available surface, including two of the five available seats. Instead of sitting, she wandered the narrow room, turning papers she walked by and smiling at Jonathon's quick, yet legible script written on nearly everything she came across.

A feminine shriek followed by quick, heavy footfalls on the stairs had Sylphine turning towards the door. Ramsey burst in, cheeks flushed, her lavender eyes glowing with enthusiasm. The dark blue fabric of her skirt swirled around her ankles as she ran, disturbing all the papers she rushed by.

"Is it true?" Ramsey asked, her eyes wide. "You really said yes? You actually agreed?"

Bewildered, Sylphine glanced past Ramsey to Jonathon leaning casually against the doorway, a small smile playing on his lips. Amusement glimmered in his dark eyes. He arched a questioning brow at her.

Realization dawned on Sylphine. Jonathon had collected his sister to be a witness. He was calling her out. Either she rejected him, likely for the last time, or she accepted what he offered. A chance at safety. Or, perhaps what she wanted, even more, an opportunity to be his. Heart in her throat, she swallowed in an attempt to ease her nerves and find her voice. "Yes, it's true."

Heat flared in Jonathon's gaze. Sylphine quickly turned away, worried she'd get lost in his stare and rooted in place.

Ramsey clapped her hands together and then began searching her brother's chaotic desk. "All right, where is it?"

"Second drawer," Jonathon answered.

On a squeal of delight, Ramsey produced a long sheet of white paper with a flourish. She laid the contract out on the desk and smoothed her hands along the sheet. After some shuffling, she found a pen and held it out. "You first, Fi. Come on."

Sylphine rounded the desk, her eyes never leaving the small printed paragraphs arranged neatly on the paper. Several blank lines stood out in contrast to all the legal sections filling up the page. She and Jonathon hadn't discussed what would fill those spaces. When she glanced up and met his stare, he swept his hand in a forward motion.

"Every decision is up to you," he whispered.

Her attention shifted back to the contract. Each choice concerning their marriage, their future was hers. With the sweep of a pen, she could tie him to her for life. Or she could take him up on the minimum five years, no promises, no financial gain, no stake in her future or that of her family. He gave her complete trust. Sylphine licked her lips and wrote in a number. Then she went to the next line and wrote in the stipulations for annulment, making sure if the Cyrano's obtained a copy, they wouldn't have anything to use against either of them to coerce a separation. Nothing personal that couldn't be proven by a third party.

When she was finished, she turned the contract to face

Jonathon and held the pen out for him. The pen left her grasp on a slow slide. Sylphine's heart pounded, her fingers tingled with nerves. In mere seconds, she'd be married… *married*… to Jonathon Hunter.

Panic welled up inside her. What if she disappointed him? What if she were as terrible a wife as she was a lover? Despite what he said, she held no misconceptions about how she'd be in his bed. Pressing a hand to her stomach, she looked away while he read over the entries she'd made.

If they'd done this same moment in Italyssa, family and friends would surround them and cheer the signing. A huge party with food, dancing, and festivity would follow. In Sziveria, the moment a promise was made between the couple was celebrated, while the actual contract signing was a more private event. For the Hunter's, the quiet signature exchange was normal. Sylphine breathed away threatening tears. She missed her parents, and the excitement they'd share over her future. The Seartavos house would have been bursting with her mother's family in celebration. Maybe even her crazy, missing great-uncle on her father's side would have made an appearance.

Then again, Sun Wind's legal team would draft a contract for the couple to sign once they set foot in Italyssa. Sylphine clung to the hope she'd still have a signing celebration after all. Jonathon leaned his forearms on the desk. Despite the dancing of her stomach, she met his gaze. He beckoned her closer.

"Ten years?" he whispered.

"Does that bother you?" she asked in the same hushed tone.

He shook his head. "No. But you should know I hope to have a child by then with you, so it'll be longer than ten years."

She slid her finger along the edge of a paper, avoiding his stare. "Only in Sziveria. In Italyssa, still only ten years."

Shock widened his eyes. "You don't have the same family laws?"

"No. If a couple wishes to remain married after they conceive, they can choose to do so. I know here, it's an automatic eighteen years from birth. Not so in my country."

"So, if you want away from me after ten years, you'll just leave?"

"No, I…" Sylphine straightened on a frown.

They hadn't discussed where they'd live long-term. Jonathon had Ramsey, and his job, both of which were incredibly important to him. Sylphine had her position within Sun Wind Trade that she couldn't simply walk away from. On a gasp of alarm, she watched him execute the final flourish of his signature. A strangled cry escaped her.

Before she could reach out to take hold of the contract, it fluttered away. Ramsey signed next, quicker than Sylphine could object. Triumph sparkled in Ramsey's eyes. She swept the document up the moment Sylphine attempted to take it from her grasp.

"I'll just go and file this now, before either one of you crazies can change your mind," Ramsey stated, her nose up in the air in an impenitent gesture that dared either of them to protest.

Sylphine raised her hand in a stop motion, but Ramsey flew past, giggling. "Wait!" Sylphine called out as the front door slammed closed. Her shoulders slumped forward, and she dropped her weight to the desk.

"Change your mind already?" Jonathon asked, crossing his arms over his chest.

"There's so much we did not discuss," she said quietly. "Like where we will live."

"We have ten years to decide."

Sylphine stared at him in disbelief. "That is impossible, and you know so. We both have important jobs and people who need us. Would a marriage work in two locations?" She shook her head and pressed her hand to her forehead. "Things we should have already talked about and decided on."

"You can do what you do almost anywhere. But yes, I understand your needing and wanting, to be near your parents. It's the same with Ramsey. Until she's married…" He sighed and dragged a hand through his hair. "I don't want to leave her alone."

"Italyssa could be good for her," Sylphine mused. "An opportunity to start over where no one knows her."

"Yes, however, I've never been, so I can't make that decision yet for either of us."

"Have you ever left Sziveria?"

He shook his head. "No. Leaving the country doesn't bode well for my family."

"How do you mean?"

"Well," he began, inhaling, "my great-grandparents decided to go see the ruins on Miami Island when they retired. Their first grand adventure, made especially to celebrate my grandfather earning our Key Guardian position. The ship never made it, however, they were lost at sea. Decades later, my grandfather decided to take my grandmother to Ruthenia in the spring since the three months the country is in bloom are unlike anything ever seen, or so the travel papers say. Their hotel caught fire on their third night in the country. Then my parents."

Sylphine frowned, her heart dropping. "I am almost afraid to know."

"Monaco Sands, the year a hurricane practically leveled the entire island. They were supposed to leave a day after landfall."

She tried to recall how long ago the storm had been. "My father sent ships for aid. He and my mother went as well to help. That was… five years ago?"

"Six." He rubbed his chin with his knuckle. "Now, on my mother's side—"

Horrified by the thought both sides of his family met untimely demises by simply leaving the nation, Sylphine raised her hand. "No, I do not want to know, please stop."

"Are you sure? One of them is rather funny, in a dark sort of way."

She waved a hand in front of herself. "I am very sure. You have me convinced I will need your life insured before you step a single foot on a ship."

A mischievous smile crossed his face. "Actually, best to do so before I even step foot on a train *bound* for the docks."

Sylphine groaned. "I will never leave this country."

"That's not true. I mean, these were all freak occurrences my family happened to be involved in. I've never genuinely had the desire to leave, now I do."

Hesitant at even the thought of risking his fate, Sylphine stared at him. "I am not convinced you would not fall overboard the second the ship launched and be gone forever. We will discuss this later, after I think of how to transport you safely."

He laughed. "I'm not made of glass."

"All the same." Then his words returned to her, and she gasped. "Only now I am married to you, and I could sink with the ship, too!"

He laughed again, louder, his whole body shaking with merriment. "We aren't cursed."

Sylphine narrowed her eyes on him. "Are you certain? Shows to me that you are."

His athletic frame straightened to his full height. In a short, fluid motion, he closed the space between them. The wave of his intent, a combination of amusement and desire, enclosed her before his arms did. His hands braced on the desk beside her thighs. Her first instinct was to shy away, to back onto the desk and put as much distance between them as possible. But she didn't. Jonathon was her husband now.

Mine.

The declaration repeated in her mind. Over and over again. A sense of unexpected possession and excitement flooded her. An overwhelming urge to wrap herself around him, fix her mouth to his and see what happened had her breath hitching in her throat. She kept still, waiting to see what he would do next.

"The word is, *appears*, not shows. How you can be so articulate and yet, miss so many words is a mystery to me," he whispered, the dark depths of his pupils pushing almost all color from his irises.

"Appears to me you are cursed," she amended, her voice nearly lost in the swirling haze of his emotions mixing with her own emerging intimate curiosity.

Sparks of blue danced in his eyes. Amusement faded, replaced solely by desire as he leaned in so close his lips nearly touched hers. "How do you propose I end this curse, then?"

Silence followed Jonathon's inquiry. He stood so close to Sylphine, that he imagined he could feel her heart pound against his chest where they touched. An almost desperate need to kiss her rose within him. She was his now. His wife. Nothing held him back except her recent confession. Anger churned inside him at learning she'd been used, deceived by her genetic talent, into accepting lovers she may not have been ready for or even truly wanted. He wouldn't be in their class.

Utilizing all his patience and restraint, he took a slow step back. Her luminous ocean green eyes widened before she bit her lip and quickly looked away. An alluring flush blossomed along her cheeks. Jonathon didn't need Sympath abilities to know she'd considered, briefly, being a temptress. And he wanted her to be. He wanted her to be bold and daring in her passion. To know nothing between them would ever be wrong or unimportant to him.

He shifted his hands to her hips, resisting the urge to fit his pelvis into hers. "Come upstairs with me."

Her gaze shot back to him, her eyes still wide, now with alarm. The pink brightening her cheeks darkened and spread all the way to her hairline. "I am not so sure—"

"Trust me. Please." His hands flexed on her hips for a second before he dropped them and took another step from her. "I'm not those men, Sylphine."

Closing her eyes, she pressed her fingers to her cheeks and nodded. "Yes, I know."

He remained silent until she opened her eyes. Leaning down, he met her gaze. "You keep saying that, and yet, I have to keep reminding you."

She inhaled slowly. "Years of mistrust will not fade away in days, Jonathon."

The words *I wasn't the one you didn't trust* were on the tip of his tongue to speak. However, his gender had placed a fear in her heart he had to undo. She *hadn't* trusted him. Jonathon nodded and held his hand out for her to take again, as he had earlier in the greenhouse.

They took the stairs in silence. Boards creaked beneath their combined weight, adding to the isolated sensation of them being completely alone. Jonathon glanced at the closed front door. Their marriage was likely official by now. They wouldn't have too much longer before Ramsey returned home.

As if she'd read his mind, or perhaps his emotions had betrayed his thoughts, she whispered, "I cannot believe we are really married. Everything happened so fast."

"Do you think it'll be enough? Will Italyssa recognize it?" Jonathon asked, leading her to her bedroom.

"I do not honestly know. I have never heard of my situation before. Will it make the reward seeker stop?"

"Yes. As my wife, he can no longer send you away, it would be considered kidnapping. Vayden Dossett may be a reward seeker, but he's honest." He closed the door, ensuring that if his sister did arrive home, they'd still have privacy.

A tremor visibly shuddered along Sylphine's body. She tried to pull her hand free, but Jonathon wouldn't let her. He guided her deeper into the room until they went behind her dressing screen. Standing at her back, he stopped in front of the full-length mirror arranged to capture window light. He laced his fingers through hers, capturing her other hand and doing the same. Slowly, he lifted both her arms from her sides and rested his chin on her shoulder. He met her perplexed stare in the mirror.

"You are so beautiful," he uttered in awe.

In a feathery, dragging motion, he slid his fingers along her palm, up her forearms, and to the sides of her dress. Her breath hitched, and her gaze fixed on his in their reflection. "What are you doing?"

"An experiment." Using the mirror to guide him, Jonathon undid the row of lace concealed buttons along the front of her gown. Every muscle in Sylphine's frame went rigid. He wanted to tell her to relax, but he knew the command would only make things worse.

"You see," he began, his attention on the gap appearing between the buttons, "I think you've been so focused on how someone else feels, you haven't realized you can experience things, too."

"And what if I do not like how I feel?" she asked, her words shaky.

"Then I will stop," he promised.

While she didn't relax completely, she did nod. Once he freed enough buttons to remove the dress, Jonathon slid the array of creamy pink silk and lace from her shoulders. The weight of the gown did the rest, falling in a whisper to her feet. Sylphine trembled and tried to wrap her arms around her waist, but Jonathon caught her wrists. She stood before the mirror in nothing more than a long, white silk slip. Small, shimmery buttons ran from the neckline to her navel.

Jonathon slid his fingers from her wrists to her shoulders and swept her hair away from her neck. Before she could block his movement, he slipped his arms around her waist. Resting his chin on her shoulder, he kissed the pulse beating rapidly at her throat. The tell-tale hitch of her breath emboldened him, and he licked a trail to her jawline.

"How does that feel?" he whispered, nuzzling the sensitive spot on her neck just below her ear.

"Um…" She swallowed, her gaze averting from his in the mirror.

Jonathon smiled against her soft skin. Tilting his head enough to see over her shoulder, he undid the row of buttons along her slip. The edges gaped, revealing the golden expanse of her skin and the full swell of the insides of her breasts. Jonathon skimmed the tips of his fingers along her revealed flesh. She shivered. The tight peaks of her nipples pressed against the thin silk covering them.

Hot desire flashed through him. He wanted to spin her around, sink to his knees and taste her all over. Instead, he drew a lazy line from her collarbone to her exposed belly-button and back up, caressing her breasts as he passed them. Up and down, over and over again. "Tell me how you feel. Not what you're feeling from me, but what I'm doing."

She licked her lips, and he copied the action on her throat. A small, urgent sound escaped her. Jonathon gently bit where her shoulder met her neck when she continued to remain silent. "I'm waiting."

"You are t-touching m-me," she breathed out, her eyes fluttering closed.

He watched his languid strokes, marveling at the contrast between their skin tones. Hers so much richer than his, nearly two shades darker. Slowly, giving her time to adjust to his touch, he slipped his hand further under the slip, capturing her breast. The heavy globe overflowed in his hand, supple and firm. He dragged his thumb across her beaded nipple and was rewarded by a shocked gasp. "You enjoy that?"

She nodded.

"No one has touched you like this?"

She shook her head, her breast pressing further into his hand with each quick breath she took.

"Do you want me to stop?"

"I am not..." She took a long, shuddering breath as he shaped and molded her breast against his palm, paying attention to the sensitive tip. "...certain."

Jonathon released her breast. She grabbed his arm on a cry of disappointment. He smiled and splayed his hand across her stomach. Gently rounded and firm under his palm, he kneaded the flesh near her hip. Her pelvis jerked, and her hand tightened on his forearm.

"Jonathon," she half breathed, half moaned.

He slid his fingers under the band of her panties but went no further. "Yes, I should stop? Or no, do I keep going?"

"No."

"No?" He eased further beneath the fabric, anticipation curling in his stomach.

"Do not stop." She turned her face and closed her mouth over his.

Jonathon wasted no time, urging her lips apart with his tongue. On a growl, he swept into her mouth, tasting and exploring. Her weight fell back, all her full curves cradling into his body. Unable to stand the wait, he slipped his hand between her legs. He found her hot and so wet he didn't waste any time pushing a finger deep into her. She pulled her mouth free on a strangled cry, her legs shifting open to allow him better access.

In quick, deliberate strokes, he worked her into a state of passion. Red suffused her cheeks and chest, her breasts rose and fell in heavy pants, brushing against his arm. "Are you feeling more than my emotions?" he managed to somehow get out, needing to know her reactions were her own and not a direct result of his own raging desire to be buried deeper than his fingers could go within her.

A high, throaty whimper was all she managed. Jonathon took that as a positive. Her hips moved in a frenzied motion against his hand, rubbing her rear into his groin. The urgency of her movements transferred to him, and drove him higher. He pulled her tightly to his body and increased his strokes between her legs until she shattered around his fingers. Her cry of release and inner muscle spasms sent him over his own edge. He embraced the rush of his own pleasure, the shared moment. Their labored breathing mingled in the sudden stillness.

Jonathon pressed a gentle kiss to her lips and pulled his hand free. "Beautiful," he whispered against her swollen mouth.

"Is there more?" she asked, her passion glazed eyes settling on his mouth.

"Yes. But not today."

"Why?" She tried to twist to face him, but he wouldn't let her, banding his arms around her waist. "We are married now. I am your wife."

"Yes," he admitted, wondering at the flutter in his stomach at her words. He kissed her cheek, her jaw, her throat. "But you'd wonder, late in the night, if what you felt was you. I want you to remember this, think on it, and when you come to me, and you will, you'll have no doubt you alone are in control of your body and your decisions."

ALONE, STANDING BEFORE HER MIRROR, STILL HALF-DRESSED WITH lingering tendrils of pleasure racing through her veins, Sylphine looked at her reflection. The same woman from this morning stared back, and yet she was *different*. Her body had been brought to a height she hadn't known existed.

Instinctively, she knew there was more, something greater to be found in Jonathon's bed. But he was right. She needed time to understand what had happened. As he'd caressed and sent her body into a spiral of need, his own emotions had coursed through her system, heightening the experience, making her want to feel more of him, while at the same time desperate to know the new sensations he brought forth within her.

The entire incident had been exhilarating and a little frightening. Why did he care about her response when no man prior to him had? Frustrated and confused, Sylphine turned away from the mirror, picking up her discarded dress. Heat still pulsed between her thighs. She slipped her hand under her clothes and touched her core, surprised to find herself damp and swollen.

She'd heard of women pleasing themselves, but she'd never been able to bring herself to experiment, figuring if her lovers had brought forth no desire, surely her own hand wouldn't do the job. As she pressed a tentative finger to her swollen nub, a shock of pleasure met her touch, and she wondered if perhaps she'd been mistaken. But as she slid her fingers along her slick flesh, the experience wasn't the same. She didn't possess the skill Jonathon had unleashed on her. All the action did was remind her of the man no longer standing in her room. Sighing, she pulled her hand free.

Bunching her dress against her stomach, she looked around. How long would he give her to understand what he'd brought to life within her? Would they eventually share a room? And after unraveling in his arms, how could she look at his face, his hands, and not remember? Heat suffused her cheeks. Oh, she was in trouble.

She'd worry about the consequences of their moment later. She needed to try to reach her parents. Being married now, she had to try to get word to them to see what the next step would be if one could even be taken. She also wanted to share the moment with them. However, she knew the chances were slim, but hope refused to die within her. While she couldn't be forced to leave Sziveria, she wasn't sure if her marriage would be recognized in Italyssa since she'd been mandated to marry Leone Cyrano.

After showering and changing into something she considered on the boring and drab side, a cotton lavender gown that darkened to black by the end of the skirt, Sylphine braved leaving her room. The house was still, except for an indistinct clanking coming from downstairs. Sylphine went to investigate and found the Hunter's three days a week housekeeper at work in the kitchen.

The older woman jumped when she noticed Sylphine, her hand sweeping to her chest, her dark eyes wide. "Oh my, Miss Seartavos, you scared me. I thought everyone had gone out for the afternoon."

"Jonathon is not home?"

"No, miss." The housekeeper wiped her hands on her black apron. "He was on his way out when I arrived. Said something about needing to run some errands and check on something at the precinct. I had the impression he won't be home for some time."

Sylphine managed to keep her disappointment to herself. He hadn't said goodbye. Then again, he never sought her out to tell her when he was leaving, why would he do so now? How much of their relationship did she want to change now that she was his wife? After thanking the housekeeper, Sylphine retreated to the library.

For what felt like the hundredth time, she powered up the radio and tried to reach her parents.

10

Jonathon flicked the open edges of the file on his desk, trying to focus on the words and not on the rings safely held in his pants pocket. He wanted to return home and see his *wife*. He wanted to slide the ring on her finger, kiss her and see if the unfamiliar sensation in his stomach happened again. Even more, he wanted to watch her open and unravel like a beautiful blossom at the full height of bloom once more. But the disturbing radio message he'd received from Tribunii Melody Ericksen had sent him into work on his off day.

All the files on the murder he'd been asked to review were missing, with the exception of what she'd brought to him. The situation was too familiar for him to ignore. Almost two years ago, Jonathon had helped uncover the truth behind the murders of Primary Guardianess Wintersfall's family. Katria Blackbain's mother and sister had been assassinated. As Jonathon looked over the file he'd put together when he'd helped investigate as a favor to the Blackbain's, he saw too many similarities to the case handed over earlier in the day.

Gathering both files, he tucked them under his arm as he stood. He could go to any of Blackbain's team members and

159

likely get answers. However, going straight to their source of information seemed the best option.

After dealing with the heavily congested corridors and stairways, Jonathon managed to emerge into the parking lot minutes later. He took a moment to breathe away the foul mood navigating the crush of people always left him in. Thankfully, he wouldn't have to deal with such chaos at the First Intelligence Office.

The ride over was smooth, as was getting an ID badge to visit the Guardian, who worked as a liaison for the Arch Guardian Synintel to the Intel Teams under his command. Files and credentials in hand, Jonathon took the wide steps up to the correct floor. Pristine white corridors with only essential personal moving between them made finding the correct office easy. A pang of envy at the tranquil, organized work environment went through Jonathon.

The hectic nature of Enforcement divisions couldn't be helped, though. Before a case went to an accusation hearing, the allegations had to be proven. The innocent and not so innocent clogged the halls vying for their chance to speak while witnesses provided necessary statements. Jonathon figured a more organized method once existed, but over the years, the auction house style of accused facing off their accuser, often times with legal help in tow, had become a custom in Sziveria.

In blissful silence, Jonathon found Ryan Voklane situated behind his desk, a file open before him while he scribbled on a notepad. Jonathon rapped his knuckles on the open door, announcing his presence. Voklane glanced up and then motioned with his free hand while returning his attention to the documents before him.

"What brings you to my office, Asherwick?"

Jonathon closed the door before approaching the seats in

front of the desk. "Something unsettling has been brought to my attention."

A pale blond brow arched, but Ryan didn't glance back up. "Unsettling seems to be our new normal."

"Sadly true," Jonathon conceded, taking a seat. He set the files on the immaculate desk.

Dying light shone in the wide window behind Voklane, illuminating the man's broad shoulders and pale, short-cropped hair. "What do you have to show me?"

Jonathon situated his ankle over his knee, knowing he likely needed to get comfortable, the conversation may be a long one. "Have you heard of the name Castien?"

Voklane's silvery-blue gaze shot up. The rest of him went very still. "I have. How have you heard of him?"

"The family." Jonathon leaned forward and pushed the top file across the desk. "Two murders and what, by my first impression, appears to be a kidnapping."

A frown darkened Ryan's face as he opened the file. "Who was kidnapped?"

"The fifteen-year-old daughter."

Voklane flipped between pages, his scowl deepening. "Where is the rest?"

"That's all there is. The rest has gone missing, including the autopsy reports."

Ryan was silent for a solid minute, his jaw working in thought. "Are the bodies still in custody?"

"I'm not sure. The case isn't mine. Another Master Tribunii asked me to take a look this morning. Apparently, this is all that remains." Jonathon hated the sense of dread that washed over him saying those words.

"Who is the MT?"

"Marck Rainier."

Ryan sighed. "Okay, he's good as far as I know. Who is the MP?"

Curiosity made Jonathon bite his tongue before he asked *how* exactly Voklane knew Rainier was one of the good guys and not part of the vast criminal network they'd been slowly uncovering over several years. "Primary Guardian Laskaris."

Ryan rubbed his knuckles along his jaw. "Atlanta Jourdain. I'm not sure about her."

"It's no secret she's ambitious. She's the first Master Prefect to earn the role under the age of thirty," Jonathon commented. "She's also, I believe, honest in her role and her desire to see Haven City safe and publicly respectful of our current Queen Elect."

Ryan steepled his fingers together. "Define publicly."

"Six months ago, when Queen Elect Arnita decided to build a task force specifically to combat the rise in drug issues, MP Jourdain agreed and selected several of her best Enforcers to apply for the opening positions within Immigration and Import. She was very vocal in her praise of the Queen's decision to take the threat of rising addiction in our country seriously."

"Others were more in Princess Verica's camp, to meet the drug situation not with violence, but with assistance."

"Yes, and both women are correct. The addicts *do* need help, but the seemingly unhindered flow of magic lily dust needs to be stopped, or the crisis will continue to escalate. There's nothing violent about cutting off the supply," Jonathon argued.

Ryan shrugged. "The drug brokers who peddle the stuff may disagree with you."

Jonathon shifted in aggravation. "Yes, but if it were up to Princess Verica, we'd park addicts on every street corner with a sign that says, 'Don't be like me' and think the problem will fix itself. It's irresponsible and naïve to think that would solve anything. Every person would walk past the poor soul and think, 'That will never be me.'"

Ryan held up his hands. "I'm with Queen Elect Arnita on this one, Asherwick, you don't have to convince me of anything. If Prince Jaiden hadn't been a late child for our elected crown, Princess Verica would be running for the nomination right now with the other four siblings. I understand her desire to gain popularity, so in ten years, when her name is on the ballot, she's pretty much a no-brainer for the population. She's thinking ahead. Most people will choose a peaceful resolution over violence, she seems to be offering such a solution, ill-conceived as we know it to be."

"Far ahead," Jonathon agreed. "Especially since the other Hayne's siblings haven't bothered to establish themselves among the population."

"Prince Jaiden is only five. The others can't even begin campaigning until he's fifteen, and no one can vote for our next elected monarch until he's nineteen. Princess Verica has a long way to go. I'd like to think she's simply stepping up as one of the nation's Princesses with benefits to her altruism down the road," Ryan said.

Jonathon couldn't help but smile. "Optimistic of you."

"I take it where I can find it," Ryan admitted with another shrug. "If Laskaris isn't hoping to gain anything by hiding this case, then she has someone else in her division who does. Likely someone who was asked to."

"Who is Castien?" Jonathon took a chance and asked.

"In my world, Henry Castien is one of the legends. In yours, probably no one."

A sinking sensation swirled in Jonathon's stomach. "A legend, how?" he asked slowly.

"He's a very talented sharpshooter," Voklane answered, shifting his attention back to the file.

Jonathon raised a brow. "An assassin then?"

"At one time, yes."

But like Aleksandrov Nachemir, he'd married, started a

family, and left the life behind. Until another assassin came calling. The situation was varied from Katria's by one difference, however. "Whoever killed the family kidnapped the daughter."

"And I'm not seeing evidence that they attempted to kill Castien."

Jonathon found that curious as well. "Why leave him alive? Retribution, maybe?"

Ryan shook his head. "Not if it's the same situation as with Nachemir's daughter. If it's the same group we've been trying to uncover, they may be using *his* life to keep his Gen-Heir in line."

"Do what we want, or we'll kill your father, situation?" Jonathon asked with a frown.

"Would make sense." Ryan stood and went to one of the many file cabinets lining the left wall of his office. He removed a thin file and returned to his seat. "Let's see, the eldest daughter of Henry Castien is Lucianna. Six years ago, she was nine. At fifteen now, she's young enough to control, old enough to be coming into her genetically inherited ability. *If* it's the same people responsible for the Nachemir murders, they appear to still be in need of an assassin. Castien would be a good success for them if they can get her to cooperate."

"They murdered her family."

"But spared her father."

Jonathon sighed. "Who will you trust to look into this?"

"I will meet with Castien. He's intelligent and will likely have valuable input, and he'll want his daughter back. I can't have him tearing through the city looking for her. However, it's his child out there, so I'll see what he wants to do." Ryan shrugged. "Who knows, maybe this will be the lead we need to find out who else is behind this mysterious group."

"Still no name for them?"

"Not officially, no," Ryan said with a sigh.

"And unofficially?"

"No one can agree on what to call them. The emblem we've found on those suspected of being involved have been analyzed to mean victory. I refuse to call them anything to do with being victorious."

"I wonder what they need to feel victorious about," Jonathon contemplated, rubbing his knuckle along his jaw.

Ryan snorted in annoyance. "If we knew that, we wouldn't be relying on only dead bodies to give us information."

"Or thoughts of conspiracy," Jonathon muttered.

"I have a few of my own, I will admit." Ryan closed the files and then set them to rights, tapping the end on the desk. "And now we have another duplicate murder situation. Right down to missing evidence and testimony. How… unnerving."

Jonathon nodded in agreement, thanked Ryan for his time, wished him luck, and headed back to East Street Division. He walked into his office to find his superior, Master Prefect Hartland, dropping a stack of files on his already overloaded desk. Jonathon froze in the doorway and blinked.

"So much for my day off," he growled.

A look of sympathy crossed Hartland's aging face. He shrugged his thin shoulders. "Someone said they saw you here earlier, I figured you'd be returning soon. I'd have called you in any way." He swept his hand over the files. "Small crime wave happened this morning."

Jonathon went to his desk and picked up the files. He flipped them open and frowned. "These are petty, violent crimes, why am I handling them?"

Hartland crossed his arms over his chest. "Since when is any violent crime *petty*?"

"Um, let's see." Jonathon regarded the files. "When they're an interrupted burglary that results in a dog attack, a drunken assault from stepping in horse manure, and…."

Jonathon took a moment and wondered if he'd be able to read this next one with a straight face. "A table dancer stabbing a patron with a fork because she caught him pleasuring himself to her show."

Hartland's lips twitched. He cleared his throat before speaking. "All right, I will admit they aren't throat slashing and torture. Are you complaining?"

Jonathon closed the files. "No, I am wondering, though, why they've been given to me."

"Because you're here. Because this morning, we had three reported rapes, two muggings gone wrong, a domestic murder, and two shootings. You can wrap these up in a few hours and go back home."

The urge to drop into his chair and bang his head on the desk nearly overwhelmed Jonathon. "I contracted this morning, I just want to get home to my bride on my day off."

Hartland smiled sarcastically. "Then you'll wrap these up in record time, won't you?"

Biting back a retort that would land him a reprimand, Jonathon nodded. "Yes, Master Prefect."

"Congratulations on the contract," Hartland said, dropping his arms and edging to the door. "I hope it's a good union for the duration. At least she'll know upfront what she's getting into by marrying an enforcer."

"She already knew," Jonathon stated somewhat grimly. "No need for concern on that front."

"Great, then there's no issue." Hartland cast another one of his not-so-happy smiles at Jonathon and then left.

The wedding rings jangled together in his pocket as he fell into his seat with a sigh. He pulled the folders close and began to read.

• • •

THE SENTENCES IN THE BOOK PERCHED ON SYLPHINE'S KNEES blurred together in the low lamplight next to her bed. Ramsey had said her goodnights hours ago, and the sound of boots on the stairs still had yet to happen. For five days, Sylphine had tried to stay awake long enough to catch Jonathon arriving home, and for five nights, she'd failed. By the time she'd managed to get down to the kitchen in the mornings, he'd already left.

In the years she'd known Jonathon Hunter, she'd learned he had a terrible knack for working himself into the ground. Very few people took their jobs seriously enough to risk their health, yet he did. She always wondered if it was a strong sense of duty or a sense of obligation to his ranked position that made him work harder than necessary. Either way, the thought of him once again disappearing into investigations with little regard for himself angered and worried her.

Tonight, no matter how difficult the task, she intended to stay awake. Scrubbing her hands along her face, she sniffled and blinked the grit of fatigue from her eyes. The book slid down her legs and flopped onto her stomach. A corner caught her ribs, and the pages crinkled and folded under the weight. Gasping, Sylphine jerked upright, snatching the book before any more damage could be done.

A muffled echo reached her from below, and she straightened, forgetting about attempting to find her lost place. Light footfalls sounded on the stairs. Seconds later, Jonathon's shadowed form passed in front of her open bedroom door. He took two steps back and stopped. The faint glow from her lamp didn't reach him, leaving him shrouded in darkness.

"Why are you still awake?" he asked, his voice gruff.

Sylphine slowly closed the book and set it on the nightstand. "I have been waiting for you to get home."

He sighed and walked into the room. With his hands shoved deep in his pockets, he stopped and leaned a shoulder against the tall rectangular post of her bed. The sleeves of his dark gray shirt were rolled halfway up his forearms. Either before arriving home or on his way up the stairs, he'd undone the top buttons of his shirt, exposing the masculine column of his throat. His dark hair was in a state of chaos, standing in whatever direction it last settled when he'd run his fingers through the short length. Fatigue etched harsh lines across his face.

"You look awful," Sylphine said when the bed frame groaned in protest to more of his weight leaning into the post.

A crooked smile lifted the corner of his mouth. Exhaustion shone in his dark eyes. "You waited up to tell me that?"

Sylphine scooted up to rest her shoulders on the headboard. The sheet fell to her lap. Jonathon's gaze shifted, and she resisted the urge to snatch the sheet and cover herself despite being fully clothed in a silk nightgown. He'd seen her in less, after all. "I waited because I am worried. You have barely been home the past five days."

He ran his hand down his face. "There's been a string of violent crimes and kidnappings. I'm pretty sure they're all tied to magic lily dust, but I need more proof."

"And what good are you dead on your feet? Surely, you cannot follow a clue when you are too tired to think."

On another sigh, he dropped his head against the post. "Haven't we had this conversation before? I feel like we have."

"Probably," she said, frowning. "I think being your wife now gives me some sort of permission to pester you about what bothers me, does it not?"

"You knew the deal before you signed the contract."

"I did, true. That does not mean I have to be happy about you slowly killing yourself over your career. If you fall over, who will help your victims then?"

"I'll be okay," he slurred, his eyes closing.

Seconds passed before Sylphine realized he'd fallen asleep. Alarmed, she sat up, palms braced on the mattress. "Jonathon!"

He started and blinked at her. "What?"

"Lay down, now."

"Okay," he muttered and then proceeded to tumble onto the bed beside her.

Sylphine gasped, quickly moving to the side to make space for his larger form. He landed with one leg hanging over the edge, his arm flopped across his belly. Heaving a long yawn, he didn't even look at her. Within a breath, he was out cold.

"Oh, Jonathon," Sylphine sighed out, gently brushing a lock of hair from his forehead. "Why do you do this to yourself?"

There was no answer except for a faint snore. She crawled out from the blankets to the end of the bed. Carefully, she removed his boots, letting them fall to the carpet with a muted *thump*. Settled on her thighs, she took in his long length, pondering if she should remove his belt. The thought of such an intimate act made her cheeks heat. Scoffing at her silly thoughts, she slid up the bed, reaching for his belt. She eased the buckle open and, inch by inch, pulled the long strip of leather free. Unable to get him under the blankets, she went to find a cover from the small closet next to her bathroom. She draped him in the blanket and then climbed back into the still warm bed.

For a few moments, she simply stared at his resting face. Dark whiskers shadowed his cheeks and jaw. He breathed slow and deep. She rested her hand over his heart, the steady beat and warmth of his body searing into her palm. In this state, his emotions were contained, and she couldn't rest caressing her hand upward to the opening of his shirt. Her fingers brushed over the skin of his throat and chest. Only the silken heat of his flesh met her touch. Gasping, she slid her hand deeper into his shirt, exploring the strong planes of his shoulders. He sighed and shifted closer. Blushing, she attempted to pull her hand free, but he caught her wrist, pinning it to his chest.

"Sylphine," he breathed out. "Stay."

"You are in my bed," she said quietly. "I am not going anywhere."

He made a noise deep in his throat that sent awareness through her body. His fingers tightened on her wrist. A sliver of desire danced along her nerves from their connection. "Sylphine."

The mere whisper of her name forced her to lean closer. His lips were parted, his eyes still closed. Temptation simmered deep in her belly. Before she could second guess, she pressed a gentle kiss to his mouth. He opened for her, accepting. The tip of his tongue flicked along her bottom lip. Sylphine closed her eyes and sank herself into the embrace. In lazy, sleepy caresses, their tongues tangled and explored.

Somehow, her hands ended up in his hair, and his hands ended up under her nightgown, gripping her rear. When he urged her to climb onto him, she didn't fight it. She straddled his hips, reveling in the hard evidence of his desire. The kiss grew from something simple to something intense. Hot, urgent emotions churned inside her, fueled by the pleasurable sensation of his hips flexing beneath her. His fingers caressed up her spine until he reached her upper back, where he pressed her close.

He broke the kiss, his lips teasing down her jaw to her throat. "You feel so good."

A sultry shudder raced through Sylphine at his admission. "So do you."

The moment the words left her lips, she froze. While the sizzle of his emotions flowed through her veins, the heat of her own desire was stronger, more intense, making demands of her body she'd never felt before. For the first time in her life, *she* was in control, not the man. She wanted to rain kisses on him, to shout with joy.

However, while the moment was life-altering for her, she couldn't help but suspect he was still asleep. At least partially. She wondered if his half-conscious state was part of the reason she wasn't overwhelmed. Curious, she closed her eyes and sank into the sensation of his emotions. Jonathon's breath teased the sensitive skin of her neck, his arms tightened in a band around her back, hugging her close. The swirling vortex of emotions she'd come to accept about him collided around and within her. No, drowsiness didn't seem to affect much. She returned his hug, amazed and excited but unsure what the discovery meant.

"Don't leave," he whispered just under her ear.

"Where would I go?"

He pressed a kiss to her neck and then relaxed under her. "Away. You always go away."

Sylphine rose enough to see him. She stroked her fingers through his hair, keeping it away from his face. Now that she knew she could touch him and remain in control, she couldn't seem to keep her hands to herself. "You are my husband now. I won't go anywhere without you."

A smile toyed at his mouth. He turned into her caress, his eyes still closed in sleep. "Yes, in my dreams." He sighed, his body loosening further. "My wife... I love you."

The truth of his words slammed into her. Powerful, almost possessive, and heartbreakingly beautiful, his love rolled in a wave through her. Tears burned her eyes, and she buried her face against his chest, taking a long, controlled breath to keep from crying. He might be sleeping, unaware of what he spoke, but the honesty of the words wouldn't be denied. Jonathon *loved* her.

Slowly, she slid off his prone form. His arms tightened for a brief moment and then fell away, slipping from her nightgown. Like tendrils snapping free between them, the strength of his emotions faded. However, as they dissipated, she realized this wasn't the first time she'd felt them. Each time he'd touched her, the unknown emotion had been present. She'd simply had nothing to compare it to, to know the truth. The love of her family was different. Warm, comfortable, safe. Jonathon's love was like the man, a force unto itself.

Sylphine fixed the blanket and then watched him sleep. Incapable of not touching him now, she feathered her fingers through his hair, caressed his cheek or his hand laying palm up between them. She settled onto the mattress beside him, lacing her fingers between his. The whispers of his emotions still echoed in his unconscious state, muted but there for her to explore. Her heart constricted as she laid her head on his shoulder. She wanted to believe the tightening in her chest, and flipping of her belly meant she loved him, too. Yet she didn't dare trust such a strong feeling as her own with Jonathon's still lingering.

"You really love me," she whispered. "How will I know if I love you?"

11

SUPPLE FEMALE FLESH FILLED JONATHON'S PALM. HE BURIED deeper into the warmth and comfort of blankets, loathe to wake from the hazy dream state he found himself in. He flexed his fingers, pleased when a soft sigh and even softer body pressed closer to him. Oh, yes. Sleeping had its advantages. Too bad he'd allowed himself to go so long without. Had he known his dreams would be this pleasant, he'd have maybe convinced himself he needed more rest.

The delicate, enticing scent of seaside flowers and woman invaded his senses. Jonathon breathed in deep, burying his face into silken hair. Leisurely, reality dawned on him. He wasn't dreaming. Blinking, he sat up in alarm. Pale yellow walls, thick dark bedposts, and a room half the size of his greeted him. Blankets shifted. Jonathon glanced down and found Sylphine, a drowsy smile on her face. Golden hair surrounded her on the pillow, a chaotic mess of loose curls. She appeared content and suddenly concerned, Jonathon looked down at himself. He blew out a breath when he saw he was still fully dressed. Whew, he wasn't missing some vital memory, like making love to her.

"Morning," she said on a stretch.

The fabric of her nightgown pulled tight across her full breasts, and his heart skipped. She twisted her hips, and the sheet that had been covering her fell away, revealing the tan skin of her belly where her nighty had ridden up around her ribs. Or where he'd pushed it, recalling all the warm skin beneath his hand. His fingers itched to feel her again.

"Morning," he somehow managed. He glanced around the room again. "How did I end up in here?"

She rested her arms above her head, seeming to be unaffected by the seductive image she painted. Under the covers, he could tell one of her legs was folded open. All he'd have to do is slide his hand beneath, and he'd discover if she ached as much as he did.

"You stopped by last night, or early this morning, when you came home. You fell asleep standing up." She looked him over, her blue-green gaze heated. "I like waking up to you in my bed."

"I'd prefer waking up to you in mine," he said before he could stop himself. What was he doing? Then again, she was his wife. If he wanted her in his bed, he was allowed now, right?

She shifted onto her side. The sheet draped over her hip, accentuating the full curve of her stomach, revealing the edge of pale pink panties. Jonathon looked across the room and focused on a thick sliver of bright light cutting along her dressing table.

"Am I invited to your room?" she asked, her fingers brushing across his wrist.

"This is your house now, too. There isn't a room you aren't allowed in." He took another deep breath, still keeping his attention anywhere but on her. "If I'm being honest, there never has been."

Her hand slid from his wrist to his thigh, forcing him to

look at her. "You would have allowed me into your room before we were married?"

"My room is not my bed," he felt the need to clarify.

"Lay back down with me." Her hand slipped under the covers, pulling them up.

Jonathon's gaze flickered to her open door. "Might not be a good idea."

A throaty chuckle made him look back down at her. "I will keep on my clothes if you do."

He quirked a brow at her uncharacteristic quip. "I appear to be rubbing off on you."

"Yes, I am learning all sorts of ways to be aggravating. Is it working?"

Jonathon settled back onto the mattress, facing her and propping his head on his arm. "You find me aggravating?"

"Do you deny you often try your hardest to be so?"

He laughed. "Fine. Yes, I do."

"I like you here," she murmured. "In my bed with me. I liked waking up to your arms wrapped around me."

"I liked that, too." He reached out, sliding his hand beneath the covers to find her bare hip.

She inhaled sharply and closed her eyes. "I have never had this with anyone. You are showing me so much, Jonathon."

The soft, smooth lilt of her accent never failed to send a shiver along his spine when she spoke his name. He took a moment for the sensation to pass. "How is that possible when you've had lovers?"

A delicate blush bloomed across her cheeks. "Rushed encounters in libraries, greenhouses, and carriages. Never truly... intimate."

He lifted a brow at her confession. "That's it? You've only been with men during what? Parties?"

She nodded, her gaze dropping as the pink tinge on her cheeks deepened. "Yes."

"There is a lot you've missed then."

"I am learning that." Gradually, she looked back at him. She shifted closer until the heat of her body reached him. "I was wondering if...." She took a deep breath. "If you'd allow me to touch you."

"You can touch me anytime, anywhere you'd like."

"Like you touched me," she clarified, her eyes downcast.

If he hadn't been completely aroused before, he was now. Every muscle in his body ached and demanded the woman inches from him. His attention flickered to the gaping shadow of the open door. "We aren't exactly in a private situation here."

Her gaze followed his, and she smiled. "Your sister is asleep, and if I am not mistaken, your housekeeper will not arrive for a few hours. But... I can close the door if you wish."

And give either of them a chance to change their mind? He leaned in close, pressing his cheek to hers, and growled into her ear. "Keep it under the blankets, and you can do anything to me you want."

In a hesitant, shy motion, her fingers brushed along the waist of his pants. The muted light and quiet solitude of morning created a sense of intimacy Jonathon allowed himself to fall into. Desperately, he wanted to sink into her, so deep he forgot where he ended, and she began, but she wasn't ready. Not yet.

"Will you be okay?" he asked, lacing his fingers through hers when she attempted and failed to undo the buttons of his trousers. "Touching me?"

Her fingers tightened around his. On measured breaths, she raised her gaze to his. "I want to know. You make me feel so much of myself for the first time. I *want* to know how we are different. I need to know."

The roar of blood pounded in his ears. His eyes locked with hers, and he helped her undo the buttons of his pants. Unhurried, he eased them down his hips, along with his boxers, until he sprang free. He didn't think he could be harder than he was. Then her fingers, warm and curious, skated across his damp tip. On instinct, his hips jerked, and a harsh groan escaped his throat.

Sylphine blinked, her eyes wide in alarm. Her hand froze. "Did I hurt you?"

"Did it feel like you hurt me?" he asked between gritted teeth.

"I cannot feel pain. You know that."

"But you can discern the emotions that go with pain. Fear, anxiety, panic. Did I have any of those?"

A bit timid, her touch found him again. "No," she breathed out, her exploration turning bolder.

"What emotions are you getting from me?" he asked, closing his eyes as her hand began a deliberate, rhythmic slide along his shaft.

"Desire. Anticipation. Need."

"And you?" He wrapped his hand around the back of her head, burying his fingers deep into the silken length of her hair. Before, when he'd touched her, he'd asked the same thing, but she'd been unable to reply. Now, he hoped she'd be more aware of her own body, of the responses that were unique to her and had nothing to do with him. "What are you feeling?"

"Hot," she said. "Aching. I want... Why? Why have I never felt this before?"

"Because you were with selfish men."

Her hand paused. "And you care?"

Jonathon opened his eyes and caressed her cheek. "So much. You can stop if you want."

She shook her head, her hand flexing around his erection.

"I want to feel your pleasure, the way you felt mine." Under the blankets, her leg shifted until the blanket rose, revealing the sensual scene hidden beneath. A jagged gasp slipped past her parted lips.

"Not what you expected?"

Her thumb slid across the slick, sensitive flesh of his tip again. A shudder of pleasure raced along his spine.

"You are amazing. I never... I have never..." She swallowed. "What do I do?"

"You don't have to," he felt compelled to tell her again.

"I want to. Please."

She didn't have to ask him again.

WARM WATER RUSHED OVER SYLPHINE'S HANDS AS SHE WASHED away the remnants of Jonathon's pleasure. Feet from her, he shed his shirt, leaving a pile of clothes on the rug in front of the shower. She tried not to stare, but when his perfect butt stepped into the bath, she couldn't help but watch how the muscles in his back and thighs flexed with the movement. A tremor raced through her at the memory of the unexpected rush that had overtaken her when he'd come. That was twice now intimacy with him had brought her to heights she couldn't wait to explore again.

When she'd wondered how he was relaxed enough to get naked in front of her to shower, he'd laughed and asked, what hadn't she seen now? Meeting her gaze in the mirror, she found her cheeks still red from his comment. What hadn't she seen indeed?

And yet, there was so much more she wanted.

All the ragged scars on his torso, the crisp hairs on his legs, all the sensitive areas between his thighs... she wanted to touch, and if she were honest, lick him all over. How would his stomach muscles feel under her tongue? How would the evidence of desire he couldn't hide taste? She wanted to know. He was uncovering parts of her she didn't know existed, didn't know she ever longed to discover. She didn't even know if he'd let her or if it was okay to want to do such things. Frowning, she sat on the closed toilet lid, drying her hands.

"Jonathon?"

"Yes?" he asked, his voice muffled by the spray of water.

"Can I ask you something improper?"

"Sweetheart, there is nothing inappropriate between us, ever. Ask away."

She took a deep, bracing breath. "Am I allowed to put you in my mouth?"

Something fell and crashed behind the curtain. He cursed, and in the next second, the curtain snatched open. Soap ran down his cheeks and neck, sleuthing across the defined angles of his chest. Sylphine blinked and followed their trail down, down, down.

"Up here," he said dryly.

Cheeks burning, her focus moved back to his face. "I'm sorry, that is why I asked, I wasn't sure if it was okay for me to want you in that way."

The curtain bunched in his fist. "Give me a second."

She focused on the bright blue towel in her hands.

"You are allowed to do whatever *you* want to do," he said. When he didn't continue, she met his stare. "I will tell you if I don't like it. I expect you to do the same. Your body is yours, and only yours. I may be your husband now, but that doesn't give me the right to do anything you aren't comfortable with or ask you to do anything to me you don't want to. Same goes for me. If I'm not okay with something, I will tell you. All right?"

She nodded. "And would you be uncomfortable with what I asked?"

He visibly swallowed. "No."

The curtain snapped closed before he could expand. A little thrill coursed through her, and she smiled. "Do you need me to get you any clothes? I don't think any of mine will fit you."

"Wouldn't that be something?" he said with a chuckle. "Showing up downstairs for breakfast in one of your pink robes?"

"I am not sure it would survive you attempting to put it on."

"Would be a shame to ruin it. Especially since I've fantasized about all the ways to take it off of you."

This time it was her turn to swallow. Heat raced through her body.

His drenched head peeked out from around the edge of the curtain. "Nothing to say to that?"

"Give me a moment."

He laughed and disappeared again. "You can get my robe for me if you'd like."

To keep from climbing in the shower with him, she picked up his discarded clothes and dropped everything into the hamper. He'd told her men weren't like women; they needed a *reset* time. She didn't think it'd been long enough to count, so she went to his room to find his robe. Though honestly, his needing time wasn't the only thing keeping her from sliding in behind the curtain.

Fear and uncertainty played havoc in her mind. *What if's* kept forming. What if she were still as terrible of a lover as she'd always been? Sure, Jonathon had uncovered a passion within her she hadn't known existed, but when the moment came upon them, what if she were the same lump she'd always been? Laying there and taking it without anything to offer. A disappointment in every way.

Sylphine shook the negative thoughts away and searched

for his robe. She found it hanging behind his bathroom door. Bunching the thick, downy fabric in her arms and bringing it to her face, she breathed in deep on the way back to her room. Jonathon's masculine scent swirled around her, reminding her of all the delicious sensations she'd experienced with him.

Jonathon glanced at her when she entered her room. He stood in the doorway to the bathroom, completely nude, towel drying his hair. Sylphine froze at the sight of him in all his unabashed glory. Every inch of her skin caught fire, and she tried to remember how to breathe. A slow, seductive smile crooked his lips and brightened his eyes. Sylphine tossed the robe at him and fled.

"Coward," she heard him yell as the door closed. She leaned against it for a second, her breathing labored, her body hot. Yes, oh yes, she was most certainly a coward. The alternative would be to test his theory on the length of time between intimate encounters. Since she wasn't ready to make a fool of herself, she pushed away from the door and headed downstairs.

The invigorating scent of coffee filled the air. Before her foot landed on the foyer floor, a heavy knock echoed through the quiet downstairs. Something clattered in the kitchen. Bare feet slapped against the hardwood. Ramsey rushed through the foyer, her black curls in disarray atop her head. She hastily tied her fluffy, blue robe tight around her waist. The knock sounded again, heavier and urgent.

Ramsey unbolted the locks and swept the door open. "The world does not revolve around you," she barked, stepping aside to allow the young enforcer to enter.

"I was told to hurry and get MT Hunter. I don't argue," a familiar, young male voice said.

Ramsey closed the door behind First Guardsman Wackerly. "How did you get stuck with bad news duty?"

Tray swiped his hat off his head, a frown marring his face.

The ends of his tawny hair stood up oddly. "MP Hartland thought MT Hunter would be less likely to yell at me since he knows me, Miss Hunter."

Sylphine scurried back up the stairs, not dressed in enough clothing to be seen by the enforceman. She turned to head down the hall to her room and crashed into a wall. Strong arms banded around her. She looked up to find Jonathon staring down at her in amusement. He was dressed in pants, his pale blue shirt halfway buttoned.

"Miss me already?" he asked his deep voice rumbling in his chest beneath her hands.

Gasping, she took a step back, but he kept his hold. "Enforceman Wackerly is downstairs for you."

"FG Wackerly, you mean?"

She nodded. "Yes, sorry."

Slowly, his arms released her, and he winked. "He earned the rank, let's not take it from him."

"I don't know," she said, sidestepping to clear the hall. "He did arrest me."

He took her hands and kissed each one. "This is true. Does my beautiful wife hold grudges?"

"How could I, when I left the poor young man with little choice," she said, chuckling. Then she sobered, glancing back at the stairs. "However, he's coming to take you away, is he not?"

Jonathon released her hands and put space between them. "Probably."

Sylphine met his unhappy stare. "I may not forgive him that."

JONATHON TRIED NOT TO BE FRUSTRATED AT THE WHISPERED words of irritation from Sylphine. Yet, annoyance twisted in his gut. He took a deep breath and finished buttoning his shirt. "You knew when you signed a contract with me my work could pull me away. Sometimes for weeks, it can get like this."

Sadness filled the depths of her ocean eyes. "That is a lie, and you know so. It is *always* like this, Jonathon. You do not know when to say no. You do not know how to tell them you have a life outside of your division."

"Say no? To who? The woman sobbing in a hospital because her husband, high on magic lily dust, beat her and sold their daughter to his drug broker to cover his next week of fixes? Or maybe I should say no to the little boy whose mother caught him being assaulted by the neighbor she trusted to watch him. Or wait, I know, I can tell the man who was stabbed and left the die in the alley for the money in his pocket that he didn't know his life would be worth."

"Stop!" she hissed, her cheeks flaming, tears shining in her gaze. "Have those things really happened? Have you really had to see all that?"

Regret filled him, and he wished he could take back his outburst. Ignorance, when it came to his job, wasn't a bad thing for civilians. "Yes."

She looked away and took a deep breath. "Fine, I understand. They need you. But your family needs you too, and you need time away…" she waved her hand as if somehow erasing the horror of his job. "From all of the awful in humanity. You do. Whether you want to admit it or not."

When he remained silent, she stepped into his space, her fingers toying with the collar of his shirt. "I know I have been your wife for less than a week…."

Grasping her left hand, he reached into his pocket and removed a braided silver and gold band from his pocket, causing her words to die as she'd spoken them. A startled gasp slipped past her lips when he eased the wedding ring onto her finger. He gripped her hand in a tight hold.

"You are my wife, and I'm glad you care enough about me to worry." He kissed her ring and released her hand. "And I don't want you to worry, not over me. I'll talk to my MP and see if he'll agree to at least one day a week where I'm not bothered, regardless of the emergency."

A frown turned her beautiful mouth into an unhappy line. "I will accept that." When he rocked back on his heels with a small smile, she lifted her finger and pointed. "For now."

He winked. "I'm okay with being the victor in our first official fight ending on a *for now*."

On a groan, she covered her face, her shoulders slumped. "I would ask if you are ever serious, but I know you are."

"I was serious," he said, sliding his fingers along the edges of his pants to make sure his shirt was properly tucked in.

The muted light coming from the hall window caught on her marriage band. She wiggled her fingers, inspecting it. "I didn't get you one."

Jonathon held up his hand, showing the matching ring. "I picked them out." He wouldn't confess how long ago. "Does Italyssa do marriage rings?"

Shadows filled her eyes, and she looked away. "Yes, but we continue to wear the promises we made, too."

He reached for her left arm. The two bracelets she still continued to wear clinked together in a delicate jingle. "We will have to do this part again, then. Another time."

When he slid his promise band free, she didn't protest. "Okay. Soon?"

Smiling, he slipped the band she'd handed him two years ago that he'd so callously thrown away back onto his wrist. The weight felt right. "Yes, very soon."

He brushed his fingers along her jaw and a fleeting kiss on her lips, the driving need to constantly touch her getting the better of him, before heading downstairs. In the foyer, Ramsey handed a cup of steaming coffee off to Wacklery, glancing up as Jonathon descended the stairs. The young man flushed and took a hasty step away from her. A board creaked beneath Jonathon's feet on the way down. He adjusted the cuff of his sleeve over his promise band.

Ramsey's eyes widened. She reached for his hand and inspected his ring. "Oh wow. Does Sylphine's match?"

"Of course."

Her violet eyes misted, and she squeezed his hand. "Just like Mom and Dad."

Jonathon returned the sign of affection. "Yes."

"They'd be so proud." Her thumb ran along the braided edge of gold and silver. "They'd have loved her."

Wackerly sipped noisily and looked all around the room. "Good coffee, Miss Hunter."

Ramsey released Jonathon's hand and grasped the edges of her robe. "Thank you, First Guardsman I'm glad you like it. You can take it with you."

"Come on," Jonathon said to Wackerly, reaching for his coat. "I'm assuming we're heading straight to a location?"

Wackerly nodded, taking another pull on his coffee. "Yes." His cheeks reddened. "I'll need to ride with you, I took a hired coach here."

"Figured that." Jonathon shrugged his jacket on, the only uniform element aside from his gun that identified him as a Haven City Enforcer.

"Did you want a cup to go as well?" Ramsey asked, motioning towards the kitchen.

"No, I'm fine." He pecked a kiss on her cheek. "Thanks."

She squinted up at him. "Why the good mood?"

Jonathon laughed and let the mischief he was feeling inside show in his smile. Her cheeks grew as pink as Wackerly's. She turned on her heel and fled into the kitchen.

The First Guardsman's brows lifted. "What did I miss?"

Still laughing, Jonathon opened the front door to the crisp, frost-laden morning. "My sister forgot I'm a married man now. I have every reason to start my day with a smile, even with interruptions."

The young man scratched his head, confusion clear on his face. "Huh. I didn't know marrying meant happier mornings."

Jonathon's mind went unbidden to earlier when Sylphine's soft hand had stroked him into oblivion. He grinned wider, closing the door. "It does for me."

12

Any lingering contentment from the start of his day fled the moment Jonathon walked into the back door of a small, single-story house. The scent and sensation of death hung heavy in the air. A group of enforcers stood in the meager kitchen, talking in hushed tones as if the dead could hear their conversation and take offense. Jonathon stilled in the entryway, observing the space.

Overturned chairs. All the bottom cupboards were open. The woodstove door was partially ajar. Someone noticed him, and a hush fell over the house. In the silence, he focused harder, taking in the fresh scuffs on the floor. Not of a fight, but in haste. Searching for something.

"Where's the body?" Jonathon asked.

Wackerly came in behind him and gestured to a narrow doorway. "It's i-in there."

Jonathon raised a brow. "It?"

Red spread all the way to the First Guardsman hairline. "Sorry. *She*. She is in there."

Jonathon placed a hand on his shoulder and squeezed.

"She's a person with someone who loved her and will miss her. Never forget that."

Wackerly nodded but failed to move from inside the doorway. The blush of his cheeks faded as he glanced at the narrow opening into what Jonathon assumed was a living area. A violent crimes investigator, this one would not be.

Sliding past the group of other enforcers, Jonathon went into the small living space. A woman walked around the body, a sketch pad in hand. She raised her head when Jonathon entered, pushed silver-framed glasses up on her nose, and then went back to work. The weak light barely illuminated the space, making her medium brown hair pulled in a tight knot at the nape of her neck darker than he knew it to be.

"FG Incorva," Jonathon said in greeting.

"MT Hunter," she returned in acknowledgment, attention remaining on her thick sketch pad. The fabric of her black jacket whispered with each movement of her arm. "I won't be much longer."

"There's no rush."

A small smile curved her lips. "I always like working with you. You're one of the few who take my renderings seriously."

He hunched down and took in the scene from the victim's level. "Preserving the scene is vital, and you're the best."

First Guardsman Aurora Incorva was a very talented sketch artist. One look at her images and Jonathon always felt transported back to the scene. She had an uncanny ability to capture every detail, right down to footprints left in dust or the slightest smudge on the body of a victim. Jonathon never hurried her away, wanting to ensure she provided every aspect she felt was necessary for evidence.

Aurora paused mid-stroke, her sky-blue eyes sad as she

viewed the woman lying prone on the floor. "I always hate to think about their last moments. The fear. The pain."

"I know," Jonathon whispered.

Dust motes floated in the air, swirling and falling in the pale rays of light crossing over the colorless flesh of the woman staring sightless up at the naked rafters. Her dress pooled between her thighs, left in an unnatural position by her attacker. One limp hand lay open on the floor, the other fell over her head as if thrown there as an afterthought. Likely from her assailant, who'd removed her clenched hands from him. The fabric of her gown was intact. A purple bruise ringed her neck. Scratches on the inside of her thighs told while her attacker hadn't removed her clothes, he'd forced himself on her all the same.

Jonathon glanced over the rest of the sparsely furnished space. An overturned side table was kicked to the center of the room. Cushions pulled from the couch. By the time whoever searched this room made it here, they were frustrated. Jonathon stood. What were they looking for?

"Any evidence of magic lily use?" he asked, hooking his thumbs in his front pants pockets while circling the room.

"No, not that I've seen. But you can ask MP Hartland, he left just before you arrived. There was another situation he had to see to."

Jonathon sighed. "How unsurprising." He looked around a second time. "Are the other rooms like this?"

"Mostly, yes. I've already captured the bedroom and bathroom, so feel free to do whatever you need to in there." She waved her charcoal pencil around. "I have her, and the kitchen remaining."

"Thanks."

The bedroom and bathroom were free of enforcers, leaving Jonathon able to solely focus on the space. He walked slowly among the debris of furniture and clothing. A little wooden toy Ariot peeking out from under the edge of a skirt caught his attention. He picked it up, looking it over, before searching for more evidence of a child. He found two pairs of small pants, a shirt, and another wooden car.

"Is there a child?" he asked, leaning back so he could see Aurora.

Her forehead pinched, and she shook her head. "No, I didn't see one or hear of one being taken into custody."

Frowning, Jonathon went to ask the others still loitering in the kitchen and outside. When everyone answered no, Jonathon found Wackerly. "Go check with the neighbors about a child."

While he waited for information, he went back to the bedroom and small adjoining bathroom and did a more thorough search, though not nearly as thorough as the intruder, who had even torn into a wall between rooms.

Wackerly returned, shoulders slumped, his face long with dejection. "The neighbors said she had a son, but he's not with any of them. Do you think he was kidnapped?"

Jonathon's stomach twisted. He looked around the chaos of the house again. "Maybe not. Return to my house and get my wife, please. Make sure you are in her presence at all times and let no one approach her."

Wackerly blinked. "Is something wrong?"

"We aren't sure about the laws concerning our marriage in her native country. I just want to be safe."

Although he nodded, uncertainty still shone in his eyes. "All right."

Hands on his hips, Jonathon tried to make sense of the mess and hoped his hunch was right.

Sylphine accepted Tray's hand as he helped her from Jonathon's Ariot. Even though the sun was high in the sky, a chill still hung heavy in the air. Ice glittered in the thick shadows around the small, single-level wood-planked house. People surrounded the structure, both in an official capacity and out of morbid curiosity. The unwholesome emotional energy rolled off the crowd, forcing her to grit her teeth against the onslaught. Tray cleared a path through the crowd, and Sylphine was careful to keep anyone from touching her.

He guided her around to the back door, where they had to wait for a group exiting, carrying a stretcher draped in a white sheet. The outline underneath made Sylphine's heart clench. A body. Unconsciously, she took a step back, coming up against the rough leaves of a shrub. The branches scraped and poked through the layers of silk she wore underneath her cloak. A twig caught on one of her *Naenzis*, pulling at her hair. She grimaced and reached up to free the strand of beads.

Tray motioned when the entryway was finally clear. Sylphine hesitated. Her attention flickered to the covered body being loaded into the HCES Medical Science Investigator's carriage. Nerves danced in her belly. She didn't want to go inside. She didn't want to be where someone had breathed their last, likely horrific, breath. Prior to a few weeks ago, life had been safe, mostly sunny. Some of her illusions had been broken, but as a whole, she existed in a plush, extravagant world where her every need was met, and her wellbeing assured.

Now, she ran from a crazy family who wanted to steal the dynasty her own loved ones had built. She found herself married, while yes, to the one man she couldn't imagine herself *not* married to, but still married other than for love. And for some mysterious reason, her husband needed her at the scene of a violent crime. Brutality was something she'd only ever read about, a casual observer like everyone else. Confronting the reality of cruelty and death left her frozen. Scared.

Like ocean waves fanning along a shore, tendrils of concern and regret, underlined by relief and love, touched her before the tidal flow of Jonathon's full emotions reached out to her. Instead of shying away like she normally did, Sylphine closed her eyes and allowed the essence of him to pull her deep into the shelter he alone now provided.

"Hey," he said, his fingers whispering along her arm, covered by the thick wool of her cloak.

She opened her eyes and tried to pull in a calming breath. "Must I go inside?"

Sighing, he looked over the gathering crowd. "Of course not." His attention shifted back to her. The shadowy depths of his dark blue eyes met hers. "However, I need your help." He leaned in close so only she could hear. Unable to resist, she touched her hands to his sides. To any outsider, it looked as if they embraced, not as though he were divulging information he didn't want anyone else overhearing. "I think a little boy is hiding inside. He may have witnessed his mother being raped and murdered. The man who committed the crime couldn't find him, and I can't either."

Horror knotted a fist around her heart. She gasped and pulled back, connecting with the bush again. Feathers and beads tangled with her hair in the leaves, but she ignored the discomfort. "There is a child in that house?"

Jonathon reached around to unravel her from the shrubbery. "I believe so, but I'm not certain. I don't have your talent. I'm hoping you can find him where everyone else seems to have failed."

Sylphine considered the situation. She didn't want to be alone in the house. The sensation of Jonathon was now familiar to her, but others weren't. "It has to be only you and I. Will that be a problem?"

"No. Wait here, and I'll clear everyone out." He kissed her cheek. "Thank you for doing this."

Not wanting to fight with the bush again, Sylphine took a step forward while waiting. Tray spoke quietly with another enforcer while a younger woman sat off to the side on one of the stairs leading to the house. A fierce look of concentration pinched her face as she smudged her blackened fingers over a thick sketchbook braced on her lap. Jonathon bounded down the stairs, careful to avoid the artist's space. He motioned for her to come to the door.

"All clear, come on in." Sylphine took a bracing breath and tried to see into the darkened doorway. Jonathon acknowledged her reluctance, holding out his hand and wiggling his fingers. "There's nothing more to see other than what has already walked by, promise."

Sylphine accepted his hand, lacing her fingers between his. The anchor soothed her nerves, and she managed a smile. Once inside, he paused at the doorway and waited.

"Do you want me to walk around with you or stay here?" he asked, his thumb smoothing circles in the middle of her palm.

The faint light of the small windows barely penetrated the gloomy interior. The tumultuous state of things only added the sense of despair. If a child was somehow lost in this tomb-like house, Sylphine *needed* to be a big girl and deal with her uneasiness and find him.

"You promise there is nothing to be seen of the murder?" she asked, her voice weaker than she intended.

"Yes. But I can't promise you won't be able to figure out where she died."

Steeling her nerves, Sylphine released his hand. "I'll call if I need you."

He caught her cheeks between his palms and pressed a delicate kiss to her lips. "Not if, *when*. When you need me. You're going to find that boy."

Uncertain whether to be empowered by his faith in her or

nervous, she simply nodded. His hands fell to his sides, and she stepped away, wrapping the cloak tight around her frame. In the silence, nothing moved except fragments of light catching on dust. Taking a moment to get used to the stillness, Sylphine shook off the protective layer of thick wool and handed it off to Jonathon. In slow, methodical steps, she slid through the kitchen, her senses open to the space, searching for even a hint of emotion in the void the house had become.

Thankful she never could perceive past emotions, she made her way through the living room, walking along the walls first and then all throughout the room. Nothing.

A whisper of fear slithered up her spine as she set foot into the bedroom. For a moment, she stood still, searching out a direction, but the sensation didn't grow stronger or give her any further hints. She walked to the bathroom. The emotion remained in her peripheral.

Back in the bedroom, she slowly walked all over the room. In the center, the distress punched harder, but she couldn't figure out from where. Frustrated, she returned to Jonathon. He spoke quietly with another enforcer at the open back door, stopping the moment he saw her.

"I can feel him, but I cannot find him," she admitted, feeling defeated for some reason. "I am sorry."

Jonathon eased the door partially closed and then crossed the distance to her. His every step focused, his expression intent. "But you can feel him, he's definitely in the house?"

"Yes, he is here."

He grabbed her hand, tugging her into the other room. "Where?"

"The bedroom."

Draped over his arm, the end of her cloak fluttered behind in his rush to get to the bedroom. Sylphine hastily accepted the flurry of fabric when he sent it in her direction, his attention on the room as a whole.

"Does he feel stronger anywhere specific?" he asked, turning a slow circle.

She pointed. "In the center."

Jonathon swept his foot in an arc, scattering clothes and toys as he cleared the floor. He dropped to one knee and felt along the floor. "Touch around here, see if anything gets stronger."

Sylphine complied, her fingers brushing the rough wooden floorboards. She frowned and shook her head. "No, not stronger."

Jonathon tapped his thumb on his thigh and looked around again. He looked up. A crease formed between his brows. Rising, he glanced beyond the bedroom door and then back to the low ceiling. "Reach up."

"Do you see anything I can stand on?"

He disappeared and then returned with a chair from the dining room. After setting it in the area he'd cleared, he helped her climb up. Keeping hold of her hips to steady her when she wobbled, he looked up at her. Sylphine couldn't help but smile. She wanted to brush her fingers through his hair, and touch his face, but now wasn't the time. Returning to the important task, she touched the planked ceiling. Terror and confusion lanced through her. She gasped and snatched her hand away.

"He is here," she whispered. Her heart clenched. "Oh Jonathon, he is so scared."

Jonathon motioned for her to climb down, helping her safely back to the floor. Once she was off the chair, he leapt on with a grace and ease that left her frowning. Carefully, he tested each board until one budged. He pulled the board free and handed it to her. The one beside followed. Using his strength, he hauled himself up, his feet dangling over the chair. Sylphine set the wood off to the side, her focus staying on Jonathon.

His muffled words made her press a hand to her chest in relief.

IN THE DARKNESS, JONATHON COULD BARELY MAKE OUT THE TINY shadow huddled in the small cave-like space. The chilly air made goosebumps rise on his arms. The boy whimpered and squeezed further into the darkness. His muscles protesting, Jonathon braced his weight on his arms and reached out in a non-threatening gesture. "Hey there, buddy. It's okay, you're safe."

Wide, dark eyes shimmered with tears in the tiny amount of light coming through the opening. The boy remained silent.

Jonathon grunted and pulled himself up more. "My name is Jonathon. I'm an enforceman. See here on my jacket?" He pointed at the bright yellow lettering on his jacket. "You know what that is?"

The boy nodded and sniffled. Jonathon sighed in relief.

"Good. That's good." He began to lower himself. A shrill, panicked scream followed by a gulping cry echoed in the small space. Jonathon heaved himself back up. The crying stopped. "Hey, hey, relax, little man, you're okay. I have to go down to get you down. Can you come here, to the edge?" Jonathon patted the wood in front of him. At first, the child didn't move a muscle. Slowly, he nodded again. "Yeah? Okay good. I'll pull you down too, okay?"

This time Jonathon waited until he received an acknowledgment. The boy nodded and made an effort to move closer to the edge as Jonathon eased himself back to the chair. He kept his fingers on the ledge. A mop of dark brown curls sprinkled with cobwebs, chunky cheeks pink from distress, and luminous dark brown eyes appeared in the space above him. Tiny fingers wrapped around the edge near Jonathon's much larger hands. Streaks of silvery tears broke up the dusty layer covering his light skin. Dirt gathered along the edges of clear mucus running to his upper lip.

Jonathon smiled up at him and touched the child's small hand. "What's your name, little man?"

"Parker Pwescott," he answered weakly, rubbing his sleeve-covered arm under his nose.

Jonathon kept his smile in place and held his hands up. "Nice to meet you, Parker Prescott. Can I pull you down?"

He leaned back, almost disappearing into the shadows. "Is the bad man gone?"

"Yes, the bad man is gone."

"Momma says stay until the bad man is gone." His chin quivered. "I want my momma."

While Jonathon didn't know much about kids, he knew *that* line meant an incoming meltdown of epic proportions if he didn't do something quick. "Hey, I promise, the bad man is gone, so let's get you down, it's cold up there. I don't want you in the cold anymore. And I bet you're hungry, huh?"

"Uh-huh," he agreed, sniffling and rubbing his nose again.

"All right, then lean out, I've gotcha."

Parker held his arms out and tumbled through the opening with little grace into Jonathon's waiting embrace. Jonathon wrapped his arms around the boy, thankful for Sylphine's sudden bracing of his lower body as he accepted the small yet unexpected weight of the child. He hopped down.

"Good job, buddy." Jonathon bent over to set Parker down. In a cacophony of sound Jonathon didn't know such a little body could make, Parker screamed, squealed, and wrapped his body so tightly around Jonathon that he stumbled forward. "Can I put you down?"

The little boy shook his head and squealed again, his arms tightening around Jonathon's neck. Exasperated, Jonathon met Sylphine's distressed stare. When he tried to peel the clinging boy-turned-monkey off, Parker kept one step ahead, lifting a foot, snatching a flapping arm away, turning his head in a different direction. The kid was a master of evade and escape tactics while still somehow managing to stick to him like frost to glass. Damn. Jonathon hadn't anticipated being held hostage by a four-year-old.

Jonathon stared at Sylphine. He dropped his arms to his side, helpless. Parker didn't budge. "What do I do?"

Biting her bottom lip, Sylphine shrugged. "I guess we have a little boy coming home with us tonight."

13

Jonathon leaned his head against the closed bedroom door and released a pent-up breath of relief. Despite the apparent break in tears, confusion, and general small child antics, he kept a death grip on the doorknob. Just in case. This was his third time to believe Parker had finally, *finally*, fallen asleep. The faint melody Sylphine had wound to soothe the boy into sleep played behind the wood.

Beside him, Sylphine leaned against the wall and flashed an exhausted smile. "Hopefully, he sleeps longer than the music box plays."

Holding his breath, Jonathon eased his hand away from the nob. They both stared at the door. Only the muted twinkling chime of a children's song disturbed the silence. Jonathon grasped Sylphine's hand and eased her quietly across the hall to his room.

At one time, their house had four rooms, but Ramsey had knocked out a wall to make her space larger, leaving the family home with three. Parker slept in what had become Sylphine's room. Jonathon would be lying if he said he wasn't happy about the new living arrangements. Having Sylphine in his bed, even if all she did was let him hold her, was an experience he'd literally dreamed about.

Earlier in the evening, they'd moved everything she'd need for a few days. He pulled her into his room and then hesitated. "Should I leave the door open?"

"You showed him where we would be." She held up her hand, fingers splayed. "Five times."

He checked the closed door across from his and then further down the corridor to the weak light burning under Ramsey's door. She'd taken the extra houseguest under her wings in the same open-armed manner she'd extended to Sylphine so many years ago. Another Hunter under the roof, even if they didn't know it yet. Nor did she care if Parker would only be with them one night.

"One night or a lifetime," Ramsey had said, "he's ours to love while we have him."

Quietly, he eased the door shut, ignoring the unfamiliar nervous sensation. "I have never dealt with kids before."

Sylphine brushed a hand along his shoulder before moving deeper into the room. "I have. My parents both have very large families, so there are many children when everyone gathers. They are fun, infuriating and confusing. Often all at the same time."

Jonathon thought back to their dinner with the boy. How he laughed at Ramsey's silly antics to get him to eat and brightened the room, only to freak out over something on his plate and throw it across the table. "Sounds about right."

"It was kind of you to let him stay. Especially when the orphanage showed up at the house to claim him."

The gentle fall of beads hitting wood made him turn away from the door. Sylphine unclasped another strand from her hair and laid it on his dresser. His heart clenched for a different reason. In the low light of the fire and single burning lamp next to the bathroom door, she was ethereal. And she was his.

"He'd have died if you hadn't found him. You know that, don't you?" he asked, turning the lock on the door to ensure privacy.

She paused mid un-clip. "You do not know that."

"I do." He went to the bathroom and stood in the opening. "Frost is already coating the rafters inside the house without a fire burning. He was in a small area, pressed up against the roof. He would have frozen, and no one would have ever known what happened to him. We would have assumed he'd been kidnapped like all the other missing kids in this city."

"You knew he was in there to be found." She set the clip down and reached for the last one. A small smile toyed at her lips. "I never… I did not know I could use my talent that way. It felt, nice, to do something so useful."

Jonathon leaned against the door jamb and shoved a hand into his pocket. "We made a good team."

She beamed at him. "We did."

"Thank you for agreeing. I know it wasn't easy, being at a crime scene."

Her smile disappeared, replaced by worry. "I cannot understand how you do your job every day."

Jonathon pointed at the closed door and thought of the little boy sleeping in her room. His entire known life ripped away from him in one, violent moment. "Parker Prescott."

Understanding brightened her tourmaline eyes. "You rescue those you can."

"Yes." Once again, her beauty hit Jonathon like a punch to the gut. He couldn't stop himself from asking, "Is everyone from your country so beautiful?"

She blinked and licked her lips, tucking hair behind her ear. Pink blossomed across her cheeks. "I do not know what you consider to be beautiful."

"You, Sylphine. You are beautiful."

She blew out a huff, unwrapping a beaded strip of leather from her wrist. "How did we change subjects from your job to… me?"

Jonathon shrugged and unbuttoned his shirt. "I don't know, I guess you distract me that way." Before she could comment, he turned into the bathroom. "I'll be out in a bit. I need to wash the crime scene off."

While the water heated, he stripped. Once inside, the hot shower sluiced over his taut muscles. He braced his hands on the tile wall in front of him and tilted his head back. The swish and scrape of the curtain opening made him look over his shoulder with a frown. Shock had him straightening his back. Naked and lush, Sylphine climbed into the shower. While her cheeks and chest were pink from obvious nervousness as she looked anywhere but at him, her body language was confident. The woman had made a decision, and she wasn't going to allow him to change her mind.

Taking in the full swell of her breasts, stomach, and hips, the arousing curves of her thighs and smooth round backside, telling her to get out was the farthest thing from his mind. When she closed the curtain, still looking anywhere but at him, Jonathon captured her wrists, pulled them high above her head, and pressed her to the cold tile, holding her captive with the strength of his body. She gasped, her eyes round and searching up at him. The softness of her cradled him in all the right ways.

He pressed a kiss at the pulse pounding a heady rhythm in her neck. A tremble raced through her body, expressed in a shuddering breath against his cheek. He licked up to her ear. "I have waited *years* for this moment."

She turned her head, her mouth whispering along his. "Me too."

The confession startled him. He drew back and met her stare. Slowly he released her arms. "Really?"

"Yes. I was scared before."

"But not anymore?"

She shook her head and pressed her palm to his chest, forcing him to take a step back. Her gaze roamed from his head to toes, lingering for a moment at the proud evidence of his arousal. Her fingers skittered along the steely length of him, and he fisted his hands and took a calming breath at the fire her gentle touch created. "No, not anymore."

Pulling her under the fall of water, he kissed her. Passion ignited. Her mouth opened, her tongue sliding into his mouth, claiming, demanding. She sank her fingers into his wet hair, her body pressing close as she rose onto her tiptoes to try and rub against him. Jonathon broke the kiss and shook his head.

"Not yet. I still have to wash."

A mischievous smile brightened her eyes. "I will help you."

Soap in hand, she rubbed the cedar-scented bar over his skin. Her fingers teased every inch of him. And when she chased the bubbles rinsing away down his torso with her tongue and sank to her knees, Jonathon had to grab the curtain rod to keep from falling over. Her velvety mouth took him deep. He cursed as pleasure rolled through his body and had to drag her back up when she sucked hard and nearly had him ending their night before they'd truly begun. He shut off the water and pulled her into his body.

"When I come this time," he growled into her ear, "it'll be inside you."

"But you liked... that?" she asked tentatively, drawing back and meeting his gaze.

He kissed her hard. "Oh yeah. *Liked* is an understatement."

Forgetting about towels, he pulled her from the tub and walked her backward, his hands on her hips, his mouth ravaging hers, to his bed. No, not his. *Their bed.* Soaking wet, they fell onto the mattress. He urged her back to the pillows, his hands caressing up the smooth length of her legs, from her ankles to her thighs, where he spread her wide. He laid on his stomach between her parted legs. Meeting her hooded stare over the full globes of her breasts rising and falling with quickened breaths, he grinned.

"My turn."

UNBEARABLE PLEASURE ROLLED THROUGH SYLPHINE. HER BACK arched on a guttural cry. One hand fisted in Jonathon's hair between her spread legs, the other in the pillow under her head. Still, he continued his onslaught. His wicked, wicked tongue took her higher. He'd started his sensual assault on her breasts, licking, sucking, and nipping until he discovered what she liked best. To her shock and his delight, she enjoyed the little stinging bites he delivered and had encouraged her to continue teasing her own nipples as he journeyed south. Something she'd done until he'd driven her to the brink and all she could do was hold on.

Covered in sweat, every limb trembling, she tried to remember to breathe as another surge of bliss threatened to crest and pull her under. His hands held her hips locked to the bed, his thrill at bringing her to climax, and his carnal desire, the strength of his love, sinking into her every cell, making the ride of her orgasm all the more potent when it crashed through her again.

Jonathon climbed up her body. He held himself above her on his forearms, his eyes dark with passion. "Put me inside you," he whispered against her lips.

All too eager for more, *needing* to know what they would

be like together, Sylphine reached between their bodies and took his thick length in hand. She lifted her hips and fit him into her, groaning with him as he slowly pushed his way deep inside. Only when her hand could no longer fit did she release him on a shuddering breath, sinking her nails into his back.

There was no easing into a rhythm. No preamble at making things gentle. He slammed into her, taking her hard, heavy, leaving her gasping for air and sending her hurtling over the edge of ecstasy as another climax roared through her body on a tidal wave. Bracing his hand on the headboard above her, he moved faster, deeper. She wrapped a hand around the straining muscles of his forearm and drew her knees up, taking even more of him, chasing another heady rush of pleasure.

Never had a man been so uninhibited with her. Never had he treated her like an equal, meeting her passion and doling out his own. This wasn't the one-sided, detached coupling she'd endured in the past. She knew the claim he made on her body went both ways. He was hers.

Panting, he rocked heavily, every muscle tense and slick with perspiration. His damp hair hung over his forehead. Sylphine had never seen anything sexier. And as another orgasm ripped through her, she took more pleasure in his deep groan and shuddering frame as his gratification flowed like a storm around her and through her nerves, sharing in his pleasure.

He stayed braced above her until their breathing evened. With a quick kiss, he shocked her a little with the sudden sense of emptiness as he pulled out and rolled away. At the edge of the bed, he stared at her for a moment, a small, intimate smile on his face. Sylphine returned the smile, her fingers trailing along her stomach, a sense of contentment unfurling inside her.

"You are so unbelievably sexy and beautiful," he said with a shake of his head.

She looked over his mussed hair, damp skin, and still semi-erect state glistening between his legs with the evidence of their love-making. Her core thrummed deep inside at the reminder. "You are, too."

Chuckling, he held his hand out. "Come on, my heiress, let's get cleaned up and dressed, or I'm going to ravish you again."

Emboldened by his declaration, she trailed her fingers higher, brushing them over her breasts. "Would that be so bad?"

Heat flared in his eyes. "No. However, I need to unlock the door. I don't want to chance Parker waking up and panicking."

Sylphine accepted his hand and stumbled out of bed, her limbs more jelly than solid. Thankfully Jonathon supported her weight, though he laughed. She slapped his chest with the back of her hand. "Hush, it is your fault."

He pressed a wet, smacking kiss to her lips on another chuckle. "I gladly accept the blame."

14

"Are you hungry, Parker?" Ramsey asked over her shoulder, her black curls swept up into a riot atop her head, her robe the same rich lavender shade as her eyes. She stirred a large pan of sizzling sausage balls with a spatula.

Sylphine smiled and urged the little boy through the door when he froze. He held a small, yellow lap blanket she'd given him when he'd awoken in the middle of the night to his face, hugging the plush length to his chest. The pre-dawn sleep interruption hadn't been as annoying as Sylphine had thought since when they'd returned to bed, Jonathon had once again sent her careening into sensual bliss.

The man had no shame and was quickly teaching her to have none either when it came to what they were capable of together. The delicious soreness between her legs reminded her that while he'd never hurt her, Jonathon was anything but a gentle lover. The intensity of his passion came as no shock to her. The strength of hers however, had. Never, in all her sexual encounters, had she been the lover she'd been with her husband. Then again, he'd allowed her to be nothing less, coaxing and urging her into not only experiencing his pleasure, but a full participant in her own. Sylphine took a centering breath. If she didn't stop thinking about him, and his incredibly gifted body, she'd find herself marching back up the stairs.

She'd left Jonathon sprawled on his stomach, deep in sleep, when she'd eased from their bed at hearing Parker's light footsteps in the hall. The boy wouldn't let her get more than two feet away before he wrapped himself around her. She figured if Jonathon were up, it would be worse. Parker seemed to prefer the man of the house.

Ramsey glanced at Sylphine in question. Sylphine dropped to her hunches in front of the boy, the length of her thick pale blue robe flaring out around her. Pulling the blanket, hiding his face away, she gave him an encouraging smile. "Are you hungry, *mayi slyazo malche*?"

"Momma makes me sweet toast," he snuffled, his small toe drawing a circle on the wooden floor.

"Sweet toast?" Sylphine glanced at Ramsey, who nodded with an endearing smile. "I think we can manage that."

Ramsey laid two butter and sugar crusted slices of bread in a frying pan. "What did you say to him in your language?"

"Hmm?" Sylphine asked, helping Parker up into a chair. "What do you mean?"

"You said something to him after you asked if he was hungry."

"Did I?" She considered her words. "Ah, yes. My sweet boy."

Ramsey nodded as if listening to something in her mind, her face drawn in concentration. "*Mayi slyazo malche*, my sweet boy. That is..." She smiled and shook her head. "Well, sweet, I guess."

Sylphine returned her smile, though a sliver of trepidation raced up her spine at the effortless recitation of her language from someone who had never been taught more than a few words over a couple of years. "Be careful, Ramsey, who you let realize your sudden gift of language."

Ramsey waved a hand, her attention back to the toast. "It's not sudden, I've always been able to read languages. Speaking is new, though I guess I never really tried before. What would it matter who knew?"

Not being involved in world travel like Sylphine, or even a form of strategy like her brother, Ramsey seemed clueless to how important her apparent genetic inherited ability could be to some. Sylphine wondered if Ramsey even knew she was a Gen-Heir, let alone one with a remarkable talent.

Sylphine brushed her fingers through Parker's soft curls. The boy zoomed a fork across the table like one of his cars, and she frowned. "I suppose we need to get some toys if you're going to be with us, little Parker."

Ramsey looked up from plating Parker's breakfast. "I bet some of Jonathon's old toys are in the attic." Smiling, she set the plate in front of the little boy. "What do you think, Parker? Want to go on a treasure hunt for some toys later today?"

He held his fork up in triumph. "Yeah, I want to find treasure! I wike treasures. And toys. Cars are my favo-wit." The tines of the fork scraped against the plate as he stabbed at a sausage ball that rolled away from his attempts. "I has lots of cars at home."

Ramsey beamed a smile at Sylphine. "I think we have a plan for today at least."

Sylphine went to the counter to make coffee while Ramsey cooked more food for the adults. Having a family cook back home, Sylphine had only learned to prepare dishes important during Italyssian holidays, and only because her mother, who hadn't grown up wealthy, insisted her daughter learn the traditions. Early on in the Hunter household, she'd learned how to at least help make coffee or tea, and she cut things up when Ramsey or Jonathon needed the help.

"Thank you for always cooking," Sylphine said, scooping a heaping spoonful of fragrant coffee into the top of the stovetop coffee-maker.

"Well, I like jasmine balls and baked lemon crusted fish as much as anyone, however, after a week, I think we'd all be done with them." Ramsey bumped her hip to Sylphine's and winked. "And I'm not the only cook in this house. Jonathon does too when he's home and can."

"When I'm home and can what?" Jonathon's deep voice asked.

A shiver of awareness raced along Sylphine's nerves. She turned to see him walk into the kitchen. Loose dark green sleep pants rode low on his hips. The edges of his robe hung open, revealing the play of muscles beneath his skin as he walked, the belt laying untied and forgotten from the loops. Every fiery moment from last night rushed through her. And when his heated gaze landed on her, she knew he remembered too.

"Make us food," Ramsey said.

Jonathon pulled Sylphine into his body. He slid one hand between the edge of her robe to the thin nightgown she'd hastily thrown on underneath while the other wrapped around to her back, holding her close. Somehow, she managed to keep from gasping. He leaned in and kissed her cheek beside her ear.

"I prefer you naked underneath this robe," he whispered.

She pressed closer, wrapping her arms around his neck.

His shuddering breath raced across her ear. Her body responded with a hot tremor. "How am I supposed to stand in this kitchen with what you do to me?"

"Hey!" Ramsey snapped her fingers. "I know you're newly married and all, but the kitchen. Family space. No lusty stuff in here, if you please."

Jonathon straightened, an unapologetic grin on his face. "Lusty stuff?"

Ramsey waved her spatula around. "Is that not what is going on right here?"

Sylphine pressed her lips together and looked anywhere but at her sister-in-law. Jonathon laughed. His hand slipped from her robe. She knew he needed to put space between them. Which, she admitted, she was in no hurry to do. In Jonathon's embrace, the swirl of his desire, love, and happiness wrapping around her was an addictive place to be.

Jonathon pressed a gentle kiss to Sylphine's lips, his eyes never leaving hers. "No, this is love."

A fist clenched around her heart. She touched her hand to his cheek. He hadn't said he loved her again since the night he'd passed out in her bed. However, she knew the truth then and the knowledge of the words since. She didn't want to have such an intimate conversation in the kitchen so she smiled through a sudden sheen of tears and caressed a path to his mouth. Her fingers traced his full bottom lip. He kissed her forehead and then stepped away.

"Are you not working today?" Sylphine asked as she returned to the interrupted task of making coffee.

Jonathon sat next to Parker, who immediately slipped off his chair and onto Jonathon's lap. Patient as ever, Jonathon accepted the little boy and slid his plate over. Without missing a bite, Parker dug back into his meal. Sylphine's chest constricted again at the sight of the two of them. She hadn't given much thought to a family, to kids. Taking a deep breath, she turned back to the coffee, pressing a hand to her stomach. After last night, she could already be pregnant, she realized.

The flutter of excitement at the prospect took her by surprise. With her other lovers, she'd worn an ovulation bracelet to track her cycle and know when to be celibate. She'd been so young, and neither herself, nor the men who'd promised to marry her, had been ready for children. Having resigned herself to celibacy for good, she hadn't worried about tracking her cycle in years, other than to know when to expect her monthly. She had no idea where she was at in her fertility. And after another glance at the heartwarming scene at the kitchen table, she didn't care. If they managed to create a life today, tomorrow or three months from now, she'd be happy. She wondered if Jonathon would feel the same.

"Sort of," he answered. "I'll be working from home the next couple days, until we figure out what's going on with the kidlet here."

Sylphine set two cups of steaming coffee on the table and went back for the third. "Do you expect someone to come and get him?"

"I don't know. So far, finding family has proven difficult," he admitted.

Frowning, Sylphine sat where Parker had been. The table, and back of the chair, were sticky. "What are you going to do?"

Jonathon accepted a plate from Ramsey, setting it beside Parker's. The boy made an effort to get a sausage ball. Jonathon blocked his fork. "No. That's my breakfast, you have your own."

"I want the ball," Parker whined, pointing with his fork.

"Mine. Eat your toast." Jonathon looked back at Sylphine. "I haven't decided. I haven't given up on finding family, yet. No one is completely alone."

Sylphine frowned. "Not everyone is willing to take on a child, family or not."

"I know. I'll deal with that if it happens."

ATTENTION FOCUSED ON THE FILES SPREAD BEFORE HIM, Jonathon worked his jaw in frustration. He failed to notice

Sylphine entering his office until the door clicked shut. She carried a wooden tray laden with sandwiches and cut vegetables. A three-quarter sleeved gown of silvery-blue at the shoulders gradually transitioned to rich indigo along the hem. From experience, he knew the shapeless flow of silk would reveal her every hidden curve in a second if she were to dance.

However, it wasn't the memory of her body moving to a seductive melody only she could hear that he dwelled on as he looked her over, but the more powerful one of her writhing beneath him, sweaty and naked. He still couldn't believe he'd known her, every inch of her body. Claimed her as his wife in every way possible now. For the first time, a lover had allowed him to be completely himself, unleashing the full extent of his passion and offering more of her own. Jonathon shifted in his seat, trying to ease the tightness of his pants across his groin. He forced his attention to the food instead of his sexy woman.

"You have been in here for almost seven hours, I thought you could use the break," she said, crossing the room.

Jonathon leaned back, flipping a pen between his fingers. "Where is Parker?"

"Taking a nap." At the edge of the desk, she searched for a clear spot to place the tray. "Ramsey is out in the greenhouse."

Jonathon glanced out the large window close to his desk overlooking the gardens and spotted the flash of color amongst all the greenery. Sighing, he tossed the pen onto the desk. "How do I get Ramsey to meet someone? I'm afraid she's going to become a spinster."

Sylphine followed his glance, the tray still balanced in her hands. "You could always host a dinner party or two, invite men you trust."

The idea of men parading around his sister, deciding

whether or not they wanted to take her to bed, let alone make her their wife, made him raise a brow. "Maybe being a spinster isn't so bad."

"Jonathon!" she chastised, laughing.

"What? I don't know what I was thinking. I doubt there is anyone who would be good enough for her."

Sylphine found a corner less occupied than the others and set the tray down. Her gaze shifted back to the window, a thoughtful expression on her beautiful face. "There is someone."

Jonathon rolled his chair closer to the desk so he could reach the food. "Unlikely. Maybe, someone, I could *tolerate*." A vision of First Guardsman Wackerly flirting with Ramsey in the foyer made Jonathon shudder. "Barely."

"Your sister deserves love," she peered up at him for a moment before fixing a plate, "and a family, if she wants it."

Jonathon braced his forearms on his desk. "Do you want a family?"

An enticing flush crept into her cheeks. She cleared her throat, handing him the plate. "I was thinking about that this morning, actually."

He accepted the plate, his focus never leaving her. "And?"

She perched herself on a chair across from his desk but wouldn't meet his stare. "And after last night...."

Jonathon's attention flickered to her wrists. She always wore bracelets, but as he looked over the silver bands, none of them were the beaded bracelets women used as a means of birth control. Not that he'd asked last night before taking her where she was in her cycle if she *had* known. "Would you be upset?"

She took a deep breath, and he held his own. Slowly, she shook her head and finally looked at him. "No. Would you?"

Jonathon imagined her round with his child and his chest

constricted. He swallowed against the sharp ache. "I can't think of anything I'd want more."

"Really?" she asked, her eyes wide in disbelief and, if he wasn't mistaken, a little shiny with tears.

He braced his forearms on the desk and leaned forward. "If there wasn't a giant window here, and my sister wasn't traipsing around the greenhouse, I'd show you just how badly I want to make a baby with you."

The flush in her cheeks deepened. "I-if we are not… pregnant, would you want to wait until we have been married a little longer before we try?"

Jonathon didn't need longer. He didn't even need another day to know the mother of his children sat across from him. "Do you?"

She regarded him for a moment and then shook her head. "I don't think so. I have known you for so long and…" She blew out a breath, rubbing her hands on her thighs. "I know it sounds so silly, but after seeing you with Parker, I know you are going to be a good father."

A sliver of disappointment niggled in his gut. She hadn't mentioned loving him as a good enough reason not to wait. Then again, he hadn't exactly declared his love for her much, but he knew she *had* to feel it from him. Just looking at her made his heart squeeze with the emotion. He'd waited as long as it took for her to come around to accepting his touch, he'd wait however long she needed for her heart to come around to him, too.

"Except for when I'm not home," he felt compelled to remind her.

"Yes, that will make things hard, but I imagine not any harder than when I return to Italyssa to see my family."

"How am I supposed to live without you for weeks?" he asked before he could stop himself.

"You could always come with me," she said.

Jonathon looked at the barely controlled chaos of his desk. "We'll have to shelve this discussion. I want to say sure, that's a possibility, but…"

She stretched her hand out across the desk. "I know. We will shelve it, as you say, because I am not willing to give up. I do not want to spend weeks without you, either."

"When are you going to try to reach your parents again?"

A worried frown bracketed her mouth. "I sent a letter a week ago. That at least should have made it by now. I included your radio number. I am hoping they find a way to reach me."

Jonathon recalled a time when he'd been in the same situation. Desperate to hear a word from anyone who could tell him the fate of his parents. Unfortunately, when news did arrive, it had been the worst they could receive. He didn't figure Sylphine would want to hear about that right now, so he offered an encouraging smile instead. "They'll radio."

She worried her bottom lip between her teeth. "I hope so." Concern pinched between her brows. She fidgeted in the seat. "You know if I do not hear from them soon, I will have to go back to Italyssa. Now that we are married, the Cyrano's cannot force me into a union. I will take our contract with me."

"Come again?" he asked, figuring he *must* have misheard her.

"If Ramsey were in danger and you were away from Sziveria, and you had no way of reaching her, would you not find a way to get back to her?"

Jonathon rubbed his thumb between his eyes. "I thought we were going to shelve the conversation of you returning home for another time. Now you say you have to return as soon as possible, while there is still a real threat to your well-being? Not a good idea."

"Then come with me. We will only be gone for two, maybe

three weeks." Her eyes pleaded as she scooted to the end of the chair.

Jonathon braced his elbow on the desk and continued to rub his forehead. Closing his eyes, he wished he'd had more time before his job seriously interfered with his marriage. "We can't. Not right now. What would happen to Parker, and his mother's case?"

Her heavy sigh had him lifting his head. "Parker. Do you have any new information for him?"

"I don't. As of this morning, he still has no family coming forward, nor any I could find. I've learned where his mother worked, and I have Wackerly getting everything he can find concerning her and the boy for me at the records department today."

"And if we leave, he will have no one," she surmised with a frown.

"I will have to surrender him to an orphanage."

Sylphine paled a bit at his frank reply. "Have you…" She swallowed, touched her chest, and tried again. "Have you ever had to do that before with another child?"

"Yes, a few."

"Why was Parker different?"

Jonathon considered her question carefully. Why had Parker been different? Each child had broken his heart. Had made his already difficult job almost unbearable when they'd been forced into a home not only full of strangers but full of despair. Something no one, let alone a child, deserved. But the little boy covered in cobwebs and snotty tears had wrapped himself around Jonathon, literally, and in that moment, Jonathon had known no one would take the boy from him without a fight.

"He trusted me, trusted I wasn't the bad guy his mother died protecting him from," Jonathon answered. And perhaps that was the clencher right there for him. He didn't want

Parker's mother's sacrifice to have been in vain. If Jonathon protected and loved the boy, what she died for wouldn't have been for nothing.

Sylphine tilted her head and regarded him curiously. "And the others did not?"

"No. They cried, screamed, hid. One even threw stuff at me, another tried to bite me, and did succeed in biting the orphanage attendant." Jonathon took a deep breath and met her gaze, wondering how she'd take what had been swirling in his mind all day between researching cases. "Would you mind if we're able to take custody of him?"

Eyes wide, she stared at him, her mouth open. She blinked quickly and glanced at the window. "Wow, um… wow." She shook her head as if clearing her thoughts and brought her attention back to him. "We have been married a week, Jonathon. A child, already?"

Jonathon had no right to the disappointment rolling through him. What he asked was sudden and not exactly fair, especially with everything she was having to deal with. He wasn't going to give up on the idea, though, or on Parker. "I know our marriage, to this point, has been a study in rushed. If you truly aren't comfortable with the idea, can we at least agree to have him under our roof until I can approve a family to accept him? We both know we want kids, it'll just be a little sooner than we planned."

She choked and waved a hand around. "A *little* sooner? At least pregnant, I will be able to get used to the idea of us as a family, as parents, responsible for another life." When he opened his mouth, she stopped her hand, palm facing him. "No, there is nothing else to say, I do understand. And the thought of someone else getting Parker is… unpleasant. I need a couple of days to get accustomed before we actually sign anything, if you can give me that."

Hope made him smile, and nod in agreement. "You can have as much time as you need. And thank you."

She tucked a strand of hair behind her ear, making the clipped feather stick out oddly. "I do not feel you should thank me for agreeing to provide an orphaned child a future."

"*You* are agreeing to provide that future, though," he said, needing her to understand the significance. "You aren't handing him over to an orphanage with money for his care and then walking away. You're deciding to raise him with me."

THE ACHING NEED IN HER CHEST TO SIMPLY *TALK* TO HER PARENTS had Sylphine rubbing her collarbone and glancing at the ceiling. Up above her, a sweet little boy napped, probably wrapped around the blanket he hadn't released since she'd given it to him. And if everything went according to Jonathon's plan, he'd be *hers*. Their child, making her parents instant grandparents. They didn't even know they had a son-in-law.

"Do you think we are doing this all wrong?" she couldn't help but ask, putting a voice to her fears. "We contracted to keep me away from another family without even discussing the logistics of an intercultural relationship, and now we want to bring a child into this chaos?"

Jonathon rose and rounded the desk. He dropped to his knees before her and wrapped his arms around her waist, forcing her gaze to his. "No, we aren't doing any of our relationship wrong. And yes, to bringing a child into our life, because it's our chaos, and we will make this work. We will."

Sylphine slid her fingers along his jaw. The stubble he hadn't bothered shaving away this morning tickled her fingertips. "So confident."

He smiled, turning his head enough to kiss her palm. "By-product of my job."

The expression on her face must have conveyed the doubt swirling around in her mind like an angry, dark cloud, for he moved in closer, his forehead touching hers. "If you really feel we need to wait, that we're making a mistake, I *will* find Parker, a suitable family. I know a lot of people, good people."

Sylphine sank her fingers into the hair at the back of his neck and breathed him in deep. "Why would you do that when you want him as your own?"

His fingers tightened on her hips. "Because I want you more."

"You already have me," she whispered, caressing her fingers through his hair. "I am not going anywhere. I said ten years, I meant them."

"I don't want just ten years, Sylphine. I want them all." His lips brushed hers. "We have our entire lives to shelter children, and have our own. If it's too soon for you, honestly, I'm not going to force you to agree. I want you to want this, too. Not just because I do."

Longing, hope, and love radiated from him, so pure and potent, her heart swelled like a sponge, taking in everything he surrounded her with. Her grasp tightened around his neck. "You should not have to choose between us, and you won't. I knew, even before we contracted, your honor and your sense of duty. While I never could have guessed it would include the need to father an orphaned boy, I will not reject your heart's request."

When he inhaled as if to speak, Sylphine continued, "Italyssians cherish children as much as Sziverian's do. They are our tomorrow, our reason for celebrating Wintervail every year, another generation to count among the survivors of a world-shattering event we know so little about. They do not need for anything if it's in our power. While I might be nervous about my ability to be the best for him, I won't refuse to be part of Parker's future. I said I would, and I will."

"Okay, then I guess we have at least settled that then." He leaned back on his hunches, his dark blue eyes warm with laughter. "What does that leave us, ninety-nine more things to resolve?"

The ability to make a scary situation *feel* normal and not a storm waiting to destroy her sanity on the horizon was a gift of Jonathon's. Briefly, she wondered if that ability wasn't his true genetically inherited talent. A knock sounded before she could reply to the quip. He rose, putting distance between them as the door slipped open.

Ramsey ushered in First Guardsman Wackerly. Beads of moisture clung to his hat and dotted his black jacket and slacks. Droplets sluiced off his leather boots. He pulled his cap off with his free hand and held it tightly, offering a folder out to Jonathon with the other.

"MT, I have those documents you requested this morning."

Jonathon accepted the files. Above them, a muffled shriek followed by a choking sob sounded. Sylphine jumped up, thankful when Wackerly moved quickly to the side.

Ramsey followed her to the stairs. "Do you need any help?"

Sylphine rushed up the steps. "I do not know," she admitted. "I know nothing about screaming children."

A wry smile turned one corner of Ramsey's mouth. "Me neither."

The tantrum didn't let up as Sylphine rushed down the hall to the bedroom. Perched in the middle of the bed, the fluffy yellow lap blanket clutched in both hands, Parker let loose a wailing sob, his face purple with distress. His chunky cheeks were wet, and snot flowed from his nose and over his upper lip. Two fat tears raced each other to his chin when he set eyes on her. He didn't reach for her, but he didn't move away either when she crawled onto the bed.

A wave of anxiety and confusion beat through her. She took a bracing breath, knowing the emotional intensity from the little boy would strengthen when she touched him. Weeks ago, she wouldn't have even entered the room, fearful the onslaught would overtake her, make her forget herself, leaving her sobbing right there with him. But Jonathon had shown *she* was in control of her Gen-Heir ability. Only she decided *what* to feel. Accepting the emotions of others, yet separating them from her own consciousness was within her power. Parker needed her, and she wouldn't shy from him.

"Oh Parker, what is this?" she crooned, pulling him onto her lap. She cradled him close, resting her cheek on top of his head while she stroked his back soothingly. "Why are we so upset, hmm?"

He hiccupped, his wet face burying into her neck. "I want my Momma."

The declaration came on a fresh wave of shockingly loud cries from such a small body. Her heart clenched. The burn of tears threatened her composure. She wanted her *Mita*, too. The urge to give in and cry with the child warred with Sylphine's need to be an adult. An actual adult. With responsibilities beyond simply making sure a transaction went smoothly or another contract landed across her father's desk.

"*Mayi slyazo malche*, I know you do," she whispered, rocking gently, her fingers caressing his soft curls.

"I want my Momma," he whined again, weaker as if he knew the request wouldn't be met but couldn't stop from asking.

Someday, they'd have to tell him what happened. Someday, the truth would need to be revealed. That day wasn't today, however. So Sylphine sniffed away her tears for a heartbroken boy curled in her lap and forced a smile she didn't feel onto her face. "I know, how about we take all those fun toys we found on our treasure hunt and see what Jonathon is doing in his office? Do you want to go downstairs and see what he's doing?"

"Yeah," he snuffled, rubbing his face along her dress again.

"Yeah? Okay good, then let's go."

FROWNING, JONATHON LOOKED THROUGH THE SHEETS OF PAPER FG Wackerly had procured for him. "What do you mean the boy doesn't have a birth record?"

Wackerly turned his hat between both his hands. The very hat Jonathon would carry a scar for retrieving. "I mean, they couldn't find one. They looked. Under his name, her name, and the names of the men from all her previous marriage contracts on file. Nothing."

Jonathon shook his head and went to his desk. "That doesn't make any sense. She wasn't keeping him a secret from anyone. The neighbors knew about Parker." He shuffled through some documentation and pulled out what he'd been looking for. "She claimed him as a dependent to receive the higher pay required of her employer. To do that, she'd need his birth record."

Wackerly shrugged helplessly.

Sighing, Jonathon braced both his hands on the desk and drummed his fingers in thought. "Check with the Birkels. Maybe we'll get lucky, and they have a copy of the boy's record in their personal files."

"Is that common?" Wackerly asked.

"They're a large house, with at least twenty-five full-time staff. If they're audited, they'd need their records in order, so it's possible." He went back to the file the young First

Guardsman had given him. "Are all her marriage contracts in here?"

"Yes. She's had four, all the minimum of a year required."

Safe affairs. Many people often took that route in the age of Human Rabies Syndrome. Had Jonathon been wiser in his youth, he would have done the same. He shook away dark memories. "The last one was six years ago. Parker is three, so either she wasn't married, or whoever made sure Parker's birth record disappeared made sure that contract did, too."

"Would make sense," Wackerly agreed. "But wouldn't a child make their contract eighteen years?"

"Not if they conceived after it expired, or she had it annulled due to abuse. A husband isn't listed on her work records, so it's likely she was a single mother."

Wackerly snapped his fingers. "I can check the records at Division, see what turns up under her name from the last couple of years. If there were abuse issues, she had to have filed an accusation against him."

"Yes, chances are good he wouldn't be able to get to those accounts if he even thought about them." Jonathon smiled at the younger man. "Good thinking, FG."

Red flamed into Wackerly's cheeks. "Thanks, MT."

When the young enforcer hesitated at leaving, Jonathon set down the paper he'd been holding. "Yes, FG? What else is there?"

Worry etched Wackerly's face. "How could someone eliminate records, MT Hunter? That... it shouldn't be able to happen."

"No, it shouldn't," Jonathon agreed. "And if we find proof someone has tampered with them, we can inform the Record's Department, and they can begin an investigation. In the meantime, we need to follow the thread we've been given."

Wackerly nodded in agreement, shoving his hat back on his head. "I will get to East Street Division right away."

Jonathon settled behind his desk, pulling the documents forward Wackerly had brought. A whirlwind of yellow and giggles bounced into the room. Sylphine's lyrical voice called from behind Parker, an alluring mixture of Italyssian and Sziverian that had him raising a brow. When she stopped at the office door, her cheeks were flushed, and she leaned heavily into the frame, panting.

"He is *fast*," she managed between breaths.

"Kids are," Jonathon said with a smile.

"I wanted to make sure before we took over your space, it was okay," she said, coming the rest of the way in, her hands loaded with toys.

Jonathon sank into his seat, accepting first the blanket that was tossed onto his lap, and then Parker, who beamed a smile and held out his hand. A detailed, carved wooden bird rested on his small palm. "I already told you, I took the rest of the week to ensure Parker was settled. This is part of it." He accepted the bird with a smile. "Very nice Parker, thank you."

"It's a pwetty bird," Parker stated with pride.

"It is," Jonathon agreed.

Parker pointed at his chest. "I found it."

The boys pride made Jonathon laugh. "Way to go, big guy. What else did you find?"

Parker scrambled off Jonathon's lap, the yellow blanket forgotten. Sylphine set all the toys on the floor. Within seconds, treasures lined the edge of the desk, each one producing more excitement than the last. Jonathon and Sylphine both made the appropriate noises of appreciation, all the while Jonathon quickly sorted through the files laying open on his desk.

"Would you mind looking through these?" he asked, holding a file out.

Sylphine accepted with a wary glance at his uneaten food. "Only if you eat what I brought."

"Deal," he said, taking a carrot off the plate.

She sat in the chair she'd occupied earlier, the file open on her lap. "What am I looking for?"

Jonathon pointed his pen at the file. "Those are all the shipping manifests I could manage to dig up for the Cyrano's company with any business they've conducted in Sziveria. I figure you'll know more than me what to look for if anything is out of place."

She chewed on her bottom lip as she shifted through papers. "Will they know you have been looking into their dealings?"

"Do you know when anyone is looking into yours?"

"Only if it is a government inquiry, like an audit."

Jonathon shrugged. "Then they shouldn't know either, should they?"

She offered a shallow smile. "I suppose not. What did FG Wackerly have?"

"Information," Jonathon stated cryptically. "Some important documentation was missing, however, so he's researching that now."

"For…" Silently, she motioned toward Parker.

Jonathon nodded. "Yes."

"Is it… bad?"

"The information missing?" When she nodded, he replied, "Could be. I don't know yet."

15

THEY WORKED IN QUIET FOR HOURS, WITH PARKER BOUNCING between them. Sylphine made a few calls using Jonathon's radio once she discovered some troubling information among the papers. Sometime after dark, Ramsey came to collect everyone for dinner. Unable to put the task Jonathon assigned to her down, Sylphine took the file with her, still perusing as she walked into the kitchen. A pressure at her hip made her pause. Jonathon's heat and scent enveloped her.

"Who can't stop working now?" he whispered into her ear, fluttering the tendrils of hair and a feather against her cheek.

Taking a breath, Sylphine closed the file and held it carefully to keep any pages from spilling out. "There is something here, I can feel it, but I cannot seem to find anything specific."

He gave her hip a quick squeeze. "I know the feeling."

Ramsey set a plate of already cut food in front of Parker as he climbed up into the chair, his blanket pooling on the floor. Sylphine picked up the blanket and hung it over the back of the seat and set down her file. After helping Ramsey place their dishes and meal on the table, she settled in the chair beside Parker and across from Jonathon.

"Tell me about the papers," Jonathon said, spooning cubed cheesy potatoes and peas onto his plate.

Sylphine placed two slices of fried herb bread on her plate. "I am confused about the manifests. The Cyrano's own three trade ships and two passenger liners. Their liners usually only travel from Italyssa to either Noreden or Thanzia. They are small vessels and can't cross the more difficult waters of the Sovereign Channel, so only carry across the Sea of Italyssa."

"And their trade ships?" Jonathon asked.

Sylphine paused, reaching for a baked pork chop. "Are capable of crossing all the waters, like ours."

"And the problem with the manifests?" he encouraged, digging into his potatoes.

"Two of them appear to be false."

"Do they have to disclose what is already on their ship?" Ramsey asked.

"No. I placed calls to contacts I have at the Italyssian Trade Bureau and Mark Inland Commerce about the two manifests. Both times, the ships appear to have left Italyssa empty, but arrived in Mark Inland full after only declaring a less than half load here in Sziveria," Sylphine answered.

Jonathon chewed thoughtfully. "Did they tell you about the cargo delivery to Mark Inland?"

Sylphine took a deep breath. "All passengers."

"And the manifest here?" he asked.

"Textiles."

He set his fork down and held out his hand. "Can I see?"

Isolating the sheets, she handed them over. Jonathon took a few moments to look at them. Butterflies danced in Sylphine stomach. She didn't like to think why the Cyrano's would fabricate a manifest in one country, while the other documented the truth. Passengers. People. Lives. Had they embarked of their own free will?

"I think we need to take these to Guardianess Raiventon. She had some issues over a year ago with forged manifests. She may be able to tell us who the company is that provided these for the Cyrano's." He handed the papers back to her.

"Is Mark Inland known for trafficking?" Sylphine couldn't stop from asking.

"Not like Cairo," Jonathon answered.

"But Cairo is different," Sylphine said with a frown. "They do not take people. You offer your service to the country in return for money for your family or a better life altogether. They don't need to kidnap people."

"And they expect a premium price," Ramsey said with a frown of her own. "No human life should be sold."

"I agree, however, technically, you are not buying the person but paying for their education and services through Cairo. The ones who do not have a choice are the children born into service." Sylphine sighed. "Sadly, too many continue to use Cairo as a convenience, and with their Sentinels, they aren't going anywhere."

Ramsey leaned forward, her eyes bright with curiosity. "Are the Sentinels as dangerous as the rumors say?"

"Yes, they are highly trained. Each unit is considered elite. When someone decides to enter into a contract with Cairo over them, they *are* paying for a life then, but the Sentinels are expected to return, and a portion of the fee is repaid." A tingle of unease ran up Sylphine's spine. "I would not want to cross a Sentinel."

Jonathon scoffed and handed her back the papers. "They aren't monsters. Raised from childhood to be nothing but a fighting force, most of the men don't know a different life."

All the talk of a dangerous mercenary force made Sylphine's stomach clench. She set the manifests back in the folder with a frown. "I wish we knew who the passengers were."

"They weren't Sentinels," Jonathon said, as if reading her thoughts.

"How do you know?"

"Cairo expects their force to be treated with respect, not stowed away on some merchant ship. It would have been a passenger liner. Besides, why hide that? If someone in Mark Inland hired Sentinel's, there's no need to arrive here first. It also wouldn't be something the Cyrano's feel they need to hide," he pointed out.

A new sense of unease crept in. "Then that means the passengers probably were not truly passengers."

Jonathon frowned. "No, I'm thinking not. They were likely not prisoners either, since the ship left from Port Scarborough, and both ships went to the same location." He set his fork down and shook his head. "If it's what I'm thinking, Mark Inland may be trying to compete in the worst way with Cairo."

Ramsey set her fork down, too. "Involuntary human trafficking."

Horror filled Sylphine. "You think the Cyrano's are... selling people?"

"Maybe not selling," Jonathon clarified. "But providing the means for it to happen, yes. I need more information."

"I will help," Sylphine stated.

"Thank you, I'll need it. Actually, I need you to do something else. It might be related, loosely, to this situation as well. I should have asked if you could do it over a year ago, but with Cora..." He blew out a long breath. "Many things were forgotten."

"And I was gone," Sylphine said, remembering all too clearly the night they'd almost lost each other forever. The night she hadn't been able to confront his sorrow or be the woman, the friend he needed her to be.

"Yes." Another heavy sigh left him. "And then you were gone."

"The past." Ramsey flashed a quick smile. "Is completely behind us."

"Words you should abide by," Jonathon agreed, returning her smile.

The smile faded into a glare. Ramsey braced both arms on the table, forcing her plate forward. "If only those outside this house felt the same, dear brother, maybe I could."

"Perhaps," Sylphine began cautiously, "if you were to be seen more often, confident in your right to be where you want to be, they would have no choice but to stop their mean chatter."

Jonathon pointed his fork at his sister. "*That* is an excellent idea."

Despite her squared shoulders and raised chin, the uneasiness rolling off Ramsey in waves betrayed her anxiety at the suggestion. "If they aren't civilized enough to accept me, why should I bother?"

Sylphine glanced across the table at Jonathon. He met her stare, his expression troubled. Was he thinking the same thing as her? What if she'd decided returning to Sziveria wouldn't be worth it if he chose not to forgive her? Or if she couldn't find a way out of her own fears, where would they be now? His foot skimmed along hers, and the worry slid from his eyes into warmth. Her heart did a funny a little flip, and she smiled at him. How had she ever believed this man would be like all the others?

"Maybe someone will surprise you," Sylphine answered, still holding Jonathon's gaze.

"They probably won't," Ramsey predicted grimly. She rose, taking her empty plate and grabbing Jonathon's.

Sylphine helped Parker finish his meal, while Jonathon and Ramsey washed dishes, continuing what Sylphine believed to be a futile argument about leaving the house for something other than groceries and books. Afterward, Ramsey took Parker upstairs, while Jonathon ushered Sylphine back into his office.

The second they were alone, he pulled her into a heated embrace, trapping her against the door. His body and his mouth stirred fire through her veins.

Knowing they couldn't possibly finish what he started, Sylphine broke the kiss and pushed him away. "Stop. I know we have a purpose for being in here, and we won't accomplish it against this door."

He nuzzled her neck, his hard body pressing closer. "Maybe this is what I want to accomplish. I have *missed* you."

"We've been together all day," she pointed out and tried not to settle deeper into his heated promise.

The tip of his tongue licked a sizzling trail to her jaw. "Not the same."

No, it certainly wasn't. Temptation warred with the curiosity he'd built at dinner. Even as she gave him better access to her neck, his lips at her pulse point sending a shudder of pleasure through her, she asked, "What about the thing you said you needed me to do at the table?"

His heavy sigh fluttered across her skin. "You sure?"

"Yes," she said, knowing any hesitation would be met with another kiss meant to crumble her already weak resolve where Jonathon was concerned.

Cold air swept into the space he occupied as he moved away. Sylphine bit back a whimper of disappointment.

"Very well." He slid a finger down her cheek. "Give me a few minutes to try to find what Cora left me over a year ago."

"Cora?" The mention of the deceased beauty twisted Sylphine's stomach into knots. She pressed a hand to her belly. Recalling the hold Cora had once seemed to have on Jonathon caused old jealousy to arise.

At the desk, Jonathon glanced up from searching a huge stack of papers. "She brought them to me, along with a folder of names. Two weeks later, she left for Westica and…" He took a long breath and shook his head as if dislodging the bad memory. "Well, you know the rest."

Yes, she knew the rest. She also knew she couldn't, wouldn't, compete with a ghost. The only grip Cora had on Jonathon was the one Sylphine allowed. While she may not know how to be a wife yet, she did know she wanted to try. The best place to start with that task was to stop dwelling on a past of which neither of them had any control. Jonathon hadn't displayed any resentment toward the men who were before him, Sylphine needed to have the same respect for him.

"Found it," he said in triumph, pulling a folder from a mountain of documents.

Sylphine took what he handed her and laid it out, smoothing her hands along the edges. "A map of Graecily?"

"Something about the rail lines and ports weren't correct, they wanted to see if you could get any additional information."

"I have a map in the library. As a settlement, Italyssa sends many shipments to Graecily, and Sun Wind usually handles them."

"While you do that," he said, coming around the desk, "I'll check on Ramsey and Parker. Meet back here or in the library?"

Sylphine glanced at the radio behind Jonathon's desk. "Here, in case I need to make a call."

· · ·

Ramsey rocked the tiny human curled in her lap back and forth, her attention on the gray world beyond her room. The chair creaked and groaned with each sweep. A comforting noise that, along with the motion, lulled the boy into a doze. Parker had been desperate for contact, something Ramsey couldn't deny him. Deep inside, she knew the innocence fighting sleep was her nephew. Her heart had recognized him the moment he'd been dropped in her arms while Jonathon and Sylphine argued with the orphanage attendant sent to take him.

Parker was, perhaps, her only chance to hold a child. Sure, she figured at some point, her brother and new sister-in-law would create something precious together. But where would they live? Sylphine had a dynasty to run, and Jonathon... his skills worked anywhere. He could search out and convict the guilty in any nation. They'd be lucky to have him as an investigator.

The couple would likely ask her to come with if they chose Italyssa for their home. And honestly, Ramsey would be foolish to stay in a country that had no use for her. She took a long breath, watching the wind toy with leaves. If she remained, there was a chance, no matter how small, the man who'd saved her life six years ago would return. He'd never find her in Italyssa. And since she'd made the rash promise to wait for him, being impulsive enough to slide her father's band on his wrist, she'd remain in Haven City.

For what he'd prevented her from doing.

For the life, he'd saved.

He deserved no less, even if he had changed his mind.

In gentle sweeps, she continued to rock and stroked Parker's back. She tried to remember details of her rescuer, who, after six years, was little more than a shadow moving through her memory. Flashing green eyes, dark hair, and a mouth... Ramsey closed her eyes.

He'd kissed her.

Not the halfhearted, pathetic kisses she'd been used to prior to that night. No, he had *devoured* her. Demanded. Captured. In a single explosive, passion-filled moment, he'd thrown all her conceptions about intimacy into the night. He'd sent fire through her veins, and despite knowing she probably remembered incorrectly, she swore the green of his eyes had glowed in the aftermath.

Wait for me. Promise, Ramsey.

I promise.

No matter how long it takes. Swear it.

And she had. Someday he'd return, and she'd be waiting. No one knew about him. He was her secret. If he never returned to claim the heart he'd stolen too many nights ago to count, no one would know her heartache. Or the embarrassment of making such a bold promise to a dark stranger. Until then, she had to find ways to keep from going insane being locked away. A self-imposed prison sentence because she'd proven too weak to handle ridicule.

Parker's snore pulled her back into the present. Smiling, she pushed curls from his face. So sweet. She balanced his weight and rose, taking him to her bed. After bracing pillows on either side to keep him from accidentally rolling onto the floor, she went to her desk across the huge room.

The folder with the manifests laid open. Ramsey sat and spread the half sheets across her desk. At the dinner table, she'd noticed odd markings along the bottom of each document. No one else had thought anything of them, but Ramsey wondered… and since she had nothing better to do, she decided to see if she could figure out what they meant.

Sometime later, a faint knock disrupted her musings. She sat back as Jonathon eased the door open, his gaze first going to the sleeping child and then to her.

"Everything okay?" he whispered.

"Yes, we're fine. He can stay with me tonight, if you like."

Jonathon smiled and slipped the rest of the way into her room. "That would be nice, thank you." He stopped beside her desk. "What are you working on?"

Ramsey pointed out the small glyphs along the bottom of each manifest. "I noticed these at dinner. I thought they might mean something."

Arms crossed, Jonathon moved closer. "Huh. It's Markinish."

"On all of them? Even the ones not going to Mark Inland?" Ramsey asked, looking over the others.

Jonathon picked one up. "Yes… appears to be."

"Can you read it?"

He shook his head and set the paper down. "No, and I don't know anyone who can. It's not a well-known language."

Ramsey chewed on her lips. "I'll go to Mr. Harold's tomorrow and see if I can find a book."

Jonathon blinked and leaned back. "Is that such a good idea, considering what happened last time?"

Heat bloomed across her cheeks. *Of course,* her brother would bring up that particular humiliation. "I will go alone this time."

"And avoid a certain section?"

She placed all her attention on the papers. "Yes. Absolutely. I'll stay far away from… there. I will walk to the other side of the store to get to the stairs."

He chuckled and shook his head. "Should I warn FG Wackerly?"

Ramsey groaned, covering her face. "I don't think the enforceman would appreciate the reminder of being caught in a compromising situation any more than I do."

"True, maybe I should warn him to make sure he *doesn't*

stop by the lusty book section after his shift. You know… just in case."

"Get out," she whispered with a glare and flicked her fingers at him. "Out of my room. Shoo."

Jonathon's low laughter followed him out. He closed the door, the muted *click* making Ramsey turn to ensure the sound hadn't awoken Parker. She'd discovered when she'd put him down for his nap earlier that a closing door seemed to equal instant alert to a small child. His little fingers twitched, but he remained asleep. She sighed in relief. Waking up was still a work in progress for the boy. He didn't handle it well. Acclimation would take time. Healing would take even longer. No one had any delusion's the trauma of losing his mother, and being stuffed in a small dark space for hours while the cold crept in around him, would be forgotten easily.

Settling her attention back onto her self-appointed task, Ramsey took a deep breath. Tomorrow she'd find a book on Markinish and hopefully figure out what the Cyrano's were hiding in plain sight.

JONATHON SAT BRACED AGAINST HIS DESK, HIS FINGERS CURLING around the edge. Sylphine let out a groan of frustration, hanging up the receiver end of the radio. The rapid-fire elegance of her language had him thinking he needed to learn how to communicate in her native tongue. Her voice took on a husky edge when she spoke the rhythmic dialect, making the ache he seemed to constantly have for this woman so much stronger.

"Well?" he asked, shocked his voice hadn't cracked.

"Well, they were confused and claimed I must be mistaken. There are no rail-lines along the UZ. That would be a waste of resources when they cannot afford to spare even a pound of iron, why would they have lines going nowhere?"

She rubbed her hands on her thighs, irritation bracketing her mouth. "Yet, why would a logistics expert be given the information if not to move a product?"

"That is what we're trying to figure out." He glanced down at the unfolded map from Raina Merrick. "Cora went to Westica to investigate the mysterious rail lines there."

"And was murdered," Sylphine said with a heavy frown.

"Yes. It's been long enough now, hopefully, you inquiring won't raise any flags."

"Whoever I spoke to seemed to think I was wasting their time."

"At least we know the lines are not officially recognized. That means something."

She shook her head. "But that means Graecily is part of whatever treachery is happening, yes?"

"Appears so," he murmured.

Anxiety pinched her beautiful face. "Graecily cannot afford to be caught betraying anyone. They have too much to lose. The alignment with Floradesol is shaky at best, with Graecily wanting to emancipate. Floradesol does not want to give up the land or the control over the colony. If Floradesol discovered stolen resources and secret railroads, the entire colony of Graecily could be evicted, leaving Italyssa with thousands of refugees."

"There is a chance," Jonathon shifted to his hunches before her, "the officials are as much in the dark as our own."

"Which could be even worse."

"True. But it also leaves some power if the dominoes tumble. They can honestly claim they knew nothing and begin building new, hopefully, stronger bridges."

She rubbed her forehead. "This is a nightmare. I *need* to reach my father."

Curious, he asked, "Do you deal a lot in politics and peace situations?"

"Not really, but knowing the stability of any port our ships dock in is essential. We do *not* send our crews into volatile situations. Ever."

"Graecily is stable, for now," he assured her. "So far, this group, whoever they are, have maintained their secrets in such a manner it's almost artful. If they weren't creating slaves, and stealing from the lands they appear to be setting up in, I'd admire the beauty of their operation. It's looking to be nothing short of brilliant."

"Do they have any clues about who could be running such an operation?"

Jonathon shook his head, his frown mirroring hers. "No. And it's inhabited countries wide. Wintersfall's Intel team has been able to track shipments sent through the organization to Imperial Qu'in, Ravenna, Westica… They're all involved, whether voluntarily or not. Now, it appears possibly the entirety of South America, as well. The organization even managed to make a ship disappear, complete with cargo."

"And both of our nations have been battling a drug epidemic with magic lily dust and kidnapped children," she said so hushed he had to lean forward to catch the words. "What if…" She closed her eyes, swallowed, and tried again. "What if they are connected?"

"I will admit to being curious if the other nations where these mysterious railroads have been erected have a similar issue. Is there any way, with your connections, that you can find out?"

"Yes, of course, I will do anything to help you. Get me a list, and I will make calls first thing in the morning."

He stood over her, framing her face between his hands. Warmth and love blossomed in his chest, along with pride for his wife. "You. Are. Amazing." Each word was punctuated with a kiss.

Sylphine laughed. Her hands slipped over his shoulders. "You are amazing, too."

Someday, she'd return the love he knew she couldn't mistake pouring out of him. Someday, she'd trust what was between them. Jonathon caressed his thumb across her glossy bottom lip. And somehow, he'd prove he was worthy of her heart, as much as he'd been worthy of her body. His blood heated as he looked down at her flushed cheeks and the desire clouding her tourmaline eyes.

He kissed her again, deeper, longer. His tongue delved into the depths of her mouth, enticing and exploring. She made an urgent sound that drove him on. In a quick burst of movement, he had their positions reversed, with her straddling his lap across the chair. *Perfect.*

"I can't get enough of you," he confessed, his fingers digging into the thick length of her hair. Feathers and beads teased his skin along with the silken strands.

"Yes," she breathed out, sinking down onto him. "But not here."

Jonathon pulled back and stared. "No?"

She shook her head and leaned close, whispering into his ear *exactly* why his office wouldn't work for her. Vivid, erotic words he didn't even know existed in her vocabulary. Gone was the timid woman, scared of her own appeal, unsure of her personal response. Jonathon had unleashed a hidden, sensual creature. Like fire, desire rushed through his veins, trapping his breath and making him ache in all the right places. *Damn.* He didn't need to be convinced further.

16

"You shouldn't have come with me," Ramsey huffed, taking the stairs faster than Sylphine could keep up.

The scent of old books and dust permeated the air. Sylphine tried not to trip on the poorly lit steps. "I am going crazy in that house, Ramsey."

Ramsey rounded so fast, Sylphine almost bumped into her. "Jonathon is going to be *so* upset when he realizes you left."

Guilt threatened to overtake the brief moment of relief at escaping the confines of the Hunter residence. When she'd caught Ramsey sneaking through the hall to leave, she'd made her sister-in-law wait five minutes. Long enough for Sylphine to throw on a dress and braid her hair. Jonathon hadn't twitched a muscle. Sylphine had learned when her husband slept, he slept like the dead. Probably because he denied rest more than he allowed. With both boys sleeping, Sylphine figured she wouldn't be missed.

"If we are quick, he will not even know I left to begin with. We'll be home before he or Parker even wake up."

Sylphine waved in an upward motion. "Let's go, you are wasting time."

Ramsey hesitated, then, growling, turned and continued running up the stairs. On the third floor with the foreign titles, Sylphine browsed the Italyssian section while Ramsey did whatever she'd come to do somewhere in the back of the room. Her native language in print brought forth a wave of homesickness so strong she found herself sliding to the floor. She hugged the popular adventure author to her chest and breathed away tears.

The gray light filtering in did little to ease her melancholy. In a few weeks, winter would officially hit Sziveria. Sunlight and warmth would all but disappear, replaced by an almost constant fall of snow, rain, ice, or a mixture of all three. From past experience, Sylphine knew she wouldn't last the winter without crying at least once. A couple of years ago, she'd been waylaid in Ruthenia, barely making it Sziveria before the Northern Pass iced over. The Sovereign Channel became especially treacherous in the winter months, with weeks often passing before it was safe to cross to Italyssa. If she wanted to return home, she'd have to do so soon.

But she married a Sziverian.

One who was important.

Needed.

A ranked guardian in a land where rankings meant duty, honor, and a voice for those unable to stand among the Gen-Heirs, hopefully using their talents to improve society. Her chest tightened. What was she going to do?

Footsteps pulled her from the dark thoughts. Quickly rising so she wasn't caught sulking, Sylphine pulled a few more books from the shelves and met Ramsey in the main aisle. The book Ramsey carried lay open in her hand.

"Did you find what you needed?" Sylphine asked,

glancing at the book. Odd glyphs filled the page. "Markinish?"

"Yes. Didn't Jonathon tell you what I discovered last night?"

Sylphine tried to think past the haze of passion and pleasure the night had descended into. "Um, maybe? I cannot recall."

Ramsey snorted. Her violet eyes twinkled. "I can't imagine why that would be."

Refusing to be baited, Sylphine cast an expectant stare. "Well?"

"All the manifests for the Cyrano's shipping company had Markinish on them."

"All of them?"

Ramsey nodded.

"How odd," Sylphine stated. "And you think you can decipher it?"

"I am hoping maybe, yes. This book is sort of their dictionary. It has Sziverian translations for their characters."

Unease trembled in Sylphine's stomach. Part of her wanted the Cyrano's implicated in all the awful things Jonathon suspected them to be involved in. It would mean her assured freedom from their clutches. Another part of her didn't, because then a trusted company from her nation was involved in something too terrible to imagine.

Together, they checked out downstairs, their purchases neatly packed in a twine-handled paper bag. Outside, a heavy fog hung low over the street and sidewalk. The echo of horse hooves, creak of wooden wheels, and the occasional *whoosh* of an Ariot driving by was hidden in the hazy depths.

Ramsey sighed. "Going to be difficult to catch the attention of a cabby in this."

"We could walk," Sylphine suggested. "Might be safer than riding anyhow."

"True," Ramsey mused, turning left onto the sidewalk. "I doubt the horses, or men, can see more than a foot right now."

Two steps in, and Ramsey vanished with a squeak into the mist between the bookstore and the coffee shop next door. Sylphine froze.

"Ramsey?" she called, peering between the narrow entry.

Nothing but a wall of swirling gray met her stare. The damp, chilled air hung like a shroud, sinking heavily around Sylphine. Panic threatened. She eased a toe along the uneven brick, trying to see even a hint of Ramsey's sage green gown. Had she tripped and fallen? Or had someone seen an opportunity and grabbed the pretty young woman? The memory of the manifests declaring human cargo forced Sylphine to find courage and venture forward.

"Ramsey!" she shouted.

There. A scuffle. A muffled cry. Sylphine moved forward. Her foot caught on something, and she fell, grabbing the brick wall for balance. A quick glance revealed the paper bag, their books spilled out, pages fluttering in the moist air. Before she could straighten to take another step, she was yanked back into a solid mass of man. Satisfaction and malicious glee curled in the air around her, thicker than the mist. Ice settled into her veins. *Oh no.*

"Hello, Miss Seartavos," a deep voice said triumphantly in a thick Italyssian accent. "What luck I have found my bride-to-be."

Sylphine's heart hammered. She twisted to see her captor and came face to face with Leone Cyrano. "I am *not* your anything!"

His grip tightened when she tried to pull free. He sucked his tongue to his teeth. His dark eyes glittered in the frustration seeping from him. Barely taller than her, his nose almost touched hers. "Now Sylphine, that is no way to talk to the man your nation expects you to marry."

"I am already married." She lifted her chin and stared at him in defiance. "I have been married for over a week. The contract has been filed. You may check for yourself."

He snatched her into his chest. A hard glint darkened his eyes further. Frustration morphed to anger in the air around her. He switched to Italyssian. "You're not married according to our country, where we're returning. Nothing has been recorded there. You are *mine*."

The cruel, elated gleam in his gaze sent a new wave of panic through Sylphine. If he could get her to the docks, he could make his version of reality true. Sylphine struggled against his hold again, trying to send her elbows, feet, anything she could, into escaping. His hold budged only for a moment, long enough to tear the fabric at her shoulder and hip, but he quickly adjusted, grasping her hair and wrapping another arm around her waist.

"Ramsey!" Sylphine screamed again, hoping to hear her friend, hoping to be heard in turn. By anyone.

A malevolent chuckle breathed into her ear. Revulsion shuddered along her spine. "The girl is a most pleasant surprise. Thank you for her. We had a few unfilled slots on our outgoing shipment. She will fill one nicely."

V**AYDEN** D**OSSETT** **COULD COUNT ON ONE HAND ALL THE TIMES** he'd landed in a situation one might consider outside his control. Since he didn't really think anything beyond his ability, creative thinking being a strength not a weakness, finding himself in the middle of such a dilemma always proved somewhat disorienting. The cherry pastry he'd purchased squished red, filling through his fingers and over his shirt as a man launched from the alley out of the mist with a terrified woman wrapped in his arms and collided into Vayden.

Witnessing an abduction in progress was a first for him. For a moment, he stared stupidly, his destroyed breakfast plopping to the ground at his feet. The beautiful, unforgettable face of Sylphine Seartovos-Hunter stared at him wide-eyed. A split second before she, and her abductor, could fade off into the thick fog of late autumn, Vayden sprang. Ignoring the sticky mess from his ruined breakfast on his hand and shirt, he grabbed the Italyssian heiress's outstretched hands and pulled, taking her captor by surprise. She stumbled into Vayden's arms on a cry. Her kidnapper fell backward, landing hard on the concrete walk.

In a rapid tumble of graceful words he didn't understand, the distressed woman pointed to herself, to the man, to the alley. Vayden held up his hand, taking hasty steps back from the shorter man rising off the pavement.

"Guardianess Asherwick, I don't understand you. Slow down, and Sziverian, if you please," Vayden stated calmly.

The man brushed off his pants with an air of importance. His stocky shoulders squared, and his dark eyes squinted in a glare. "She is mine, return her to me, and I will forget this insolence."

Vayden cocked a brow. *Oh really?* "Guardianess Asherwick doesn't *belong* to anyone. And I'm sure her husband wouldn't appreciate my handing her off to some stranger."

"I am to be her husband." The short man puffed out his chest and stabbed his finger into the center. "*Me.* Italyssa has granted me her hand, not some *gsaputri khamand itperdeza!*"

Sylphine stiffened in his grasp, and then she lurched forward, fingers curled into claws. He managed to maintain a hold on her upper arms. Barely.

"Tva eis na gsaputri izrasmet khamdore!" she screamed.

Vayden figured it must have been some sort of insult, for

the man's face turned purple and his hands fisted. On a shout, the Italyssian lunged. Vayden spun, taking Sylphine with him. She continued to hurl words, squirming to get free. The man's fist connected with Vayden's shoulder blade, where Sylphine's face would have been if he hadn't twisted.

In a flash of insight, Vayden realized the furious, plum-faced man with perfect dark hair, expensively cut clothing, gold and silver draping from his neck and adorning every finger must be Leone Cyrano. A former employer. Vayden had never personally met the man. Their only communication via radio and messenger notes. The second The Records Department had stamped and filed the Hunter Contract of Marriage, the reward to send the Italyssian woman back home had become void. She was now a Guardianess of Sziveria. His to protect and defend, just as her husband was tasked to do, for their great nation. Never mind, as a gen-common, Vayden couldn't have the same opportunity, he *would* follow the same honor driven code.

"I'm sorry, Mr. Cyrano," Vayden said, ignoring the sting in his shoulder. "The only place Guardianess Asherwick is going is home, to her husband."

Sylphine froze.

Leone sputtered. "You have no idea who you are talking to. I will make sure no one in this putrid country ever deals in any business with you, I will—"

The last of Vayden's patience disintegrated. Keeping one hand on Guardianess Asherwick's arm, he rotated on the balls of his feet and reached for Leone. His fingers, still covered in thick filling and bits of pastry, wrapped around the weaselly man's neck, cutting off his promises. "And I will make sure no one finds where I leave your body."

Vayden increased the strength of his grip and hauled the man close, until only the alarm in Leone's near black eyes filled Vayden's vision. "I suggest you run. Faster than I can."

Leone stumbled as Vayden released him. A choking gasp escaped the man's pale lips as he reached for his throat with trembling fingers. Spinning, he took off. The echo of his falling steps faded into the heavy mist.

Confident the threat was over, Vayden released his hold on Sylphine. "Are you okay?"

"Yes, but Ramsey." She pointed urgently and headed back into the alley. "Someone grabbed her, too."

Vayden rushed to take hold of her, keeping her back. "Stop. There's no outlet to this alley. They're probably waiting to hear from their leader, who has abandoned them. Go back into Mr. Harold's or to the coffee shop, and wait for me."

She hesitated, looking between him and the alley. "You are on my side now, our side, right?"

A niggle of guilt made him scratch his neck. "Yes, though, to be honest, I was never *against* you. I was hired to see a law in your country met, nothing more. However, the issue is moot. You're married to Key Guardian Asherwick."

She nodded and then crouched to gather a small collection of books together on the ground. Vayden waited until he heard the muffled tinker of the bell from the alley door into the book emporium before venturing deeper into the hazy alley.

Hushed voices speaking the same lyrical language he didn't understand filtered through the thick fog. Vayden eased along the wall slowly. Shadowy forms materialized. A large man held Ramsey Hunter's arms behind her back, while another reached for her breasts, pushed tight against the front of her dress. She fought against the hold and glared. Blood trickled from a split in her bottom lip. Angry marks marred her pale, slender neck.

The big guy hissed harsh words at his friend, who waved them away with an annoyed flick of the wrist. Ramsey lashed out, spewing angry words of her own in their language. Her black curls had long come free of their binding, dancing wildly around her. Her captor struggled to maintain his hold. The two men stared at each other in shock.

Vayden took their moment of surprise to his advantage. He leapt from his mist-shrouded cover and sent the heel of his palm into the larger man's cheek. The man's head snapped back, and he released his hold on Ramsey. Vayden grabbed hold of her and pulled her out of her captor's reach. "Tell them their boss has run off, and they will too, if they know what's best."

When Ramsey only stared at him with wide, lavender eyes, he pointed at the men. "Tell them! You speak their language, don't you?"

She blinked and then faced the men and said hopefully what he'd told her to. Like the idiots Vayden figured they were, they gaped at them. Vayden stepped to the side and swept his arm in the direction of the sidewalk. The two men edged by and then dashed away with the same stealth as their leader.

Vayden released his hold on Ramsey. He inspected her cut, frowning. "Is this the only place you're hurt? Do you need a medical scientist?"

"I'm fine. Thank you, Mr. Dossett." She took a step away from him with a deep breath. "Why are you helping us?"

"Why wouldn't I?"

"The reward..."

"Was for *Miss* Seartavos."

Understanding dawned across her pretty face. "Ah. Right. Where is she?"

Vayden motioned for Ramsey to move ahead of him. "Worried about you, waiting inside at the emporium."

Ramsey stumbled.

Vayden reached to keep her from falling and frowned. "Are you sure you're okay?"

"Yes. I tripped," she clarified, stepping carefully through the thick mist. "They were arguing about my value if they hurt me. Aside from pinning me, which is where I was hurt, they didn't do anything."

"I'm sorry you went through that," he said.

She shrugged, reaching for the alley door to Mr. Harold's. "I've mostly given up on people's decency. Granted, being almost taken by human smugglers is new."

Vayden stared at her in astonishment. "How are you so calm? Most women I know would be sobbing or passed out."

Sadness filled her gaze. "Sobbing does nothing. Passing out only makes it easier for them."

Before he could comment, she disappeared inside the building. The sound of Sylphine's relief carried through the doorway. The two women returned to the alley.

Vayden sighed, knowing he couldn't leave them. "Come on, I only live two blocks from here. You can wait in my building, while I radio Asherwick."

"Thank you," Sylphine said as she fell instep beside him.

Vayden glanced over his shoulder, where Ramsey trailed a little behind, the dense haze in the air flowing around her like a cloud. "Miss Hunter said they wanted to take her, to sell. What do you know of this?"

The beautiful Italyssian frowned. "Not much, I'm afraid."

"A close friend of mine, his daughter has gone missing. Do you think this Leone Cyrano would know anything about that?"

The question was a long shot, Vayden knew. If Enforcement Services, with all their resources and Guardian investigators, couldn't even find one thread to follow, his efforts were likely to be equally useless. But he had to try. He'd made a promise. The loss his friend, who was more like an uncle, had taken was felt by the entire Dossett family. While Vayden's investigative skills weren't considered useful by

Sziverian Gen-Heir standards, he'd made a name for himself in the private sector. He'd do the best he could.

"He may, but he is likely on his way out of the country if he is smart. Ask Jonathon, perhaps there is a way to search his ship, or ships before they leave a Sziverian port," she said.

"Then he *is* kidnapping people and taking them from the country?"

"Again, I do not know for certain, but after what he said...." She sighed and shook her head. "I think so, yes."

A sick sense of dread settled in his gut. Vayden had more than Jonathon Hunter to radio when he returned home.

Jonathon was out of the bed and standing before he knew what had awoken him. Breathing hard and listening, he waited. A long, healthy cry sounded. He dug a hand into his disheveled hair, noting the empty bed and silence in the rest of the house. Where were the women?

After jerking on a pair of sleep pants, he rushed down the hall, calling soothing words to Parker with each step. The distraught boy met him at Ramsey's door. Tears streaked his face and his arms were raised in demand. Jonathon picked him up, rubbing Parker's back as the boy wrapped his arms and legs like a vice around Jonathon's torso.

"Hey, little man, where's your Aunt Ramsey, hmmm?"

Parker snuffled, rubbing his face on Jonathon's shoulder. "I all by myself."

"I see that."

Jonathon tried to tamp down the unease prickling along his spine. And failed. Holding tight to the boy, he went downstairs. More silence greeted him. With a muttered reminder that panicking wouldn't do anyone any good, least of all himself, he made a cursory search of the downstairs to be certain.

He knew where Ramsey had gone, which meant Sylphine likely went with her. Getting angry over her ignoring his wish to remain home wouldn't help matters. Up until a couple of weeks ago, his wife had been very independent, traveling the world alone, conducting business, and socializing. Forced into hiding in a country so different from her own was clearly getting to her. He couldn't fault her desire to get out for a little while. He only wished she'd opted to include him.

With Parker still on his hip, Jonathon went into the front room and looked out over the dense gray morning. "Doesn't look too good out there, does it?"

"Where did the sun go?" Parker asked, pointing out the window.

"It's hiding from us this morning. The clouds came to say hello to you."

Parker laughed in delight and waved. "Hello, clouds!"

Jonathon allowed the child's amusement to ease the anxiety still balled in his chest. "Let's go get dressed before the ladies return home."

Halfway up the stairs, the radio chirped an incoming call. Jonathon hurried to his office. Parker squealed, his arms squeezing tight around Jonathon's neck. "MT Hunter, Key Guardian Asherwick," he answered, hoping he didn't sound too breathless.

"Asherwick," a deep voice acknowledged. "Vayden Dossett. I have your sister and wife safe at my building. They're in Madeleine Fenwick's apartment with her grand-daughter, Delanee Ralston."

Jonathon tamped down his shock at the caller's identity and message. He started to say *Report*, but somehow remembered Vayden wasn't one of his enforceman. "What happened?"

"Leone Cyrano."

A curse formed on Jonathon's tongue. He bit it back with a

glance at Parker, who reached for a radio knob. Jonathon angled the boy away from the unit. "Are they okay?"

The radio crackled for a second before Vayden's reply came through. "Yeah, they're fine."

"Thank you, Dossett. Let me have your address, I'll be there as soon as I can with this weather." He wrote as Vayden relayed the request, then he disconnected the transmission.

Parker's big brown eyes met his when he glanced down. "Our girls managed to get into some trouble."

"Uh oh!" Parker said, eyes growing wider. "I'm not in trouble. I still get yummies."

Jonathon couldn't stop his laughter. He hugged the boy. "Let's get dressed and go make sure they're okay."

Parker lifted his little hand into the air. "We will bring them yummies! Yummies make ev-wee thing okay."

Jonathon didn't know if something sweet would fix this particular mess, but he liked the idea all the same.

"I THINK THE BOOKSTORE IS A PLACE YOU TWO SHOULD AVOID," Delanee Ralston proclaimed as she handed steaming cups of tea over the living room table.

Both Ramsey and Sylphine took one. Sylphine wrapped her hands around the warm porcelain, breathing in the sweet, spiced scent drifting from the milk infused contents. As she took a slow sip, she allowed her attention to move over the journalist. With skin the color of the tea in Sylphine's hands, warm, golden eyes, and spiraling, dark red hair falling just past her shoulders, Delanee was nothing like Sylphine expected.

Sure, Sylphine knew Cora Dandridge had been a stunning beauty in her own right. And while Delanee lacked the curves so popular in Sziverian society, her tall, lithe frame fit her perfectly. She seemed content in her body. The woman was absolutely gorgeous and made Sylphine a little jittery, knowing Jonathon would arrive any moment.

Sylphine also knew deep inside, the jealousy was unwarranted. Yet the ugly emotion insisted on taking hold anyway. Jonathon loved her. He'd spoken the words into their relationship. She *sensed* them every time he touched her. But she hadn't returned the sentiment. How long would he wait until he became as frustrated with her as he had with her refusal to be touched?

Contemplating her anxiety over love, and whether she even knew what the emotion felt like within her personally, wasn't something she needed to focus on sitting in a stranger's living room. Especially when said strangers were a journalist and a matchmaker.

"Are you sure I can't get you some wine or champagne?" Madeleine asked, perched like a queen in a tall, wingback, white wicker chair. "You both had quite a scare today. The wine will relax you."

"I'm fine," Ramsey said with a smile, sipping at her tea. "This tea is delicious."

Madeleine's intriguing golden-green eyes sparkled in a face touched by time, but no less elegant. "I'm so glad you like it, darling. I added a hint of Italyssian spiced rum." Her gaze shifted to Sylphine. "Your nation sure knows how to make the spirits."

As the tea settled on her tongue and rolled in a warm ball to her stomach, the citrus and spice infused liquor warmed her tongue. "I have never had it in tea before. This is lovely."

The matchmaker beamed. The silvery threads woven into her maroon gown shimmered as she wiggled her shoulders with delight. "I know, I serve it to all my nervous or otherwise emotionally distraught clients. Calms them right down."

Ramsey took another healthy sip. "Unless they accept your offer of wine or champagne."

Madeleine smiled slyly. "Of course."

The thought of women stumbling drunk from the Fenwick-Ralston residence after agreeing to some random marriage set-up had Sylphine easing her cup onto the table. "Thank you for letting us wait here."

Delanee's golden eyes sparkled with amusement as she sat on the couch beside her grandmother. "Don't worry, there isn't enough in each drink to do much more than provide flavor. My *Bakishka* forgets she is in her sixties and enjoys teasing."

Madeleine scoffed and brushed a flippant hand across Delanee's wrist. "Oh, come now, child. I wouldn't have a single client if I wasn't taken seriously. A little rum or wine never hurt anyone."

Ramsey tipped her cup back and finished. "I'll have another cup if I can?"

"See?" Madeleine held her hand out in approval. "It's medicinal."

Delanee rose enough to pour another cup from a pretty rose painted teapot on the table. She also handed Ramsey a plate of cookies and small pastries. "As for thanking us, having one of the most socially popular women in my apartment is hardly an imposition. You'll forgive me if I must ask, are the rumors true? Have you really contracted with Key Guardian Asherwick?"

"Is that not public information?" Sylphine asked, glancing first at Ramsey, and then back to Delanee. "Mr. Dossett knew, I figured everyone did."

Delanee poured a cup for herself, a smile toying her full lips. "Yes, the contract is public information, but I haven't seen it myself, nor did either of you make a formal announcement about the happy event."

Suddenly the cup of liquid courage looked appealing again. "And you want one."

"I am the societal pages journalist," Delanee said. "And you are Sylphine Seartavos, the most eligible bachelorette, most sought-after foreign heiress, the most lusted for—"

Having heard more than enough, Sylphine raised her hand to stop the diatribe. "Right. Yes, Jonathon Hunter and I are married."

"Are you a Hunter or is he a Seartavos?" the troublesome journalist asked.

To hide the heat in her cheeks, she dipped her head and took another sip of tea. "We haven't decided."

"Delanee," Madeleine chided, and brushed her granddaughter's wrist again. "They are guests, not subjects for an article."

"But Haven City is dying to know, *Baki*," Delanee argued.

"Be that as it may," the older woman said, shoulders squared. "My house is a sanctuary, you know that. If you wish to know more, make arrangements to meet at their residence."

Feeling like she'd been saved from an inquest, Sylphine smiled at Madeleine in gratitude. Sooner or later, Sylphine knew her marriage would need to be made public. Nothing she did stayed quiet for long. As Delanee had pointed out, she was a renowned heiress to a trading fleet that had helped not only launch economies but kept many functioning. Simply entering a country was often a very public affair. Being married in secret, without fanfare or additional witnesses was surely causing a stir in Sziveria. Since she'd been sequestered, she had no idea *what* people were saying. Sylphine also had to admit, making a public statement would only help solidify the union. A union, if Leone Cyrano were to be believed, could be in jeopardy if she were taken back to Italyssa without proof.

"Has anything been written about my marriage so far?" Sylphine asked.

"*The Havener* has been speculating, which is what they do," Delanee answered with a shrug. "There are whispers you'd have to be pregnant to have agreed to marry Asherwick.

"Guardianess," Delanee said, her tone imploring, "your wealth alone would bring *kings* to your doorstep. Was your first promised not an heir to a portion of the Westican Trading Fleet…"

My first disastrous lover, and mistake. "Yes."

"And was your second not a prince?"

"Eighth in line," Sylphine felt the need to reveal.

"My point," Delanee cast an arch stare at Sylphine, "is they all would have elevated your status, brought something to the table so to speak, same as you would have for them. Jonathon Hunter is a Key Guardian, the lowest ranked Guardian position. He's an investigator of violent crimes, he doesn't even have access to the circles you usually move in."

"His role in your country is very important. Is he not the top investigator in the entire city?"

"Oh, he's vital. There's no question. And he should have married up into a higher-ranking family. With his skills and his family history, parents would be fighting for the chance to marry their daughters into the Hunter line. Securing a future within, say, the Master Guardian Laindrigan family. Their daughter is available, and the family has a long history within the Sziverian National Investigative Division. With that alignment, he'd be set up to take over the Master Guardian position, or at the very least strengthen his Gen-Heir progeny." Delanee leaned forward, setting her cup down and bracing an elbow on her knee. "So you see, the question swirling is why? Why would two people, who offer nothing to each other, marry? There has to be a significant reason."

Aghast, Sylphine stared at her. "Besides love?"

Delanee scoffed. "Love? In your circles? Asherwick's, maybe."

"My parents married for love. Status meant nothing to them. I was raised the same, to find love, not prestige. Love is…" Sylphine slid her finger down one of the thick feathers in her hair. "Everything."

"Love is everything," Madeleine chimed in agreement. "Without love, there is only misery." She turned her focus to Ramsey. "Isn't that correct, Miss Hunter?"

Ramsey peered over the top of her titled cup. "Mmm?"

Madeleine smiled. "I knew you'd agree."

Sitting back, Delanee rolled her eyes. "Love is a myth, *Bika.*"

"Your parents' marriage is a myth?" Madeleine's brows rose high. "What of Dalila, Deverick, or Darianna, who are very much in love with their spouses? They are not living a fantasy, Delanee."

"They are an exception, most certainly not the standard," Delanee argued. Then her attention shifted back to Sylphine. "But, all right, love. Great. Haven City would enjoy a romantic, feel-good story. I haven't been able to write about one since Kynhaven's marriage, and readers have been asking for more. Actual love being so rare, they've been disappointed. So, when can I come over and interview you both?"

Sylphine stilled. When indeed? Her marriage to Jonathon was by no means fake. However, she didn't know *what* it was just yet, and she didn't want that revealed to all of Sziveria. Especially before her own parents learned of the union. A quick, sharp knock saved her from answering. Delanee jumped up and went to the front door.

Parker's small, excited voice sounded before the small group appeared in the living room. Jonathon carried the boy, and Vayden followed. The moment Jonathon stepped into the open room, his anger, frustration, and anxiety crashed into

Sylphine like a wave breaking against a rock. She clenched her hands, her gaze meeting his. The serenity of his features told a lie his emotions couldn't hide. She knew his eyes missed nothing as he took in her torn dress and Ramsey's bruised and split lip. Sylphine couldn't stop from rising, couldn't contain the need to be in the shelter of his arms.

Jonathon set Parker down. The boy clung to his leg, looking around the new space in uncertainty. "Are you both really okay?"

Sylphine stopped before she reached him and nodded. "We were lucky Mr. Dossett was there, and on our side."

Distress twisted across Jonathon's face. His hand wrapped around her wrist, and he pulled her into his side. Sylphine went willingly, closing her eyes and breathing the warm cedar scent of him in deep. His love, relief, and the lingering remnants of fear, thrummed across her senses. Seconds later, Ramsey joined them. Jonathon held them close, his face buried between their heads, his breathing ragged.

"Don't ever, *ever* do this to me again," he whispered. "Please."

"We're okay," Ramsey assured.

"Had no one been there, you wouldn't have been, and you both know it. According to Dossett, one of you would be on a ship bound to Italyssa, the other to who knows where. Mark Inland, likely, for a very bad reason." He tightened his hold around them on a rough curse. "Come on, let's get home. We have some unpleasant things to talk about and not in front of a journalist."

"The journalist wants to know why we married," Sylphine said.

Jonathon lifted his head, smiled down at her, and then looked at Delanee. "I married her because I love her. What else is there?"

17

Jonathon paced in front of his wife and sister, desperately trying to figure out the best way to break his suspicions to them. Neither would be happy with the news, nor with the course of action required to keep them both safe. The relief of having them home still hovered on his peripheral, making him not really care *how* they felt about how he planned on keeping them protected.

"At least we know the Cyrano's are definitely involved in some sort of trafficking," Ramsey said, breaking the tense silence.

"Yes." Jonathon paused mid-step. "And how, exactly, did you learn enough Italyssian to carry on a conversation with your would-be abductors?"

Ramsey fidgeted. "I don't know. I heard them, and I just… understood."

Jonathon rubbed at the tension building in the front of his brain. "I need you to keep that to yourself, okay? If anyone asks, Sylphine taught you. No one will question that."

"Why?" Ramsey tilted her head in question.

"Please just trust me, okay?"

"Can you do anything?" Sylphine asked, her fingers massaging the ends of her knees. She'd changed from her torn gown into a simple, comfortable, pale blue one. "Since we're positive, can you seize his ship?"

"No. All we have is their word against yours. Words are not enough. They never have been. We need evidence," Jonathon said.

"But the evidence will be on the ships!"

"You know you couldn't go to Arch Guardian Immetana with what you have. Friend or no, she couldn't do anything with the information without actual proof." He took a deep, calming breath. "I know you both came dangerously close to being kidnapped today. No one wants this scab more than I do at this very moment. But we have *nothing*."

"But..." Sylphine took a shaky breath of her own. "What about all the people aboard?"

"We have to find more proof than what was spoken. Now that we know for certain, he's confirmed it, we just need to find evidence." He raked a hand through his hair. "Which leads me to the next problem. You both are witnesses against Cyrano, and he knows it."

Sylphine's spine stiffened. "How am I a witness?"

"Did he not confess to you he'd be taking Ramsey, and that he didn't care about your new status as a Sziverian citizen?"

She blinked at him. "Oh. Yes, he did."

Jonathon shifted his attention to his sister. "And if you hadn't said anything, they'd think you didn't understand a word. But you did, and now Cyrano will know they discussed that not only were you being kidnapped, but you'd be sold into slavery."

Ramsey grimaced. "I'm sorry, I didn't think about that."

"You have nothing to apologize for. I just need you to understand you're now in the same situation as Sylphine," he explained.

Resignation settled across Sylphine's beautiful face. "And what situation would that be?"

Meeting Sylphine's unhappy stare, Ramsey sighed. "The one where we're stuck in this house unless Jonathon, or someone he approves, is with us."

Jonathon winked at her and pointed his finger. "Figured it out in one."

Sylphine groaned and dropped her head in her hands. "I never should have gone."

"Actually, I don't think it would have mattered," Jonathon admitted. "Leone Cyrano appears to be getting desperate. He would have done something with Ramsey, either way."

"We need to reach Italyssa," Sylphine said.

"I agree completely. Do you think you could convince the IIRA to let you use their radio again?" While Jonathon had some pull, being an investigator, Sylphine's connection was one of the highest, unless she could count their Queen Elect among her friends. Which Jonathon realized with a little niggle of unease, he didn't know if she could.

"I will radio Arch Guardian Immetana and see if she will approve it." Sylphine tilted her head in contemplation. "Are you thinking it would be wise now to contact someone else in my country?"

"Yes. If nothing else, maybe we can wait while someone sends word to your parents in person and advises us where to go from here. Maybe there's more to be found in your nation than mine."

"I want to know if they are safe, more than anything," Sylphine said quietly.

Hunching down in front of her, Jonathon took both her hands into his. He rubbed his thumbs across the back of her hands. "I know. I do, too. But I want you safe, more than anything." He glanced at his sister, remembering all too clearly the loss of another. "Both of you. These people don't care who they eliminate to keep their secrets. They don't care who they hurt."

"You think it's the same problem Wintersfall is dealing with?" Ramsey asked.

"I think it's possible. Too many things are similar. The manifests, the strange routes…" He shook his head and sighed. "Throughout history, human trafficking has been a lucrative business. No reason to think someone hasn't decided to take advantage of that to fund the underground growth of an empire."

Sylphine took a sharp breath. "And if the Cyrano's are involved…"

"Getting hold of your family's shipping enterprise would be like hitting a coal mine. Not just in current revenue…"

"But in what they could load onto the ships," Sylphine finished grimly. Her eyes met his, filled with dismay. "They will not stop coming after me, will they?"

"You married me for a reason, remember? They don't get to have you," Jonathon vowed, squeezing her hands, hoping she heard, and felt, the depth of his words. "You're mine."

THE STEADY DRONE OF CONVERSATION, BOOTS ON TILE, AND paper shuffling filled the vast foyer of the Immigration and Import Regulation Agency's building. Large lamps burned high overhead, providing light the huge overhead windows couldn't due to dense, dark clouds. If not for the sea of humanity ebbing and flowing below, the patter of rain would echo in the open space.

Sylphine took a deep breath, smiling at those she passed as Laurel Karisse, the Arch Guardian Immetana, walked her up wide, white marble stairs. The Guardian's thick navy skirt brushed against the layers of lavender to dark purple of Sylphine's silk dress. A knitted, tunic-style cream-colored wool sweater hid Laurel's thinner frame.

"Your husband was quite worried about you, wasn't he?" Laurel asked, her dark green eyes curious.

Sylphine couldn't help glancing over her shoulder, where said husband faded into the crowd. He'd left her only *after* getting the sworn word of Laurel, an *Arch Guardian* for artic's sake, to protect Sylphine. Had staring down a powerful Guardian of Sziveria phased her husband? Nope. Not one bit. She knew he'd have preferred to stay with her, but he had other issues he needed to handle.

Namely, Parker, their soon-to-be-son, not existing according to Sziverian records.

Ramsey and Parker had been safely ensconced with Master Guardian Raiventon and his wife, who was going to look over Ramsey's findings of the manifests. While Jonathon had made the visit seem like a business arrangement, one look at the fortified property, and Sylphine knew Jonathon had left his sister in the safest place she could be, besides with him. Same as Sylphine. No one was going to take her out from underneath an Arch Guardian, from a national building. If Sylphine had to guess, she figured she'd be seeing the inside of the Raiventon house soon, too.

"Yes, he is," Sylphine agreed.

Upstairs, the Arch Guardian's assistants greeted Sylphine like a long-lost friend. Some congratulated her on her recent marriage, which Delanee Ralston had broken to the city in this morning's edition of *Haven City Chronicle*.

"Have you really been here for weeks?" Kelsey, one of Laurel's assistants, asked.

"I have," Sylphine said, "I actually came here for documentation when I arrived in the country."

"Well, I wish I would have remembered that. I would have requested you sit in on the Italyssian trade agreement we hosted between your country and a Monaco Sands merchant."

Sylphine frowned. "We already had one with Monaco Sands. For champagne, wine, and citrus."

Kelsey waved in dismissal. "Oh, no this was for something silly, like three shipments of shells or something like that."

"And it needed a witness?" Sylphine glanced at Laurel, who had a brow raised in question.

"That does seem a little odd," the Arch Guardian agreed.

The assistant shrugged, accepting a folder that was handed to her by a passing clerk. "Something about establishing trust, that's all I gathered. Like I said, had I known you were in Haven City, I would have sent for you. I was *really* not the right person for that job."

"I don't remember this meeting," Laurel said with a frown.

"You approved it," Kelsey insisted.

Agitation pinched Laurel's forehead. "Can you bring the documentation to my office?"

Kelsey nodded. "Yes, Arch Guardian. I'll send them right away."

Laurel paused outside the spacious, glass room of her office. Her fingers wrapped around the long silver necklaces hanging to her stomach in an unconscious motion. "Did you want to sit with me or go to the radio room?"

"I won't be interrupting your work if I go to the radio, will I?"

Smiling, Laurel shook her head. The tightly coiled glossy brown hair atop her head barely moved. "No, of course not. You'll be safe there, I don't need to go. But if you don't mind returning and looking over this Italyssian deal, I'd appreciate it."

"Of course, I will."

Laurel nodded in approval, her smile broadening. "Great."

On the way to the radio room, Sylphine tried to ignore her nerves, clenching and unclenching her hands. Yes, she'd tried this before and had been met with radio silence, just as she had at Jonathon's. Even with a new plan, if the signal didn't connect, she was still worried about the outcome. She wished Jonathon had been able to stay. If the worst... *No*, she wouldn't think that way.

The room buzzed with activity. Operators connected calls to other transceivers within the building. Agents made necessary outbound transmissions at various stations. Sylphine waited until one of the larger, international units came available. She opened a directory of location codes for Italyssa, just in case. With shaky fingers, she input her parents broadcast code.

Static crackled. Sylphine pressed the transmit button and sent her plea off into the vast airspace. For long seconds nothing. Then the faintest whisper of words reached through the speaker. Sylphine pressed her hands to the small work surface with a gasp and leaned forward. She urged the messenger to repeat, leaning closer, trying to make out anything familiar about the wavering voice on the other end.

A technician noticed her dilemma and rushed forward, adjusting dials and nobs until the static-laden murmur became clear. Acrisius Seartavos's voice came through like sunshine breaking through clouds. Sylphine cried out, touching the speaker, tears burning behind her eyes. She thanked the technician with a smile of gratitude.

"*Pata!*" she nearly shouted in relief. Words tumbled from

her in her native tongue, "Are you okay? Is *Mita* okay? Why haven't I been able to reach you?"

"Are you okay?" Cris asked.

Sylphine dropped her head into her hand and tried to breathe through the tears so her voice would remain steady. "I'm fine, and I'm safe."

"Are you with your Guardian? Did you make it to him?" Nathalia asked, distress clear in her voice.

"Yes, I did, and yes, I am." She couldn't help but smile and give a little laugh. "Actually, he's your Guardian now too, or rather your son. I've contracted with him."

Her parents raucous delight made several eyes look her way. "Oh, this is great news, my dove! You are happy, yes?"

"I am so happy," Sylphine admitted, wiping away an errant tear. "I wish… I wish you had been there."

"We will have a celebration when you return home. Don't you worry," her father promised, "he'll be welcomed into our family the way he's meant to."

The way he's meant to. With sunshine, music, dancing, laughter, flowing drinks, and a seemingly endless table of food brought by family and close friends. And during the joyous celebration, guests randomly threw flower petals over the couple whenever they were together, as a good luck gesture of fertility, and for a blessed, beautiful union. Sylphine had been to her share of them in her life. After her third failed promising, she'd lost hope in ever having a celebration of her own.

"What happened that I couldn't reach you?" she asked, shelving the dreams of celebrating. Since she had no idea when they'd be able to leave Sziveria, she didn't want to focus on an event she couldn't have.

"Someone took down the radio tower that covers our part of the island," Acrisius answered.

"Your father and a handful of workers have spent the last

two weeks getting it back up," Nathalia said, frustration clear in her words. "We've had to place guards around it."

"Why would someone do that? Has there been more unrest?" Sylphine asked.

"No," Acrisius answered. "We think it was intentional to block communication from this side of the country. To what purpose, I haven't figured out yet."

"Were you trapped in the house?"

"Kind of," Acrisius answered vaguely.

Sylphine tapped her fingers on the small work space in impatience. "What does that mean?"

"It means," her mother began, "we've dealt with felled trees, a boulder, a destroyed bridge, and a heated merchant argument."

Sylphine covered a giggle with the last one, imaging all too well the impassioned movements and words of two merchants so embroiled in turf warfare they blocked traffic.

"We tried," her mother's voice broke.

Acrisius took over. "We tried to reach you every day, my love."

Sylphine touched the radio as if she could reach across the distance to soothe her parents. "I know, and I have tried to reach you. We're talking now, we're all safe."

Her father inquired about their weeks apart, and Sylphine did her best to inform him of everything that happened. When she came to Parker, she couldn't bring herself to tell them the news about him over the radio. Instead, she skipped to her near abduction at the hands of Leone Cyrano. Acrisius said a rare, foul word over the line. Sylphine flushed, thankful no one in the room appeared to understand Italyssian.

"Have you been able to learn anything more about the petition?" Sylphine asked.

"What does that matter anymore?" Acrisius asked in turn.

"You're married now. Leone is an idiot. Even if he brought you back—"

Her father's words were cut short by Nathalia. "You must file here. If he can force a contract before you file the one with Jonathon, Italyssa won't recognize the Sziverian union. I told you I would learn more, and I have. The law was put in place to protect Italyssa. An Italyssian union will be honored before all others, unless you file the documentation before he can."

"What is stopping him?" Sylphine snapped, her heart racing with frustration and fear. "He could claim me as his wife right now if he wanted."

"In Italyssa you need a signature and…"

"A thumbprint," Sylphine finished on a groan, dropping her head in her hand. She had forgotten about the little security feature her country required for all marriage contracts.

"Yes. While your marriage *will* be recognized here, you'll both still need to file with our records department with our customs. Until you do so," her mother's sigh crackled across the speakers. "The Cyrano's petition is still active in Italyssa."

Once again, the surrealness of her situation hit Sylphine, stealing her breath. *How* could she be in such a dire predicament? A prisoner in Sziveria until she could travel, with her husband, to be legally married in her own country.

"I don't know when we'll be able to leave. Jonathon's job…" Sylphine choked back a cry and sniffled. She quickly composed herself and tried again. "Jonathon's job doesn't allow much time away."

"And traveling alone is out of the question," Acrisius stated, more as a law than fact.

"I know," Sylphine said. "Don't worry, I won't travel alone."

The hum of conversation drew her attention, and she noticed with a frown a crowd had gathered, waiting to use the radio station. She reluctantly said her goodbyes to her parents, promising to try again from Jonathon's house, and cut the connection. Back in Arch Guardian Immetana's office, Sylphine accepted the documents handed across the desk to her. She settled in a comfortable padded chair, thankful for the lack of conversation while she tried to process all she'd learned from her parents. Rain and ice kept a constant *tink-tink* against the exterior glass walls of the office.

When she barely managed to read one paragraph in what felt like hours, Sylphine gave in and looked over the desk to Laurel's working form. The woman, not much older than herself, was deep in thought, her attention moving between two open folders. Laurel gnawed on the end of a pen, a weak habit that told Sylphine the Arch Guardian was comfortable in her presence.

"What have you learned?" Laurel asked, not looking up from her task.

Sylphine blinked and glanced back to the documents. "This appears to be exactly what Kelsey said, a simple trade agreement between a Monaco Sands merchant and a small Italyssian shipping company for three orders of shells."

"But?" Laurel looked up and clasped her hands together.

"They're orders. I see no mention of the merchant on the Italyssian side. Why use Sziveria to oversee the arrangement? It makes no sense." Sylphine pulled out a document. "And here is your authorization to agree to the usage of the IIRA for the meeting between them."

"Yes, I did see that. Only…" Laurel shook her head and reached into her desk. "Three years ago, I decided to start journaling what I signed. I had heard some rumors, you see. I won't get into all that, but they made me uncomfortable. I *did* sign a meeting agreement last week, but not for anything to do with Monaco Sands and seashells. I would have refused something so trivial."

"Then for what?"

Laurel shrugged, her round face falling in defeat. She turned the book to face Sylphine and pointed a polished fingernail at a blackened line. "I don't know. I sign so many documents in a day, that's why I keep track in this book. And someone made sure I'd never remember."

18

<hr>

WITH ONLY THE ENDLESS PATTER OF RAIN FOR COMPANY, Jonathon waited for Ryan Voklane to return to his office. They'd been interrupted when an urgent call had come in for Synintel from Immetana. Jonathon had almost insisted on being included since his wife was currently in the care of the IIRA's Arch Guardian, but one look from Voklane had told him arguing would be useless. So he sat. And waited. If not for one more very important matter to discuss with the FIO operative, Jonathon would return at a more convenient time.

Glancing at the clock over a wall of filing cabinets, Jonathon tried not to think about the minutes being wasted that he could be working. The sheer *nothingness* of his situation had him rising to search for the missing Guardian. Before he could reach for the doorknob, Ryan walked in, his face pinched.

"Key Guardianess Asherwick is fine, you can relax," Ryan said, closing the door. "The matter was unrelated to her. Mostly."

Jonathon arched a brow. "Mostly? What does that mean?"

"She helped Immetana with some translations and documents, nothing more." Ryan took his place behind his desk, easing back in his chair with a long, weary sigh. "You said you needed to talk about one more thing?"

For hours, the two had poured over all the available documentation Jonathon had on Parker Prescott's murdered mother and the mystery of the non-existent boy. In the days since obtaining responsibility over Parker, Jonathon had managed to procure enough evidence to show the boys mother hadn't kept him a secret. He was listed on her employment records. He had a Medical Science Officer he went to for regular visits. Two neighbors often watched the child when his mother had to work late or run errands she didn't want to bring him along for.

Someone had deliberately expunged the boy's existence.

While Ryan knew of the human trafficking involving prisoners and had heard rumors of missing children, this development created a new troubling depth to the problem. If someone could simply erase Sziveria's children, who would even know to look for them? The bigger question now became, *how many*? Finding out was a task Jonathon didn't have the manpower, or the resources, to take on.

"Yes." Jonathon tried to force down his unease at yet another topic he wished he never had to bring up. "I need you to promise me something."

"Promises can be hard to make when I don't even know the issue," Voklane said, laying his laced hands over his flat stomach.

"I know, but this is important or I wouldn't ask."

Ryan's pale blue eyes narrowed. "Everyone says as much."

"I'm sure," Jonathon muttered. Then, against his better judgment, he took a deep breath and forged ahead. "I need a sworn oath that neither you nor anyone else from any branch of the Sziverian national government will attempt to recruit my sister, Ramsey Hunter, for a Guardian position."

Voklane's gaze stayed narrowed. His mouth thinned to an almost nonexistent line. "And what if she wishes to serve her country?"

"She has no understanding of what that truly means. And since she already *did* serve her nation as far as I'm concerned and was ostracized for her efforts, I think you can understand my desire to protect her from further abuse."

Ryan flinched. "Right. So why are you even concerned? Outing serial rapists isn't a job we look to civilians for."

Jonathon fidgeted in his seat. "You might start to hear other rumors concerning her. Rumors, if at all possible, I'd like you to head off *if* they do occur."

"All right," Ryan said slowly. "Will the rumors consist of truth?"

Jonathon took another deep breath. "Yes. I recently learned Ramsey's Gen-Heir talent is a cryptographer."

Ryan shot up in his chair. "What level?"

"I don't know, and I don't want to. Probably high. She spoke fluently after limited exposure."

"And she just *now* came into her talent? She's what, twenty-three?"

"Twenty-four," Jonathon corrected. "I think she only recently decided to utilize it, for whatever reason."

Ryan opened his mouth, snapped it closed, tried again, and then shook his head, his face a mixture of frustration and wonder. "You should have her tested."

"No."

"Asherwick—"

"No," Jonathon snapped. "Her name is not to show up on anyone's desk in any capacity. Understood? I have helped you, to the best of my ability, regardless of the risk to myself or my career. Leave my sister out of it and alone."

"Can I ask for her help personally if I need it?" Ryan inquired.

Jonathon considered the question for a long moment, his attention on the rivulets of water chasing each other down the window behind Voklane. "As long as she remains anonymous in any reports, or not even mentioned at all."

"Thank you." Ryan's troubled gaze met his across the desk. "And what if the underground group gets ahold of her?"

"They won't have a chance."

Ryan flexed his jaw. "You keep telling yourself that."

DESIRE SWEPT SYLPHINE ALONG IN A TIDAL WAVE OF NEED. Jonathon's mouth glided across her jaw, to her throat, and further to her collarbone. His hands fisted in the length of her skirt, casting the weight aside in an annoying toss. Like threads of silk intertwining between them, his need tangled in her nerves until she wasn't sure who wanted the other more.

The second they were alone after putting Parker to bed, he'd pounced on her like a starved cat, sending them both careening onto the bed in a heap of limbs and desperate kisses. And after retelling the conversation she'd finally been able to have with her parents, she couldn't deny the comfort and distraction his passion provided was welcome.

However, he had yet to tell her what he'd learned concerning Parker. They'd been apart all day until well after dark. While they'd bathed the little boy, Sylphine had told him about her day. He'd relayed what Raina Merrick had helped Ramsey uncover. More questions, not many answers, except yes, all the manifests had Markinish on them, some sort of code both the women were certain.

His palm skimmed the length of her thigh, and oh, sweet summer sun if he touched her…

Yes, there.

Sylphine moaned, unable to stop her legs from falling open or the inevitable loss of intelligence as his touch discovered how very much she wanted him. The haze of yearning he weaved so expertly around her intensified. Each shifting, probing, pleasure inciting stroke sent her further under.

"I missed you," Jonathon murmured, his fingers moving to deftly undo the buttons between her breasts.

His words caused some errant brain cells to form into a coherent thought. Sylphine stared at the wavering shadows cast by the woodstove across the ceiling and blinked. "We need to talk."

A growl of disagreement followed him pulling her nipple deep into the velvety warmth of his mouth. "We can talk later."

Pleasure sizzled straight to her toes, which curled into the thick covers. The onslaught of his hunger beat against her like an out-of-control tempest against cliffs. In the midst of the chaos, she called upon everything he'd taught her over the weeks about her inner woman, and somehow managed to find herself. Somehow managed to focus and separate from the enticing lure he created. "Jonathon… please."

He lifted his head. The sapphire depths of his eyes burned in heated longing. Slowly, his tongue flicked out and touched her erect nipple, glistening from his attention. His teeth nipped. A thrilling arc went straight to her core. Oh yes, he knew how to play her. Knew every way to wring sensuality from her body better than she ever would. But he'd been an excellent teacher, and the awareness, the knowledge that *she* maintained complete control, had her keeping a level head.

Despite her dress being around her hips, legs spread, and her breasts exposed, she called upon the power of the woman who could silence a room full of angry men with nothing more than a look. If they upset *her*, they'd be left with empty ships and empty pockets. Jonathon had shown her *that* woman always existed, sometimes she just needed to look a little harder. Like now, when all she wanted was to be swept into his erotic storm.

"Jonathon," she whispered, brushing her fingers across the rough stubble of his jaw, forcing him to look at her. Really see her.

He stilled. On a ragged sigh, he hugged her to his body and laid his head on her chest. "I'm sorry. I'm not better than they were."

She caressed her fingers through the silken lengths of his hair. "You stopped. They never did."

He rested his chin on his hand to keep it from digging into her breastbone. "Not even when you asked?"

Continuing to stroke his messy hair, she smiled, her heart swelling. "I never knew I could. Not until *you* showed me how."

He rose up on his forearms and kissed her. A slow, love-infused melding of his mouth over hers, his tongue easing and retreating with a sensual pull that nearly made her forget she'd asked him to stop for a reason. Thankfully, Jonathon seemed to remember as he withdrew and returned to his spot, laying across her torso.

"I love you," he said, the firelight softening the serious angles of his face. "You can always tell me to stop, and I'll listen. Always." His mouth twisted in a wry smile. "Though, it may take me a little while to notice, like I did tonight."

She laughed and caressed his jaw again. *I love you* was on the tip of her tongue, and yet, she hesitated. The emotion clenched in her chest like a fist, but somehow seemed weak, more a reverberation to the surge of her husband. Love seemed too complex an emotion for her to sift away as her own.

Jonathon sat up, rearranging her dress. He propped

himself against the thick headboard and crossed his ankles. "Now, what is so important that we're both sitting here fully clothed instead of naked and lost in each other?"

Well, now that she had to voice the interruption, heat suffused her cheeks, and she sat up, straightening her clothing further. Was her reason foolish?

"I wanted to know what you learned about Parker. Today. We cannot adopt him without his birth record, correct? And if he's taken..." The words caught in her throat. She couldn't finish speaking her fears that if Parker were loaded onto one of Cyrano's ships, they'd have no hope of finding him again or a way to get him back even if they did.

Jonathon reached out and twined their fingers together. "Hey, it's okay, he's safe. He's not going anywhere."

She nodded and took a calming breath. "What did you learn?"

"His father's name."

The troubled shadows across his face made Sylphine shift closer to him. "And?"

"He's not a good man."

"Do you think he murdered Parker's mother?" Unease churned in her stomach.

"Yes. Emily Prescott knew her attacker. Knew enough about him to know to hide her son." Jonathon scrubbed a hand down his face. "Word on the street is Brock Ivans is a magic lily abuser. He will do anything for his next fix, including kidnapping and selling kids."

Sylphine gasped. "And he planned on kidnapping and selling his own son?"

"Near as I can tell, that's the reason he showed up at Emily's house. She hid the boy, and when she refused to tell Brock where he was, he beat and raped her. I think killing her was an act of passion, not a planned moment."

"Do you know where this man is?" Sylphine asked, trying

to keep her anxiety from rising and sending her fleeing to Parker's room, where she'd crawl into bed and stay with him the rest of the night to make sure he remained safe.

"Not yet. All of this is speculation based on the evidence and witness testimony I've been able to gather. I could have it wrong," he said gravely.

"But you do not think you are."

"No." He sighed. "I don't think I am."

"We have to get documentation for Parker," Sylphine said.

Jonathon tugged on her hand until she sprawled across his chest. He sank his fingers deep into her hair. One by one, he undid the clips of her *Naenzis*, setting them on the nightstand. "I am already working on that. Parker obviously exists. That his father has connections in the Records Department with the ability to remove Parker's file is troubling. Who knows how many kids this has happened to? Thanks to Emily *not* keeping her son a secret, despite her obvious fear of her former husband, Parker has enough proof of life, and citizenship, to be issued a new record, with you and I listed as his parents."

Sylphine frowned. "But, what of his mother?"

"She will be noted as his biological mother. We will be listed as mother and father." He massaged her scalp, his gaze searching. "Are you okay with that?"

Sylphine climbed across his hips. "I said I would be, and I have not changed my mind. I just do not want him to forget her."

Jonathon rose and brushed his lips across hers. "We won't let him forget. We'll be honest and answer all the questions we can. It'll be hard, though. Emily didn't have any family for us to learn more about her or even allow Parker to visit. I've asked Aurora to draw a picture of her, as best she can that isn't a crime scene image, for Parker to have so he can remember what Emily looks like."

She wrapped her hands around his biceps, reveling in the steely strength beneath her touch. "That was sweet of you."

"I may have lost my parents as an adult, but I know how significant remembering them is. It'll be no less important for Parker just because he's a kid."

Sylphine pressed her chest to his and pulled her knees in tight to his hips. She slid her fingers along the taut muscles of his shoulders to his neck. "You are amazing," she breathed against his lips.

"Have I satisfied your curiosity enough?"

She nodded and kissed him.

"Good," he growled. "Let me satisfy the rest of you."

The constant shouting, hum of a hundred voices speaking, and shoes on tile left Sylphine feeling overwhelmed and stressed. A closed door barely muffled the intense volume of the hall outside Jonathon's office.

"How do you handle the noise?" she asked Jonathon in disbelief.

He shrugged, jotting a note inside a file. "I'm used to it. I don't even hear it most days, honestly."

"I do not see how anyone can accomplish anything, least of all having a conversation about guilt or innocence," Sylphine stated, frowning.

"They figure it out. Has been this way forever. The chaos is all part of the experience. Don't want to deal with an ocean of people, don't commit a crime."

Sylphine braced her arms over the papers she'd been helping him review. "And what if there is a Human Rabie's Syndrome occurrence? Seems dangerous with so many people packed in like they are."

"Same for anywhere," Jonathon said. "Train station, ballroom, theater performance."

"Maybe," Sylphine conceded, glancing over her shoulder when the door shuddered from some sort of impact. "Has it ever happened?"

"Yeah, about a year ago, on the fourth floor." He made a note and flipped to a new page. "Every Guardian employed under Master Tribunii Enforcement ranking rotates for HRS duty every month or so. When you're on the team for the day, you can't leave the building."

"How many on a team?"

"Four."

Sylphine's attention flickered to his jacket, where his dual rankings stood out in gold lettering. "So, you do not have to?"

"Not anymore. Did my fair share of HRS duty days before my promotion, though."

"When is your next promotion?" she asked, curious about his job and future goals.

"Whenever I apply for an open position."

She tilted her head and regarded him. "Will you?"

"Not anytime soon. I'm not ready to be stuck behind a desk yet. As First Tribunii I'd direct teams instead of work on one." He nodded to the papers she still leaned over. "Have you found anything?"

Sylphine straightened and looked down at the documents. "I have been able to highlight a lot of names for you, yes. From the transfers to the prisons in mainland Sziveria that never arrived compared to the ones that have. I think I might almost be done."

He held his hand out. "Can I see what you have so far?"

"Thank you for letting me come with you today and do something useful. I was going crazy in that house," she said, gathering the pages together.

"I really appreciate you helping. I was given these pris-oner lists almost two months ago, and I haven't had time to…" His words died, and his brows furrowed in a heavy frown. "Can I see the other pages, please?"

At his impatient gesture, Sylphine handed him the entire folder. She went around the desk to look over his shoulder. "What is it?"

"I don't know yet. Hold on." In quick, jerky motions, he looked over each sheet, flipping so fast Sylphine barely had time to see one row of names, let alone the dozens listed. "Is this all of them? Are you sure?"

"All you gave me this morning, yes." Sylphine jumped back when his chair scraped on the tile without warning. He went to one of the cabinets along the right wall. "What is it, Jonathon?"

"Hopefully, nothing." When his search seemed to prove fruitless, he went to the radio across his office. He punched in the code and waited. The static clicked into a connection.

"Kynhaven residence, this is Tybalt speaking, how may I assist?" a male voice carried over the waves.

Jonathon gripped the edge of the radio table until his knuckles turned white, hoping with everything he was wrong. "Are either Primary Guardians available?"

"Guardianess Kynhaven is in residence. May I tell her who calls, please?"

"Key Guardian Asherwick, Master Tribunii Jonathon Hunter."

Moments later, the velvety, female voice of Jessi Dandridge spoke. "Jonathon? How are you?"

"I'm fine. I'm sorry to cut through niceties, but I'm calling to see if you're in contact with your father. It's urgent."

"Yes, but it's a bit complicated. I can reach him if necessary."

Jonathon snapped the page where a name leapt off like a

red-hot coal in the snow. "It's necessary, and I think he'll agree when you reach him."

"All right, what do you need me to tell him?"

Jonathon took a deep breath. "Not tell him, I need to find out if a prisoner is still incarcerated at Stonebreak."

"Okay, is there a reason?"

"I have a prisoner transfer list from Stonebreak in the Northern Boundary to Glass Fields Correctional here in the mainland. Glass Fields is showing no arrival of said prisoners."

A sigh crackled across the speakers. "We knew that was happening. My father admitted as much."

"Yes, but I don't think he would have allowed one of the prisoners in particular to vanish. The Arch Guardian never would have agreed to the transfer, let alone knowing the transfer would mean *this* prisoners release."

"You don't know what he would have agreed to," Jessi said so quietly Jonathon had to strain to hear.

Leaning his forehead on the wall, he closed his eyes. Six years ago, Arch Guardian Praekasdian's life was turned upside down when his daughter, Jessi, was kidnapped by a madman to instill his cooperation against the current reigning leaders of Sziveria. Despite knowing the specifics, Jonathon still struggled to understand just how far the man had gone to appease an enemy force. Sylphine's gentle touch fluttered across his arm before closing around his bicep. He pulled strength and grounded himself in her simple touch.

"Right. Can you ask him about the prisoner stamped as SZ-SB-25225."

Jessi repeated the sequence. "I'm assuming this is important?"

"I think I'll be hearing from the Arch Guardian, that's how serious."

"I'll tell Mason then, he'll know the quickest way to reach him."

"Thank you, Jessi."

"Of course. And congratulations on your marriage. From what I've heard, Sylphine Seartavos is beautiful."

Jonathon glanced down at his wife. Her gorgeous ocean eyes sparkled up at him, full of warmth. He laced their hands together, enjoying the sensation of their meeting skin. "Thank you. She's remarkable, yes. We'll try to come by and see you both soon."

He disconnected the call.

"What was that about?" Sylphine asked, kissing and nuzzling the back of his hand.

"One of the prisoners on the list, SZ-SB-25225, is one of the fake transfers."

"I gathered that by your conversation. Why is it important?"

Jonathon's fingers tightened around hers as anxiety flooded his stomach. "Because it belongs to Joel Blackbain."

She gasped. "The man Ramsey testified against?"

"The same."

"What are you going to do? Will you tell her?"

Jonathon slid a hand down his face with another long, uneasy sigh. "I don't know."

DARKNESS HAD LONG SINCE CHASED AWAY THE SUN, LEAVING ICE to creep along the edges of the windows and turn the outside into a crystal-infused dreamland. Sylphine leaned against the wall in Jonathon's office next to the only window not overlooking the greenhouse. The moon cast a silver glow across the yard. Each blade of grass and quivering leaf sparkled like so many diamonds. Sziverian nights were mysterious and beautiful in their own way. She wondered in the quiet, why she'd never seen the allure before now.

Behind her, Jonathon spoke in low, serious tones to the Arch Guardian Praekasdian. He'd been correct in his assumption that the Guardian over all the prisons in the country would reach out to him once he learned of Joel Blackbain's escape. Though, in the week it took, Jonathon had nearly worked himself into the ground trying to obtain more information on his own. Sylphine wasn't even sure if he'd come to bed or not. After helping with Parker at meals and at bedtime, he'd disappear into the study again or even back to the Enforcement building, where he had access to more information.

Not everything he investigated pertained to Joel Blackbain. He also searched for Brock Ivans. Between following each thread he could that the two men created, Jonathon had little time for much else. Once again, he'd disappeared into the sphere of his job, and this time, Sylphine knew getting him out would be harder. She didn't want to feel jealousy towards his work. Neither did she want to consider where on the scale of Jonathon's life she fell in importance because doing so led nowhere good.

She tried to be supportive. Tried not to let frustration or insecurities rule her. The tightness in her chest told her she was failing. Looking back over the silvery world outside, she inhaled to clear away the unease. The lower the temperatures plummeted daily, the more she longed for the warmth of Italyssa, and the comfort of her large family spread all over the island.

Though returning to the sheltered bubble of her previous existence seemed impossible. News articles read differently to her now. She'd forever wonder if ships contained the cargo they said they did, including those of Sun Wind. After assisting Jonathon where she could, she was no longer so naïve as to believe a captain or two on her family's payroll wasn't corrupt enough to accept what he shouldn't. The moment she had access to the business's records, she'd begin an investigation of her own to ensure the integrity of Sun Wind Trade.

Jonathon ended the call and cradled his head in his hands, more out of the exhaustion Sylphine could feel radiating from him than the hint of anxiety. Pushing off the wall, Sylphine closed the distance between them. She perched on the arm of his chair, not surprised when he let out a long sigh of fatigue and laid his head on her thigh. Unable to resist temptation, she combed her fingers through his silky hair.

"Well? What did he have to say?" she asked, trying to ignore the heat that rose in her belly as his warm breath fluttered along her thigh.

"It took him so long to radio because he had to be certain. They conducted a search of every cell and checked inmate stamps. Blackbain is gone." His arms wrapped around her waist, hugging her hip tight into the hollow of his shoulder.

Sylphine glanced up at the ceiling, where Parker slept, and Ramsey did whatever she did in her room alone. "You need to tell her."

"Tell her what exactly? That Joel Blackbain is running loose somewhere in the inhabited world? I have no answers for her. While I can pinpoint what day he appears to have stepped foot on a train, from there, nothing. We've assumed all the prisoner-to-slaves had been loaded on ships in Port Tabria, but Joel is special. For all I know, he's somewhere in south Sziveria, running devious plans from Sunwater Cove."

"What makes you think he is not slave labor like the others?" Sylphine asked, her fingers sinking deeper into the thickness of his dark hair.

"He'd be wasted that way. No, someone had plans for him. Someone who knew how smart and capable of building master strategies he was. They needed him for something, or it was a plan all along after he was convicted."

A log popped and crumbled in the fire. Embers floated and rolled in the air, disappearing up the chimney and turning to ash around the grate. Sylphine focused on the dancing flames. "How long ago was he released?"

"Two years."

"And in that time, you haven't known, and neither has Ramsey. Do you think suddenly being aware would make a threat to her worse?"

Jonathon lifted his head. Hard lines of weariness etched his face. Sylphine caressed her knuckles down his cheek and to his stubble-covered jaw. Her heart clenched. How she hated to see his job reduce him to a shadow of himself. "*Augabesca mayi*, why do you do this to yourself?"

He leaned into her touch. "I don't mean to."

"Then listen when I tell you no more." Like she had four days ago, when he fell face-first on their bed at three in the morning and somehow managed to pull himself back up four hours later. She'd begged him to stay in bed and catch up on his rest. But he'd changed and walked out the door.

"I have to know where he is. I have to figure this out. And I have to find Brock Ivans, who has simply vanished."

"Have you considered whoever was waiting for a little brown-haired-boy may not have been happy to not receive one?"

He raked a hand through his hair. "Yes, I have. It's not exactly a secret that we have the boy now, too. Which means Brock Ivans became a huge liability when his son became a ward to an Enforceman."

"Not just any Enforceman," Sylphine felt the need to point out. "A violent crimes investigator."

"Who is also a ranked Guardian." He let out a long huff.

"Yeah, my chances of finding this guy alive are slim. But I'm still trying."

A knock echoed through the empty downstairs. Jonathon made a motion for her to stay put. Sylphine wanted to follow, just in case, someone decided Jonathon was needed back at East Street Division. If she had to become an irritating wife to keep him home tonight and let him get some much-needed rest, she wasn't above sinking so low. When he didn't return within a few minutes, she left his office.

In the inky darkness of the foyer, he leaned against the closed front door. The chill of night clung to the air. Sylphine rubbed her arms, staying in the waning light from the office doorway. "Who was it?"

He held up a slim folder. "The chances of finding Brock Ivans alive went from slim to none. His body was dumped in front of the East Street Division building."

20

THE OVERWHELMING SCENT OF PINE DISINFECTANT, MEANT TO sanitize and help cover the odor of death, delivered a punch to Jonathon's senses when he pushed open the swinging door to the morgue in the Health Services building. Ryan Voklane waited for him outside one of the many exam rooms, hands shoved in the pockets of his dark blue slacks. He looked through an observation window, an expression of intent hardening the angles of his face. The bright glow from the exam room washed out the pale blond of his hair, making it appear more white than golden.

Jonathon's shoes echoed on the gray tile floor. Ryan flicked a glance his way, then returned to the window. "You're late."

"I have a stack of cases, you know."

"And a missing convict, I heard."

Jonathon raised a brow. "I'm pretty sure there's more than one."

"Yes, many, but not as high profile as Joel Blackbain. I thought Wintersfall's head was going to explode when I told him."

"He wasn't the only one," Jonathon muttered. "Is he looking into it now?"

"Everyone is, as quietly as we can. If Blackbain learns we're after him, he'll go so deep underground, we'll never get a location."

"Do you think he's still in country?"

Ryan made a face and shook his head. "Doubtful. He's too high profile, someone would have seen him and spoken about it. I'm looking into the ships that departed within twenty-four hours of his release date, trying to see what I can track that way."

Jonathon stopped in front of the window. Inside the narrow room, two Medical Science Investigators worked over the body of a thin man. A pale blue cloth covered his genitals. Silver clamps kept his chest cavity open. On a small table at the head of the exam bed, containers held organs they'd removed and studied already. Autopsies were never his favorite. A clinical, impersonal study of a body someone once lived in. Loved in. This time he couldn't muster even a kernel of pity.

"Have they found anything interesting? Other than him being beat to death?" Jonathon asked, crossing his arms over his chest.

"He was beaten to death, all right. One of his kidneys ruptured. His liver was torn. He bled out within minutes of being dumped on the sidewalk in front of your building." Ryan tilted his head. The glass reflected his troubled expression. "He has the tattoo."

Shocked, Jonathon looked at Ryan. "The one Phipps Greier and Tamina Peyton had? The nasturtiums inside wings?"

"The same."

Jonathon's attention returned to the gaunt man, who

clearly hadn't taken care of himself in a long time. "He was a drug addict. A street brute."

"Yes, and bullies have their uses. Especially ones who have no moral standards," Ryan said. "They asked him to kidnap his own son, and he agreed."

"Do you think it was a test?"

"I think it was a trial run for something, yes." Ryan turned to face him, leaning a shoulder against the thick glass. "I did a little digging, and none of the other children reported missing have had their records stolen. Your Parker Prescott is unique."

Jonathon had been hoping to make his own inquiry into the records department, but as a Haven City official, not a Sziverian level Guardian, access had been limited. "To see if anyone noticed?"

"Perhaps. I don't know yet. The kid is nothing special." When Jonathon opened his mouth to argue, Ryan held up his hand. "Except that he's a kid and is automatically extraordinary. I mean, his mother was gen-common. His entire family tree is gen-common. Not one ranked Guardian or Gen-Heir among the bunch. Same for the father. There's no inherited wealth, or lucrative business interests."

"Parker was the perfect kid to disappear and no one to care about him."

"Pretty much. I mean, we've seen that a lot, to be sure. However, this is the first time they tried to *erase* someone. Why?" Ryan shook his head as if to dislodge an unpleasant thought.

Jonathon considered his words for a moment. "I think they'll try again."

"Oh, I know they'll try again. If they can get away with it, no one will ever be the wiser when citizens, young or old, go missing. Especially if they don't have any family to miss them. I'm sure we have so many already in that situation. Stolen, with no one to raise the alarm to their disappearance."

Jonathon settled back on his heels in thought. "Nations with uninhabited zones are being resourced in secret. But Sziveria doesn't have any zones to exploit, so for contribution, or even to increase the necessary income to run this secret group, or make its members all the wealthier, our very people are being traded."

"I would agree that appears to be the situation."

They stood in silence, both watching the two MSI's poke around inside the victim. The investigators were frowning and making unhappy gestures amidst their conversation. Jonathon tapped on the glass. When they looked his way, he asked if they could enter with a motion. The MSI closest nodded and waved *come in.*

"What have you found?" Jonathon asked, holding the door for Ryan.

"We aren't sure yet." Her lab jacket read Master Tribunii Caitlin Marks, M.S.I.

Her companion, Tribunii Craig Norcross, M.S.I. swept his bloody gloved hand over the near hollow torso before them. "There is some odd internal tissue damage we've never seen before."

Ryan leaned forward, braver than Jonathon, and peered at the evidence in question. A quirky expression twisted his face. "Looks… slimy."

"Yeah." Craig slid his fingers around somewhere Jonathon was glad he couldn't see. "It is. So strange."

"Any guesses?" Ryan asked, taking a step back.

"Whatever it is," Caitlin began, "it's not post-mortem. This damage has been happening for some time."

"Not an illness?" Jonathon asked.

She shook her head, her hand disappearing back inside the body. "No, I don't think so. At least not one caused by natural means."

"HRS in mid-stage?" Jonathon wasn't sure how the fatal

contagion progressed, other than it happened over a two-to-three-week period, ending in a frantic race for the infected to spread the syndrome to as many hosts as possible before death.

"No, not that either." Caitlin removed her hand, rubbing her fingers together and inspecting the glossy fluid. "I have an awful suspicion this is something he consumed."

"Food or drink?" Ryan asked, crossing his arms over his chest.

"Perhaps, but laced with poison," Caitlin speculated. "This *feels* like poison. But it's nothing we've ever seen before."

"Maybe a venom toxin?" her partner speculated.

Jonathon groaned. "I don't want to hear that."

Craig cast him a look of sympathy, pulling one of the containers containing an organ closer. "We'll know more after we investigate further. You'll get our full report."

"Can you deliver it to me personally?" Jonathon asked, not trusting the recent events that could keep something vital from landing on his desk.

Caitlin glanced up, her dark brown eyes wide. "Are reports going missing?"

"Yes. And I don't want this one to accidentally be misplaced."

She tsked and went back to her work. "East Street needs to get it together. Guess you should consider applying for that MP position when it comes open again, hmm?"

Jonathon's lips twitched. "Not me, someone else can deal with their mess."

Caitlin shook her head. "Someday, you'll change your mind. The sirens call of normal hours and no more body duty will become too strong to ignore."

Jonathon and Ryan thanked the two MSI's and headed out. Outside, Ryan stood next to his Ariot, his arm perched atop it. Gray clouds floated quickly above. Heavy gusts of wind promised more storms for the approaching evening.

"If you don't get the report, let me know, I'll make sure you get a copy," Ryan said.

"How? If it doesn't land on my desk, how will you make sure it lands on yours?"

"I'm going to be there when it's signed," Ryan said, a false smile on his lips.

"Ah, that's one way to make sure it won't disappear."

"Right. And if it disappears before it makes it to you, the number of people who handled it will be small. I might find another rat."

Jonathon shook his head and turned to leave, then remembered something Ryan had mentioned earlier. "You said something about looking into the ships leaving Sziveria. Did you find anything yet?"

Ryan drummed his fingers on top of the vehicle. "Actually, I have. Almost every ship leaving Port Tabria is going to a harbor in Mark Inland."

The news made Jonathon's stomach tighten. "That is interesting. I wonder if someone else noticed. Shield Guardian Northclyffe was called into IIRA a couple of weeks ago. She didn't look happy."

"She has a lot to account for, as the First Prefect for Enforcement Services up there. If people are being smuggled through her city by the shiploads, she should be aware of it, and if she's not, why? I'd want the answers to those questions, too."

"You mean to tell me the FIO hasn't already asked?"

Ryan opened the door to the Ariot. "Not our place. That's for IIRA. If we get information that's helpful for Immetana, we hand it to her. Our job is to keep it from needing to get to her."

• • •

THE FAMILIAR CONVERSATION AND OCCASIONAL LAUGHTER OF A small group comfortable with each other filtered around Sylphine. She sat alone, trying not to pull her unhappiness around her like a warm cloak. The adorable infant kicking and punching at the air while lying on her lap helped keep her depression from sliding into outright anger. Scrunching up her face in a manner only babies appreciated, Sylphine helped the tiny human raise into a sitting position. He gurgled his pleasure at the action.

"I see you've found another person to be your slave," Raina Merrick cooed. "Such a spoiled little boy."

Sylphine chuckled, her hands swinging with the force of Tanis's random flailing. "As he should be." When the baby babbled happily, Sylphine made another face. "Yes, you should be, that's right."

Raina laughed, her pretty, pale brown eyes sparkling with a happiness Sylphine envied. "We are doing our jobs well, then. Did you enjoy the dinner?"

Ah, the dinner. The celebration over her marriage by the close friends of Jonathon's that Sylphine had only met briefly in the past. She'd been ecstatic to receive the invitation four days ago. Even more excited when Jonathon had agreed to accept.

Only Jonathon hadn't arrived from work to escort his family.

The Hunters had loaded up into a carriage and arrived without him. During dinner, Sylphine had held out hope, but nope. No Jonathon. The extra glass of wine had helped keep her from screaming. Barely.

Breathing through another bout of hurt, Sylphine hoped the smile she offered her hostess didn't betray her embarrassment or fury. "Yes, it was delicious, thank you."

Sylphine's gaze slid to the other side of the room, where Parker sat on the floor between Ramsey and Kevin, Raina's husband. Sean, their team leader, watched Ramsey intently while his wife, Katria, sat on the floor at his feet, rolling a ball to Parker. Mason and Jessi occupied a small couch. Jessi watched Parker and Katria play, laughing at the boy's joy. Mason listened and added to the conversation Sylphine figured revolved around Sean's missing brother and the steps being taken to locate him. The person absent from the gathering felt like a giant glowing ember in the corner, smoldering away. Everyone knew it was there, but no one wanted to mention the impending disaster.

"Are you looking forward to Wintervail in a couple of weeks?" Raina asked, brushing her fingers through the curly strands of her son's hair.

"It will be my first one away from home. I am not sure what to feel," Sylphine answered honestly.

Raina patted her arm. Sympathy slipped from her touch into Sylphine, who wanted to shy from the emotion. "Sziveria is beautiful during the holiday, I promise, you'll love it here. We almost always have a white Wintervail, and when the Wintervail Orchids bloom, not even the greenhouses can contain their sweet fragrance. I don't think there is anything more lovely than sparkling snow and perfumed air. And I can promise every bloom party you attend will have some of your country's Wintervail wine on hand."

Which Sylphine figured wouldn't comfort but rather make her long for home more. Still, she forced another gracious smile and nodded. "That will be wonderful."

Raina sighed and shook her head. "You don't have to fake happiness with me. I was trained to be the epitome of grace regardless of the situation, so I know the allure to fall back into it. No one here will judge your displeasure. I'm sure things are very stressful right now for all of you."

"I am sorry Jonathon had to work. He thought he would be able to be here."

Another conciliatory touch from Raina brushed Sylphine's arm. "We achieved the goal all the same. We were able to get you out of the house."

The visit continued until fussing children forced the evening to end. Parker fell asleep before they pulled away from the Raiventon compound. At home, Ramsey helped Sylphine change a floppy little boy into his pajamas and tuck him in.

In the dark, still clothed in her evening gown, jewelry, and her *Naenzis* falling through her hair, she sat on the stairs and waited for her husband to walk in the door.

21

THE MOMENT JONATHON ENTERED THE HOUSE, HE KNEW HE wasn't alone downstairs. Easing the door closed with a gentle *click*, he turned all the locks and waited, not quite ready to face the impending storm. However, he'd never been one for cowardice, so he removed his shoes and jacket. Then wordlessly slipped into his office to lock up his badge and gun.

At the bottom of the stairs, he met Sylphine's colorless gaze. In the near dark, he was thankful he couldn't see much of her expression. He figured he knew what he'd see if he could. Disappointment, anger, hurt... All directed at him. All justified. His chest tightened, knowing he'd messed up, hating he'd put her in that position.

"I'm sorry," he said quietly, resting his hand on the banister.

"Where were you?" Her voice betrayed nothing, giving no indication to her state of mood.

He took a long, deep breath. "They found a deadly toxin in Brock Ivans. I received the autopsy reports today and had to hold a Division briefing regarding the discovery and what it could mean for Haven City."

"An important situation," she said. Her fingers plucked at a swath of lace draped over her knees.

Jonathon had nothing to say to that. They regarded each other in tense silence. Slowly, unsure of his welcome, Jonathon climbed the stairs. When she didn't move, or lash out, he sat beside her.

"I am *trying*, Jonathon. I am. I am trying to understand how important your job is," she whispered. In the stillness, her words fell like glass on marble. "And where *we* are supposed to fit. Where *I* am supposed to fit."

Looking out over the inky void the foyer had become, Jonathon couldn't help the uneasiness at realizing they'd been here before. Hurt. Lost. Seconds from disaster. The outcome *had* to be different this time. He had to make sure of it.

"I know I made the choice for ten years." The words were faint, restrained, laced with the emotion he knew she tried desperately not to show. "But I am beginning to wonder if I will be spending them alone, in Italyssa, where I will at least have my family."

"I am your family," he said, his words just as hushed. "Parker and Ramsey are your family, too."

Her ragged breath echoed in the darkness. "Yes, but this is not my home."

The stated fact twisted like a knife through his heart. No, this wasn't her home because he'd made little effort to make it so. "Do you want it to be? *Could* you live here? Make Sziveria, my house, your home?"

"I would not have agreed to marry you if I did not believe I could." She turned to face him, her knees brushing along his. "But Jonathon, what reason are you giving me to try?"

"I can't change my job. I can't stop bad people from doing bad things. We've had this conversation before, many times."

"I know. But you do have control over how many hours in

a day you give them. You have a family now, not just a wife, but a son. I know your job is important, but we are, too, are we not?"

Needing to touch her, to feel her soft, warm skin under his, Jonathon laced their fingers together. He brought her hand to his lips and brushed a kiss across her knuckles. "You know you are."

"We keep having this argument because you keep making a promise you are not keeping," she said quietly, her fingers tightening between his. "And I cannot figure out another way to reach you. To show you how important this," she motioned between them, "is."

With a quick tug on her hand, he pulled her closer, until his forehead rested against hers. "You have to know you are everything to me, Sylphine."

The cool sensation of her fingers sliding along his jaw forced his eyes shut. "I can feel the truth of your words. I always have. You show me such passion and have taught me so much, but then you just..." She sent another long, shuddering breath in a rush across his lips. "You disappear on me. For days. How can I be everything to you when your job is the real priority?"

Jonathon couldn't deny the honesty of her words. He had no argument against them. Deep inside, he wanted to be angry, wanted to lash out and demand she understand. But as he sat in the darkness, the success of his brand-new marriage hanging in the balance, Jonathon knew he had a decision to make. Either his job took precedence in his life, or his wife did. They couldn't compete for his attention. She didn't deserve to be in second place.

"I wish I could help you understand what it feels like to have an open case running around in my head." He pressed a kiss to her mouth when she went to speak and whispered against her lips, "No, wait, I'm not done. You also run around my head all day. All I seem to want to do recently is get home to you. But then a new case lands on my desk, or a little boy is made an orphan, or a new drug creeps in under our noses, and all I can think about then is making this city safe. For you. For Ramsey. For Parker. Before I realize, one day of work has morphed into ten."

"How do I pull you from this cycle?"

"I don't know," he said honestly, not wanting to lie to her. Unable to do so with her ability even if he did.

"You saved me from myself." She shifted closer until they were thigh to thigh, and the lush curves of her torso pressed along his. "Help me learn how to save you. I refuse to take no for an answer."

He tucked a thick length of her hair behind her ear and caressed his thumb along the smooth angle of her jaw. "Shouldn't I be the one trying to fix things when I'm the one who's caused all the trouble?"

"We are Jonathon *and* Sylphine." Her lips brushed his, once, twice. Elegant, seductive pulls that set his blood on fire. "Not only Jonathon. Not only Sylphine. That means we work together, no matter who is to blame, to find a solution because we must both live with the result. Yes?"

The blinding light of clarity struck Jonathon. He didn't deserve this woman. Passionate, beautiful, kind, intelligent, she was damn near perfect. And here he sat, messing up the achievement of his dream to be hers. He grasped her cheeks between both hands and kissed her with all the emotion he suddenly found he couldn't speak.

On a gasp, her mouth opened. His tongue slid past her lips. He plundered. Claimed. Demanded. Her fingers dug into his shoulders while her body moved to get closer. Fire exploded between them, as it always seemed to. The slightest tinder and they erupted into flames.

Jonathon devoured her mouth until their breathing labored, their hearts pounded, and they shook with equal desire. His fingers tangled in her hair and the ornaments dangling within the strands. At some point, she'd climbed onto his lap, straddling his thighs. With herculean effort, he ended their kiss, but held her head firm, pressing his forehead to hers. He knew what he had to do. What he should have done over a week ago.

"I will take you to Italyssa," he whispered.

Her sharp inhale echoed in the darkness. "When?"

"As soon as we can go."

RAMSEY TRIED TO KEEP ENVY FROM SHOWING ON HER FACE AS SHE watched Sylphine fold yet another article of clothing into a travel trunk. Leaving Sziveria would probably be an exciting adventure. For a woman who arrived on their doorstep wearing the equivalent of a burlap sack, she was making sure the trip home was a different experience.

"Are you leaving for good?" Ramsey couldn't help but ask. "Because you're packing all your things."

A flush crept along Sylphine's cheeks. Ramsey had always admired the rich shade of Sylphine's skin. Idly Ramsey wondered if she spent enough time on the shores of Italyssa if she'd look just as exotic or if she'd turn as red as a tomato. Looking down at her ivory skin, she figured the tomato scenario would be the more likely outcome. Oh, well.

"No, we'll be returning. The trip will be over a week."

"And you packed enough clothes for three," Ramsey pointed out.

"I guess I am just…" Sylphine sighed and returned several hanging gowns to the armoire.

"Worried you're going to end up in an itchy, baggy dress again?"

The smile Sylphine cast in her direction was anything but cheery. "No, I am…" Her sister-in-law rubbed her hands up and down her thighs in a nervous gesture.

Ramsey sat up, concerned. "What's wrong, Fi?"

Waving a hand in dismissal, Sylphine turned back to the armoire. "It's nothing. Really. I just cannot decide what to bring, and I guess I was bringing everything."

"Don't you have a closet full of clothes at your family house?" Ramsey knew the answer. She also knew full well Sylphine was lying.

"More than I will ever need."

Ramsey crossed the short distance and made Sylphine turn to face her. "Then you'll be fine, right? Try again. What is bothering you?" Normally, Sylphine wore confidence in a manner Ramsey wished she could imitate. Right now, her friend seemed small, scared. Ramsey reached out and rubbed her arm. "Hey, it's okay, you can tell me."

"Are you sure you will be okay with Parker, here by yourself?"

Ramsey shook her head and wagged her index finger. "Nope, nuh-uh, you aren't deflecting the question. Answer me first. What's wrong?"

A shaky breath rushed past Sylphine's lips. Uneasiness pinched her brow and shone in her eyes. "I am so nervous."

"Why?" Ramsey asked, taking Sylphine's hand. "You'll be safe on the trip. Jonathon said Primary Guardian Wintersfall and his wife are going along."

"What if he hates Italyssa?" Sylphine whispered, her eyes filling with tears. "I do not think I could stand it if he does."

"Oh…" Ramsey cupped Sylphine's jaw tenderly and squeezed her hand. Her heart swelled in adoration for the woman her brother had *finally* claimed as his. Someday, Ramsey would know the stress of worrying for another more than she worried for herself. Someday, she'd experience such profound devotion between two people. Until then, she'd be the best support she could for her family. "My dear sister. He will love it there because he loves you, and you are part of your country. Don't you see? Love changes everything. Jonathon won't be able to help but fall in love with where you came from, what has made you the woman you are."

"They have not been the best example of a welcoming nation," Sylphine said with a weak chuckle.

"And Sziveria has?" Ramsey rolled her eyes. "Or have you forgotten being chased by Vayden Dossett, and being arrested in the lusty book section, which then made it into the morning paper? Not the arrest, mind you, just the part about us being, gasp, amongst illicit literature."

That brought forth the laughter Ramsey was hoping for. Sylphine pulled her hand free on a sigh. "Yes, all right, well stated. I will try to be less nervous and enjoy my husband on my shores."

"There you go." Ramsey cuffed her gently on the shoulder. "Good attitudes only. As for your earlier question, yes, I will be fine with the kidlet. I need help planting seedlings in the greenhouse anyway. Hopefully, his paperwork will be done by Wintervail since you won't be able to travel due to ice flows come the winter season. If not, we'll have ourselves a lovely Wintervail together. Making paper birds and baking is always more fun with a child."

Sylphine covered her mouth. "Oh no, Wintervail. I think Jonathon forgot about that. He won't want to be separated from Parker on his first holiday as a family."

Ramsey shrugged, unconcerned. "Then we'll celebrate when we're all together again. It's just a date. The importance of Wintervail can happen anytime. Won't be the first time this family has had to do so."

"Thank you, Ramsey." Sylphine pulled her into a tight

hug. "I am lucky to have you for my sister. I always have been."

Warmth spread through her, and she patted Sylphine's back. For the first time since her parents died, Ramsey felt as though her little family were stitching together again and becoming whole. "We are lucky to have each other."

22

WARM, SALTY AIR GREETED THE GROUP OF FOUR AS THEY STEPPED off the ship and onto the Italyssian docks. Crowds bustled along the wide wooden walkways, clothed in vibrant colors, many moving in a swaying rhythm only they could hear. Sylphine breathed in the oceanic breeze, mingling with scents of *home*. Sweet, citrusy baked goods, roasting meats, fish from the piers, and the ever-present delicate scent of flowers in bloom. No matter the season, something flowered on the island.

The fragrances didn't seem to sit well with one member of their party.

Katria rushed for the edge, barely making it before she lost the contents of her stomach into the blue water lapping gently under the walkway. Sean held her hair and rubbed her back, a frown marring his handsome face. The bulky weight of Kat's gun case hung from his shoulder by a thick, leather strap. The markswoman had been ill the entire voyage.

"I'm starting to feel really bad about asking them to come with us to make sure we'd be safe," Jonathon muttered.

Due to the volatile situation they may find themselves in

while visiting her country, Jonathon had requested the markswoman to join them. No one had anticipated Katria falling horribly ill on the voyage.

A group of men walked by and loudly voiced their approval of Sylphine. Jonathon wrapped an arm around her and tucked her into his side. Sylphine smiled up at him, his possessive move making her heart swell. Yes, she was his, and she didn't care who knew. In fact, she hoped soon everyone did. The wind toyed with her hair, tugging and dancing the strands, feathers, and ribbons around her face. "She should feel better soon, now that we are on solid ground again."

More than a little gray, Katria stumbled to them, her fingers brushing in annoyance at the limp hair dangling around her face. The ocean breeze was as unforgiving to the sick woman as it was for Sylphine. "Let's get those documents signed so I can go lay down wherever we end up for the day. I am so sorry."

"We can go straight to my parents," Sylphine offered. "Our luggage should be on the way now, too, so everything you need will be waiting for you."

Katria shook her head, which caused her to sway. Sean pulled her into his body, banding his arms around her torso. "No, we came here for a reason, let's make sure it happens. If I get sick, I get sick, it won't be the first time I've traveled in less than ideal conditions."

Sean sighed but remained silent.

Wide cobblestone roads occupied by bicycles, open horse-drawn carriages, and lined by merchants selling everything from candy to fabrics, produce to furniture opened up before them. Vine-covered clay and sandstone buildings cast peaceful shadows over the street market. A riot of color—draped fabrics hanging from windows and balconies, flowering vines, and wares of the vendors— so different from the drab gray and consistent red and gray brick of Sziveria, made tears burn in Sylphine's eyes.

Competing music from street performers mingled with the ocean waves and clomp of hooves and clack of wheels. The urge to join each dancer they walked by rode her hard. By the time they reached the Offices of Records and Registry, Sylphine's feet moved in time to the nearest drum beat and her hips swayed. On a laugh, she grabbed Jonathon's hand and held it up while she twirled underneath his arm.

He joined her laughter and shook his head. "I'm glad you're so happy to be home."

"Just wait until I see my parents." She twisted free of his hand and skipped away, up the short steps to the official building.

Natural light spread golden warmth within the cream interior of the two-story building. An older woman sat behind a wide, wooden desk, her graying red hair piled high on her head in a cascade of curls interspersed with the traditional feathers, ribbons, and beads. She greeted the group with a welcoming smile on her face and in her bright, blue eyes.

Sylphine requested the documentation for marriage, supplying a copy of their records from Sziveria. Nervous flutters dominated her stomach. She kept glancing over her shoulder, half expecting a Cyrano to burst through the door and demand their right to matrimony. Sean and Katria waited outside, though Sylphine wondered more if for the woman's upset stomach, than for security reasons.

The records keeper placed the papers and an ink pad before them with a flourish and an excited congratulations. Sylphine showed Jonathon where to sign and where to press his thumbprint, knowing he couldn't read the words written in Italyssian.

"So, my house, my raimarks... what else am I giving you?" he asked jokingly.

"Your heart," Sylphine answered, signing her name on the next line.

He stopped long enough to press a tender kiss to her mouth. "You already had that."

The swirling emotions of love, happiness, excitement, and wonder spread through and surrounded her. Sylphine returned his kiss, unable to stop from opening her mouth and taking it deeper, not caring about the witness in the room with them. The paper slipped away on a sly smile from the keeper. Sylphine leaned into Jonathon, wrapping him close in a hug.

"Thank you," she whispered against his lips. "Thank you for coming here, for doing this."

He returned her hug, burying his face in her hair. "I want to make sure you're my wife everywhere you legally need to be."

After a thanks to the records keeper, who waved them off with another rowdy congratulations, they met the Blackbains outside. Jonathon inspected his black thumb and held it out for Sean to see with a grin. Katria leaned against the wall, her head leaned back, eyes closed. Sylphine clucked and pushed a damp lock of hair behind the woman's ear.

"Do you think you caught something?" Sylphine asked.

Without opening her eyes, Katria answered, "I have no idea. But every smell seems to be disagreeing with me right now and the ground won't stay still."

"We have to take a carriage to my parents. They live on the other side of the island. It's about an hour's ride. Usually, my family has one waiting when I disembark, but I did not know how long it would take at the registry," Sylphine said.

Jonathon squeezed her hip. "It'll be fine, we'll manage with a hired one."

Sylphine couldn't call a driver fast enough. Holding out her hand, she waved and practically jumped in front of the first for-hire coach that went by to make sure it stopped. Sean helped Katria up first, who huddled pitifully while waiting for her husband to jump up after Sylphine. Jonathon settled in the seat beside her, his arm draping across her shoulder. Sean gathered his wife into his arms. Katria went without protest, closing her eyes and laying her head on Sean's chest.

On the scenic route to her parent's cliff side mansion, Sylphine spent more time watching Jonathon's reactions to her country than to the familiar land passing by. He asked questions and seemed to soak in the surroundings. She found herself hoping he'd be excited enough to return after the first thaw in Sziveria. The sun beat down, warm and comforting. A constant breeze kept the air fresh and crisp.

When the terrain changed from gentle sloping to a steady climb, Sylphine grabbed Jonathon's forearm and squeezed. Perched on the top of the hill, framed by the brilliant blue sky, sat her parents three-story, white marble house.

"Look, there it is! We're almost there," Sylphine exclaimed.

Jonathon grabbed her to keep her from standing in the swaying vehicle. "It's beautiful."

Katria tried to look over her shoulder, but the effort appeared too much when she immediately changed her mind. "I'll see it soon, I'm sure."

Sean kissed the top of his wife's head. "How long has your family lived here?"

"Five generations. It used to be full of Seartavoes, but all my aunts and uncles left to live with their spouses' families until only we remained after my grandparents passed. My great-uncle, if he's still alive, lives with us, too," Sylphine answered.

Sean raised a curious brow. "If he's still alive?"

Sylphine shrugged. "He is… what is your word for it… misplaced in the brain? He thinks some evil enemy is lurking in every shadow. When we do manage to see him, he is usually in the basement or on the top floor, looking through binoculars and relaying the minute-by-minute activities on the neighbors."

Jonathon leaned close and whispered, "We call that crazy."

Sylphine laughed. "He takes care of himself just fine. We do not worry about him doing anything foolish." She pursed her lips and considered the past. "Well, he did paint all the red flowers in my *Mita's* garden a much calmer shade of pink, because he said red attracted the enemy, which of course killed the flowers."

"No wearing red then, while we're here?"

Sylphine thumped his chest with the back of her hand. "You do not own anything red."

"Sounds safer to me. Do you?"

"No," she admitted, laughing. "No one owns red in our house, at least not that we wear when my Uncle is around."

The carriage came to a stop at an open gate. The footpath to the house was too narrow for anything more than a bicycle or walking. Katria was helped down first. Jonathon handed the gun case down to Sean. She immediately sat on the cobblestone path, breathing deep. Jonathon jumped off and assisted Sylphine, who paid and thanked the driver.

Nearer to the water, a stronger wind whipped around, flapping the turquoise and white curtains draped from the open spaces of the house. Seagulls flew high above, calling and sailing on the stiff currents. Brilliant green butterflies danced between bright white and yellow blossoms growing along the trail. Far below, waves crashed into rock and rushed away. The constant essence of motion meant life, and Sylphine absorbed it all.

Sean helped Katria slowly rise. Sylphine considered going to the house to get her mother, who knew all the local flora and fauna, to help ease ailments. However, she knew once she saw her parents, she wouldn't let them go for a while. Best to wait for the reunion after everyone was settled and comfortable. Hands clasped together, Jonathon and Sylphine followed close behind Sean and Kat, wanting to make sure they were there if the poor woman needed sudden assistance.

In the serenity, the *crack* of a shot being fired took a moment to register. Katria noticed first. Despite looking like death warmed over, she grabbed for her rifle, alerting everyone else to the sudden danger. Jonathon dove for Sylphine, knocking her into her mother's beautiful bushes. Twigs and leaves crushed beneath her weight. The hard ground slammed into her back. Confusion and fear fought for dominance against the wave of Jonathon's determination and anger.

"STAY DOWN!" JONATHON ORDERED WHEN SYLPHINE SQUIRMED beneath him.

Jonathon glanced over his shoulder to see Katria take cover behind a massive painted terracotta pot with a tree. Sean went to the one left of her, handing her parts as she called for them, efficiently building the BACR-18 into a formidable rifle. Two more shots puffed the dirt around Jonathon, and he shifted, urging Sylphine to keep to the ground as he sought cover similar to the Blackbain's. Katria put the stock to her shoulder and engaged, her pale face a mask of purpose. While he could never hope to use the weapon at her skill-level, he envied the control she had over their situation.

"They're hidden in the small outbuilding down at the bottom of the hill," Katria revealed. "At least two shooters."

She popped off two shots and shook her head. "They're well covered, probably sandbags."

"So you need to get closer?" Sean asked.

"Different angle. They were prepared for this one," she answered.

"And they won't be prepared for another one?" Jonathon asked, crossing the short distance to the pot to the right of Katria. A chip of clay went flying, and he ducked. When silence reigned, he motioned for Sylphine to cross the short distance. The second he was able, he grasped her fingers and pulled her into his body, needing the physical contact to assure himself she was safe.

"Probably not," Kat said with a sly grin, "they didn't know I'd be here."

Sean cast his wife a concerned look. "Are you feeling okay to move?"

The markswoman waved away her husband's concern. "Adrenaline is flowing, I should be fine for a bit. Best anti-nausea available."

"All right," Sean said, exhaling. Then he looked at Sylphine. "Can we get to a higher floor in the house?"

She nodded. "Yes, but how will we get there safely?"

"I'll provide cover," Kat answered. "I think one of you is the target."

"You'll become one the moment they realize you're a threat if they haven't already." Jonathon kept hidden as a brick splintered in the walkway.

"I know." Kat returned her attention to her scope, shifting the barrel and pulling the trigger. She snapped her teeth in frustration. "Like rats in a hole."

Lifting the barrel of her weapon, she glanced from the out-building to the route and back. Jonathon tried to keep his anxiety low, knowing anything he experienced, his wife felt too. Enough stress surrounded them, he didn't need to add more.

"All right, I'm going to relocate closer to the door of the house. When I say go, that means go. No hesitation. Understand?" She waited until both Jonathon and Sylphine nodded before sprinting to a boulder glittering with quartz near the front stairs. Sean followed close on her heels. Tiny disturbances followed her journey but failed to reach either of them.

Sylphine's hand tightened around Jonathon's. Her wide, terrified eyes, the color of the water below them, met his. He pressed a reassuring kiss to her mouth. "We're going to be fine."

"Why here?" she asked. "Why wait until we are at my home?"

Jonathon glanced around. "No crowds. No one else to worry about. Up on this hill, we're easy targets." Jonathon met her gaze again. "Or rather, I am."

She shook her head in denial. "No... no..."

"Sylphine," he said again, forcing her attention back to him, cupping her face between his hands. "It'll be fine. That's why I brought the Guardians Wintersfall, okay?"

"Now!" came Kat's barked order.

Jonathon leapt up, taking Sylphine's hand. Her arm went rigid when he went faster than she seemed to expect, her weight almost yanking him back. Keeping his balance, he sprinted around behind Katria to keep from interrupting her cover fire. The front door flew wide open. Whoever opened the door appeared to know the danger, keeping from being exposed. Jonathon swung Sylphine around in front of him, using his body as cover when they leapt up the stairs.

The sting of heat through his right shoulder and across the outside of his right thigh barely registered with his need to protect his wife. Safety loomed so close. He shoved Sylphine hard into the interior of the house. She screamed in alarm, tripping on the edge of her dress. Still holding her hand, he followed her down, grunting when he landed on her soft frame.

He tried to rise, but his right arm gave out under his weight. Incredible pain he'd only experienced once before, after taking a dive from a five-story-building, erupted through his entire right side. Roaring a curse, he collapsed back on top of his wife. At least, if nothing else, he figured as darkness crept across his vision, she was safe underneath him.

STICKY, COPPERY-SCENTED WARMTH SPREAD ACROSS SYLPHINE'S chest. At first, she panicked, thinking for sure she'd been shot. But when nothing hurt, anywhere, except her butt where she'd landed on the marble floor, and the remnants of a pain-filled, masculine bellow registered in her mind, her panic turned into outright terror. Jonathon lay limp across her body, his head pillowed on her shoulder.

"Jonathon?" she whispered, shaking his shoulder. The liquid heat spread further until it saturated her stomach.

Silence.

"*Jonathon!*" she screamed, scrambling out from underneath him. She looked down at her dress saturated in blood, and then to her unmoving husband. She closed her eyes and focused, trying to latch on to even a glimmer of his usual emotions. Nothing.

No.

Her husband did not land on her shores, at her insistence, to be murdered in her home.

No.

Jonathon was *not* dying in front of her.

No.

Clear as a flash of blinding light striking across her

consciousness, Sylphine realized she loved the strong, brave, patient man lying in a growing pool of his own blood. She loved him, and she'd never had the courage to speak the words aloud. To acknowledge the power they filled her with, the power they had over her relationship, over her life. Now, she may never get the chance. He would never know how much he meant to her.

Something in Sylphine snapped. An awful, guttural cry echoed in the spacious first floor. If the sound came from her, she didn't know. "I cannot feel him!" she screamed until her throat burned from the effort.

Mired in fear, she hardly registered someone's arms banding around her, holding her tight. Fighting, she tried to reach her husband's side, only to be pulled farther away. Sean skidded across the floor on his knees beside Jonathon. He pressed fingers into Jonathon's neck and then rolled him over with her father's help. Sylphine blinked. When had her father arrived?

In jerking, efficient motions, Sean tore Jonathon's shirt open and yanked it halfway down his arms, exposing the torn, bleeding flesh of his shoulder. Blood covered half of Jonathon's torso, forcing Sylphine's heart into her throat. Sean only paused long enough to give the wound a cursory glance before ripping open and tugging down Jonathon's pants to reveal the gash in his thigh dripping blood onto the pale marble beneath him.

Shaking and back to looking near colorless, Katria slid down the wall behind the door to sit on the floor. She wiped a trembling hand across her mouth and used her foot to kick the door closed. Sylphine wanted to rail against her, to demand why the woman hadn't been able to keep them safe. But the tear that slid down Kat's face stopped her. No one was at fault here except the unknown assailants down the hill.

"Is he going to be okay?" Kat asked, her voice wobbly.

An odd look crossed Sean's face before he went back to looking over Jonathon. "He'll be fine, if I can get the bleeding under control."

"We have an infirmary at the back of the house," Acrisius said, taking Jonathon's legs while Sean looped his arms to lift Jonathon's torso.

"Really? How convenient," Sean grunted.

"At one time, over fifty people lived under this roof. Having medical means was necessary," her father explained, a bit breathless as they heaved Jonathon past her. Blood splashed to the floor with each labored step they took.

Sylphine tried to follow, but the arms holding her hostage tightened. "*Nuoh, porubra mayi,*" her mother whispered. "Let them settle him before you go in there and possibly make things worse. Is he in good hands?"

"Sean is a Medical Scientist," Katria answered, eyes closed, head dropped against the wall. "He'll save him."

"See?" Nathalia forced Sylphine to turn in her arms. She brushed the tears Sylphine hadn't realized she'd cried with a tender touch along Sylphine's checks, and smoothed wayward hair in a motherly manner. "How about we get you cleaned up, and then prepare your suite for him so he has a comfortable place to rest and recover when they are finished, hmm? And see your friends to their suite as well. We will be useful in a different way."

Fresh tears spilled in a heated trail down her face. Her doubts reared, ugly and vicious, twisting a knife through her heart. This was not the way she'd envisioned her homecoming turning out. "What if it's not okay, *Mita*?"

Nathalia squared her shoulders and looked down at her, eyes the same jewel-tone as Sylphine's, looked at her in warning. "We do not have those negative thoughts in this house, and you know that. Your husband will be fine. The Cyrano's have not won, and they will not."

"You think it was them?"

"Who else?"

Right. Who else indeed? Anger scorched Sylphine's stomach and bunched in her muscles. "They cannot get away with this."

"Jonathon is a threat to them, not only with their plans where you are concerned but also to their business interests as a whole. The two of you have made discoveries your father has urged our nation to investigate. Trust me, my dove, they will not get away with anything."

THE DOOR TO SEAN AND KATRIA'S SUITE CLOSED ON A *SNICK*. A single flickering candle illuminated the spacious room. If Sean had to guess, the space was easily the size of his entire upstairs back in Sziveria. While Acrisius Seartavos had helped him clean, stitch and dress Jonathon's wounds, he'd explained the massive marble dwelling had once housed the entirety of the Seartavos clan. With each more recent marriage, his brothers and sisters had opted to live with their spouses, until only he and Nathalia remained. Now empty, they'd made dozens of rooms into only a few.

Sean searched the inky darkness for his wife with no results. He finally found her huddled on a chaise lounge on the balcony. The moon cast a silvery line across the shifting waters and illuminated the outdoors enough to make out her silhouette. He sat across from her. She flickered her gaze his way, then returned to looking out over the endless dark ocean.

"Remind you of home?" Sean asked.

"Only the water. Everything else is different." She looked at him again, taking in the bloody clothes he hadn't yet changed. Shoulder's hunched, she shrunk into herself. "Is he going to be okay?"

"He lost a lot of blood, but he's going to be fine."

Across the distance, her relief reached out to him. A sniffle followed a delicate whimper. Silver tracks raced down her cheeks. Sean's heart clenched. He sighed and rubbed his hands on his thighs to alleviate the combined contradiction of excitement and anxiety. Earlier in the day, he'd suspected the cause for his beautiful wife's illness. Now? He was certain.

"It's not your fault, you know," he said.

"Sure, it is," she whispered. "If I hadn't been dry-heaving because there was nothing left for me to throw up, I'd have been able to keep them covered."

"Katria," he admonished, "you can't stop an involuntary action of your body."

Her defiant glare said she disagreed.

"Are you feeling better?" he asked.

"Yes. The tea Nathalia made for me helped enough for us to use the tunnels to get to the outbuilding the scabs were hiding out in."

When she didn't elaborate, Sean urged her on. "And?"

She took a shaky breath and sniffed again. "One tried to be brave, but having his rifle shot from his hand changed his mind. Whatever Nathalia said to them had them running. She felt confident they won't be back."

Sean believed the matriarch's influence over island ruffians. The Seartavos's held a lot of power on Italyssa. That someone had agreed to pop off shots at their front door spoke a lot for how desperate the Cyrano's had become, and how much the rival family must have been willing to pay.

"Good, I'm glad we won't have to worry about snipers anytime we're visible at the front of the house," Sean said.

"I just hope this tea keeps working." She wrapped her

arms around her legs and dropped her head onto her knees. "What is wrong with me?"

Unable to stand the short distance between them, he joined her on the chaise lounge, gathering her into his body, messy clothes be damned. He kissed her temple. "Do you really not know?"

"Bad chef? Sick passenger?" she guessed.

Sean chuckled. "Let me go change really quick. I wanted to make sure you were okay when I came in."

She twisted and grabbed his biceps. "You swear Jonathon is all right?"

Smiling, he pressed a kiss to her lips. "Yes, I promise. I was able to push some fluids, and I'll do so again tomorrow. Acrisius was a capable assistant for me. We took good care of him."

He kissed her again before going to the room and finding the chest with their clothing. After washing his face and arms just to make himself feel better and putting on a clean shirt, he returned to her side. She immediately crawled onto his lap, and he settled back onto the comfortable, plush recliner. Katria's need for comfort in his arms when she was stressed would never get old for him. He gently rubbed her back and glided his fingers through the length of hair falling between her shoulders.

"You're pregnant," he whispered against her temple.

Every muscle in her body stiffened. She sat up and stared down at him. Disbelief, wonder, and joy sizzled along his nerves. Normally, Katria was as placid as a lake surface without a ripple. Calm. Her emotions ran deep, where he only sensed them with a touch. Right now, her reactions were so strong he could practically see them.

"How do you know? I mean, how can you tell?" She tucked hair behind her ears and blinked down at him. "Can you *feel* our baby?"

Sean laughed and pressed a hand to her flat stomach, where the life they'd been trying so hard to create for over a year now grew, safe and nestled inside her. "Wouldn't that be something? No, I can't feel the baby. Not sure how much there would be to feel just yet anyhow. If my guess is correct, you're probably around two months."

On a long sigh, she laid back on his chest. "Wow. What are we going to do? We never really thought past wanting a baby to what it would mean for the team."

Sean hugged her tight, resting his cheek on top of her head. "Kevin and Raina are expecting again, and he's already told me he's done. He'll serve in-country, sitting in a stupid seat if he has to. I figure I'll do the same. Mason hasn't decided, but Jessi would obviously prefer he remain home, too."

"Maybe we can be an asset to Sziveria, be utilized for the National Investigative Division, or if Enforcement Services needs us."

"I'm hoping they see that, too." Then he shrugged, the future unknown, yet bright on their horizon. "If nothing else, there's the private sector. With all this crap going on, a company like Sun Wind Trade could use our skills to make sure the corruption hasn't leaked into their midst."

"Hmm, that could be very good," Katria agreed.

"Would keep us from getting bored."

She lifted enough to settle her mouth over his. "Are you getting bored, husband?"

Sean took her lips in a slow, languid kiss. Allowed himself to taste and explore without the rush his body wanted to demand otherwise. He pulled back enough to see her passion-glazed eyes and stroke a finger along her jaw. "With you, my love? No such thing."

23

AGONIZING PAIN AND GLIMPSES OF LIGHT AND DARKNESS blurred through Jonathon's consciousness. The gentle glide of fingers through his hair and sweet murmur of a familiar female voice occasionally broke through his unconsciousness, easing the misery. Time ran fluid, unknown, and irrelevant. Hours or days, he had no way of knowing.

Awareness gradually seeped into his fog-filled brain. The calming *woosh* of water and distant sound of birds cawing and tweeting pulled him into the warm, gentle spill of light through open balcony doors. Actually, as he grimaced into a sitting position among a collection of pillows, he realized there were no windows or doors. Only thick marble beams broke up the open space revealing scenery worthy of any artist. Heavy turquoise drapes and sheer white curtains billowed and danced in the sultry breeze. A wide balcony wrapped around the outside as far as he could see.

Jonathon glanced around, wondering where he was. The large bed was positioned against a wall the exact size of the whitewashed headboard. What was around the other side, he

323

didn't know, but a sitting area was in front of the terrace, complete with a woven rug and potted, green plants spilling their leaves in a long cascade to the floor. The discomfort radiating from his shoulder and thigh made him inspect his body. He pressed at a dense pad wrapped around his torso, and another around his upper leg. Thin, loose, white cotton pants covered his legs. Huh. The cobwebs in his brain refused to lift as he tried to remember what had happened. What he *did* know was that he wanted out of the bed. Now.

The first attempt left him thankful he was alone. The second went a bit better, not much, but he somehow managed to hobble, shuffle and grit his way onto the porch. A plush reclining chaise lounge rewarded his efforts. Collapsing onto the blue padding, Jonathon lifted his face to the warmth of the sun. The breeze ruffled his hair and teased the thin length of his pants.

A giant, glowing ball in the sky, the sun cast everything in bright light and harsh shadows. As far as he could see, the ocean stretched into a line touching the horizon. Deep sapphire waves in the distance rolled into a vivid cerulean blue and eventually crashed out of sight against the cliff he sat perched over. If he'd felt better, he'd have leaned over to get a better look.

Gentle chiming and jingles announced his wife's presence in a familiar melody he hadn't heard in weeks. Anticipation tightened in his chest. The motion of sound paused before continuing closer. Jonathon was thankful he sat when she emerged onto the porch. Rippling silk in vibrant orange draped low on her hips, showing off sexy, full curves. A matching, sheer-sleeved top wrapped her breasts and tied around her ribs, leaving long ribbons to trail past her butt. The honeyed skin of her stomach was bare. Each step became an erotic play of sweet, feminine flesh. Her sun-kissed hair was unbound, the breeze picking it up and playing in the strands. Her blessings danced in a riot of colors and textures.

"You are impossible," she chastised. "I cannot believe you came out here alone."

Words seemed to flee his already muddled brain in her presence. He looked her over again, noting her bare feet, except for a chain wrapped around her ankle connecting to a ring on one of her toes. Hot desire flowed through him, making the echo of pain an afterthought. She looked exotic, playful, and wholly female.

"You are stunning," he finally managed.

She held out her arms and spun in a slow circle. "I am home."

"Home is a good look for you," he admitted.

Her gaze wandered him, from his bare feet to his bare chest and the thin pants in between that couldn't hide his very male interest in her. "My home looks good on you, too."

"How long have I been out?"

"Three days," she said, a frown darkening her features.

Jonathon scooted over on the chaise when she closed the distance between them. She perched on the edge near his thigh. "What happened?"

"You do not remember?" she asked, shocked.

Fuzzy bits of memory tried to reveal themselves, but in the end, Jonathon gave up and shook his head. "Not really. Other than us making it to your parent's open door."

"Ah, well, we sort of made it. You were shot in the shoulder, and another bullet grazed your thigh. You needed quite a few stitches all around. Sean is pleased with your recovery so far. No signs of infection."

He looked her over again, noticing not even a scratch on her beautiful body. "You weren't hurt?"

She slid her hand along his stomach. The muscles jumped and contracted at her touch, and Jonathon closed his eyes.

"No," she said.

Relief made him relax. He cast her a lopsided smile. "I did try to warn you traveling with me was a bad idea."

She shook her head and sighed. Her hand trailed a teasing path along his hips. "Are you in pain?"

Was that a trick question? Jonathon blinked at stared at her. "Define pain..."

She laughed and traced the waistline of his pants. He groaned and dropped his head back. Like a cat stretching, she eased onto the lounge beside him, her arms sliding along his side until her weight rested along his uninjured side. The sheen of tears brightened her eyes. Jonathon caressed her jaw to her throat, reveling in the smoothness of her skin.

"What's wrong?" he asked.

"I almost lost you," she whispered. She pressed a trembling kiss to his chest. "I almost lost you, and I never even told you I love you."

His heart clenched, and he stared at her in wonder and disbelief. *Finally* he heard the words he'd been desperate for. Unable to rise, he cupped her neck and pulled her close, capturing her lips. She kissed him with wild abandon, climbing over his torso, her foot braced on the ground to keep from bumping into his injured thigh. Cool silk billowed over his chest and thighs, blanketing him in softness as she pressed closer. Her mouth devoured his while the rest of her remained still.

Being only three days from death's door, he knew he shouldn't want her with the desire coursing through his veins, but he couldn't stop his reaction. She was as necessary to him as the air surrounding them.

"We should get you back in bed," she murmured into his mouth.

He kissed her again, long and deep. "I like it here, in the sun."

She slid her fingers into his hair and pulled back, her gaze moving over his face. "I tried to imagine you here, in my country, underneath our sun. I wondered if your hair would lighten while your skin turns darker, like mine."

Jonathon shifted his attention from her glossy, just-kissed mouth to the tanned expanse of her chest, darker in the days since she'd been home, clearly taking advantage of the rays. "I'm not sure about that, I'll probably burn."

She laughed and kissed him again. "We will take it slow."

The husky words made him think of another thing they could *take slow*. He smoothed his hand underneath her skirt, meeting skin just as delicate as the silk shifting over his arm. A groan tore from his throat and he dropped his head back in defeat when he found her bare. The fight to deny what he so desperately craved was already lost. Her weight shifted forward again, while her hips scooted low, until her heat teased at the waist of his pants.

"I was hoping," she whispered, "you would need me as much as I have needed you."

He glided his hand to the smooth globe of her rear, squeezing the firm, supple flesh against his palm. The fire in his veins turned into an inferno. "I always need you."

His name became a cry, a plea, on her lips. She did all the work, easing the loose cotton to his thighs without rising. In sweet, tender pulls, her mouth worked over his. She teased and tasted until Jonathon began to question his sanity. Helpless, he had to allow her to set the pace, even as she took his erection in hand and slid all her hot, slick heat onto him. Jonathon's world narrowed to her. To him. To the flames erupting between them.

Dancer's hips brought him to the brink, only to shift, change focus, extend their moment in unhurried, sensual circles. Her tongue pleasured in equal movements inside his mouth, heightening his awareness of their connection. Chest to chest, breath to breath, she *loved* him. And Jonathon poured the sentiment back into her, knowing she felt every nuance of his emotions. Needing her to know.

Only when the deep tremors of her release crept up on them did she pull her mouth free, burying her face into the side of his throat, and whimpered. Jonathon held her as close as he could with one good arm, wondering what was brighter in that moment as his own pleasure stole over him, the sun above or the woman in his arms.

A throb of pain erupted from his shoulder as his muscles relaxed and he grimaced.

Sylphine gasped and sat up. "Are you okay?"

"I'll be fine," he said, closing his eyes against the discomfort.

"Maybe we should not have…"

He squeezed her thigh and shook his head. "Completely worth it." Fatigue settled heavily over him. "But I think I need to sleep now. I'm sorry."

"That's fine." She pressed a kiss to his forehead, then to his mouth before settling into his side. "I will be here when you wake up."

ONE WEEK LATER…

UNSURPRISED TO FIND THE BED EMPTY YET AGAIN, SYLPHINE padded across the cool marble to the balcony. Sunlight flowed around Jonathon like the wind teasing his clothes and hair. The midnight blue ocean in the distance made the white pants and open yellow shirt fluttering around him stand out in stark contrast. He leaned against the thick, stone rail on one arm. Sylphine froze, struck by his masculine beauty. All hard lines and predatory grace that she'd noticed yes, but not quite like *this*. Surrounded by the elegance of her homeland, he stood out as the Guardian she knew him to be.

Her body heated in a way only he could create. But she hadn't come in search of him to remind them both he was alive and healthy. Something they couldn't seem to stop from doing no matter how hard they tried. A secret smile toyed with her lips. Later. Stepping out of the shadows of the interior, he twisted and looked her over. She knew what he saw. Silk wrapped around her breasts, crisscrossing over her stomach to flow into a vivid blue and peach skirt to her ankles in uneven, sheer layers. Gold chains slung low over her hips chimed with each step. Two thick bands wrapped around each of her upper arms.

"My *Mita* wanted to see if you were feeling up to a group meal tonight."

He turned and settled his weight onto the rail. "I guess I've hidden long enough."

"I have enjoyed having you to myself for so long," she admitted, sliding up to him and wrapping her arm around his waist. The heat of his skin settled along her bared stomach. "Sean said another week and your stitches can be removed."

"I know he told me last night when he checked them." His fingers caressed at the small of her back. "He said I'll have a nice set of scars, too."

Sylphine kissed his chest next to the thick bandage still wrapped around his shoulder. Her heart fluttered, and she tried to keep the twinge of anxiety from showing. "I will take a scar over what would have been the alternative."

"How do your parents feel about me? Really?" he asked, tugging on her hair to get her to meet his concerned stare.

She smiled and touched the stubble covering his jaw. "Jonathon, my parents love you already. And once they know you, they will love you even more."

"But…"

She covered his mouth with her hand, knowing what his argument would be. "There is no *but* because you are good enough for me. My mother was a street dancer when my father met her. She is seven years older than him. He did not care. My parents want only happiness for me like they have. You love me that is the requirement for them."

He pulled her hand free. "Even if I take you from here?"

Giving a loving smile, she nodded. "Yes, because what you do is important, and I won't ask you to give that up."

A shaky sigh rushed past his lips. He looked out over the land, shadows darkening his eyes. "I've been thinking, maybe we shouldn't leave."

Stunned, Sylphine could only stare at him for a second. "What? Why?"

He swept his arm wide. "Look at this... it's perfect."

"You will not get an argument from me," she said carefully. "However, Italyssa is not Sziveria. Our crime, while we have some, is different. You would be wasted here. Sziveria needs you, Jonathon. They made you a Guardian for a reason."

"I inherited my rank," he said with a frown.

"After you proved you were capable of holding it, and honoring the commitment to take on the responsibility. Italyssa will be here when we need the time away. And we will. I will. I want our children to know their heritage, including Parker. But..." She let a sad rush of air free. "This will not be *home*."

"That upsets you."

"New chapters in life can be intimidating, but I'm ready to start ours. I'd even like to continue to help you, if you'll let me. I enjoyed using my talent for something so important."

He pulled her close, resting his chin on top of her head. "I am lucky to have you."

Sylphine smiled against his chest, her heart full and warm. "We are lucky to have each other."

Turn the page for a sneak peek at

ERICKSEN

Releasing Nov. 2022

The *tick, tick, tick* of a clock broke the bleak silence permeating the house. Once laughter, life and love had filled the brick home. Now the lone, steady beat of cogs ticking away time sank the space deeper into melancholy. Vayden Dossett sighed and went in search of his mentor, wishing he had something, *anything* of value to reveal.

Vayden searched the singe level home, each empty room a reminder of all Henry Castien had lost. A scattering of toys still covered the living room rug. A half-read book rested pages down, open and waiting for a reader who would never again discover what the novel held. The only clue to the emotional distress of the owner were the torn down and discarded Wintervail decorations littering the floors and hallway. Dishes, who knew how old, sat stacked in the sink. Four plates and cups. Henry hadn't used the room since tragedy had struck. Continuing through the dining room and a short hall to the library, he found Henry sitting in the wash of gray light filtering from the wide greenhouse doors. Not even a fire burned in the hearth to ward off the deep-set chill of impending winter.

On another sigh, Vayden went to the cold fireplace and started a fire, hoping the soft glow of light and heat would alert Henry to his presence. One did not surprise an ex-assassin. Especially one suffering in the midst of a personal nightmare no man ever wanted to face.

The chair creaked. Henry's flinty dark brown eyes widened when he noted Vayden crouched before the fireplace. His hands moved in the rapid motions of his language. "How long have you been here?"

Not wanting to disrupt the quiet, even if Henry couldn't

hear, Vayden used only his hands to answer. "Long enough to notice you haven't eaten. When was your last meal?"

"I'm not hungry," he signed with jerky, angry motions.

Vayden crossed the distance between them, dragging a chair along with him. He positioned it next to Henry and sat. "Lucianna is still out there, somewhere. You know she is." Vayden waved a hand up and down before signing, "What will she come home to? A starved husk of her father?"

Henry shook his head, his face aging before Vayden into harsh lines. "You don't know anything. She could be lying in a field somewhere, worm food, like her mother and brother."

Vayden clenched his jaw at the ugly imagery, at the angry delivery, and at the pain the words brought to his own heart. He took a moment to compose himself, looking out over the stunning greenhouse grounds Fiona Castien had been so proud of. "Do you know something I don't?"

An odd snorting puff of air escaped from Henry's nose and mouth. He waved a dismissive hand. His signs were equal parts frustration and annoyance. "The First Intelligence Office thinks they can make sense of it all."

"You don't?"

Henry shook his head. "There is no sense to be made when a nine-year-old is murdered."

Okay, Vayden would give Henry that truth. "What about learning why? Did whoever visited say they would try to find out why, or even who? Did they give you any information?"

"The man's name was Ryan Voklane," Henry signed. "He had no information to give me, only questions to ask."

"What sort of questions? And is this Voklane a ranked Guardian?"

"No, just a Guardian, no rank. He asked about the day, a complete account." Henry's attention shifted back to the greenhouse. Long moments passed before he faced Vayden again and signed, "Why would he need that when Haven

City Enforcement Services met me at the crime scene? Wouldn't they have everything he needed?"

Vayden shrugged. "You are asking the wrong person, Henry. HCES wanted nothing to do with a gen-common like me."

A grunt of aggravation accompanied a flippant wave. "Idiots, all of them, I told you that when I was training you. I trust your opinion over any of those *Guardians* any day. Now, tell me, what do you think it means?"

Knowing he needed to tread carefully here, that his mentor, a man more like an uncle than a friend, suffered. However, Henry was smart. Vayden couldn't ignore or gloss over the question. "I think he either wanted to hear the information from you himself, or HCES didn't share."

"FIO has dominion, they can request access to any case the HCES has."

"Yes, but that doesn't mean they gave it."

Henry seemed to mull the information over, his focus once again sliding to the immaculate greenery past the windows. When his attention returned, determination hardened his tired face and edged the aggressive motions of his hands. "I want you on this case."

Vayden slowly shook his head. "We've talked about this already. The situation is too high profile, I won't get any information and I'll be stonewalled at every turn when I do go looking. Government services don't like their territory intruded upon."

"You've taken harder jobs, and succeeded. I know you have."

Vayden scrubbed his hands down his face. He had. But never so personal. Never with so much to lose, and someone so important to him to disappoint. In a rare move, Henry reached out and grabbed Vayden's forearm. Squeezed. Vayden stared at the stark grief in Henry's eyes. The desperation.

"Cia won't be found without you," Henry signed, each elegant sweep of his hand emphasized with the fear blazing in his eyes for his only living child. His daughter, not even fifteen yet.

"I learned some information that may or may not make a difference," Vayden signed. "I came to share it with you, so you could pass it on to whoever is handling the case."

"You," Henry snapped the gesture, "are handling it."

"I don't think it's a good idea," Vayden tried to disagree again.

Henry jumped from his chair and paced before the conservatory doors. His signing aggressive and over-exaggerated in his anger. "They don't care about her! She is a no one to them."

"She is a missing child," Vayden insisted. "Of course she matters."

"I have received no other visit expect by that Voklane man. No updates. No assurances. How is that mattering? If you don't do this Vayden, she is lost to us."

Vayden flexed his jaw in thought. On a drawn-out sigh, he dropped his head in defeat. "Very well, I will do all I can. But you know I can't promise anything. HCES doesn't have to share anything with me."

"But they can't stop you from talking to people, from doing your own investigation."

"No, they can't," Vayden acknowledged. But past experience told him the behemoth government agencies filled with men and women who looked down upon his gen-common status, regardless of his mother being a Shield Guardian, could make things considerably difficult. Especially if they felt their territory was being intruded upon.

"What did you learn?" Henry asked and sat back down.

"Have you heard of a family named Cyrano? They own a small shipping company out of Italyssa."

Henry shook his head. "I have not, why?"

"There is evidence they are kidnapping people from the streets of Sziveria and shipping them off to be sold," Vayden explained.

"Why kill Fiona and Joshua, only to take Cia to be sold, then?"

"I don't know," Vayden admitted. "I just thought the information was interesting, since she has gone missing. I wanted to tell you about it. The two may be unrelated."

"Or not." Henry sighed. "She is young, female, and beautiful. Perhaps too beautiful to kill to punish me for my past."

Vayden agreed. If the order to murder the Castien family had been from a past grudge, the assailant could have decided to make extra income by stealing the girl instead of killing her. Henry suffered all the same. He lifted his hands to say as much when a knock echoed from the front.

Henry's gaze narrowed on Vayden. "What is it?"

"Someone is at the door."

Henry glanced over his shoulder and then back to Vayden. "I am not deaf to anyone who is there. If they come in, speak," Henry said.

Rising, Vayden nodded. He knew Henry liked to keep the upper hand. Only those the retired assassin decided ever knew he couldn't hear. Had never been able to. On wit, his Gen-Heir talent, and a drive few exhibited, Henry Castien had built a career as a dangerous man working for the Sziverian crown. "Very well."

Before answering the door, Vayden picked up the stranded garlands of silvery birds, orchids, and greenery cast aside in the hall. He tossed the glittery mass into the living room and closed the door on the expressed chaos of loss. One final look assured the home appeared more like a bachelor residence than that of a broken man.

He opened the door, not sure which surprised him more, the cold shock of air or the visitor with her hand poised to deliver another knocked. Unable to control the inner-trouble-maker she seemed to bring out in him, Vayden crossed his arms and leaned against the doorframe. Lazily, he allowed his gaze to wander from the top of the pretty strawberry-blonde curls brushing her shoulders, down the length of her petite frame, to her booted feet. He tried not to enjoy the visual journey. And failed. Everything about Melody Erickson worked for him. She squared her shoulders and straightened her spine, pulling up all her five-foot-six-inches, issuing the clear challenge of who had authority over whom.

Ah yes, how dare he forget his lowly gen-common status.

Vayden smiled.

"Guardian Erickson, how may I assist you this morning?"

The light smattering of freckles covering her cheeks and nose stood out as color crept up her face. Her spring-green eyes nearly glowed with annoyance. She pointed a finger at the bright gold lettering printed on the front of her black HCES uniform jacket. "Tribunii Erickson, Dossett. Respect my ranking, I worked hard to earn it."

"Ah." Vayden straightened and grabbed the edge of the door. "All right then, easy enough. Hope you have a great rest of your day, *Tribunii*."

With another smile, Vayden let the door slam on Melody's attractive face.

Dumbstruck, Melody stared at the closed teal painted door and blinked. What had just happened? Her cheeks burned with mortification and anger. The pounding of her heart made her chest ache. Taking a calming breath, she pressed her hand to her chest and willed a sentiment of calm to flow through her.

Okay, so she hadn't expected the overly handsome reward seeker to answer the door to her current case. A man she'd turned down months ago when matched to him by a matchmaker she figured understood the necessity of proper genetic compatibility. As a Gen-Heir, Melody *needed* to marry another strong Gen-Heir talent. The rejection on her part had been nothing personal. Only the gen-common seeker had never seen it that way. No, the infernal man had taken it entirely *too* personally.

Unsure how the enterprising seeker had found out about poor Henry Castien's situation, Melody raised her hand and pounded on the door, determined to make sure the grieving man didn't squander any money on hiring Vayden. Cold wind blew at her back, skittering leaves and scraping naked branches together. Winter teased the edges of fall. Soon the short days would never thaw. Melody shivered in her pants and thin uniform jacket, not having expected to spend more time outside than what it would take her to walk from her Ariot to a building. She pounded on the door again, hoping this time the owner would answer.

To her disappointment, Vayden, with his breathtaking golden-blue eyes, dark brown hair a little too long to be considered professional, and a masculine physique Melody couldn't seem to make her own traitorous body ignore, swept the door open. He quirked an eyebrow. "Yes?"

"I would like to speak with Mr. Castien, please," Melody ground out.

The much too sensual curve of his mouth tilted up. Mischief danced in his gaze. He took a step back and swept his arm wide in an invite to enter. "By all means, I'll take you to him. I'm sure he'll be interested to know the latest development on his case."

Anxiety churned in her stomach. Melody swallowed and stepped past him. She tried to ignore the earthy, citrusy, dark scent of him. Somehow, she resisted the urge to breathe in deep, to inhale his essence, thereby thoroughly embarrassing herself. In the end she resorted to holding her breath. After closing the door, he led her down a short corridor, where they turned right into a kitchen and dining area, went through another short hall and into a cozy library. A fire warmed the space.

Henry stood when he spotted her and held out his hand in greeting. Melody accepted, squeezing his rough textured fingers. "Mr. Castien, thank you for seeing me."

"Do you have news for me?" he asked, his dark eyes full of hope.

Melody removed her hand from his and cleared her throat. "Not exactly, no, I'm sorry."

Henry looked at her and then over her should to Vayden, who must have made some sort of expression, for Henry's changed to one of resignation and disappointment. "Ah, I see. Please sit."

Melody took one of the two chairs situated in front of the greenhouse doors. She couldn't help but admire the beautifully cultivated garden with a brick path for viewing and benches for leisure.

"So," Henry began with a slap to his thighs, "if no news, what is the reason for your visit?"

"I had some additional questions for you, if that's okay?" She reached into her inner jacket pocket and removed a pencil and small notebook. "My Master Prefect has given your case to me and I had some things I wanted to clarify."

"Is anyone looking for my daughter?"

Melody glanced over at Vayden, noting his scowl and crossed arms. A new set of nerves danced in her belly. She had to play this right. Henry watched her intently, which only served to increase her anxiety. "Um, yes, we… we're doing what we can, but the information is um, of course as you know, limited. I haven't been able to find any leads, as of yet, which is why I was hoping you could give me a more detailed statement of patrons in the park that day."

"I told the MT who took my statement of every person I saw. I pointed them out, most of them were still in the crowd of onlookers," Henry said, a heavy frown settling across his face.

Melody looked down at her notepad. "Well, I—"

"The least you can do is look at him when you tell him bad news," Vayden said, his deep voice low and dangerous.

A shiver raced up her spine. "Who said I'm going to give him bad news?"

"Bad news?" Henry's back straightened, he looked at Vayden in concern. "What is this bad news?"

Vayden made down motions. "Relax, she has said nothing yet." He turned his beautiful eyes her direction. Like sapphire wrapped in gold, Melody mused. She must have pondered a little too long, for he snapped, "Tribunii?"

Blinking, she looked from him, to Henry and back to the empty notebook page. "Yes?"

"You have something to tell Henry?"

"No, I have questions to ask, that's all," she assured. "You are the one who made assumptions. There is no news to report."

Henry chuffed an odd snort and stood. "I have no answers to give that you don't already have. I have asked Vayden to find my daughter. From now on you can deal with him, he's my agent in this whole affair."

Melody hastily closed her notebook and stood, shoving everything into her pockets. "Mr. Castien, I highly recommend you leave this case to the professionals. HCES is more qualified than a reward seeker to find your child."

For long moments Henry stared at her, then his gaze shifted to Vayden, who'd leaned against the mantle, hands in his pockets. Annoyance flashed through Melody. She forced the unhelpful emotion down and cleared her throat.

"Look, I know it seems like we haven't been able to do much so far, but HCES is committed to helping Haven City residents in any way we can," Melody said.

Henry barked a laugh. "You should have been a saleswoman, Tribunii Erickson."

Heat suffused Melody's cheeks. "Have I convinced you?"

"No."

"Then I would have made a poor saleswoman," Melody stated.

"Are you a better investigator?"

Vayden's deep voice drew her attention back to him. Really, she decided, a man shouldn't be allowed to look *that* good. The faint shadow of stubble covering his jaw accentuated the hard edges of his face. Long, thick black lashes made the unique coloring of his eyes seem more intense than probably would be otherwise. Maybe. The rich, caramel of his skin had to be an inherited trait from one of his parents, unlike her milky white so common in the sun-poor nation of Sziveria. She blinked to reset her thoughts. She *had* to stop getting lost in his looks.

In her world, the people she crossed paths with most daily, had a single shade of color to their irises. Pure blue, green, amber or any other shade, with variants of the same color, but never a mixture of one with another. Eye-color was the general way to determine if someone was Gen-Heir or gen-common. The first time she'd met Vayden, she'd been speechless. He'd taken her breath away. Then she'd been angry, because he shouldn't have, and she couldn't do anything about her attraction anyway.

"They didn't promote me because I'm pretty," she said dryly.

"And yet you've made no progress," he pointed out.

She wanted to glare and snap he needn't be Mr. Obvious, but that would take down her professionalism a notch or two, and she wouldn't give him the satisfaction. Melody decided the truth, or at least a version of it, would serve best. "The case is new to me. I took it on this morning. Any lack of development to this point is due to the rise in crime across the city. We're understrength as you well know."

Vayden smiled, an expression she was learning had nothing to do with happiness. "That happens when hiring is a restricted process."

Uneasiness made her shift her weight. The prejudice against the gen-common population of Sziveria was known and accepted. For the greater good of all, the elevation of Gen-Heirs within society served on many levels, ensuring the best, most capable of protecting were chosen. They were called Guardians for a reason. Some, like Melody, hadn't achieved a ranking within the Guardian system, but the title was still theirs to claim. A fact Vayden usually never failed to mention in some snide manner, reminding her of her failure so far to procure the greatest honor of her nation. Someday she'd be able to affix a rank before her name that had nothing to do with her Enforcement position. She'd achieve the status her parents had bred and groomed her for.

The problem was, she realized as she stared at Vayden, she'd never actually met a gen-common individual affected by the genetic inheritance guardian law. Being faced with the bias, knowing she'd never truly understand, made her uncomfortable to admit. She sighed and looked away from him. "The genetic inheritance law is—"

"Put in place to best serve the nation as a whole with no intent to harm, or hinder, the professional growth of any

Sziverian citizen... blah, blah, blah," Vayden flapped his fingers together in mock speaking. "I know the law."

"Vayden will handle the investigation for me personally," Henry cut in. "If you work together, all the better, but he *is* handling it."

Work? With Vayden? Melody glanced between the two of them and wondered when her reality had taken a sharp turn. "But he's... a reward seeker."

"Yes," Henry said. "I am aware. I suggested the profession to him when he was told he'd never be able to be a Guardian. The next best thing, a reward seeker. Helping those the government can't, or simply won't assist. I trained him myself."

"I can't be seen working with a reward seeker," Melody choked out before she could stop herself. Diplomacy had never been her strength.

"Vayden, would you mind seeing the Tribunii out, please? I have told HCES all I need to," Henry stated, looking past her as if she'd already left.

Great. She'd really stuck her foot in it this time. If she didn't find a way to salvage the situation, she'd never forgive herself. Henry may think Vayden qualified for the task, but Melody was a *Gen-Heir* for the love of sun, she was better equipped, and more capable. Finding the missing girl couldn't fall into the hands of someone who *might* be able to see the recovery through.

"All right," she conceded, holding her hands up in defeat. "I will work with him."

Henry narrowed his eyes. "On all things?"

Melody worried her bottom lip between her teeth. "I'm not sure—"

The earthy, citrusy scent of Vayden reached her before he did. He took hold of her elbow and steered her towards the library door. "Come on, Guardianess, the owner of the house has spoken."

Shocked by the heat of his touch through the layer of her jacket, and the strength of his fingers wrapped around her bicep, Melody gaped at him. She stumbled, failing to send the message to her feet to move. Before she could fall, she found herself hauled up against solid man.

"Sorry," he said, taking a step back. "I shouldn't have moved so fast."

Would her entire visit in the Castien house be one long string of mortification? At this point she'd be lucky if her cheeks didn't become stained red for the rest of the day. Huffing her aggravation, she yanked her arm free. "I can walk on my own, thanks."

Vayden made an *after you* sweep of his arm. Melody cast one last glance at Henry, who had settled back in his chair before the greenhouse, ignoring both of them, lost in thought. "How long have you known Mr. Castien?"

"Almost my entire life. He's friends with my father."

"He is very fond of you."

"Because he trusts me to handle something so important?" He stopped at the front door, his hand on the knob.

Melody tucked a curl behind her ear. "Well, yeah, I suppose. I mean you charge people a fee for something enforcement handles for free."

He held up an index finger. "Actually, I charge people for what enforcement deems too unimportant to take on. There is a difference."

Melody pursed her lips. "No one ever said the Castien case wasn't important."

Vayden crossed his arms over his chest and leaned back against the door. "And yet we're going on three weeks and no movement. A fourteen-year-old girl is missing. You do realize at this point she may not even be in Sziveria anymore, right? The incompetence of HCES is staggering."

Melody looked around the small entry hall, noting the lack of festive decorations for the Wintervail season. Then again, her own house was decidedly bleak, without the excuse of personal loss. She wished she could refute his claim. She also knew if she didn't fix the mess she'd made of things, there would never be answers for Castien. "Actually, you're correct, I am embarrassed to admit. I wasn't so much assigned this case, as I've taken it upon myself."

Melody took a deep bracing breath and forged ahead. "All the evidence and testimony has gone missing."

My Dearest Reader,

Sometimes the noise of this world drowns out the things that are important to us. We allow our lives to get too busy, too cluttered with the unimportant that we fail to realize we've let something vital slip from our fingers. Relationships. Projects. Dreams. And the moment we realize they've faded, we have a feeling of panic, because how will we ever find the time to revive them? So much is demanded of us, that the quiet things, usually the things that bring us the most joy, become mere shadows, forgotten and sometimes lost.

But what if we could realign ourselves to shift focus back to what matters? What if we didn't check social media every time we sat down, but instead, while home, went and picked up those colored pencils we've been dying to test on a coloring page? Or maybe we ignore the 'What to Watch Next' recommendation and instead go out into the sun and plant those seeds you dropped in your cart with dreams of putting food you grew yourself on your table? Maybe instead of lamenting the fact that you weren't invited to something, you find that person who's been trying to forge a connection and invite them to lunch, or bowling, or a movie. With or without the kids. Fun moments can be captured even with the littles in tow, and maybe even more so. Memories don't happen without moments.

Start small if making time seems too big a task. Dedicate less time to scrolling and more time to reviving passions. Less time watching other people live their lives, and more time exploring the amazing gift of your life. Find an art festival and be inspired! Stop by the craft store on the way home and be bold, buy that canvas, and then carve out a chunk of time each night to touch a brush to it and create something unique to you. Don't let clutter steal your joy.

Sarah

Let this hope burst forth within you, releasing a continual joy. Don't give up in a time of trouble...

- Romans 12:12a (TPT)

ABOUT SARAH

SARAH WESTILL lives in Alabama with her US Army-retired husband. They have two sons – one they've successfully raised to adulthood – the other is still a work-in-progress, navigating middle school. As a full-on creative, Sarah lives to write, paint, teach, and meet amazing people while doing portrait photography. A veteran in the publishing industry working as a cover artist under the name Elaina Lee, she has been blessed to help hundreds of authors to achieve their own publishing goals for over a decade. To learn more about Sarah as she blogs her adventures, and about her Guardians, please visit her at sarahwestill.com or follow her on Instagram @authorsarahwestill

9 781955 293082